"When you talk to thos▮ ▮▮▮▮▮ **don't think they'll believ**▮ ▮▮▮▮▮ **the people are ready to** ▮▮▮▮▮ **they'll believe it when y**▮▮ ▮▮▮▮ ▮▮▮▮ ▮▮▮re close **enough to the ground to speak for the dirt."**

I didn't like that analogy, but he was right. In the limited time I had spent with the nobles as Theodor's guest, I felt both their disdain and their curiosity. "So you hunted me down just to ask me to talk more?"

"Be our voice." He clutched the well-worn hat. Its top was bleached gray. "Help us. I—I know I wasn't exactly kind to you this winter, and your brother never understood you or your insistence on spending your talents on nobles. You certainly didn't make any friends spurning poor Jack in favor of being a noble's doxy." I bit my lip. "But I have to admit that you're in a position we never could have dreamed of. It might lead to nothing, in the end. But damn it all, Sophie, use it."

The lump in my throat grew again. I had managed to ignore, most days, that I returned alone to the row house I had shared with my brother every evening, to bury any sorrow over his absence in anger at how he had used me at Midwinter. But I did miss him, and deep in the pit of my stomach, a bitter kernel of worry often swelled into full-blown fear for him. I wanted, desperately, to ask if Kristos had any hand in seeking me out, if he had said anything about me. But I couldn't. I didn't want to know any more about my brother in exile, not really. Knowing meant being responsible for keeping that information safe. I needed the distance.

I straightened. I needed the distance from Niko, too. I couldn't be tied up with a fugitive, and I didn't want to risk Kristos's life by knowing any more about his whereabouts. "You have my word, Niko. I will advocate for what I can, when I can."

Praise for *Torn*

"One of the best novels I've read this year! *Torn* is masterfully written—full of fascinating politics and compelling characters in a vividly rendered, troubled city. Sophie is a believable, layered, and wonderful heroine; her journey from ordinary to extraordinary is a joy to read. I absolutely loved this book!"

—Sarah Beth Durst

"*Torn* challenges readers to thoughtfully consider all sides of social change by humanizing each perspective. Readers interested in classic fantasy, feminism, adventure, and a bit of romance will enjoy this thought-provoking book." —*Booklist*

"Miller weaves a fresh, richly textured world full of magic-stitched ball gowns and revolutionary pamphlets. The vivid, complex setting and deeply human characters make for an absorbing read!"

—Melissa Caruso

"A gorgeous weave of romantic fantasy and urgent politics."

—Anna Smith Spark

"Real stakes combined with a clever, unique magic system."

—*B&N Sci-Fi & Fantasy Blog*

"Miller deftly weaves a thrilling tale of revolution and turmoil in a complex fantasy world." —Cass Morris

"Strong research, moral ambiguities, and an innovative magic system." —*Kirkus*

FRAY

By Rowenna Miller

The Unraveled Kingdom

Torn

Fray

FRAY

The Unraveled Kingdom: Book Two

ROWENNA MILLER

www.orbitbooks.net

Copyright © 2019 by Rowenna Miller
Excerpt from *Rule* copyright © 2019 by Rowenna Miller
Excerpt from *Empire of Sand* copyright © 2018 by Natasha Suri

Author photograph by Heidi Hauck
Cover design by Lisa Marie Pompilio
Cover art by Peter Bollinger
Cover copyright © 2019 by Hachette Book Group, Inc.
Map copyright © 2019 by Tim Paul

Orbit
Hachette Book Group
1290 Avenue of the Americas
New York, NY 10104
orbitbooks.net

First Edition: June 2019

Orbit is an imprint of Hachette Book Group.
The Orbit name and logo are trademarks of Little, Brown Book Group Limited.

The publisher is not responsible for websites (or their content) that are not owned by the publisher.

The Hachette Speakers Bureau provides a wide range of authors for speaking events. To find out more, go to www.hachettespeakersbureau.com or call (866) 376-6591.

Library of Congress Cataloging-in-Publication Data
Names: Miller, Rowenna, author.
Title: Fray / Rowenna Miller.
Description: First edition. | New York, NY : Orbit, Hachette Book Group, 2019. | Series: The Unraveled Kingdom ; book two
Identifiers: LCCN 2018049172 | ISBN 9780316478632 (trade paperback) | ISBN 9780316478649 (ebook) | ISBN 9780316478663 (library ebook)
Subjects: GSAFD: Fantasy fiction.
Classification: LCC PS3613.I55275 F73 2019 | DDC 813/.6—dc23
LC record available at https://lccn.loc.gov/2018049172

ISBNs: 978-0-316-47863-2 (trade paperback), 978-0-316-47864-9 (ebook)

Printed in the United States of America

LSC-C

10 9 8 7 6 5 4 3 2 1

For Randy, my partner, and always ready for our next dance

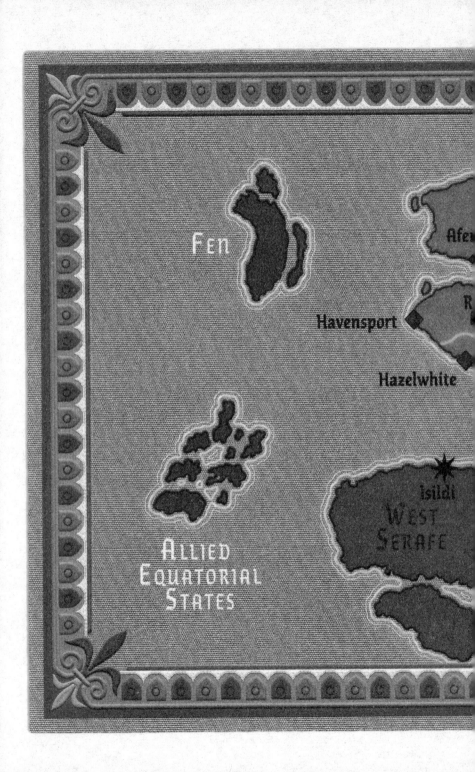

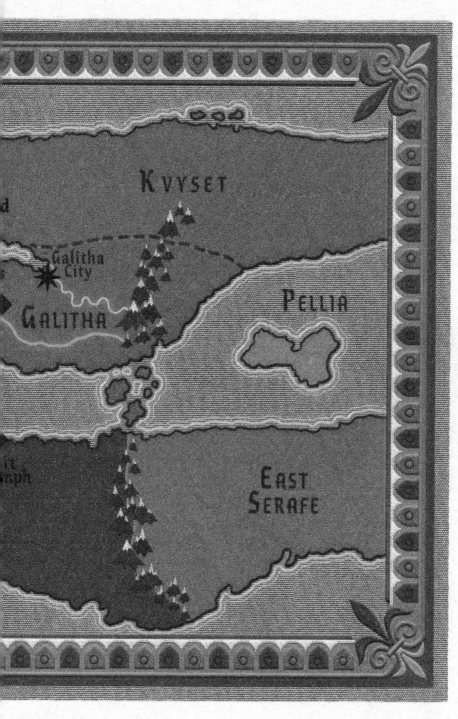

1

—⁂—

THE SILK FAIR HAD DESCENDED ON FOUNTAIN SQUARE IN THE middle of Galitha City, flooding the gray flagstones with color. I inhaled, catching the scent of silk fibers, block-print dyes, and some pungent damp wool on the faint summer breeze.

"All right, Alice." My assistant caught up to me, already red-faced in the summer sun. She carried a list of necessary purchases and a ledger to keep track of our expenses, just as I usually did at the fair. This time, Alice was tabulating our purchases and watching our budget, practice for managing a shop herself someday. "Where should we start? Brocades? Wools?"

"We need more cotton," Alice answered. "Those chemise gowns have been our most frequent commission in the past two months. I've already cut into our last bolt of voile."

Though painfully pragmatic even when faced with row upon row of brilliantly hued silk, Alice was right—ever since I had designed and created a frothy, floating gown for Lady Viola Snowmont, crafted of finest voile and deftly gathered into a full bust and sleeves, our shop had been swamped with orders for similar pieces. The daring design had turned the tide for our shop; for one, only about a third of these fashion-forward women even requested my signature charms stitched into the hems and tucks of their chemise gowns.

"Fair enough—cottons first. Then silks." My conspiratorial grin coaxed a smile from practical Alice. The promise of silk was hard to resist, even for Alice.

"Poor Emmi," Alice said. Our newest hire was relegated to minding the shop and finishing some hems.

"Should I have brought Emmi instead?" I teased.

"No, of course not," Alice replied. "After all, I'll be managing the inventory, so I should learn the purchasing process. And, well, silk." She finally cracked a grin, and I laughed. "Have you considered hiring another assistant?"

I sighed, sobered even as we passed a stall crammed with beautiful brocades. "I have. I'm just not sure—this could be a temporary uptick, and I would hate to fire someone a couple months after hiring her."

"If I may, most out-of-work seamstresses would prefer a couple of months to nothing," Alice said. "And there are plenty of out-of-work seamstresses."

Alice wasn't wrong—caution had followed the failed revolt at Midwinter, with some nobles leaving the city early for their summer estates, stalling building projects and limiting spending even from the city's most confident consumers. Another side effect, I thought ruefully, that my brother and his coconspirators would never have guessed. My shop was unusually busy compared to my neighbors, and I had only the connections with Lady Snowmont's set to thank for that.

"Wise counsel. And this is why you'll make an excellent shop owner someday." Once the Reform Bill that Theodor had been drafting since the Midwinter Revolt passed, starting a business would be simpler, unimpeded by the archaic legal thorns that currently snagged every step of the process. I was sure Alice would leave me someday for an atelier of her own.

"Cottons—here we are." I passed several booths of less finely woven goods before finding the one I was looking for. I fingered the crisp edges of muslins and the soft drape of voiles. The merchant, a slight man from the Allied Equatorial States, hovered just inside a comfortable radius. Alice followed me like a puppy, waiting to note which selections I made.

"Do you like the voiles?" The merchant edged closer. "I have another five bolts just like that one—and this one is particularly fine," he said, producing a lighter weight cotton.

"No, this weight is better—don't you think, Alice?"

She nodded. "Too light and you'd see their underthings," she said. The merchant cocked his head, confused.

"Alice, that's brilliant! Imagine one of those gowns—with a bright pink sash—or deep blue—and an underpetticoat, matching. It would show through, just faintly."

"But—you'd see their underthings," she protested even as she yielded and handed me the lightest weight bolt to test the drape.

I bought two bolts of the lightest weight and three of the more substantial voile. Alice was right—the concept was daring. But I was sure some of Lady Snowmont's set would be delighted with the idea. The merchant promised delivery within the hour. I knew it was more likely to be three, as his helper—probably one of his sons—attempted to navigate the side streets and alleys of sprawling Galitha City.

We stopped at one of my favorite silk merchants next. Over the years, I had made the West Serafan woman several health charms and she had always saved the best of her wares for me. As usual, Aioma was effluent in her enthusiasm when I entered her stall.

"Miss Sophie!" She bowed, which made me blush, even though I knew that deference to a guest was proper courtesy to Serafans. "I feel more alive, more full of health than when I made your acquaintance three years ago. I will dance at my daughter's *sheen-ata* night this year!"

"Oh—I—very good," I said, unsure what she meant.

"It is a tradition for wedding celebrations." She laughed. "The women dance all night long before the bride and groom are joined. I will dance, thanks to your charms!"

I smiled awkwardly, and her gangly teenage son brought several bolts of fabric from under a table.

They were exquisite. I traced the lines of an intricate brocade, gold and pink and yellow on pale ivory, imagining the court gown it could make. A brilliant green was almost too bright to look at, but I thought of the silk-covered hat or pert caraco jacket it would make and grinned. And a pale, almost foamy blue organza seemed to float off its bolt.

"All of it," I whispered.

Aioma insisted that we join her family for the midday meal. Alice gratefully accepted a mug of cold tea, and though I wasn't familiar with the lettuce-wrapped meatballs and milky sauce Aioma served me, I enjoyed my lunch thoroughly.

We were halfway to the wool merchants before I remembered that I had wanted some fine book muslin for kerchiefs. The sun was hot, stronger than usual for early summer, and Alice was already wilting a bit, perspiration glistening at her hairline. "Why don't you take a rest in the shade, and I'll go find the muslin." She agreed happily.

The square was growing more crowded. A pair of jugglers tossed slim orange rings to one another near the fountain, and strawberry sellers jockeyed for the best corners to hawk their wares. The Silk Fair pulled plenty of people, not only shop owners and seamstresses, from their everyday work into the center of Galitha City. The rich excess of fabrics, the brightly colored Serafan tents, the Kvys wool merchants who traveled with painted sheep—all a spectacle that any Galatine could enjoy.

I stopped between stalls of near-gaudy printed cottons and sturdy woven checked linen. One bolt caught my eye, a blue-and-white windowpane check that looked just like one of my brother's shirts. I took an edge between thumb and forefinger; it was good-quality linen, but nothing special, nothing I couldn't buy anytime. The indigo-blue crosshatches were common on working men's shirts and women's kitchen aprons, garments I didn't make. Still, I smoothed the folded edge of the linen back onto the bolt with a gentle hand.

"Not really your specialty, is it?" The voice, too close to me and unsettling in its familiarity, made me jump.

Niko Otni leaned against a crate of osnaburg, flipping the frayed edge of the undyed, coarse linen between two fingers. My eyes widened, but I recovered my composure quickly. Despite his vocal disdain for me and his willingness to torch Galitha City to further the Red Cap goals, Niko couldn't hurt me here. Especially given that he was, technically, still wanted for his participation in the violent insurrection and regicide.

"No, it isn't," I replied, forcing a level tone and sounding more prim than I intended. "Though fabric, on the whole, isn't really your specialty, either."

He cracked a smile. "I'm not exactly sharp with a needle," he conceded. I could see why my brother had liked Niko; they shared a quick wit and I could sense bright good humor buried underneath Niko's sharp tongue. Yet there was something unsafe about him, even now, under a blanching summer sun, a lack of compassion and an unrestrained motivation. If my brother was the pen of the revolution, Niko had been the blade. "But I'm not here for silk."

I considered him as he fell into step beside me, his unbleached linen trousers and a short linen jacket left open over what had to have been his best shirt, with a finer-than-average ruffle at the opening. "If you wanted to have a chat, Mr. Otni, you could have dropped by my atelier."

His smile faltered, slightly. "You know I couldn't. I can't exactly run around the commercial district making social calls. Still a wanted man, aren't I?"

"I suppose the pardon did exclude the leadership of the revolt, yes."

"It certainly did. They've been rather half-hearted about actually hunting us down, but the likes of me, trotting into your pretty shop?" He shook his head with a scolding cluck. "Noticeable. Reportable. Here? Half of Galitha City is here." He shrugged as we passed a clutch of dockworkers buying strawberries from a round-cheeked country girl with bare feet. "And here I blend in. These blokes aren't likely to turn me in even if they do recognize me," he added, nodding toward a trio of men in patched trousers who laughed at a trained monkey fleecing the pockets of a fourth unfortunate man. The monkey's keeper, in bright harlequin costume, met Niko's eyes and bowed subtly.

"Fine." I was losing my patience. The last person I wanted to see was Niko Otni, and the last thing I wanted to do was engage in a prolonged conversation with him. "You wanted something?"

"I think we both want something," he answered. The smile faded, replaced with urgent gravity. "We want those reforms passed."

"Of course we do." I sighed, annoyed. "We all do. If you hunted me down just for that, you've wasted your time."

"I wouldn't say we *all* do." Niko caught my arm and drew

me into the shade of a sprawling flaxwood poplar, its seeds in their tow-colored tufts drifting past us on the faint breeze. "Plenty of voting members of the Council of Nobles don't want reform, do they? Things are too nice for them just the way they are. And sure as shit they'll vote against the reforms your prince is pushing."

"Yes," I replied carefully. I didn't know every vote on the council, but many were vocally opposed to the reforms that had already been months in the drafting. "But I don't vote, remember?"

"You talk to plenty of people who do," Niko said. I assessed him, his best shirt starched at the collar, his hair clubbed carefully under a weather-beaten cocked hat that he pulled off in an awkward, earnest gesture. "This vote has to pass, or there will be another uprising."

"You don't have to threaten—"

"I'm not making threats." He slapped the hat against his leg. "I'm just—I'm telling you. Drop the prissy act, will you?" He sighed. "At this point, you're the closest thing to an ally in high places those of us still slogging through day wages have."

"Believe me, Theo—Prince Theodor is taking all of this into consideration, and his small council will bring the Reform Bill to the Council of Nobles within the fortnight."

"And if it doesn't pass, what happens?"

I hesitated. The revolt had failed at Midwinter, but another uprising would be better thought out, less incumbent upon a single man's plan, and fueled by what could only be seen as an utter failure by their own government. The people had risen up once, and their anger still simmered, ready and willing to boil over again. "I know," I replied softly. "More blood."

"Not just another revolt. A real revolution, fully organized and unwilling to yield. If they allow you to try this your way, with politics, and you fail them?" He shook his head with a low whistle.

"The price of failing will be unimaginable."

"But the future doesn't have to cost blood," Niko said, earnest belief in the words.

A lump formed in my throat, awkward to talk around as I tried to ignore it. "That sounds like one of Kristos's catchphrases."

"It is. It's new," Niko said.

"You—is he here?" Panic pressed against the lump and made my voice catch. "He can't—they might not catch you, Niko, but he's not—"

"Calm down, and maybe don't use my name." Niko's dark eyes narrowed.

I met them, stony and unflinching. "You don't get to tell me to be calm, not about this. Tell me. My brother."

"I've been keeping him informed of the situation here, and he's been writing. I found a new printer and of course we still have our old distribution channels. No, I won't tell you how or where or what his address is."

"I wouldn't ask," I retorted.

"But it brings me to the point, Sophie. We're working, on our end, to make promises that we can't keep alone. Your brother's writing is encouraging the people to hold fast and wait for the Reform Bill. That it's enough. That they don't need to riot or burn anything down." He smirked. "I'm guessing you have no idea how many times I've told Red Caps down at the Rose and Fir to put the pitchforks away and wait. But they need to get something worth waiting for."

"I agree completely," I said. A tuft of flaxwood seeds settled on Niko's shoulder. I resisted the impulse to pluck it off.

"Then do something. When you talk to those nobles, be a voice for us. I don't think they'll believe it when your prince claims the people are ready to take up arms again the way they'll believe it when you tell them. You're close enough to the ground to speak for the dirt."

I didn't like that analogy, but he was right. In the limited time I had spent with the nobles as Theodor's guest, I felt both their disdain and their curiosity. "So you hunted me down just to ask me to talk more?"

"Be our voice." He clutched the well-worn hat. Its top was bleached gray. "Help us. I—I know I wasn't exactly kind to you this winter, and your brother never understood you or your insistence on spending your talents on nobles. You certainly didn't make any friends spurning poor Jack in favor of being a noble's doxy." I bit my lip. "But I have to admit that you're in a position we never could have dreamed of. It might lead to nothing, in the end. But damn it all, Sophie, use it."

The lump in my throat grew again. I had managed to ignore, most days, that I returned alone to the row house I had shared with my brother every evening, to bury any sorrow over his absence in anger at how he had used me at Midwinter. But I did miss him, and deep in the pit of my stomach, a bitter kernel of worry often swelled into full-blown fear for him. I wanted, desperately, to ask if Kristos had any hand in seeking me out, if he had said anything about me. But I couldn't. I didn't want to know any more about my brother in exile, not really. Knowing meant being responsible for keeping that information safe. I needed the distance.

I straightened. I needed the distance from Niko, too. I couldn't be tied up with a fugitive, and I didn't want to risk Kristos's life by knowing any more about his whereabouts. "You have my word, Niko. I will advocate for what I can, when I can." Even, I knew, if it meant driving a deeper wedge between me and the nobles that made up Theodor's world. "But don't contact me again."

"I will have little trouble," Niko replied with a grin like cracked porcelain, "keeping that promise."

2

—⁂—

"DID YOU FIND ANY DECENT SILK?" THEODOR EXAMINED THE tightly closed bud of a yellow rose next to him; pink and cream climbing roses bloomed in a cascade of petals in the arbor. He had carefully trained them himself, nudging their fledgling vines up the trellis as they grew, year after year.

"Oh, loads. Cottons, too. And a nice set of wools—good colors, not drab stuff. Alice and I spent all day, and I'll be going back tomorrow for a few more pieces. You want to come peruse the wares?" I joked.

"I wish I could. The small council is finalizing the Reform Bill. It goes to the Council of Nobles for debate as soon as we can hammer out the election regulations."

"Finally," I breathed in near reverence for the bill that had taken months for the group of council members under Theodor's leadership to draft. "Elections—for the councils replacing the Lords of Stones, Keys, and Coin?"

"Those elections exactly, and the Council of Country." A smile crept over his face at saying the name borne of a concept cobbled together from political theory books, my brother's revolutionary writing, and hours of discussion with his small council. What was only an idea would be, if the bill passed, real seats of government filled by real people, elected by their peers, in the fall, serving as a second and equal governing body alongside the Council of Nobles. *When the bill passed*, I amended. I had to believe it would.

"So close," I breathed. "You included the voting provision for women, yes?"

"Let's not push," Theodor said. "The suggestion horrified enough of the small council that it will have to be put off for now. The bill has to be as perfect a presentation as possible," he added. "If it's too radical, they'll call for a quick vote and eliminate it right off, then recess and trot off to their estates for the rest of the summer."

"But it has to be enough," I countered. My relationship to the movement I had thought of for so long as "my brother's revolution" was messy and difficult, but I knew that trivial changes wouldn't be enough. Not for Niko, and not for the thousands he certainly spoke for.

And not, I accepted, for me, either. I had never peddled pamphlets in the streets or been willing to risk fire and scythe in a coup, but change could come without violence now. The past months had shifted that, working quietly with Theodor to build and revise this monumental piece of legislation. Of course I wasn't welcome in the chambers of the Council of Nobles, but Theodor had asked my opinion, and I had carefully considered what insights he needed from the commoners of Galitha, as well as I could represent them. Moreover, working alongside one another, our relationship had changed in myriad minute and lasting ways. Spark and flash of early romance had softened and built into comfortable coals of earnest partnership.

Now reform—true, enduring change—was so close that it hung ripe and heavy like the early blackberries in Theodor's garden, and still as fragile as the unpicked fruit.

"I think," Theodor said with a statesman's deliberate care, "that it will be. The most important, most oft-repeated theme of the literature preceding the Midwinter Revolt was elected representation. Replacing the Lords of Coin, Keys, and Stones with elected bodies and creating an elected council to serve alongside the Council of Nobles should accomplish that."

"Yes," I said with some hesitancy. My brother and his friends would have happily seen the nobles' control removed completely. I knew, of course, that eradication of the Council of Nobles would have been the kiss of death for the bill itself. "And taxation? The imposition of taxes has always been contentious among the people."

"Indeed. I suggested a popular vote for all taxes, as your brother's pamphlets all suggest, knowing it would be rejected." I sighed, but Theodor held up a hand. "Knowing it would be rejected, but that requiring approval from their elected representatives in the Council of Country would, then, sound far more appealing."

"You're actually quite good at this," I said with a grin. I nodded. "Will this—all this—be enough?"

"I think so." He reached into the inside pocket of his coat. "If this is any indication."

He tossed a smudged pamphlet to me, its cheap binding already coming apart. *The Politics of Reform and the Duty of Conciliation: A Peoples' Responsibility.* "That sounds like one of my brother's titles," I joked weakly as I paged through it. *These reforms are hardly adequate, but they open a door of progress . . . We must not mistake compromise for concession . . . Our voices will be heard over the clamor of tradition, as reason and logic that convince the aristocracy of their own injustice.*

I set the paper down slowly. "This sounds like my brother's work," I whispered. So familiar in its cadence and diction, so like him. It was like holding a part of him in my hands, letting an echo of his voice speak over incalculable distance.

"He said he would find a way to keep working. I suppose I should be grateful he's working in our favor. Somewhat," he said, nudging the page open to a particularly incendiary diatribe against the liberties taken by the nobility.

"I—he's not the only one." Even here in Theodor's serene garden, leaning against his chest, surrounded by roses in explosive bloom, Niko's charge followed me. "I saw Niko at the Silk Fair."

Theodor sat upright, pulling me to face him. "Niko Otni? He's evaded the Lord of Keys for months."

"He says you're not trying hard enough," I replied blandly.

"That may be true," Theodor said. "Things have been blessedly calm and the Lord of Keys hasn't wanted to upset the quiet with a manhunt."

"Well, Niko says you have him to thank for the quiet, too." I traced an over-bloomed rose with my fingertips, and its petals fell in a fragrant shower into my lap.

"What did he want?" Theodor brushed the rose petals from my skirt impatiently until I stayed his hand.

"To impress upon me my responsibility," I said loftily, then softened. "I need to advocate for the Reform Bill."

"You?" He caught himself. "Not that you aren't as well versed as anyone, but you're—" He stopped abruptly.

I watched the flush break over his fair cheeks, embarrassment at what he almost said. "Yes, it's because of who I am. A common woman. They'll believe me when I say the people are ready to rise up again if reform doesn't pass."

He nestled into quiet reflection of the yellow rosebud nearest him. "I suppose," he said finally, "that you may be correct." He pressed his lips together. "I confess that I've been...protecting you a bit."

I pulled his hand away from the rose and searched his face. "Protecting me?"

"If you were noble, if this match was more...conventional, we would be appearing together at social events far more often. Publicly, not quiet evenings at Viola's salon."

I nodded, appreciating this. I had only attended a couple of social functions with Theodor since the Midwinter Ball, and those had been small events, hosted by Viola at her salon or, more recently, by Theodor's brother Ambrose, who had insisted with firm kindness on making my acquaintance and including me in his monthly card parties. "You didn't want to put me through what the nobility would say. How they'd look at me."

"No, I didn't. They're not all like Viola and Annette and Ambrose. Some of them are far more wedded to tradition and the elevated separation of the nobles for the good of the country and all that rot. They're not pleasant when someone skips serving a fish course at a dinner, let alone something of this magnitude."

"I couldn't avoid them forever. I mean, not if..." I left that hope, that future unspoken but tangible.

"I know," Theodor confessed. "I suppose I figured they would eventually accept it without pushing them. That is, I had hoped that time would simply relieve them of their curiosity or surprise, but the tension surrounding the Reform Bill...there's no chance for them to calm down enough."

"I think," I said, hesitant but unwilling to back away now, "that it's time. I...I could have done more last fall and winter. Maybe. I don't know. But trying to hold the ground in between sides only resulted in..." I stopped, overcome for a moment remembering Nia, and Jack, and the hundreds of dead, nameless to me but known and fully loved by others. They had been neighbors, faces I passed in the street. Perhaps the nobility couldn't account for their loss, but I could. "I can't stand by again. Speaking for the common people is all I can do, so I will."

I paused, absently pulling a few petals from a rose. I didn't want to bring up the one additional thorn to appearing with Theodor at more social events, but I had to. I hadn't pressed the issue, but I had not been invited to the spring concert series his mother hosted at the palace, or the official coronation ball—of course, I hadn't particularly wanted to attend, either. If I was honest, I was content to avoid that potentially painfully terse situation as long as possible.

"What about your parents?"

"What about them?" He handed me a new rose, taking away the bare stem I held. "Oh. You mean—right. You'd certainly see them at some juncture and—yes." I waited. Theodor stared at his hand. I gently kicked his ankle. "I'm sorry, I'm sure once they meet you, they'll be delighted—"

"I doubt that they'll be delighted." We were going to have to deal with Theodor's reticence to face his parents about me at some point, but it didn't have to be today. "Maybe it's better if we don't attend anything with them, at least not right away."

Theodor studied my face with the same careful, delicate examination he usually reserved for botany. "Very well. That won't be difficult—we're often invited to different events. I can think of several opportunities. There's a dinner at the foreign minister's house, a concert, and a garden party."

"All this summer?"

"All in the next fortnight." He laughed at my shocked face. "And this is the off-season—most of the nobility are at their estates for the summer. Be glad it's not the height of the social season. We'd be swamped. And then that does introduce the question…you will be viewed as taking a more official role with me. As my intended."

"And the politics of that…"

"Damn the politics," he said, pulling me toward him and cupping my face. "You sit here and tell me you're willing to be ridiculed and outcast, you're willing to lose clients for your shop, all for the sake of the reform, and I'm not supposed to simply love you for you, no politics?" He kissed me, impulsive and bright, and knocked more petals into my hair.

"As much as you like," I said, tracing his cheek as I pulled back, "but you know that for you, marriage, and this one in particular, is acutely political." I was an outsider—perhaps harmless, perhaps a trivial novelty, but perhaps something too destabilizing for the already wounded system of nobility. Perhaps, even, an outsider viewed as a malicious threat. "Will the nobility read a threat in that? Will it push them away from reform?"

"You're not forgetting a large group of people we can surmise will be quite pleased at the union, are you?" I shook my head—of course I couldn't forget the people who surrounded me every day, who rented the row houses next to mine and bought strawberries in the street in front of my shop. "And given the fact that they're waiting for some real sign of progress on reform, I still say," he said, an arm tightening around my waist, "that this is a politically expedient marriage. The old bats can balk all they like, but what could possibly convey how serious I am about the common citizens of Galitha more than marrying one?"

"Getting the reforms passed." I laughed.

"Fair enough. I'm working on it." He tweaked my nose, and I swatted his hand away with a grin. "Formal dinner next week then?"

I mustered my resolve and offered him a gentlemanly handshake, which he returned, then kissed my palm. "You have a deal."

3

—〰—

"I want to eat this," Emmi said, pulling a bolt of shot silk, cross-woven with gold and pink warp and weft, from the shelf. It was newly arrived from the Silk Fair and had already been picked up for an order. "Really. It's just too delicious."

"But can you imagine a whole gown of it?" Alice asked, screwing up her mouth. The dual colors produced a brilliant sunset hue, and the effect was bright—almost too bright.

"Yes," replied Emmi dreamily. "With a sheer white apron to break it up? Trim of the same fabric?"

"On some fat old countess dripping gems, toting a tiny dog that smells of the scullery? That's who would pick that color, not some fashionable young lady." Alice shook her head. "You'll see."

Emmi just laughed. "What fell in your tea this morning?"

"Plaster, actually," Alice said. "The roof is leaking again. At least it's cropping up now and not in the middle of winter."

Alice did seem in a more dour mood than usual, and Emmi more effervescent. The two usually coexisted quite peacefully, almost complementary in their moods. Today, I feared, might be an exception. Still, Alice had the management of the shop's schedule, ledger, and staff of two so well in hand that I felt more and more at ease leaving it in her charge when I had business elsewhere. Someday, I knew, Alice would make a fine shop owner. The thought came as a sharp, almost painful, surprise, that if I ever left shopkeeping, for marriage or politics, having Alice take over my shop and its license would be a nearly seamless transition, in everything but the charm casting.

"At least this time we needn't worry about whether the customer can carry a whole ensemble," I said. The silk was for a sash, for one of the frothy white chemise gowns in the style I had created and that Viola had made so popular. All of the ladies at Viola's salon had one, created by me or by one of the dozens of other seamstresses who had quickly copied the style for their clients. A welcome bit of unadulterated professional pride swelled in my chest—I had set a new style. The city's elite seamstresses, the private hires and upscale shops, were copying me. Though I had built my business on charm casting, becoming known for my designs and the quality of my work had always been a quiet, driving goal.

"And for that, it's absolutely perfect," Alice said, holding the length of silk she cut next to the white cotton voile.

Emmi couldn't disagree, and she set to stitching the bright edges into a tiny hem. "One more down," she said, "and the board still full."

"Very good," I said. "I'm going to try to catch up on pieces that are waiting on charms." That list was growing—and only I could complete those orders. Emmi was a charm caster in the traditional Pellian methods of clay tablets and herb sachets, but our limited lessons with charm-cast stitches had proven ineffective, and there wasn't time to spend on refining her technique.

I slipped behind my screen in the workroom, taking a deep breath to push the list of orders and deadlines to the back of my mind as I sank onto the divan. The piece was one of my favorites from the spring's commissions, a dainty blue riding habit trimmed in sharp black. The young merchant's wife who had commissioned it had been content with imbuing the trim with the protection spell she wanted. It allowed for precision with the charm and, better, let Alice and Emmi handle the construction of the jacket and petticoat themselves. I threaded my needle with black silk and began with an anchoring stitch. The black wool tape was already pinned in place with Alice's careful workmanship. I took a few uncharmed stitches to begin to tack it securely into place.

Then I took a deliberate breath and began to pull the charm into the thread as I stitched. The golden light gathered around my needle and thread, and I fell into the easy rhythm of drawing the charm into each small stitch I made. I had only finished a few inches when my needle slipped.

At least, that was my first assumption—the golden light I was so used to controlling hiccupped and then receded. I caught it and drew it back, and resumed sewing. But it happened again, and as I squinted at the fabric under my hands, I almost dropped my needle.

Black sparks like hard obsidian speckled the pale blue—not that anyone else would see them. They were the marks of a curse, the dark magic that a curse caster would deliberately pull into their work. But I wasn't curse casting—I was casting a charm as I had done hundreds of times before. Impatient and more than a little frightened, I waved my hand over the black sparkle and it dissipated quickly.

But now the golden light was fickle and reluctant, fighting my needle and my thoughts like it had a will of its own. More than once I saw the black glittering lines encroaching on the golden lines of stitching, as though they thought I was calling them into my work, as well. I wasn't—I deliberately pushed them away, but they hovered, threatening to tie themselves into the stitches as firmly as the pale light. I struggled to complete the row of trim, frustrated with the sloppy stitching and weak charm that my work produced.

Confused, I lay the piece aside. Was I just tired? Was there something about this piece, about the young woman it was for, about the materials? Nothing about the piece itself seemed out of the ordinary, and the recipient of a charm had never mattered before. Had I been reusing materials, I would have wondered if, somehow, they had been previously charmed, but these were brand-new woolens and threads. As I examined them, they bore no signs of charming or cursing—and I would have seen either clearly.

Startled, I realized that the proximity of the curse magic had not made me feel ill, either. Controlling the glinting black as I had stitched it into the queen's shawl had made me nauseated and fatigued, even as I progressed in my control of it. Maybe if I didn't try to control it, I was free of its effects. This made me feel a bit better—I hadn't drawn the darkness into my work. It hadn't worked through me; if it had, I surely would have felt ill.

I stood up, shaking my hands as though I could shake the problem away. I was tired, I concluded, overwhelmed by the influx of orders. The conclusion didn't satisfy me, but I pushed the concerns aside and returned to the main workroom, determined to finish cutting a new gown instead.

"Is this the right fabric for the bodice lining?" Emmi asked as I scanned the specifics of the order, a deep wine silk gown for a minor countess. Imbuing different stomachers with different charms had been her ingenious idea—one for love, one for luck, one for financial fortune—to interchange as she needed. The gown itself, however, could be sewn entirely by Alice and Emmi, and would avoid further backlog for me.

I glanced up and nodded. "You've picked up on the linen

weights very quickly," I praised her. It had taken my former assistant, Penny, the better part of three months to finally discern the difference between linen lining fabric, hemp drill, and linen sheeting.

"I enjoy it," she said. "It's so much more interesting than helping at home or working for Nanni Defaro at the fishmonger's." I didn't doubt that. Nanni was a cranky old bat from everything Emmi had told me, and fish . . . I didn't relish the idea of handling fish all day, either. "And it's—it's a real trade, you know?"

I did. Even if Emmi never progressed to the level that Alice had achieved, she would always have adequate skill to be an assistant in a seamstress shop. I had no doubt she could do even better. I sighed—I needed to take the time to train her more thoroughly, not only for the benefit of my shop's bloated to-do list, but for Emmi's future, as well.

"Help me draft out these sleeves," I said.

"Oh, I've never—"

"I know." I handed her a ruler. "I'll show you how, and then you repeat the process. It's just translating these measurements to the fabric—and we'll cut a muslin for fitting first. Make a mistake, and we can just put it in the scrap bin."

Emmi smiled nervously, and soon we were so engrossed in patterning Countess Rollet's sleeves that I had almost forgotten my loss of charm-casting control.

4

THE PUBLIC GARDENS SPILLED OVER WITH BLOSSOMS AND GREENERY under the steady summer sun, and the quiet of the winter months was replaced with promenading couples, ladies having picnics, and rumpled children singing rhymes as they were herded away from fountains by patient nursemaids and harried mothers. The broad avenues were as bright as the beds of flowers, with ladies in walking gowns of cheerful cotton prints and men in vibrant silks, dressing to be seen. The poorer classes, not to be outdone, wore sashes and kerchiefs of crimson silk and indigo printed cottons, economy allowing for these small indulgences of color.

"It's not quite so private in the summer, is it?" Theodor asked as we walked toward the greenhouse. The doors were open and the greenhouse, though currently lacking the novelty of a living garden in the midst of winter, was flooded with people exploring the aisles of exotic plants, exclaiming in wonder as they read the placards Theodor had written.

"No, but I'm glad your work hasn't gone unnoticed," I said. "Even if it means it won't be as quiet next winter, I hope they come back to see it then. In winter, it's magic."

"If I hadn't built it, I'd agree with you," he said. "And even then, flowers in winter do seem a bit like something your charms ought to produce, not metal and glass." He led me past the greenhouse. "I think I know a spot that will be a bit quieter," he confided. The formal gardens gave way to the wooded park, where several picnickers stopped their progress to whisper as we passed. I tilted my head down, hiding my flushed face behind my enormous silk-covered hat. Theodor, with gentlemanly bravado, lifted his ebony walking stick in a show of pleasant greeting.

"Let's go this way," he said, diverting down a narrow path of crushed shells into the forest.

I lifted my skirts over a wayward root. I didn't know the gardens well; though Theodor and I had spent countless hours here, most of them were in the greenhouse, often with Theodor in shirtsleeves and me with a large bib apron, repotting saplings or pruning roses. It was Theodor's escape from the endless haggling and needling of the Council of Nobles, and though I never cared for dibbling in the dirt like he did, there was something close to normalcy about working alongside one another. I could forget, with matching lines of dirt under our nails, that he was noble and I was common-born.

"Ah, as quiet as I expected," Theodor said. He ushered me into a quiet glade at the top of a hill, the branches above fracturing the sunlight and casting intricate, ever-moving shadows on a clear pool in the center. The pool cascaded to another just below it, and another, all the way down to a stand of willows, fronds brushing the water like languid golden fingers.

I gasped as I realized where we were—the waterfalls Theodor had brought me to when we had left Viola's card party, shaken and afraid in the tumult of the weeks preceding the Midwinter Revolt. They had been frozen and staid in the cold, not the laughing cascades they were now.

"You remember?" He took my hands in his.

"Of course I do," I breathed.

"Good." Theodor grinned. "If you didn't, it would make this rather awkward." He pulled a thin chain of gold from his pocket, the links so minute that it looked more like a thick thread of winking metal. My jaw loosened and my eyes brimmed with sudden, sweet tears—I knew this tradition even if I had never seen the ritual unfold.

"I would tie my lot to yours," Theodor said, draping the chain over his left wrist, "and bind our lives together." He held out his hand to me. "Would you take the same vow?" I found I had no voice, but I laid my trembling fingers over his, and he brought the chain over my wrist, sealing a Galatine betrothal.

The gold bound our hands together only temporarily, but I knew what I was agreeing to, letting its cool links settle on my skin. I could swear that I almost tasted the traditional words Theodor had recited as he kissed me. I exhaled as he pulled away.

"Are you all right? To my understanding, most women eventually say something," he coaxed.

"Yes, I—"

"You do want this, don't you?" He lifted my chin to meet his eyes. "I know it doesn't seem an easy road, potholed with stodgy old nobles, but I know this is right. For us, for Galitha—"

"Yes, this is what I want," I stopped him, the gold chains on our wrists clinking gently together. I didn't need to be sold on the prospect of marrying the man I loved, and better positioning myself to look out for the interests of my neighbors, my friends, the common folk of my country in the process. I had faced the fears I no longer needed to say, that I would never be accepted, and that I would have to give up the security and, indeed, identity of my shop. I had come to accept those fears, their attenuate risks. I understood now that inaction meant risking more than making a choice did.

"I know this means giving your shop up, eventually," Theodor said. "I know that you don't take that lightly, and neither do I."

I nodded, then gripped his hand. "I know. I even know what I want to do—there are fewer charmed commissions than before, and Alice is already taking over more and more." I couldn't keep the shop, but the shop didn't have to close. All my years of relentless work didn't have to end with empty shop windows, a cold grate in my atelier, and the loss of my employees' jobs. I could close off charmed commissions, finish those I already had in the queue, hire at least one more seamstress if not two—it was as easy to plan out as it was difficult to imagine my life without the shop.

"When the reforms pass, you can even sell it to her," he said. "At whatever rate you think fair."

Somewhere between all the money in Galitha and nothing at all, I thought with a wistful smile. "She could never afford the cost of what it's worth. I would sign it over as a bequest."

"Now, let's see if I can do this right," Theodor said, turning our still-bound wrists. He crisscrossed the chain, revealing a pair of minute clasps. With a gentle hand, he unhooked them, revealing that the chain was in fact two lengths of gold, one to wear on each of our wrists. I traced the gold with a tentative fingertip; I'd seen bracelets on wealthy clients, while poorer Galatines usually used silk ribbons. The slight weight felt strange, a foreign, if welcome, presence. A constant presence, I reminded myself, as the binding wasn't traditionally removed until the wedding. By then the ribbons poorer people used were ragged and stained, but, just like the metal wristlets the wealthy used, were saved as family keepsakes, sometimes worked into baby gowns or made into rosettes on a prized piece of embroidery.

The gold winked at me in the bright sunlight as I wrapped my arms around Theodor and let him sweep me off my feet and into a long embrace as the cascading water played a bright melody.

5

I COULDN'T KEEP THE NEWS OF MY ENGAGEMENT TO THEODOR quiet for long. Emmi spotted the gold chain within moments of arriving at work the next morning and squealed loudly enough that a farmer selling snap peas outside our door stopped to peer inside.

"And it's real gold," she said, touching it and then retracting her hand as though she'd been burned. "Not that it wouldn't be, of course, but I've never seen a real gold betrothal binding before. Only ribbons!"

"We really ought to have anticipated this," Alice said, almost chiding in her careful tone. "I suppose the wedding will be before fall?" she added.

"We haven't decided," I said. A noble wedding was an involved affair, especially with the heir to the throne involved. His priority—and mine—was bringing the Reform Bill to a conclusive, passing vote. Still, Galatine engagements were not typically more than a few months long. That gave me until winter, at most, to ready the shop. Alice's measured gaze on the thin gold marking my wrist told me that she had thought of this, too. Of course—in her mind, the engagement meant the closure of the shop, unemployment for her, and an uncertain future.

I would alleviate her of that concern soon, and for now there was little uncertainty for the coming months. The slate hanging above the counter that held the list of orders was so cramped that Alice's neat handwriting couldn't keep them from running into one another. There wasn't time to spare.

"All right," I said as Alice and Emmi packed orders in brown paper behind me. "Emmi, take these orders out for delivery." As she gathered the teetering pile of packages and scurried out the door, I turned to Alice. "I can't be the Prince of Westland's wife and run a shop. But you already knew that," I added with a soft smile.

"I'm sorry, I didn't mean to be rude." Her hands fidgeted through a pile of receipts.

I took them from her and tucked them into their box. "It's not rude. It's business. And I'd like it to be yours."

Alice blanched, the roses in her cheeks fading as she sat, hard, on the bench behind the counter. "Mine?"

"Who better?" I laughed. "For now, I want to clear our slate of charmed orders, stop taking more, and let you take over day-to-day operations. When the Reform Bill passes," I added, purposefully avoiding the *if* I knew was more accurate, "I'll sign the shop over to you."

"I can't possibly buy the shop, not now—maybe in a year, or two, if I can save and get my family to—"

"I don't want payment. Legally, it will be a bequest," I said quietly. There was no amount of money that seemed fair, in exchange for the years of life I'd spent on building the business, establishing clients, making a name for myself. Yet I didn't want that work to go to waste, and if someone talented and invested didn't take the shop under her guidance, it would shutter. "Legally, practically, and in every other manner, I cannot keep this business and marry Theodor. I've made my choice, and

I have to leave it behind." I paused—I spoke of my shop almost like a person, a traveling companion whose road finally diverged from mine. I had a new vocation now, as a voice for the quiet majority of Galatines, leveraging my position among the nobility. Even after the reforms passed, that voice would be necessary.

"I—I can't accept that," Alice said, repressing the excitement in her voice. I knew she wanted to open her own shop someday, and I'd always anticipated losing her to her well-earned ambition.

"You can. Understand, this isn't purely a favor, a gift to you. This shop has been a place of employment for…" I counted quickly, surprising even myself as I said, "For over a dozen women since I opened. I've given women a place to earn a fair wage, to gain skills and experience." The options most commonly granted to women for work—servants, laundresses, market women—were sparse and few offered the potential that dressmaking did. "I very much want it to continue to be that sort of place, not just for experienced seamstresses, but for less practiced girls, too." Emmi had taught me the value of looking past a girl's current skill level and toward her ability and willingness to learn. Though Emmi had not been a seamstress by trade when I had hired her to help me just before the insurrection, she had proved quick with a needle and thread. She had been so successful—and appreciative of an opportunity usually beyond her—that even Alice, dubious of the decision at first, had come around on her intrinsic value in our shop.

"And in that vein," I continued, "we need to hire more seamstresses. If I won't be here much longer, you'll need to have at least one, if not two, new staff ready, and soon."

Alice nodded. "I'll place an ad in the *Weekly* tomorrow." Once practical tasks superseded talk, Alice's unease dissipated. Accepting such a proposition was not easy for Alice, who liked to see clearly that she had earned what she had gained, one of the many reasons I knew she had the steady head and pragmatic temperament necessary to continue the work I had started.

"One more thing," I said. "I'd like you to hire at least one Pellian, if you can."

Alice exhaled carefully, weighing her words. "We got very lucky with Emmi. But Pellians—few are trained in fine sewing. You know as well as I do that we need more help than someone sweeping the back. Emmi still isn't quite up to where Penny was."

"I know," I said, "and I won't argue that it doesn't make more work, up front. But, Alice—they're not trained in fine sewing because they're not hired by the milliners and dressmakers as day laborers and apprentices. If any of them wanted to learn, we're the only chance they have. And Emmi works harder than Penny. She knows she has a lot to learn, and she dedicates herself to it."

"There are Galatine girls who need work, too, you know," Alice said gently. I knew she meant it kindly, reminding me I was helping a girl support herself no matter what.

I had helped many Galatine girls over the years. And though I wished I could say that I had done so solely because they needed my shop, in truth, I needed them. I wanted the façade of a fine Galatine atelier, with the polished wood counter and the plate-glass window framing my best work and primly dressed assistants in starched caps and aprons. I had built a proper Galatine shop, and I had populated it with Galatines. I had been, I accepted, neglectful.

"You're right, of course," I replied, "that any girl we can hire and give a reference to is better off because of it. And I certainly don't mean to say that we oughtn't to hire Galatines, too. But a Pellian girl—you know as well as I that very few shops will take a risk on her."

Alice pursed her lips. The color had returned to her cheeks in sharp points, whether of frustration or embarrassment, I didn't know. "You were right about Emmi," she finally said. "We'll see how it goes for another time."

Impulsively, I hugged Alice. Her arms stiffened, then relaxed. "You'll be a wonderful shop owner. Better than me, I'd wager." Then I glanced at the slate. "And now, to get these charmed orders finished."

I returned to the riding habit I'd left the last time I'd tried to charm cast. I began to sew, and finished one side of the jacket's front before I sensed something strange, like a constantly moving itch or a person standing just outside the periphery of my vision. The charmed light I held to my needle faded, spreading out like ink on wet paper, and the itch intensified as the dark glint of curse magic encroached on the space.

Quickly, I tied off my thread, leaving the jacket half-charmed as curse magic hovered around my needle. My hand shook, the needle warbling between diffuse charmed light and dark sparkle. I couldn't pull the light away from the dark, and began to panic.

No, I told myself silently, forcing myself to set the needle down, stabbing it into the riding habit's pale blue wool. I was shocked when a dark smudge embedded itself alongside the needle. I hadn't meant to include charm or curse at all. Drawing on a skill I hadn't touched in months, I removed the curse using the method I had learned for the queen's shawl. It disappeared back into the ether.

I set the jacket down carefully and stared at it. What was I going to do? We had a full slate of orders, a good number of which required my skills. If I couldn't reliably charm cast, how could I finish them? The last thing I wanted to do was hand a business with a faltering reputation over to Alice.

I wasn't sure how I could find out what was wrong with my

charm casting, either. None of the other charm casters I knew, Emmi included, cast curses. It was taboo. How could I explain the sudden, unwelcome presence of what only a curse caster would recognize to begin with? There was still only one person who knew I had cursed the queen's shawl, and Theodor couldn't help me with this problem.

There was nothing to be done about it today, at any rate. Maybe I only needed time, a short break, some focus.

Shouts outside foretold that focus was not going to be in great supply.

I followed the noise to the front room, where Alice and Emmi were already pressed against a window.

"Did I miss a holiday?" I asked, though I couldn't help but feel apprehensive. Not after the riots the summer before or the revolt that started in the streets at Midwinter.

"I think we all did," Alice said, pointing at the crowd gathering, waving sticks with bright strips of cloth attached. To my relief, they looked happy.

I opened the door, the bright afternoon sun baking the stones outside and painting a glistening sheen on the people I now saw clearly were revelers, not rioters. They waved colorful red banners, some brilliant scarlet and some a duller madder red—whatever their bearers had managed to find on short notice.

"Hurrah for the Prince of Westland!" A coherent voice emerged from the joyful shouting. And another, "Reform is coming!"

"It passed?" Emmi asked, incredulous.

I shook my head—the bill had only just been drafted, and I knew contentious debate was still to come, not to mention the vote itself.

A passerby pressed a broadside into Emmi's hands. "The

prince's reforms were officially introduced to the floor today!" He brandished his banner, the vermilion cotton matching his red cap. "Read these—these will make for a better Galitha!"

Emmi and Alice read the broadside, listing the high points of the Reform Bill I already knew like a well-worn book from hours talking with Theodor, but as the merry band paraded down the street, I couldn't dissuade myself from worry. The people were in clear favor of a bill that would only pass after a fight. Would this merriment turn to violence in the wake of disappointment?

"We should get back to work," I said quietly, watching the brilliant scarlet fade as the crowd moved into the summer haze.

6

—〰—

I THREW MY COMB DOWN, READY TO GIVE UP ON DRESSING MY hair for the formal dinner I had agreed to attend with Theodor. I knew how nobles managed elaborate hairstyles—they had their maids trained in hairdressing or hired professional hairdressers. I had no such luxury, but a formal dinner demanded a formal hairstyle nonetheless. Even more now, with the prince's gold wrapped around my wrist, I had implicitly agreed to looking the part of royal consort. The rose scent from the powder wafted into my nose. I had liked it when I had selected it at the apothecary's, but now it made me want to sneeze.

The bells from Fountain Square warned me that it was six o'clock already, and Theodor's coach would be at my door in half an hour. I hadn't dressed yet, wanting to spare my new gown an unhealthy dose of powder from my hair. I shook a little more powder into the front, took a breath, and rolled it onto the wool pad again. This time the modest pompadour was smooth and at least reasonably even. I quickly pinned it in place and gave up on the idea of more elaborate curls on the sides, settling instead for a simple chignon and loop of hair at the nape of my neck.

I hoped that the new gown, a brilliant turquoise silk with perfectly stitched pleats cascading down the back, courtesy of

Alice, and trimmed with box-pleated strips of the same fabric, my own work, would distract anyone from the near travesty on my head. The prospect of accompanying Theodor to more public events had spurred me to remedy the severe lack of formal clothing in my own collection. I had made the turquoise gown, had begun another gown appropriate for a ball or dinner in a pale coral pink, and sitting in pieces in my bedroom were the beginnings of a court gown for the most formal occasions.

New gowns could only prepare me in part for accompanying Theodor anywhere, however. Any public appearance with an heir to the throne was complexly coded, read by the nobility as a message of intention and, often, political machinations. When the son of a minor noble appeared at his aunt's birthday dinner with a duchess above his station as his guest, Viola's salon had buzzed for a week over the alliance growing between the families.

Rumors had already circulated the city that the prince had bound hands with, depending on the source, a "heroic seamstress" or an "infernal doxy." I had, of course, anticipated gossip. There had been intermarriages between commoners and minor nobility in my recollection. Accounts of the weddings made it into the better monthly magazines; salacious gossip filled the cheap rags. It had been clear that money, or a lack of it for the nobles, had motivated most of the marriages. Successful merchants, especially speculators who wagered well in the gamble of imports and shipping, could accrue more money than nobles whose estates were unlucky or mismanaged.

No one would assume that Theodor was courting me for my money. I laughed at the thought, but the laugh was spiked with nerves. It caught in my throat. There was no turning back, not now that I'd begun to uncouple myself from the shop, not now that I was about to appear on Theodor's arm wearing paired wristlets.

I had a reason to be there, I told myself strictly, and that reason was the betterment of Galitha and her people. I repeated this little mantra to myself as I pinned my stomacher and then my gown into place, checking in the mirror that the robings covering the gown's front edges were even and straight. The turquoise hue worked particularly well with my Pellian complexion—warm tones and dark hair that were unusual in the Galatine nobility. And that, I knew, meant that few other women would have a gown in this color. I consulted on enough gowns to have mastered the art of pairing silk hue to skin tone, complementing hair and eyes with the right touches of accent colors.

I plucked jewelry from my modest collection, deciding between paste peridot and real pearls from Theodor, knowing that the imitation peridot worked better with the gown but that the pearls wouldn't be sniffed out as inexpensive costume jewelry. Ultimately, I chose the peridot.

I hovered by my door, watching anxiously for Theodor, not wanting to make him wait or come to my door. My neighbors were gossiping enough as it was, and I didn't relish the attention. When the carriage maneuvered around the narrow corner, I was out the door in a flash.

"It's not the hippodrome," Theodor said as I rushed to close the door. "We aren't in the midst of a race. Though, speaking of races, there is a horse race I thought you might—"

"One thing at a time," I reminded him, though I couldn't help but laugh. "Perhaps we'll attend the dinner on your terms and the race on mine. Fancy a picnic on the general lawn?"

He smiled at my joke. I wished the suggestion hadn't been made in jest.

The foreign minister's house was on the outskirts of the city, in a relatively new district full of limestone façades and grand brickwork overlooking the bluff where the river began to widen into the harbor. I had rarely been here, save an occasional consultation with a newly moneyed merchant's wife or shipbuilder's daughter. Viola and Theodor both lived in older, though no less wealthy, districts.

We were escorted down the long hall, wider and more full of echoes than either Viola's or Theodor's townhouse. Each footfall sounded louder than I intended, uncontrolled against the marble floor. I took in the dining room in one look—nothing intimate about this place, not like Viola's salon. If I had thought myself at all prepared after spending afternoons and attending parties with Viola's set, I was quickly disabused of that notion. This was a level of formality and presence I had not experienced since the Midwinter Ball—and my mission here was entirely different. I realized I was less prepared for it than I had been to remove the curse from the queen's shawl.

I was relieved to be seated next to Viola. "I convinced Lady Juline to swap my seat for the Duchess of Pommerly," she whispered, nodding toward a bird-slender woman with a pompadour of pure white hair, surrounded by other octogenarians at the far end of the table. "I think they'll all be more comfortable if they're allowed to nod off during the sorbet course, don't you?"

"Thank you," I replied. With Viola beside me, at least I had an ally.

She sat, smoothing her delicate lavender gown. Amethysts bobbed in her ears, catching the candlelight, and a brilliant scarlet cockade winked at the edge of her neckline. "Your gown is delicious," she said as I took my seat next to her.

"Thank you," I said. "I haven't sewn for myself in ages."

The woman across the table from us glanced at me. I wasn't

sure if she had heard me, but I flushed anyway. Sewing for myself—no other woman here did that, save embroidered trifles and beadwork that they gave one another as gifts. I felt my cheeks growing red, but after all, this was what gave me the clout to speak for the common people, wasn't it? My calloused hands and long days of work?

"The color is superb," Viola continued. "I suppose you went to the Silk Fair this year?"

I swallowed against a dry mouth. "Yes, it was well attended."

"I hear that the Serafan silk production has suffered a bit from the droughts—the worms are overwarm or something," she said. "But that their dyes are as brilliant as ever."

I couldn't help discussing fabric. "They've dealt with the quality issues by producing some silks with larger slubs in them—rougher texture—and thinner, so it won't do for formal gowns, in my opinion. But it could make interesting wraps or dressing gowns. Dyed just so, the texture looks as though they even intended it."

"So cheap silk becomes the new fashion." Viola laughed.

"I think so," I said.

The woman across the table didn't seem interested in our conversation; no one did. Next to me, Theodor chatted amiably with a man with a graying mustache wearing full military uniform. Viola's tactic was immediately clear—she had made me seem completely at ease, discussing any old topic, knowing full well no one else was listening to what I was actually talking about.

"Speaking of silk," Viola said, digging into her pocket. "I nearly forgot. I know I should leave the sewing to you, but I made up a few of these." She pressed a cockade of scarlet and gray silk into my palm. "To support the Reform Bill. Red for obvious reasons, gray for the granite most of Galitha City is built on. Like building on a good foundation. Clever, no?"

I turned the silk cockade over in my hand. The gray reminded me of ink, and of winter, too, of the Midwinter Revolt. "It's perfect," I said.

"I know it doesn't exactly match your gown, but here," she said, handing me a pin. I affixed the cockade like a breast knot at the center of my gown.

"And I was looking forward to sitting next to Lady Juline!" I looked up—the speaker was Theodor's brother Ambrose. He grinned as he sat next to Viola.

"You can see if one of the prune and porridge set would like to trade." Viola laughed.

"Then I couldn't sit by Sophie," he said with a half-serious seated bow. "Congratulations are in order, I understand. Welcome to the family, and my apologies."

"Thank you," I said with a nervous laugh. The woman across the table was staring now, at the gold bracelet, and abruptly caught herself and turned away.

Ambrose took a quick swig of wine. "Did you finagle a date for the wedding? Autumn, I suppose? But then again—Mother hasn't been well lately, and she'll certainly want to take the helm." In truth, I hadn't even begun to consider the multilayered machinations of a noble wedding.

"Her migraines?" Viola asked. "Is she leaving for Rock's Ford for the summer soon, then?"

"Mother's trying to hold out until the council recesses, but Polly's working on her to go now. She even started flirting with that entirely reprehensible rake of a man Duke Tye of Underhill, just to convince her to leave the city earlier rather than later. Or too late, when she's late." He laughed.

"You're terrible," Viola said, "and your jokes are worse. Ah, the salad—tomatoes? Who plates a tomato and calls it a salad?" She prodded the runny crimson and gold disks on her plate with some disdain, but I enjoyed them, enhanced with salt and a dash of vinegar.

As we finished the salad course and moved on to the fish, conversations percolated from observations about the weather, the meal, conspicuous or absent guests. It was almost as though any topic of potential contentiousness was neatly avoided, the woman across the table from me even steering discourse nimbly away from summer weddings with a pointed glance at my wrist. This continued until the meal was nearly finished. Viola had been correct—the clutch of older guests at the end of the table had grown very quiet. I nudged her and we both laughed behind our hands.

"I don't think there's anything going for it," the man next to Theodor said, too loudly for the room, breaking the quiet hum of conversation. "Enough with reforms already. There's been enough concession as it is." Ambrose glanced at me and rolled his eyes with a subtle shake of his head. A keen student of law, he had supported Theodor's bill from the first, helping him draft and revise the nuanced codes and regulations that would provide legal structure to a new system.

"So I suppose you'd favor a return to last fall's riots and last winter's coup, then?" The woman across the table from me had a high, piercing voice. "General Whiteacre, perhaps you have the benefit of having missed this particular engagement, but I assure you, none of us wishes to repeat it."

"I didn't miss anything," General Whiteacre bellowed. I assumed she had touched a sore point. "I'm not afraid of rabble with pitchforks, but you lot can't see what you *should* be afraid of, and that's their grand ideas—not only stuff and nonsense, but dangerous poppycock. Impossible for a government to put into practice."

"How so?" Ambrose asked, the careful control in his tone

making even more plain Whiteacre's histrionics. "Are there particular legal theories or comparable government frameworks one could reference?"

Whiteacre avoided the request for a scholar's specifics. "The common man can never be expected to govern himself. That's what they want, at the end of it—you'll concede yourselves right out of governance. And when you're gone, what will the country have? Anarchy."

"Not a government of elected men?" Theodor said. "Hypothetically. That is what most of their writings aim at—elected representation."

"Commoners electing each other—yes, let's allow the pigs to rule the sty."

Viola glanced at me, her wide brown eyes taking in the entire scene at once, scanning the players and the setting as though arranging a painting. I could see it laid out on canvas, in a classic style, the quarreling statesmen-nobles arrayed on either side, the opulent setting, the remnants of the meal laid out like a still life, and me at the center, turquoise gown drawing the eyes to an unwilling focal point.

"I thought I was coming to dinner, not the hall at the council," Viola said. "I've avoided sitting in the gallery there long enough and now you're bringing it to me!"

There was some polite laughter, but General Whiteacre would not be quieted. "The common people don't have the gumption to sustain a revolution," he said.

I took a hesitant breath. "I believe, sir, that you would find yourself on the losing end if you laid stakes on that bet."

Viola's eyes widened, surprised that I'd spoken, and Theodor pressed his lips together until they turned white, clearly nervous on my behalf. Ambrose gave me an encouraging lopsided smile. I straightened my shoulders. "They were quite capable of fomenting one insurrection and will be all the more motivated if their patience is rewarded with inaction."

Whiteacre's bulbous nose turned a shade of crimson that the best dyes would have difficulty reproducing. Before he could reply, the woman across the table who had dealt him a swift retort turned her shrewd eyes on me. "Is this to be read, I wonder, as a threat from the insatiable masses?"

If I had thought her an ally in the cause of the reform, I had been mistaken. "I hardly think so," I stammered. "Merely a comment on their dedication."

"And I think it important," Theodor rushed to add, "that they are being very patient, given the circumstances. Why, half of the broadsides circulated are celebrations of the legal process and exhortations to patience, patience, more patience." His laugh was nervous, but I noted that several nobles, silent in this debate, were nodding.

"Speaking of wagers, I understand we're to be given quite a treat with the series of horse races this summer," Viola said, prompting several voices to fill the silence with chatter centering on the summer social events in the city. Even this topic, however, was tinged with conflict—the only reason so many nobles were staying in the city this summer was the Reform Bill. Most of them, in a peaceable kingdom, would be spending the summer away from the city, on their estates.

"I'm sorry for that outburst," Theodor said as we drove away. "I shouldn't have pressed Whiteacre—he's a blowhard. Knows the military but couldn't maneuver through passing a new law for his life."

"He's certainly not the only one with those particular opinions," I replied. If Theodor's goal for the evening had been to encourage an elite nobility to consider and begin to accept a commoner as a consort, I wasn't sure that we had been even remotely successful. "And it isn't only reform he's rejecting," I said, staring out the window. It was the idea that he was equal to someone like me at all. I was glad my side of the carriage overlooked the bluff and the river rather than the oversize houses on the other side of the road.

Theodor edged closer to me and laced his fingers through mine. "Men like him can bluster all they like, but they can't unmake this alliance. They can't go against legal reform. We'll outlast him."

"What if—what if we don't?" I recalled something from one of Kristos's books, one of the thick tomes I now suspected he had borrowed from Pyord Venko. Despite the dubious source of the material, the line stuck with me. "Stasis is easier than change, and it has its own momentum, entrenching itself," I paraphrased. "What if they won't change?"

"If reform passes, they have to change. Whether they like it or not."

"Do they?" My voice was small, barely a whisper. It challenged everything we had built our hopes on, but I had to voice the creeping doubts that Whiteacre had stirred in me.

"For them to go against the law would be treason. Just as much as assassination or secession or any other unthinkable act." He edged closer to me as we jounced over a particularly deep rut. "Reform won't be theirs to give or withhold any longer."

"But they still have the money, and control so much of the provincial regions—how will you make them?"

"They'll follow the law," Theodor repeated.

I hesitated. "Theodor, I—I don't mean to mistrust you, but these nobles—they've been working within a system of governance that gives them all of the authority for generations. Isn't it—perhaps—just a bit too optimistic to assume they'll bend to new laws?"

"Are you suggesting that the nobility would—what? All turn criminal overnight?"

"No," I answered, frustrated. "But when you see them, you see them as equals. I see them as people who have been at the top of a very unfair game of king of the mountain for a very long time. They don't know what the view looks like from anywhere but the top."

"Are you saying I'm...stepping on you? Keeping you below me?"

"No!" My hands clenched into fists around my silk petticoats. "That is, not on purpose. You can't help that you were born on the top of the mountain and I'm farther toward the bottom, but can't you see how you're allowed power that we're not?" I breathed out, quick and relieved to have finally said it out loud.

"But I'm trying to help! I'm trying to do right by you and everyone else in Galitha without the whole damn country falling apart!"

"I know! But—damn it all, Theodor, can't you see how *you* doing it is part and parcel of the problem? How it feels like something is being given?" I sucked in a breath. "How it feels like it could be taken away?"

He stared at me, at the crumpled silk in my hands and my stalwart confidence. He took a measured breath. "I can try to understand that better."

"Thank you."

"In the meantime, I think we can proceed with some assurance that even if they don't truly want to change, they're not interested in fighting a long-scale rebellion, so they'll pass the bill."

I accepted his confidence with a tentative smile. "I don't suppose they fancy fomenting civil war, disobeying the reform once it's law."

"Indeed not," he blustered with mock indignation. "Leave that to the upstart common rabble who think they can govern themselves! Poppycock!" I laughed—his imitation of Whiteacre was on the nose. "For now, there's piles of work to be done, and plenty of long evenings like that ahead of us." He took my hand. "I'm glad I'm facing it with you beside me."

7

SUNLIGHT ALREADY GILDED A PATH ACROSS THE COVERLET WHEN
I woke. Theodor was still sleeping, his hair falling into his face.
I gently extricated my arm from under his and slipped out of
bed, draping myself in the rosy silk wrapper Theodor kept for
me and tiptoeing to the window. Another rich summer day
bloomed outside, the sun burning the nighttime chill from the
distant harbor in a golden haze.

A knock at the door woke Theodor and startled me. "Come
in," he called lazily. I flushed—I still wasn't used to being seen
here, to the servants knowing I had spent the night. I imagined
them gossiping about me in the kitchen and their quarters.

The footman opened the door with his usual careful ceremony and deliberately avoided looking at me in my undress
clothing. "Lady Viola Snowmont is here for you, Your Grace."

"Viola? What time is it—she can't have already gotten up."
Theodor laughed. "Tell her she can wait in the boudoir if she's
willing to let me receive her in a banyan."

"Very well, Your Grace."

"I'll just—I'll wait here," I said awkwardly after the footman
closed the door.

"No need, I'm sure. Viola could have guessed you'd be

here." He rolled out of bed, running a hand through disheveled hair and reaching for his shirt.

"Let me get you a fresh one." I laughed. I took a newly pressed shirt from a pile of neatly folded clothes in his clothespress. "Socks, too?"

"I suppose that would be appropriate." I tossed him his underthings and he snatched them in midair. "You look presentable already."

I tugged on a pair of shoes. "Barely. What could Viola possibly want this early in the morning?"

Theodor shrugged, buttoning his breeches. "Who knows." He shrugged his shoulders through his chintz banyan and rubbed the last of the sleep from his eyes.

I was still blushing when Theodor opened the door for me into his boudoir. Of course Viola must have assumed that I spent plenty of nights here, but the acknowledgment in seeing one another here was different.

My apprehension melted when I saw Viola. Still wearing the gown and jewelry she had worn the night before, she was pale and pacing the boudoir, wringing her hands.

"Viola!" Theodor crossed the room in three strides to her. "What's wrong?"

She gripped his hand and took a deep breath. "I'm so sorry, Theo. I didn't—it wasn't anything I ever meant for anyone else to see."

"Viola, calm down. Sit down." Theodor guided her to a settee and she sank into the cushions. "I'll call for tea," he added, clearly gauging that his usual morning coffee would not help Viola's nerves.

"I can't just calm down, you've no idea!" She inhaled sharply, her collet necklace rising along with her voice as she added, "It's not that it's such an imposition for me, but it reflects on the royal family and—oh, I can't believe this."

I sank farther back against the silk-covered walls. "Sophie, I'm sorry to barge in on you like this," Viola said, taking a shaky breath. "But this—it affects you, as well. So please, please stay and listen, too?"

I nodded, trying not to look as worried as I felt.

"Theo, I just—I didn't know what else to do. I didn't want you to find out from anyone but me." She looked up at him with pleading eyes as she used the childish nickname.

"Vivi, please. You have to tell me what happened." Theodor sat patiently across from her, taking one of her trembling hands.

"After the dinner last night, I wanted to finish a...sketch I had started. Of Annette." She hesitated. "I pulled out my portfolio and charcoals, but that sketch, and several others, were missing." She flushed deep pink. I had never seen Viola embarrassed before. "Someone must have taken them during the dinner party I had the day before."

"I don't see why that matters so much. It's no secret that you and Annette are great friends and that you paint the royal family."

"They weren't for public viewing," she answered in a flat tone. "They were private. They were just for us."

My brow constricted in confusion, then released in surprise. Of course—I should have realized it, with all the time I had spent with them. Their dedication to one another, their shared grief when Annette was going to be married. The tranquil depth that ran between them like a swift-running river. Quietly, without naming it aloud, they had practiced a devotion that extended beyond friendship, and these sketches were Viola's expression of that intimacy.

Viola looked toward me. "I'm sorry, Sophie, I know it's...
we have always endeavored to be discreet, for the reputation of
both of our families. Very few people know, I hope you're not
offended that you were kept in ignorance."

"Of course not," I stammered. Affairs were understood but
rarely acknowledged in Galatine society, and romance between
two women could only be an affair, never sanctioned by the
legal name of marriage. I felt suddenly foolish and childish, first
acknowledging that Annette and Viola were the first such pair I
had ever known, then the slow and embarrassing realization that
I had probably known others with unspoken but enduring bonds
and been too blind to see them.

"But these sketches, Vivi. Someone took them," Theodor
said. "You don't know who. You're absolutely sure you didn't
misplace them, that Annette didn't take them home?"

"Of course I'm sure! I've been up all night searching the
house, and Annette would never have taken them home, are you
insane?" She stood up again and resumed pacing.

"Maybe someone took them as a joke," Theodor offered.
"And even if not—what? Who doesn't know already?" he asked,
a little too cavalier.

"No one knows, you know that. My dearest friends only.
Annette has, bless it, never even been one of the rumored vic-
tims of the insatiable nymphomania the gossip rags invented for
me. This is—this is your reputation, Theodor."

"I really don't care about that, Vivi. So there will likely be a
spate of rumors, some unflattering things printed in the magazines, maybe you won't be invited to some of the best parties this
season. But it will blow over."

"This reflects very badly on the royal family," she repeated.
"Your father's reign is very new, and anything that damages the
family damages him."

"Really, I wouldn't worry about it. All of this matters much less than how my father manages his politics." Theodor turned and walked toward me for a moment, meeting my eyes only briefly. I could tell he was lying. "This will blow over. You did nothing wrong."

Viola shook her head. "I can't even begin to make this up to you." Her big brown eyes misted over. "I'm sorry."

"Just keep your head down for a few weeks," Theodor said. A knock on the door announced the tea. I took the tray from the maid and shooed her away with a whispered apology.

I poured Viola a cup and dosed it with the splash of cream I knew she preferred. Her hands shook, the sound of rattling porcelain like the sound of nerves themselves.

"Thank you," she whispered to me.

"I just poured the tea," I said with a pale smile.

"No, for being…understanding. I know this is not exactly orthodox, and dragging you two down with me—you would have every right to be upset."

"Over what?" I picked up my own tea, then set it down, laughing. "Viola, I'm currently one half of the least orthodox romantic pairing in the entirety of Galitha."

She almost laughed along with me, but her smile stalled and she sipped her tea instead.

"Well," Theodor said after she had departed. "That worries me."

"I'm sure—I mean, it's fodder for vicious gossip, but hasn't Viola always been at the center of gossip?"

"Of course, yes. I feel badly for Viola, and my cousin, but what worries me is why someone would do this now."

"Isn't it just a nasty joke?"

"I hope so." Theodor sighed, leaning back. His banyan flopped open and I saw that the silver buckles at the knees of his breeches were still undone. "I worry it's a deliberate attempt to cast the royal family in a poor light, and right now, while the Reform Bill is under review."

"Why should this particular affair matter more than the usual lineup of salacious gossip?" I asked, knowing full well that it probably did.

"No one cares about our little dalliances and affairs, within reason. But of course we are expected to do our duty and marry and produce heirs, eventually. The noble families have always cared about that even if the populace doesn't. It's insurance for our own stability, keeping titles in families."

"And one affair threatens that?"

"In a way, yes." The maid arrived with Theodor's customary morning coffee. "We may be rather more open than the populace in terms of mistresses, but this is still beyond the pale. The implication is that Annette actively avoided marriage in favor of Viola. That interferes with the system. And the fact that, while daughter of the reigning monarch, Princess Annette could have compromised her duty for such an affair—it won't read well."

"I see," I said, balancing a delicate coffee cup on its saucer. "And you and Annette and Viola are particularly close, and that Annette is the king's niece—you all look irresponsible."

"Irresponsible and careless, to an old-guard noble's view." He sighed. "And given that proximity, my assumption has to be that someone stole those sketches as a deliberate attempt to undermine my father or me by association. Or both."

"Or the reforms." I swallowed this along with my coffee. My view of the conflict had been simplistic, the populist struggle Kristos had introduced me to—the common people against the oppression of the nobility. Theodor and Viola had complicated this already, making me understand the delicate international balance and economics these political questions affected. This added an entirely new wrinkle—that "the nobility" was no more homogenous than the populace, and could faction and infight on their own accord.

Theodor set his coffee cup down, staring at the dark liquid as though it could tell him what to do next. His shoulders slumped.

"I'm not making this easier, am I?" I whispered.

"You're making my life far more bearable right now."

"You know I mean in terms of reputation."

"I don't care. I didn't want you to speak, last night, at the dinner, didn't want you to have to feel that kind of scorn. But you did, and you—you only saw Whiteacre's face, didn't you?" I nodded. "But I saw the others around me, and they were listening, to you."

"To the harbinger of bad news," I replied. "Lovely."

"To the future." He sipped his coffee. "I'm not ready for this," he said, and I wasn't sure if he meant the coffee, the morning, or the entire situation as he plucked me from my chair and carried me back to bed.

8

I WAS RIGHT IN GAUGING THE POPULARITY OF THE WHITE COTTON dresses for daytime social events—they bloomed and bobbed along the riverbank. Different seamstresses had lent different touches; some sleeves were slim and fitted, others ballooned like sails in the wind; some added tiers of ruffles to the low-cut necklines, others, to the hemlines.

"You didn't wear one?" Theodor asked, gesturing toward Viola, Pauline, and a trio of women I didn't know, all wearing chemise gowns and huge silk-covered hats that looked like partially deflated mushrooms.

"I wanted to be different," I said blandly. I had remade an old pale gray silk gown to cut away in the front and reveal a red stomacher, a plain homage to the colors of reform.

Theodor suppressed a laugh. "It seems your success ran away with itself a bit."

As I looked over the sea of white gowns, I noticed something punctuating each of the white cotton dresses—red and gray, in sashes and cockades and ribbons. Like wine on a tablecloth or blood on snow, impossible to miss. I smiled, faintly. The chemise gown of my design was not only a fashion statement but, it seemed, part of a political one as well. I brushed the cockade nestled into a large double-looped bow at the top of my gown.

A gentleman in a dark blue suit approached Theodor. "I had hoped you'd be here, Your Grace," he said. Theodor forced a smile at the deferential title; this was a social occasion, but unlike Viola's salon, formality of rank persisted here.

"I had a question of clarification on the election procedures outlined in the Reform Bill before I feel, shall we say, comfortable placing my vote."

Theodor's resigned sigh was barely noticeable. "Of course." I slipped quietly away, drifting toward Viola.

"Sophie!" She caught my hand as soon as I was close enough to snare. Pauline greeted me as well, but two of the three women they had been talking to glided toward the rose arbor. "I'm glad you came. Theodor said you might not," she added. I was grateful she didn't continue—that my reasons for refusal would have been the back order at my shop.

Pauline smiled. "It's been ages since I've seen you!"

"You really should come to the salon more often," Viola said. "Or are you too busy selecting bridal silks and tasting cake recipes with Her Majesty the Queen?"

I forced a laugh; it sounded like a nervous squeak. "There's been so much to do," I said. I hadn't told Viola that Theodor's parents had yet to acknowledge the betrothal. "But you're both staying over the summer?"

Pauline shook her head. "I'm planning to leave for the old family haunt down south within the fortnight. Mother and I were waiting for Father to be free to come, but..." She hesitated, glancing at the other three women standing nearby, and decided not to continue.

"Old family haunt, indeed!" Viola laughed. "Sophie, the

Hardinghold family has the loveliest estate on the Rock River, with an orchard you couldn't believe."

"We grow the best pears in Galitha," Pauline confirmed. "And make the best pear cider," she added.

"I've need of another case for my cellar," the woman I didn't know replied. She was older than us, with faint lines of gray in her brown hair that, rather than detracting from her appearance, touched her hair like sunbeams.

"Of course," Pauline said. "Oh! I imagine you don't know Lady Sommerset."

"No, I haven't had the pleasure," I replied demurely.

Lady Sommerset held me in her level, precise gray eyes. Pauline continued the introduction. "Lady Dorsette Sommerset, this is Sophie Balstrade. Sophie, Lady Sommerset is the wife of Lord Sommerset of the Council of Nobles and the daughter of Lord Oakes. Lady Sommerset, Miss Balstrade is—"

"I know quite well," Lady Sommerset replied with a cool smile. "Her affiliations are certainly no secret in this company."

I swallowed a sharp retort and instead let my hand wander to the betrothal binding on my wrist. My meaning was clear—I was not going anywhere. "It's an honor to make your acquaintance, my lady," I murmured, keeping my gaze on her delicate pink silk slippers lest I allow the ice I had successfully kept out of my voice to show in my eyes.

"Indeed," she replied simply.

Viola brushed my arm. "I'm completely parched," she said. "Care for a sip of something?"

I agreed readily and let her pull me toward a vine-woven loggia spread with tables of petite cakes and grand displays of fruit. A large crystal punch bowl hid among a voluminous display of roses. "It's not just you," she said, dipping us each a cup of punch. "It's that Sommerset woman. Her husband is barely an anybody and he's a horrid estate manager. She thinks she can hang on by lording her old name over everyone."

"It is me, Viola," I said, keeping my voice low. "I'm sure she's no pearl, but I—I know that these occasions are not going to be like the salon."

"Well." She shook her head and sipped her punch with near-violent indifference, sending a tiny sliver of orange careening toward the rim. "It shouldn't matter what her political persuasions are; one is polite regardless."

"Politics," I muttered. "Everything comes back to politics."

Viola poked her orange slice back into her glass. "And you— with that little wrist flick, showing off your gold. Quite the subtle gibe."

"You know better than I do—how many people here actively hate me?"

Viola waved the question away like a fly. "I won't pretend to know how everyone's politics shake out. Anyone in support of reform sees your impending marriage as a beautiful symbol, and anyone opposing reform sees that marriage as political machination at best and dereliction of duty by Theodor at worst. If you wanted to know how the vote on the Reform Bill will swing, send out wedding invitations and see who replies with their acceptances and regrets." She laughed, but I knew that she was only half joking.

I glanced back at Lady Sommerset, curiosity overcoming my better instincts. She had returned to her gaggle of friends. None of them wore the white chemise gowns, and I noticed that three of them had gold and brilliant blue ribbons fashioned into complicated bows pinned to their gowns. Another had decorated her white silk-covered hat in blue and gold rosettes. She slipped a small book from her pocket, disentangling it from the fine cotton of her skirts with a harried flick of her hand. I squinted, but I couldn't see the title. The smirks on their faces, however, hinted at the content—a libertine piece, a saucy dialogue, or maybe a satirical work raking some current target over coals built of metaphor.

Theodor joined us, looking faintly drained. "I thought we were supposed to be playing croquet," he joked, "but I feel rather more like the ball, and the Reform Bill, the wickets."

"We ought to start a game," Viola said. "Just the thing to keep everyone behaving civilly toward one another—let them whack at something with sticks."

She sauntered toward the croquet pitch, already set up in a level promenade in the far end of the garden, motioning toward several ladies to join her. My only experience with the game was attempting to fight the ball over the divots of my first employer's tiny garden at a Midsummer party, but I was pleased to discover quickly the equality in our match—none of us was particularly good. I found myself actually laughing and joking with the ladies and gentlemen playing alongside me and—remarkably—they with me.

"Tell me," said one plump lady with azure-blue eyes and a silk hat to match, "is it true that the common folk actually want to elect representatives?"

I arrested the incredulous reply that came to mind first, and instead demurred, "Of course it's true. Why wouldn't it be?"

"I've heard so many people say that they don't think the common people are capable of the responsibility," she replied, lifting her croquet mallet and flicking a bit of clover from it. "I daresay it will be a new experience for them, if the bill passes."

I swallowed. This was why I was here, I reminded myself. "They are very used to responsibility," I said evenly. "The responsibility of feeding their families and heating their houses and caring for their children and their aged parents. They are well suited for the responsibility of maintaining their country's good health, as well."

She paused, taken aback by the seriousness of my reply. "I see," she said slowly. "Ah, dear, it's my turn. Quite the game, isn't it?"

I was flushed pink by the time the croquet games ended, having finished solidly in the middle of each match but feeling as though I had won something more. Several ladies and one lord had openly inquired or left an open avenue for my opinion on the reforms, and I had imparted, as confidently as I could, the pressing need and hopeful dedication of the common people. The common people, I didn't need to state in so many words, like me.

"You seem happier than after that stuffy dinner," Theodor commented as we drove away. "I didn't know you played croquet."

"Clearly, I don't." I laughed. "I didn't realize most nobles were so poorly practiced."

"It may have been the honey mead punch," Theodor confessed, "that led to quite a few missed wickets. At any rate, by the end of the match, you seemed rather at the center of things."

"I really don't enjoy being at the center of anything," I confided.

"I know. And there is something more I wanted to ask you to do, but I fear it's too much."

"Too much?" Irritation prickled in my voice. "You could let me decide about that."

Theodor resisted, then laughed, seeing that I was determined. "Every five years, the leaders of Galitha, Kvyset, East and West Serafe, and the Allied Equatorial States gather for a summit. We meet this year, at Midsummer, in West Serafe."

"West Serafe in midsummer. That sounds miserable," I

replied amenably, anticipating a request for summer-weight clothes for the queen or some other dignitary and mentally adjusting our already-tight schedule.

"I didn't pick it." Theodor sighed. "Clearly, this year poses some difficulties. The king does not want to leave Galitha so soon after the insurrection. The involvement of Kvys mercenaries—which the Kvys officials continue to claim they have no knowledge of, for what it's worth—is making that particular tension worse. And the only acceptable dignitary to send in place of the king is completely untrained and doesn't know his head from his ass."

"And who is that?"

"Me." Theodor's mouth twitched into a wry smile. "It's me, Sophie. I'm supposed to lead a diplomatic envoy to West Serafe in—what? A month?—and I have no idea what I'm doing."

"Oh," I said. My most pressing concern—how much I would miss him—surprised me with its strength, but I pushed it aside. "You have some experience, with international delegates coming here to Galitha. And you've traveled."

"Well, yes," he admitted. "I've sat in on dozens of meetings with the East and West Serafans, some with the Allied States, and a very cold late-autumn meeting in Kvyset. I suppose I did assist with hosting the delegation that came for Annette's marriage contract, too." He sighed. "It doesn't seem like enough preparation for actually representing the entire country."

"There probably isn't enough training in the world for that. But you'd best get used to it, Crown Prince." My laugh felt dry as sawdust—if he had to get used to representing an entire country's interests, I wasn't many steps behind him.

"I had hoped to convince you to accompany me." Anticipating my doubts, he rushed to add, "It's only a fortnight. Maybe a few days more if travel doesn't favor us. In almost any other circumstance, it would be customary for a spouse or fiancée to accompany a delegate. I recognize that this is not entirely typical, but I feel it sends a very important message for you to attend. To the common people of Galitha, to the nobility, to our allies."

I had not expected this. "I—I'm afraid I won't have the slightest idea of what to do."

"That will make two of us." He grinned. I rolled my eyes at his exaggeration. "I figured I'd alleviate our suffering a bit and invite Annette to accompany us. She's as savvy about foreign affairs as most of the council, but what's more, she understands the social nuances of all the dinners and receptions and whatnot." He traced his gold bracelet. "And then when we get back, we can get to planning a wedding in earnest."

My eyes widened, but I nodded. "All right. But if I'm being honest? I'm terrified."

"I know," he said. "I am, too."

9

EMMI AND I LEFT EARLY ONE MUGGY AFTERNOON TO JOIN OUR Pellian charm-casting friends at our favorite coffeehouse. The months after the Midwinter Revolt had been difficult for some of the casters; Venia's brothers had been involved and their livid father had thrown them out of the house, and Lieta had lost a son in the fighting. We didn't meet for months, with the city under a cold veil of mourning and its various factions—workers, merchants, nobles, Galatines, Pellians—uncertain in trusting one another. As spring thawed the city and the snow and ice released their hold on the streets, the meltwater began to flow, and we resumed our visits.

Lieta waited on the steps of the shop, facing the sun with her eyes closed in her weathered face. Emmi tapped her arm. "Ah!" she said with a grin. "The sun feels so wonderful, doesn't it?" I was surprised to see a red-and-gray cockade pinning closed her traditionally Pellian, busily printed cotton neckerchief. Viola's statement had caught on among her salon and spread through the class strata of Galitha City quickly enough, but I hadn't realized it had penetrated so deeply into the Pellian quarter that octogenarian Lieta would wear one.

Emmi and I had to laugh—the hot sun felt like choking

oppression to both of us. "It's just your dusty old bones that want to drink up the heat," Emmi joked.

"You two never knew Pellia. This—this is a fine summer's day in Pellia."

I shook my head. "Right now I think I'm grateful I've never known what a scorcher in Pellia feels like."

Lieta laughed. "Yes, the sun stretches—that's what we called the long midsummer dry spells—are a bit strong. Venia and Parit are inside."

Parit was Venia's cousin, a new member of our regular charm-casting group with a quick wit and a dry sense of humor. Like Venia, she had come from Pellia as a child, but like Emmi, she was more acclimated to Galatine culture than her cousin.

The women exchanged pleasantries, Emmi chattering happily about the new gown she was draping and Venia sharing a new recipe for saffron rice she had perfected.

"Sophie, are you going to teach Emmi how to cast with needle and thread?" Venia passed me a cup of strong cold-brewed coffee.

Emmi flushed. "I'm not that good at sewing yet," she said, protectiveness raising her voice a bit. We hadn't discussed charm casting in stitches becoming a more regular part of her training yet after Emmi's initial attempts hadn't worked. Given my difficulties in casting, I had been putting it off.

"Emmi's progressing wonderfully. I do think we'll work a bit more on the finer stitches and draping—I think it's easier to incorporate the casting into something you're confident with," I said. I hesitated. These were the only people I knew who might have some insight into my problem, but I feared that admitting my difficulties could open the door to other admissions—curse casting.

"I need to work on my prick stitching," Emmi confided to Venia.

Parit giggled. "That sounds rude. And painful."

"Top stitching. Tiny stitches," Emmi amended, blushing.

I decided I had to ask. "I wonder—has anyone ever struggled to cast a charm?"

"Oh, lots of times," Venia said. "When I was first learning, I had trouble concentrating, trouble making the clay tablets themselves, trouble keeping the charm going..." She ticked off reasons on her fingers. "I wasn't good at it for a long time."

"I don't think anyone is," Lieta said gently.

"I meant more...recently," I said. "I mean, after you've learned. Does anyone backslide? I've never taught anyone before," I added hastily, covering my reason for asking.

Parit scrunched up her mouth. She used a deep carmine on her lips, accentuating the faces she made as she talked. "Not that I know of. At least, it's never happened to me."

"Me either," Emmi said. "But I've never really learned anything new beyond basic casting."

"I stopped casting for a while," Lieta said. I sat up straighter. "After my husband died. It was as though...as though I didn't have the energy," she explained.

I sank back, slightly disappointed. She didn't describe the dark magic infiltrating her work as she continued, "I tried several times, but it was as though I couldn't focus enough. The light kept slipping away. It only lasted a few months. I probably shouldn't have tried to work while I was still in mourning," she added.

"There's a reason we have the quiet fortnight," Venia replied, referring to the Pellian custom of families retreating after the burial of a loved one, usually for two weeks but sometimes more. Others in the community brought them food, ran their errands, and did whatever work was necessary for them.

"Galatines don't," Emmi said.

"Galatines don't know a good thing if it doesn't come from Galitha," Parit said. "But how are you supposed to manage a quiet fortnight if you need to make your day wages?"

Lieta nodded in agreement. "I tried to work too soon. It was Galatine thinking, not Pellian," she said. I bit my lip; this wasn't pertinent to my problem at all.

"At any rate," Parit said, "I had a question for you, Emmi— you said your mother used different tools for her tablets?"

I let the conversation flow away without me, its current dipping into clay types and the wording of inscriptions that had been passed down from mothers to daughters to granddaughters.

"Is something troubling you?" Lieta said quietly, laying her hand on my arm, the motion familiar and maternal, though we were not related.

I shook my head as Parit related a story about the Pellian quarter's market day. The others laughed as she mimicked a Pellian market woman shooing rambunctious children from her stall. "Everyone has moved on," I said, almost without meaning to.

"From this winter?" Lieta pursed her lips. "Not quite, I do not think."

Her son. "I'm sorry, I wasn't thinking."

"No, you're not mistaken. It is like any other Galatine summer in so many ways." She sighed. "My *miri'ta*—she is struggling. It pains me." She used the Pellian term for a daughter-in-law. There was no good Galatine translation for what I knew meant something closer to "given daughter" or "gift daughter" than the Galatine phrase, which sounded more like a legal relationship than a familial one.

I nodded, thinking quickly. "She is taking in work?"

"She sews, actually. She's quick with mending. She tried to pick up work at the laundry, but the forewoman didn't like her."

I wondered why—was it because she was too close to the Red Caps, or that she was Pellian, or something altogether unrelated?

I hesitated—Alice had already placed the advertisement, and already had inquiries. I didn't want to imply that I didn't trust Alice to find a new hire, but I wanted to help this woman. "Tell her to inquire with my assistant," I said.

Lieta looked surprised. "But she—she is no couture seamstress!"

I glanced at Emmi with a smile. "If she can learn, she can become one. And if she can't"—I shrugged—"I am like any other business owner. I will give her severance and she'll be no worse off. What is her name?"

"Heda," Lieta replied. "She's a good worker." She paused before adding, "And soon you will be someone's *miri'ta*, as well. It is a blessing, to be given another family." She didn't need to add that I had no family of my own left, and in the Pellian traditions, this made me worse than a pauper.

"Yes," I said, "though I am not sure they will welcome me as kindly as you've welcomed your *miri'ta*."

Lieta smiled sadly. "Yes, it is a different world that you move into. Are they kind to you?"

The question took me entirely off guard. I hadn't stopped to consider whether I had received or even expected kindness from some of the most powerful people in the country—and my future family. "Some of them," I said. "Theodor's parents… there is some distance there. But his brothers here in the city are kind enough. Ambrose is a student of law at the university, and Ballantine is in the Royal Navy—on occasion he's here. They are both welcoming, but of course they're also very close to Theodor.

"Gregory and Jeremy—the twins—are both at the military school in Rock's Ford. They'll be sixteen in a year and will both commission in the army, so I doubt I'll see much of them in any case. Jonamere is too little to know any better, but I made him a stuffed lion and so he likes me well enough. Polly—Lady Apollonia—isn't quite sure what to think of me, I believe." I knew enough of Theodor's golden-haired, whip-tongued sister to know that she loved her brother fiercely and, given who I was, reserved her trust when it came to me.

Lieta nodded. "You know that you always have family here, too."

I quietly took her hand while the others talked. Lieta had been like an aunt or a granny many times, unassuming and gentle in her advice. Even when I had gone to her months before, knowing the risks inherent in a relationship with Theodor, to ask certain embarrassing questions about delaying starting a family. There were ways, I understood that much, but I had never known who to ask—certainly not my brother, who wouldn't have known women's methods anyway. So, shame-faced and stumbling over my words, I had gone to Lieta. I had a feeling I was the only adult woman she had ever enlightened regarding a woman's cyclical fertility, but she was calm and kind and tried not to make me feel like a fool.

And now, she didn't make me feel foolish for joining myself in marriage to a Galatine and a noble whose family would never welcome me as a Pellian family would have, as her family would have. Whose customs felt cold and created to build boundaries rather than welcome newcomers. Whose mores might mean seeing far less of my Pellian friends in favor of duties to Crown and country instead of family, whether born of blood or choice.

She poured me another glass of strong coffee. "When someday you are princess and then queen," she said, "you will be the first royal lady, I wager, to cast charms in the palace." She laughed. "I suppose you can't begrudge an old Pellian for being proud enough of that."

10

—m—

"I'd be happy to meet with her," Alice said carefully. I'd explained Heda's limited sewing experience and my hope that we could hire her. In truth, Alice had already selected several, far more proficient, candidates from the response to the advertisement.

"I know she's not going to be the most qualified, but as I said before, I would very much like to—" I stopped, noticing Alice's dour countenance. "You can't be worrying over her being Pellian, can you?"

Alice's grim stoicism broke into a heaved sigh. "Not at all! No," she repeated, composing herself. "It's that you're—how can I explain this?" She pursed her lips, considering for a long, uncomfortable moment. "Do you want me to take over the shop, or no? Am I going to have my name on it, make the decisions, or are you going to—stay on? Directing from behind the screen?"

I blinked, began to argue, and stopped. I had carefully mapped the practical steps to hand the shop over to Alice, but I had failed to actually untangle myself. In my mind, the shop was still mine.

"I'm sorry, Alice." Tears rimmed my eyes, and I swiftly

wiped them away. "I should have—I should have made this your decision. You'll have to manage the new employee, after all. Because I am stepping away. Completely. As soon as the transfer is finalized." I bit back more tears—there would be time to mourn the loss of my shop later, not in front of Alice.

"If you don't want to—I mean, I wouldn't be unsatisfied with a manager's job instead of owner. If that's what you wanted instead."

"I do want that, dearly. I want to hold on to this place until they pry the business license from my gnarled, liver-spotted old fingers." Alice cracked a faint smile. "But I can't. I can't own a shop and be—Theodor's wife." I let a single tear slip and wend its way down my cheek. "And that's the more important thing for me to be, now. I gave women a place to work, I started—too late—giving Pellian girls a chance to learn a trade that they could succeed in, here in Galitha." I smiled. "Now? Now I can do much more than help a few women at a time."

Alice nodded. "I understand. You love this. The shop, the work." She laughed. "You really love work. For what it's worth, I would have hired your friend's daughter-in-law anyway, if she wasn't a louse. I wish you'd given me the chance to do it on my own."

"From now on, you will run this business on your own," I promised.

"Good. Because we wasted money on the advertisement in the *Weekly* if you were just going to trot someone in here anyway." Alice hesitated, then patted my hand. "I'll take care of the shop. On my honor," she added with the closest thing to a grin I'd ever seen grace Alice's face.

Heda started within the week. She didn't have any experience in a formal atelier, but she had made a quick business taking in mending and had even sewn a few sets of baby linens for sale, making her far more skilled with a needle than Emmi had been when I hired her. Knowing that she would have little enough chance at being hired by any other seamstress in Galitha City, I signed her wage contract.

Though I couldn't trust her with any fine sewing, another set of hands basting and cleaning caught us up within days; at least, it had caught up the non-charmed cutting and construction for our orders. I was still woefully behind on my charms, struggling to cast without the darkness creeping into my work. Fortunately, Alice and Emmi were so caught up in their work that they didn't notice me falling behind, or that I took work home with me most nights, wrangling it mostly unsuccessfully.

I found that I had only so much energy to cast in a day before the effort in keeping the light and dark from warring with one another in each seam became so taxing that I was fully wasting my time, so I felt only some guilt leaving Alice in charge of the shop one bright afternoon to meet Theodor. He waited for me in his study, papers strewn across his desk and his violin case propped open on top of them.

"How were the debates?" I asked, not even giving him time to greet me with a kiss.

"I think we're making real progress," he said. "That is, no one is happy with the state of the bill at the moment, yet no one is ready to walk out on it."

"What has your father said?" Theodor hadn't said much about him, but the king had distanced himself from the reform efforts. I didn't bring it up, but he still had not publicly acknowledged our betrothal. Theodor's mother had sent me a kindly worded if rather perfunctory letter expressing her felicitations, apologizing that she would be unable to receive me before leaving the city for the family estate in Rock's Ford, and suggesting a late fall wedding. Between the rote politeness of her words, I sensed her avoidance and her hesitation, almost as though she hoped that the passage of a few months would erase this aberration to the plans she had certainly held for her eldest son.

Theodor's slumped shoulders confirmed my suspicions. "He's cowed by all of the nobles opposing the bill. Unfortunately, some of them are the richest, and their taxes fill the coffers." I read what Theodor meant without further explanation—his father didn't have the political capital to spend challenging them. But without his vocal support, plenty of nobles would continue their confident opposition. "Most of the nobles coming to session have taken to wearing blue-and-gold cockades to counter the reform red and gray."

"Brilliant blue?" I recalled the bright ribbons on Lady Sommerset and her friends at the croquet party.

"Royal blue," Theodor said with a wry smile. "They're currying favor with my father, picking the color of the royal standard, and of course gold, for the crown, as their emblem."

"What do the students call that at schools—licking boots, I believe?"

"One of the more polite terms," he said, handing me a glass of iced citronade. "But I know this much—that your influence has been a positive one so far. More than once one of the lords has, in formal debate, insisted on the determination of the common people."

"Niko would be so pleased," I said, smile brimming with taut sarcasm. "And we won't ask how they feel about the little wasp of an upstart stinging everyone with threats at social functions."

Theodor pulled me to him. "It was never a role that would win you friends," he conceded.

"Don't I know it."

"Let's talk of something else. Not politics, not the infernal heat. I've been practicing with the violin and thought I might get your thoughts. I don't want to boast, but I think I've gotten better," he said. "I can hold the charm longer and draw it out more quickly."

"When have you had time to practice?" I asked. Theodor's ability to cast charms through music, golden light following the bow as he played, had surprised both of us. I hadn't realized that the gift might strike outside my Pellian community, and he had no idea that he could manipulate magic at all until I showed him. "With the reforms and the council, I figured you wouldn't work on casting for months."

"I probably shouldn't," he said, checking his tuning. "But it's relaxing. I feel—I don't know, happier when I've practiced an hour or so. It's been like a tonic the past months."

"I know exactly what you mean," I said, recalling the veil of tranquility and contentment I felt after a long session of casting. Recalling, because that feeling had eluded me for weeks now.

Theodor began to play a cheerful, bright melody. "New composition," he said. "One of Marguerite's." Then he concentrated on his work and began to cast.

His casting was stronger. The golden light bloomed more quickly and steadily and grew comfortably, without the hesitation of his earlier casting.

"Let me try something," I said. As I had done as the dome collapsed at the Midwinter Ball and as we'd practiced a dozen times since, I caught threads of his charm casting and drew them together. This time, instead of weaving a net or manipulating the charmed light in the air around us, I pulled a thin strand toward me. Thinking of the way that a spinning wheel or drop spindle twisted and bound fibers of wool, I pulled the disparate golden light taut and fine. It spooled as I twisted it.

Could I use this charm thread, drawn from the ether by

someone else, in my own work? I directed the end of the spooled thread—thicker and less smooth than sewing thread, but visible only to a charm caster—toward the hem of a curtain. Concentrating, I drove it between the weave of the silk. It resisted; without my physical motions of a needle, it wanted to remain on the surface of the silk. I pushed it harder, and to my shock, it began to meld with the silk fabric itself, a thin gold line permeating the gray fabric, embedded like a slim line of dye.

"Well, what exactly did you do?" Theodor asked as he set his violin down. "Aside from—charm my curtains?"

"The curtains were just convenient," I apologized. "I used the charm that you cast to imbue a physical item with a charm— what I usually do with my own casting."

"Interesting. I mean, as an experiment. Hardly useful if you can cast yourself, though," he said with a laugh. I forced a smile. It would be hardly useful if my work wasn't somehow tainted.

"Unless," I said, thinking out loud, "you could double a charm's potency, or relieve a tired charm caster, or—I don't know, I haven't really thought it out." Not to mention, I realized, I had bypassed any physical process to embedding the charm. No sewing, no inscribing in clay, no mixing herbs. I had simply pressed my plan upon the golden light, and it had complied. "I'll have to check for its durability, though," I added, mostly to myself. Still, I thought as I examined the golden light now a part of the fabric itself, it was possible I had opened the door to something new and potentially very practical.

11

—⁓—

I saw very little of Theodor in the days that followed our casting experiment in his study. The debates over the Reform Bill sapped his time, hours extending past the official council meetings and into the evenings, where every noble seemed to demand some fraction of his attention. Every one of them believed he had some brilliant insight that the council couldn't move forward without, and even the pro-reformists became a nuisance as each wanted to finagle their personal touches into the final resolution.

For my part, as summer grew hotter, our orders of formal gowns for the winter social season grew. We opened every window in the atelier, thankful for the iceman who pulled his wagon of dirty ice blocks down the street once a day. Alice made a delightful citron tea that we cooled with carefully washed chips of ice, and Heda taught us a brilliant Pellian trick of wearing neckerchiefs dampened with cool water. It left wet marks on our gown necks and our kerchiefs dried stiff and wrinkled, which was why I imagined my mother had never suggested trying it. I didn't even care that it might not be properly Galatine, and neither did Alice. Our only respite from the heat came when thick gray thunderheads rolled in, showering the streets with torrents of rain and turning the wheel ruts and gutters into rushing streams.

One of those storms had just cleared the thickness from the air as I joined Theodor to attend what was set to be the first of a series of horse races showcasing Galitha's finest equines. We rode to the racetrack, just outside the city proper, passing landmarks I knew from making the same trip on foot.

"We're being hosted by the Pommerly family—well, the troupe of them that's here in the city."

"Troupe? Like acrobats? Or monkeys?"

"Yes, very much like monkeys. The Duke of Pommerly has enough brothers and children and cousins to fairly well fill the primate house in the West Serafan menagerie, and I've doubt they'd behave better than the yellow-crested langurs and blue-nose macaques." He paused. "They have a tendency toward lewd jokes. And rump slapping."

"What?" I choked.

"You've been warned." He was genuinely embarrassed. There were nobles less educated than Viola's salon set, less ethical and motivated than Theodor—why shouldn't some be rude and uncouth? "At any rate, the Pommerly estate produces some of the finest racehorses in Galitha. So we all best act impressed or they'll be offended."

"You really dislike these people." I laughed.

"I really do. The Pommerly family is one of the oldest and most distinguished noble houses in Galitha, related to our house somewhere along the line, so of course we had to see quite a bit of them growing up. I always—always!—ended up locked in a closet or dumped in a pond during one of their games."

I held back a laugh. Growing up, I had been quiet and not terribly outgoing, but Kristos had been one of the most popular boys in our quarter, gathering groups of fellow Pellian ruffians for games of tag or charades or marbles. I was protected from any bullying by his popularity. Theodor, more interested in the gardens than in hunts or horse races, had likely been an easy target as a child.

"And of course they're vociferous opponents of the bill."

"I can't say I'm surprised," I said.

"No, and to make this more complicated, the Pommerly family has been boasting to anything with ears that they're hosting the king of Galitha. So Father and Mother and the whole family will be there."

"Oh." I let my fingers fret the trim on my sleeve ruffle. "The first time we'll see them since—"

"Yes. I had hoped to have a private dinner with just the family, but with the debates in council I've been so wretched busy and Mother hasn't replied to my note yet—" He stopped. "I'm not sure how to play this one, Sophie. Between the bill and the betrothal, those box seats are going to be a damned hornets' nest."

"We could pretend it's merely a social event," I said. "Just watch the races, sip some wine—please tell me the Pommerlys are not such boors that they don't at least serve wine?"

"Pommerly grown and bottled, I'm sure." Theodor tapped the side of the carriage, a nervous tic that made me want to slap his hand. "Even if I wanted to, someone will bring up the bill, corner me into debating it. We will have to discuss the Reform Bill, like it or not."

"What's so different, then? I'm well versed at this point with the amendments to the bill, the adjustments to the election procedures—"

"I know you are," he snapped. "But my father—"

Ice sharpened my voice despite the heat. "Your father. You don't want me to embarrass myself in front of your father."

"No! I don't mean that."

I waited. And grew exasperated at the silence. "What did you mean?"

He heaved a sigh. "I don't need his blessing for this marriage, but I'd rather not be the reason it causes any disagreements."

"You wouldn't be the reason. I would be. You know you can't marry me and keep everyone happy." My voice rose. "You dropped me in this damned boat, insisting it was watertight, and now you're upset that I'm rocking it just by sitting here."

"I just don't want to give him a reason to disapprove." He avoided my eyes.

"You mean confirm his suspicions that I'm a lowborn churl, or that I'm a pitchfork-wielding revolutionary?"

"He doesn't think either one of those things."

"How do you know? Have you talked with him about me recently?" I snapped.

We both knew that he hadn't. "Forget I said anything. It's like any other event." He turned his face toward the window, away from me.

"Except it isn't." There was no avoiding that the reforms and our impending marriage were inextricably linked, two parts of the same whole just as our betrothal bands were forged of the same chain. Neither was a comfortable reality for the king and queen.

"No, it's not." He sighed. "It doesn't matter whether they're supportive, you know. Legally. Or, to my mind, ethically."

"But it does matter. It's your family."

"We didn't ask Kristos what he thought of you marrying me," Theodor reminded me with a saucy grin.

"It really is a good thing Galatine law doesn't require consent from anyone's family," I said in agreement.

I focused my gaze out the window, watching happier

commoners walking toward the racetrack, swinging baskets of bread and wine and carrying blankets for the lawn. We would be trapped in a box, high above the ring, with paid seats filled by merchants and shipbuilders and mill owners below us, and the general lawn below that. It struck me that each tier had more comfortable seats and less comfortable company than the one below it.

Theodor took my hand and I let him hold it more tightly than was comfortable as we joined the Pommerly family and their guests. As liveried servants in Pommerly-pink uniforms passed canapés of some sort of bland gray mousse and slivered cucumbers, I reflected that the food might well be better down on the lawn, too. Summer races were social events in Galitha City for the common folk as well as the nobles who owned the horses and paid for the training of the jockeys who rode them. A basket of the best white bread, aged rounds of cheese, and plum confit for the races was perhaps the only indulgence of the year that Kristos didn't have to fight my tight purse strings to buy. I could almost taste the brilliant purple-pink jam and pungent cheese—imagination wasn't difficult when its rival was a shaved cucumber with too little salt.

The king, attended by Ambrose and Ballantine as well as several high-ranking lords, acknowledged our arrival with an obligatory nod. His wife and daughter stood close to him, both delicately blocking their view of me with slim sandalwood fans. I had finally made myself one of the cotton gowns my shop had churned out for others; it had begun to be understood as a pro-reformist statement in and of itself. Besides, I thought with some satisfaction, it was far more fashionable than the queen's elabo-rate flounces. I proudly wore a new triple-looped scarlet-and-gray breast knot, but it didn't escape me that most of the nobles present had royal-blue kerchiefs or cockades.

Theodor was quickly snatched up into conversation with two portly lords, including, I believed from the metalwork device pinned to his coat, a Pommerly. His brother Ambrose quickly took a position next to Theodor, and I slipped away by myself. A faint breeze carried the scent of new-mown grass into the box; I stood by the railing and watched as the first set of horses was paraded before the spectators.

Ballantine, a near beanpole in his well-fitted Royal Navy dress uniform, saw me by myself and joined me. "Do you like horses, Miss Balstrade?"

I didn't know much about horses; I had learned more about wagering than about the animals themselves from Kristos and his friends at races in the past. Still, the way their bones and musculature moved in fluid tandem reminded me of a well-constructed gown, pieced precisely on a deftly crafted structure. "I like watching them run," I answered honestly. "I'm not sure I like them, precisely. I'm not sure I understand them well enough to know."

"I confess, I prefer ships to horses. Ships do as you tell them," Ballantine confided. I laughed. "I understand he's been teaching you to ride."

"Yes, he gave me a few lessons." After accompanying Theodor on a ceremonial hunt Viola hosted for the New Year in the spring, I had insisted on learning the rudiments of riding. While Theodor and the hunting party had sprinted ahead, chasing a white hare through the broad, green Royal Park outside the city, I had watched from the pavilion set up for the elderly ladies and nursing mothers. Theodor had taken me to the royal stables, at times when no one would see my embarrassing falls and awkward seat on the horse. "I can manage a comfortable walk and can almost tolerate trotting."

"Tolerate is a good term for it," he said. "Like some other

things I could mention." He nodded toward Theodor, pinned near the trays of petits fours by a pair of nobles.

"It hasn't been presented in the bill, no," Theodor said.

"The Livestock Act is outdated," the older of the two declared. "The concept of restricting trade on proven breeders hasn't been supported since my father was a pup."

"I don't disagree, Lord Fairleague, but the Reform Bill as it stands is not taking that particular issue on," Theodor replied. I could hear the forced calm in his voice. Whether this was an obtuse suggestion borne out of ignorance or a deliberate attempt at distraction from the true reforms facing the council, I didn't know. In either case, it grossly misunderstood where the Galatine system was broken, attempting to tack down a loose shingle instead of reinforcing the foundation of a collapsing house.

"Well, what does the king think?" Though phrased as a jovial question, it was a challenge—which side would the king take? I glanced at Ballantine, whose lips were pressed together in a hard line. My mouth was dry. Would the king openly argue against the reform with his son, here, in a public space? Or, in a bright miracle, would he side with us?

"A complicated question," he hedged, and then let Lord Fairleague begin a long diatribe on the grievous laws hampering his estate's cattle-breeding efforts.

"Well, this is impolite conversation," Annette, who had arrived without my notice, said under her breath. "I didn't need to hear about bulls mounting his heifers, did you?"

Ballantine blushed. "Lady Annette." He bowed in greeting to his cousin.

"I was trying to ignore it," I said, though it wasn't exactly true. The king's deflective response had been spineless, and I waited for him to correct Lord Fairleague.

The king didn't correct the lords, even as Theodor interjected.

"That's all very well, and you ought to draft something for the council's next session. For now, our focus is on creating representative bodies with regular elections and—"

"Elections!" the Duke of Pommerly sputtered. "We'll see if such a thing ever comes to pass."

I could almost feel Theodor's sinews tightening from across the room. Ballantine laid a steadying hand on my arm. "Don't let them rile you," he whispered to me. "These men will never change their minds; the world will go on changing without them."

The king's smile was tepid. "Well, well, we'll let the councillors debate, shall we?"

Theodor shot him a frustrated glance, adding, "Something has to be done to address the concerns of the populace. I happen to believe in certain ideals, but for pragmatism's sake—we can't leave the Fourth Regiment encamped in the park forever to prevent the riots you know will resume if the people aren't assuaged."

"Nothing *needs* to be done," Pommerly retorted. "Everything that is done is a choice. Our choice."

"The nobility is indeed the backbone of our great nation," the king said, his soothing tone like something I'd heard less competent governesses use with very small children. I watched Theodor seethe quietly, feeling the same fiery exasperation muffled under thin civility. I caught his eye. He shook his head slightly—don't bother, the defeated gesture said. The country was teetering on the edge of collapse, rotten at her core, and if the people kept picking at it, with revolts and coups and riots, the resulting conflict would be ugly, long, and bloody. These men weren't able or interested in seeing it, and a very new king didn't have the political capital to oppose the most powerful people in his own country.

"Let's all let this drop and enjoy the wine, shall we?" Lady Apollonia, Theodor's little sister Polly, had a voice like the highest bells in the cathedral's carillon, and it punctured the tense silence. I tried to meet her eyes with a grateful smile, but she turned her head away from me. She wore royal blue draped in a swath across her silk gown, and it fluttered in the breeze she made walking away from me.

Theodor returned to my side. "I think we probably ought to make our pleasantries with my parents," he said.

"Is that what we're calling it?" I asked with a raised eyebrow. Pleasantries—it sounded like a social call over Midwinter.

He took my arm, deliberately placing my hand on his, and escorted me to where the king and queen of Galitha stood overlooking the racetrack.

"Mother, Father," Theodor said with a subtle bow. I smiled, rote and faintly idiotic. Was I supposed to curtsy? Kiss their rings? I had a feeling I was not about to be embraced and given a familial welcome.

"Theodor," the queen said with genuine affection for her son in her eyes and a terse smile on her lips. "You are looking well. And you've finally brought her to meet us," she added, turning to me with all the cold poise of an ice sculpture.

"I'm so glad we are able to spend the day together," I said. I had carefully selected and rehearsed the line—"lovely to meet you" only highlighted that we should have met a long time ago, and "pleased to see you" suggested some sort of familiarity that we didn't have.

"Indeed." She continued to regard me with an expression I couldn't quite place. "I'm sorry we haven't time to host you and Theodor for dinner before we leave the city. I spend the summers at our estate near Rock's Ford."

"Will you see Gregory and Jeremy?" I inquired. The twins

were at school near Rock's Ford, attending the prestigious Galatine military academy.

"The school will host several exhibitions over the summer
for families to attend, and the boys will come home for a short
break between the terms." She turned back toward the racetrack, and I finally placed her expression—complete and utter
disinterest in me. Not disdain, not hatred—nothing.

She wasn't angry with me or threatened. Her emotional
investment in our exchange was nothing at all. She discounted
me now, and she would go back to ignoring me as soon as I was
out of sight.

"Too bad, too bad I'll miss the boys this year." The king
sighed. He regarded me with clearer emotion—distrust. "This
Reform Bill of yours is keeping everyone in the city longer than
they would like, dear boy," he added, turning back to Theodor.

"I feel it's necessary," he replied. "Don't you?"

"Necessary, well." The king turned to Polly, who was standing by a tower of white cake and strawberries. "Do cut me a slice
of that, Polly, won't you, dear?"

"Of course, Papa," she said, her smile like sunshine as she
served the most powerful man in the country a plate of sweets.
She grazed past me, the false rump under her blue silk gown
nudging me out of her way. "Theo, you should work less. Those
dark circles are getting worse."

"Maybe cake would make them better," he said with a grin.

"Get your own cake." Polly brushed him off. Theodor
looked hurt, more so than by his mother's cold reception or
his father's rejection of his work. He and Polly had always been
close. I hadn't considered that she might not support his marriage or his political work, but it was clear—there was a divide
in the family, and she had sided with her parents.

"Ah, they're ready!" Annette said, grabbing my shoulder but

speaking loudly enough that I knew she was hoping the royal family would hear as well. Between the starting shot and the last horse thundering across the line, I had a short respite from the thick tension that seemed to bind us all together while forcing us all apart.

"Good showing, Pommerly," the king said, raising a glass to the lanky bay who had come in a tight second place.

Pommerly huffed a bit, accepting the congratulations, but insisted that his next horse would place first. His wife leaned in and whispered something in his ear, tittering.

"Well, why don't you ask her," he harrumphed loudly, turning his eyes on me.

Theodor sidestepped ever so slightly in front of me, his hand on his sword hilt in an unspoken protective reflex. "Ask about what?"

Pommerly glowered under a lacquer of politeness. "I figure my horse could use some extra luck to place first. Can she sew a saddle blanket? Is she any good with leatherwork?"

The box was silent, save for a faint buzzing that I recognized was in my head. I felt the rustle of Annette's skirts behind me, moving closer. Ambrose glared at Pommerly, though he didn't take notice, and Ballantine stepped beside Theodor, as though offering another sword in defense if it came down to it.

"Come now," Pommerly added with a forced laugh, "from what I understand she doesn't even charge for most of her... services." Theodor gripped the hilt of his sword tightly. No one could have missed the suggestion in Pommerly's rude joke.

I looked to the king and queen. They had an opportunity, now, in front of everyone, to claim me as part of their family, as under their protection. No one would have made such a comment about Polly or Annette. If they did, they would have been quickly rebuked.

The king and queen stood silently. A faint smile played around the edges of Polly's lips.

"I'm afraid I'm not any good even mending leather," I answered, forcing my voice steady. "And though I'd be pleased to charm something for your jockey, I do think the turnaround would be a bit too tight at this point."

Pommerly shifted, uncomfortable. He hadn't expected me to reply. I glanced at the king, who stared at a spot between the toes of his boots.

I couldn't help myself. "Indeed, if you or one of your staff would like to visit me at my atelier, I would be happy to comply. Do I have one of my cards?" I stuffed a hand into my pocket, knowing full well I didn't have any trade cards with me.

"Sophie," Theodor said, low, like a faint growl. I shook my head at him. If his parents wouldn't stand up for me, I would stand up for myself.

"I am sorry, I haven't a single one," I said with a broad smile. I turned on my heel, fuming yet deliberate and precise. "Annette, tell me—which do you think for the next round? The dappled gray or the roan?"

She forced a smile and Ambrose joined us to place wagers on the next race, and though I had an inkling we wouldn't be invited to any more races with the Pommerly family, I felt I had won some small victory.

12

ALICE HAD THE EVERYDAY WORKINGS OF THE SHOP WELL IN HAND, and though I didn't intend to finalize my departure until closer to the wedding, I found I was less and less needed in the shop. A few administrative tasks remained on my docket before I could leave the shop in Alice's hands permanently, including finishing the charmed commissions and reconciling all of our accounts. I had struggled with a recalcitrant health charm all morning, and so took on the task of inventorying our stock so that Alice had an accurate accounting. I was in the midst of tabulating fabric bolt yardages when I heard yelling from the front room, where the staff were packing orders. I dropped my notebook like I'd been stung—Alice never raised her voice, yet there was no doubt that the shout was hers.

I hurried toward the front room to see Heda cornered by Alice near the counter and Emmi slinking her back against the far wall. Alice's round cheeks were red. "I won't allow this... this smut in here!"

"I didn't think—it's a joke," Heda stammered.

"It's hardly a joke. It's...it's propaganda, and it's cruel, and it's—" I stalled in the doorway to the front room as Alice tore something out of Heda's hands and threw it on the counter. "You should leave."

"You have no right!"

"I most certainly do as the manager of this atelier. I will consider your continued employment here."

Heda was out the door before I could intervene.

"Alice, what in the world is going on?"

"Heda brought—she allowed political propaganda of a particular nature—it's simply disrespectful!"

"From the way you reacted, I thought someone must have been bleeding or she set the cottons on fire." I glanced at the now-crinkled, paperbound book sitting on the counter. "That's it?"

I picked it up and felt the warmth drain from my face as I paged through the opening paragraphs.

"I thought you must have seen it already," Alice said, gently taking it from me before I could read more.

"No, I had not read the novelized version of my personal affairs relayed as the Cuckold Prince and the Nymphomaniacal Witch." I was shaking. It was mean-spirited and ugly, no doubt, but, as I snatched the book back from Alice's protesting hands and skimmed further, it was more toxic than that. Political aspirations fueled the fictionalized version of me, bent on avenging a scheming brother and instigating a new revolt. The illustrations depicted a grossly caricatured Pellian woman, with unruly dark hair and brawny shoulders.

A hollow fear grew in the pit of my stomach—could there be some truth, some tiny grain of reality embedded in these pages, that would reveal my well-kept secret? But no—from a grotesque depiction of a blood sacrifice ritual victimizing an alley cat and a bizarre magic-fueled orgy, it was clear the author of the piece knew nothing about real casting. The author did, however, place particular emphasis on the curses as Pellian traditions, and on the leadership of the revolt as Pellian. If anyone believed the trash excuse for a novel, they would understand the Midwinter Revolt and the Reform Bill both as borne out of a cabal of scheming Pellians.

I threw the book on the counter with shaking hands, and it skittered onto the floor.

"If I'd known you hadn't seen it...I'm sorry." Alice pursed her lips.

The meaning behind Alice's statement dawned on me, horrible and clear. "You mean you've already seen this? It's widely circulated?" I recalled the book Lady Sommerset had slipped into her pocket at the croquet party and her cruel clandestine laughter. How many had read it, had digested the wretched propaganda about not only me but the validity of the Reform Bill itself? "How did you come across it?" I asked, my tone sharp.

"I didn't mean to!" Alice protested.

"I know," I said, softening my voice.

"They pass them around in the taverns and sell them in front of the coffee shops," Alice said. She hesitated, and added, "There are others. They all have that you practice magic—they don't get it right, though. I thought you knew."

I traced my fingers over my ledger, which lay closed and bound on the counter. Years of charm casting out of this shop, the discretion for the benefit of my clients and the mystique for the benefit of my business, all tainted and tawdry in the light of some badly written propaganda. I had endeavored since opening the shop to practice my art with deft integrity, and it didn't seem to matter at all in the face of vicious rumors.

"My sister brought another one of them home...it was meant to be about Lady Viola, I think."

My hands felt cold, even in the warm humidity of the summer air. "What about her?"

"I didn't read it past the first few pages—it was all dirty sex stuff. That she likes women, that she seduces nobles and maids and even princesses." Clearly uncomfortable, Alice edged farther into the counter, as though it could swallow her.

Of course—a piece exploiting the rumors that had always circulated about Viola, coupled with new ones about a long-standing affair with Annette. I was sure, if I read the piece, it would insinuate not only improprieties in her private behavior but dereliction of noble duty and languid indolence, as well.

"I'll dispose of this," I said, more to myself than Alice. I plucked the book from the floor and glanced at the printer's mark, recognizing it as one of the more upscale printers in Galitha City. Likely printing, I acknowledged, at the behest of nobles to suggest to the people that the champions of the Reform Bill were immoral, unhinged, and unduly influenced by Pellians. "Now. What about Heda?"

Alice flushed deeper pink. "I'm sorry if I overstepped."

"Hardly. You're quite close to being the mistress here, and in any case—it's not proper to have such trash circulated here. Hopefully she'll consider such propriety in the future. But— what about Heda?"

"I . . . I don't think it would be right to fire her over it," Alice said carefully. "It was only a first mistake, even if it was a big one. And . . ." She stopped herself.

"Yes?"

"Well, she hasn't worked in a fine shop before." Implicit in her remark was Heda's background, her upbringing, even her complexion.

"Very few of the girls we hire here have," I cautioned Alice. "Pellian or not. Get used to training them to be proper employees, not only to be seamstresses."

Alice nodded, chastised even though I had said nothing to scold her. We continued the day's work quietly and she set off early, mouth in a taut line, to pay Heda a visit. I locked the shop door behind me an hour later and almost tripped over a boy in a red cap, perched on my doorstep like a sentry.

"Can I help you?" I asked as he scurried to his feet.

"I'm supposed to deliver this," he said, presenting me with a folded and sealed letter. The paper was cheap; then again, so was the delivery method. Hiring a boy to run errands cost less than a pint of ale.

I fished out a coin to tip him. He held up his hand. "Just doing my service for the cause, ma'am."

"The cause?" I raised an eyebrow at his earnest face, smudged with the red dust of the street. He was all of ten years old.

"The Red Caps. I knew your brother," he added, with confidence in the standing this gave him among the juvenile hangers-on of the Red Cap movement.

"I see. Thank you," I said as I opened the letter. He dashed away.

I didn't recognize the handwriting, and the letter was unsigned, but it was clearly from Niko. *I wouldn't dare intrude on your wedding planning and stitch counting, except that I've heard rumors that you're so badly disliked by the exalted elite that there's some talk of making you disappear. Talk only—but talk from the mouths of those in the king's circle. Don't ask my sources, I won't name them.*

We aren't the only ones who can foment violence, his note concluded. He'd included a clipping from the *Gentlemen's Monthly*, which catered to nobles and the wealthy untitled, of a dark-haired woman clutching a cap—presumably red, despite the grayscale printing—with an oversize needle woven through it, thread waving in an imagined breeze. She was standing on a gallows.

I folded the note and put it in my pocket, hands shaking. Of course there would be talk—talk of eliminating a loud voice in favor of the reform, a voice with the ear of the prince and his circle. Of eliminating an embarrassing interloper to the royal family. Surely it couldn't pass beyond talk, not without driving distrust between members of the ruling elite, without breaking the laws that the nobles saw themselves duty bound to uphold?

Surely it was just talk, and Niko had no right to frighten me with it. Still, I shivered as I walked home despite the lingering summer evening sun.

13

THE REFORM BILL HAD THE CITY BY THE NAPE OF THE NECK, with broadsides printed as rapidly as the debate on the floor of the council changed. Emmi said that Red Caps gathered under the windows to listen to the arguments, noting the proposed changes and each kink and bend in the logic of the nobles who debated each provision. They printed the broadsides on cheap paper at the end of each day and circulated them through the city by morning, fueling debates and speculation in every coffee shop and chocolate café in every quarter of the city.

Alongside the news and the commentary written, published, and posted on a near-daily basis were cartoons and satire printed in the cheap weeklies and even in some of the better magazines, celebrating or lampooning one side or the other, as their editors' opinions lay. I was featured more than once, including an unflattering portrait of an ugly Pellian in a chemise gown like a sack, with knitting needles and a jug of rat poison.

I showed this particular offense to Theodor one evening as we retreated from the war of words that ignited taverns and concert halls and noble salons, secreting ourselves away in the peace of Theodor's house.

"Do you even know how to knit?" he asked, scrutinizing the clipping.

"Not well," I replied. "This is how the educated populace believes casting works, I guess?"

Theodor shrugged. "It's not worth getting upset over, I hope," he said, wadding the paper up.

He tossed it into a bin by the empty fireplace, kindling to save for autumn. But he couldn't burn every copy of every broadside and novel, every cartoon and column. They flowed through the city like runoff after a rainstorm, staining every block and corner and tainting the honest efforts of reform.

I tugged at the circlet of gold on my wrist. It was delicate but strong; it would have taken strength I didn't have to break it.

"Are we doing the right thing?" I asked quietly. "Your parents aside—are we causing more harm than good, marrying each other?"

"Sophie!" He pulled my hands into his with a laugh, then sobered when he saw my face. "By the Galatine Divine, you're serious."

"I can't keep dragging you down with me. You can't pull me up to where you are. They keep pushing me back down."

"No!" He held my hand, fiercely, so that his nails dug into my skin without his meaning to. "No. They drag down what threatens them, and they do it to one another, too."

"This is different than that, and you know it." I raised my hand, stopping the protests he was ready to levy. "I love you. I will always love you. But what if..." I choked a little on the words. "You know as well as I do that the country needs the reforms, needs them or we crack open and rot like overripe fruit. What if I'm only an obstacle to that?"

"You're a good part of how they came to be!"

"What if my part is over now? What if we're being selfish?" I disentangled my hand from his.

"Nothing is more important to me than you," he said, reaching for my hand again.

I pulled away. "And that is selfish!" I snapped. He started, and then pressed his mouth into a hard line.

"I'm tied into knots over getting this bill passed, and I'm selfish?"

"Yes!" I half shouted. "You keep thinking of me, of the country, of the reform—all as neat pieces you can put together into a tidy finished puzzle. But they don't fit nicely. They haven't fit all along, no matter how much you wish they did. This won't be easy, Theodor. It's as though you can't understand that."

He stopped, growing very quiet. "Maybe I can't. Maybe... maybe I expected that everything would fall into place."

"Because you're a prince, because everything has always worked before?" I forced myself to speak more gently. "This... this is only the start. Maybe in ten years people would talk less. Maybe in twenty they would trust me more. But the rumors, the exclusion, using me to call you into question—it's not going away." I didn't stop, even though I wanted to. "And if my presence is detrimental to the Reform Bill, if the rumors are worse because I'm here, and there are nobles who will cast their vote against it because of me, I shouldn't be here anymore."

"If I didn't believe it was right, marrying you, I wouldn't do it. The risks from the elite having their noses tweaked is out-weighed by the benefit in the trust of my people. We need that trust."

I fell silent. The rumors, the shunning by his family, the cold receptions and scalding gossip behind people's hands—I could bear it for the country, but I was tired of seeing it alone. They didn't speak of Theodor like this, not really, and he could go on believing it wasn't so bad. "If you've chosen your people over the nobility, if you've chosen me—this isn't going away. And I can't keep bearing the burden of that reality for both of us."

"I can't stop them!" he protested.

"Yes, but you can stop telling me it's not as bad as all that." I sighed and took his hand. "It is that bad. Please—put aside your optimism and see how difficult this is for me."

Theodor leaned against the sun-warmed wall. I saw the glimmer of tears in his eyes and knew he finally understood. I felt hollow, but strangely relieved. I couldn't keep living a fairy tale built out of soap bubbles—iridescent and light, but ready to collapse at any moment. If we were going to continue, those bubbles had to break, settle like film on the hard edges of the life we would have together.

"There's something I want to show you," he said softly.

I followed Theodor into the parlor, where we had cast the charm together, his music and my manipulation of the magic working in tandem.

The charm still glowed, embedded in the fibers of the curtain. We had made it together, that indelible light sunk into the velvet. I took a shaky breath.

"It's lasted this long, at least. Any likelihood it will fade?"

I gripped his hand tightly. "My charms don't fade until the stitching itself wears out and the fabric frays away. So I doubt this will."

"The life we make together won't, either. That's not selfishness on my part. That's faith in you."

I paused, questioning whether I could, whether I should ask Theodor for help. "I'm in a bit of a bind," I said. "I'm to go with you to the summit, yes?" Theodor nodded. "And after that, well—there isn't a terrible lot of time to finish all the charmed commissions I have on my docket, is there?"

"I don't suppose I can ask you to delay those deadlines, or put anyone off."

"You most certainly cannot," I replied crisply. For all Theodor understood of the duty of a noble, he had difficulty translating it into my own work ethic. Sometimes I feared he would never quite take seriously the pacts I kept with my customers, my employees, and myself. "I have a responsibility to give a shop with a good reputation over to Alice. But you could help me. I've been having some...difficulty with casting, and it seems easier for me to use the charm you create with your violin than to craft and embed my own."

"Difficulty?" His brow constricted with worry.

"It's nothing, I'm sure." I was not at all sure, but Theodor's neophyte understanding of charm magic couldn't help me unpick the problem. "I'm having a hard time...sort of holding on to the charm. I didn't want to burden you with it, not with the Reform Bill and the summit."

"You do realize what a marriage is, don't you?" I shook my head, taken aback by the question. "It's the state in which you're legally, morally, and ethically invited to share your problems with someone else."

"You know what I meant," I argued. "The timing of everything—there are more important things at stake."

Theodor assessed me with a long, uncomfortable scrutiny. I knew he wanted to say more, but he decided against it. I knew what he left unsaid, and he was probably right—years of independence had left its mark. I could certainly take care of myself, but I was rubbish at letting anyone help.

I put this aside. "At any rate. If you cast, and I pull threads into the already-stitched work, the piece is charmed, and from what I can tell, it's as effective and permanent as if I'd sewn the charm in."

"I'm game," he said. "It will be good practice for me."

"Yes, I suppose so," I replied, surprised. "I hadn't realized you were so invested. Of course, I have no idea how to train you in that, so it's going to be stabbing in the dark for both of us."

"I think we can manage. When shall I report to your shop? The council recesses every day quite promptly. Leaving that stuffy hall is the one thing they all agree on."

"I thought I'd just bring things here."

"Make you schlep all of that silk and bustle here, when I need carry only a violin? Seems impractical."

"Well, it seems improper to have you come to my shop," I answered. "A prince, fiddling in an atelier?" I laughed. "What kind of rumors would that start?"

"Nothing that isn't already circulating," he joked. "Besides," he added with sly grin, "we've not seen enough of each other lately."

I slid closer to him, happy to close out thoughts of angry reformists and anti-reformists. "What, social engagements and discussions of reforms isn't seeing enough of each other?"

"I meant seeing more of you quite literally," he said with a teasing laugh, tugging my kerchief away from the neckline of my gown.

He leaned forward, the scent of his clove pomatum washing over me as he kissed me, hot and thick and with the abandon of a man with far fewer responsibilities. I twined my arms around him, and he surprised me by drawing me up, cradling me in his arms, and making for the stairs. I laughed and kicked as he peppered my collarbone and shoulders with kisses.

A sharp rap on the front door interrupted us before he could leave the room carrying me. "Let the maid get it," Theodor mumbled, kicking at the parlor door, trying to close it without putting me down.

The front door swung wide and he set me down abruptly. I tugged my kerchief back around my shoulder, and Theodor sprang forward. "Ambrose, what in the world?"

"You should answer your door quicker," he snapped. "Evening, Sophie. Sorry for the...intrusion." He glanced at my hair, blushing. My cap was askew and several tendrils had escaped.

"What could possibly warrant barging in like this?" Theodor said. "We're not both kids sharing the nursery, you know, there are certain—"

"There's a riot in the square," Ambrose replied, voice stern and face taut. "It's bad."

14

〜〰〜

AMBROSE CLOSED THE DOOR WITH A WORRIED GLANCE OUT ONTO Theodor's still-placid street. "The Fourth Regiment has already been assembled, and Father gave the order to use violence if it was warranted."

"What?" I gasped. "No, this can't be right." Niko had promised that the people wouldn't rise up until we'd been given a chance to address their concerns through the bill.

Before Ambrose could answer, the report of rifles echoed through the stone corridors of the city. Faint but clear, shattering the evening quiet.

"Shit," Theodor said, rushing toward the door and shouting to the servants for a carriage. "Ambrose, where was Father? Palace or Stone Castle?"

"He's at the Stone Castle, but Theodor, honestly. What are you going to do?" Ambrose countered. "It's going to be over before you even get down the street. Riflemen and soldiers with bayonets, against a riot? It will be a rout." The reports of gunfire and shouting peppered the conversation, distant voices raised in support of Ambrose's argument.

Theodor paused. "That's true enough. But it's what comes next that I worry about," he answered. "I need to talk to Father."

Ambrose sighed. "I don't know that it will do any good. He's like a cuckold husband with the conservative nobles playing the role of tyrant wife. He knows the danger of ignoring the common people, but it's not enough to jar him out of a lifetime of playing upper-crust politics, where the nobles with the most money and influence have the power."

"Maybe this did the trick," Theodor argued. He plucked his hat from the chair beside the door. "At the very least, someone needs to be there to counterbalance whatever draconian suggestions Pommerly and the other old bats are probably making regarding punitive measures for those caught."

He was out of the door before Ambrose could answer. I found I didn't have anything to say in any case. "What do we do now?" I wondered out loud. Already the gunfire had ceased. Fears that the bill was dead before it could be voted on, that someone I knew was lying bleeding in the square, that this was only the start of a true civil war all ran together.

"I'm going to follow that idiot brother of mine to the Stone Castle and see if there's anything we can do." Ambrose sighed. "It's probably not safe to send you home alone. I'll take you. Unless you'd rather stay here?" I shook my head. Ambrose's legal training gave him the dry, deductive rationale of a barrister, which was strangely comforting in a moment like this one.

We took his carriage toward the center of the city. The streets were clear, but knots of people crowded in doorways and corners, under the eaves of side-street taverns. We skirted Fountain Square, but I could see past a unit of the Fourth Regiment onto the cobblestones beyond. I saw blood.

"I wish—" I clamped my mouth shut. It didn't do any good to voice it out loud, that I wished there was something I could do. There wasn't, not here, not now. I would only be in the way of the medical corps, the regimental surgeons and nurses surely already setting up a makeshift hospital in the Stone Castle or the cathedral. If only I had time to sew charms into their bandages, or embed one of Theodor's musically summoned charms into the linen strips. Of course there wasn't time for sewing, and Theodor was busy wrestling with the politics of a potentially disastrous blow to the Reform Bill.

Ambrose didn't wait for me to open the door of my row house—the modest, quiet home I had shared with Kristos. It wouldn't be mine much longer; the lease expired in several months and then I wouldn't have an inconspicuous home of my own. Everyone knew where the Prince of Westland lived. I fumbled with my key.

"Sophie."

I whirled. Niko beckoned from the slim alley between my building and the next set of row houses over. The eaves overhung the dirt path, casting thick shadows, and I could have walked by him a dozen times without seeing him.

"What are you—"

"Over here," he ordered. I bristled at his tone, commanding me like an officer barks at a private, but I slipped my key back into my pocket and followed him into the alley. His shoes and the hems of his trousers were spattered with mud, and I thought I saw streaks of blood on his dark brown linen coat.

"How many hurt? Dead?" I managed to ask. My most pressing fear—how bad had it been?

"They didn't even get to use their bayonets," he said, as though this would placate me.

"So they only shot my neighbors, they didn't gore them to death." I gripped his arm in mine. His sleeve had blood on it. "How many, Niko?"

"I don't know yet. Maybe twenty, thirty hit, maybe more. Look, the soldiers entered Fountain Square from the Stone Castle, fired in ranks a few times, and the rioters scattered. It was a damn good thing for the soldiers that the rioters hadn't had time to properly assemble with weapons, that's all. It would have been a brawl." He pursed his lips, as though calculating their odds.

"Would that have been preferable?" I almost shouted. Niko shot me a sharp look, and I lowered my voice. "A brawl? Hand-to-hand fighting in the square?"

"No, of course not, I'm just saying—this wasn't exactly planned."

"Then explain how it happened."

"Explain what? A crowd-size temper tantrum I didn't orchestrate or condone? Sweet hell, Sophie. You'd blame me for the mosquitoes if you could."

"Then what," I forced through tense lips, "happened today?"

"They're impatient," Niko said. "Yesterday's debates didn't go so well. Folks gathered to talk in the taverns, they got heated, they started moving from tavern to tavern and eventually into the streets; the crowd gained momentum." He shrugged. "It just—snowballed. These things do that, you know."

"Why?" I held up my hand to his exasperated retort. "I mean, why now? The vote is coming. Reform is coming."

"Yeah, well, their patience is getting thin. And there was an amendment to the bill recently, remember?"

"Yes, they removed the anti-conscription provision—mercies, Niko, they didn't riot over that?"

"They sure as hell did. I tried to stop it but this got out of hand, quickly. They don't trust a governing body that keeps taking things away from them!"

"It was..." My breath shook. "The anti-conscription provision was a bargaining chip. We knew that piece would probably fail, but having something less vital to be able to remove—Niko, it's invaluable to the process."

"You set that part up to fail? You meant to remove it?" I thought, for a brief moment, Niko might actually hit me. "You're a worse snake than I thought."

"It's politics, Niko! It's negotiation. There has to be something you're willing to give up—"

"What is the nobility willing to give up?"

I fell silent for a long, uncomfortable moment and made him wait for me to speak. "Plenty of them aren't willing to give anything up and we have to be able to vote them down."

"Do you trust them?"

"What?"

"The nobles. Once this vote is done, say it passes—you trust that they aren't going to go back on this?"

The fight I'd had with Theodor echoed in memory, recalling words so similar to Niko's but spoken by me. I took a shaking breath. "Yes. We have to. There's no other way forward."

"You were born down here with the rest of us rats," Niko retorted. "You can play pampered palace pet all you want, but you know better. You know that their game is rigged. They hold all the power. They can give it or withhold it and all we can do is—what?" He snorted. "Riot until there's none of us left. And we will. You know that."

I ached, from the soles of my feet to my throbbing head, but deeper than that, in my soul. For Galitha, for the common people, for a nation ready to tear itself apart. "Legal reform will work. It has to. You know that, or you wouldn't have asked me to help you."

He sighed, the lines around his eyes showing plainer than before the Midwinter Revolt. "Yeah, sure. I did. Call me a hopeless optimist."

"That," I assured him, "is something I have never called you, nor will I."

15

THE RIOT CAST A LONG SHADOW OVER THE CITY. I SPENT A QUIET
afternoon at Viola's salon a few days later, ostensibly to discuss a
new book of poetry but in reality to digest the impact of the riot
on the Reform Bill's chance of success. The nobles were quieter
with their objections to reform, frightened like chastised children, just as they had been after the Midwinter Revolt. All my
warnings seemed to percolate into their conversation. I spoke
little but felt a sense of relief despite my grief at the bloodshed—
the nobility now understood the depth of the common people's
dedication. They weren't giving up. *We* weren't giving up.

The date was set, swiftly and unceremoniously, for the
vote on the Reform Bill. With the final moments of the work
of months hanging in the balance, I didn't expect Theodor to
be able to help me with the charms as we had planned, but
he insisted that he needed to get away from the scrabbling and
clawing of the nobles the day before the pivotal council session. He arrived inconspicuously at my shop in the late afternoon. "All right," he said, unpacking his violin. "I'm at your
service."

"Did anyone see you come in?" I asked, glancing at the
quiet streets through the window. The hours between midday

and the end of work tended to be quiet in my shop's quarter, as morning errands were finished but the bustle of trades-people locking up and going home or out to the taverns hadn't yet begun. The dozy quiet of a hot summer afternoon even seemed to seep inside between the panes of glass.

"I don't believe so, but does it matter? A prince does as he likes," he said with false gallantry.

I rolled my eyes as though it were a joke, but I didn't like that cavalier attitude. "Alice and Emmi are washing the windows in the back. The dust is so bad this summer that we can hardly see to work sometimes. They'll be done shortly."

"Of course, you wouldn't want them to know about—"

"No," I replied hastily as Emmi trotted into the front of the shop, dust smudging her cheeks and painted in a thick stripe down her pinner apron. "How goes it?" I asked her.

She glanced at me, and then blanched at seeing Theodor. "Almost done," she squeaked.

"You needn't be afraid, I won't bite," Theodor said.

"Don't tease her," I said, more irritated than I intended. What of it, if Emmi was a bit struck by the presence of the heir to the throne in our shop? The reality of my situation was so strange that I often felt separated into discrete pieces, one that lived in my shop, and one that lived with Theodor. Perhaps my employees felt that division, as well.

Alice and Emmi shook out their cleaning rags in the alley and tidied up as best they could, though the reddish street dust had nearly dyed Alice's fair hair pink. "Pink and blue hair powders were the fashion ten years ago," I joked. "If anyone asks, tell them you're reviving the style."

"I wouldn't have worn them then, either," Alice grumbled, arranging her black silk-covered hat to hide the worst of the dirt streaking her white linen cap.

"I'm going to have to spend half the night washing this off—it's gotten places I hadn't dreamed of." Emmi laughed, then remembered that Theodor was standing a few feet from her, and her bronze cheeks reddened. They both clattered out into the street before Emmi could embarrass herself any further.

"To begin, then," I said, leading Theodor into the back of the shop, into our workroom.

"First," Theodor said. "Between that letter from Niko and the riot, I'm worried about you living alone." He raised a waiting eyebrow.

"It's all just talk, I'm sure, Niko's letter!"

"I'm not so sure. Obviously it wouldn't be said in my presence, so I asked Ballantine and Ambrose—"

"Theodor!"

"What? There shouldn't be any secrets kept from them. They admitted that they'd heard plenty of…unflattering… things, but it's hard to tell if anyone is serious about them." He sighed. "Still, I can't help but worry—perhaps you should stay with me. Until we go to the summit, until—well, we're going to be living together soon enough, anyway."

A hundred weak reasons ran through my head: that I hadn't packed, that I still owed three months on my current lease, that I hadn't washed the windows and couldn't move out of a rented space and leave it dirty. In truth, the thought of accelerating our eventual domestic arrangement was overwhelming. In my little townhouse I had peace and quiet and could do things the way I always had. "I'll consider it," I said, more curtly than I intended.

Theodor's mouth was a thin line. "Consider it, then. And perhaps consider making yourself one of those protection charms you charge your clients for."

"How can you suggest that?" I nearly shouted, remembering my open windows in time to keep my voice down. "You know I don't use my own charms—I never have, and I never will," I declared.

"I know you never have, but I didn't think you were so stubborn as to set yourself a rule that you never would."

"Stubborn?"

"Inflexible, yes. Refusing to consider new situations previously unimagined."

"The entire point of a rule," I said, my voice tight, "is that it applies regardless of the situation."

"Why?" he challenged.

"Because," I snapped. "Because that's the rule, the rule we all follow, passed down from mothers and grandmothers and aunts."

"And no one has ever broken that rule? It's a superstition, Sophie, not a law."

"It's real to me. My mother taught me, and she didn't break it, even when she got sick with a fever—and she died, Theodor."

"I don't want you to die just to prove a point," he said, voice softening a bit. "I don't understand why a rule your mother taught you as a child, a child who was never going to do anything but sell charms to her neighbors, has to hold up now, for a woman who's so much more than that. A woman who's influencing the fate of nations."

"Because with power comes responsibility, and rules govern that responsibility," I said, echoing words my mother had said once, long ago. "I think that applies all the more to who I am now."

Theodor shook his head. "I can't convince you."

"No," I said. "But I will tell you—if you ever figure out how to make a physical good-luck charm, I'll take it. First—practicing your casting. We can start with this," I said, producing a jacket whose bright rose silk shimmered beautifully but was bereft of the charm that had been commissioned for it.

"You have a deal," he said, "and I have motivation to learn more about casting. Now—do I just play? And let you do whatever it is you do to draw the charm?"

I hadn't considered one finer point of the process—I imbued my pieces with particular types of charms. Luck, love, money; Theodor didn't have the control for that yet. Fortunately, this piece was for simple good luck. "I suppose," I thought out loud, "that the kind of music you play might have an effect on the precise nature of the charm. This is for general good fortune, so try to play something...lucky. Cheerful."

He played, drawing the charm quickly from the ether. The song was a vibrant, plucky country air, and the accompanying charm as close to pure luck as I could have hoped for. I deftly drew it into my control and wove it into the fibers. "It's working," I confirmed as I set a line of light around the hem and then embedded it down the center front. "And that's enough."

He finished the piece with a flourish; simply stopping in the middle would not, apparently, do. "Already?"

"Yes," I said. It had taken perhaps a quarter hour, far less than my usual method of stitching the charm in. I could only hope it was as strong and indelible, but nothing I had seen from the experiment with the curtain led me to believe anything else. With various melodies and adjustments to them, we tailored the charms to the pieces on my schedule. It took merely the better part of two hours to move through the remainder of my backlogged projects, finishing with the sky-blue riding habit I had struggled with. When we were done, the protection charm clung tightly to the fibers of the riding habit, glowing in the wool as though it had been woven there.

"Keep going for another minute," I said, curiosity eliciting inspiration. "I want to try something." I pulled a thick thread of light, twining like yarn, toward the shelving on the far wall of the atelier. Fabric was my medium, what I knew innately. I understood the weave and hand of a piece of cloth before I even touched it, and allied myself with it when I draped and sewed. Wood, metal, stone—the materials of a building weren't my usual canvas.

I pressed my intentions on the golden thread. I manipulated its movement, trying to drive it deep into the wood, to hold it there. To my surprise, it slivered itself into the wood grain and held, but at an odd angle, like a bent nail, with the tail of the thread dangling behind it. I looped the thread and tacked it into the wood, creating an uneven pattern on the surface.

Thinking of some of the finer furniture I'd seen at Theodor's house, I tried something else, cutting the thread off and picking a new shelf. I flattened the threads into something more like thin sheets of metal, and imagined them pressed into the wood like an inlay. It worked; the charm settled into the wood like mother-of-pearl into barely perceptible grooves in an inlaid box or tabletop.

Theodor stopped playing as I inlaid another set of shelves with the charm he had cast. "Do you think it will hold?" he asked.

"I have no idea," I said. "It might fall out as soon as we walk away."

"More experiments," Theodor said with a laugh. "Keep it up and we'll have to get you a university post," he joked, then his face fell. "I'm sorry—I didn't mean to compare you to him."

"Not at all," I replied, though the thought shook me. Was what I was doing comparable to Pyord's studies? I thought of something he'd said, that we'd only scratched at what charm casting could do. I shook off the thought, though the idea of being able to imbue anything with charm—or curse—was unsettling. Would charmed rifles never miss? Would cursed fortresses crumble?

"But Pyord thought of this," I said. "If not this, exactly, he knew there could be more to charm casting. He studied this, in ancient texts."

"Not to sound insensitive, but if the Pellians had this figured out...well, either it's not very powerful at all or they weren't terribly good at it."

"I know, they're not exactly world dominating today—Pyord seemed to think it was just a rash of bad luck that kept them from developing casting further."

"That's irony for you."

"It is," I said, disconcerted. What exactly had the Pellians discovered? How far had they stretched magical influence? "There's really no way to know without another Pyord digging up ancient texts."

"Few enough people know how to read those defunct languages. Of course..." Theodor flashed his best imitation of a conniving smile. "The university in West Serafe is considered the best in the world, with scholars in every discipline and a library that makes our Public Archive look like a second-hand bookbinder's."

The prospect was intriguing. Away from Galitha City, where very few people could read the ancient language that shrouded any studies of my skill, could I hire someone to research and translate for me? I was reluctant—after all, Pyord had been a scholar of Pellian antiquity and he'd been far from trustworthy, but Nia had been willing to help me. Any concerns I had about someone recognizing me and growing suspicious of my work would be allayed in a foreign country. Theoreticals aside, perhaps I could discover what was wrong with my casting ability—and recover my skills.

"Beyond that," Theodor said, his voice intensifying as he laid his violin in its case. "It does make one wonder. There have always been rumors that the Serafan court magicians were, well, actually magicians."

"Not just better-than-average tricksters and showmen?" I scoffed.

"Rumors are rumors," Theodor conceded, "but quite often, where there is smoke, there's fire. Is there any possibility, do you think?"

I wanted to dismiss the prospect completely, but short months ago I wouldn't have believed one could control musical casting at all, let alone manipulate it into physical objects. "I suppose it's not impossible," I said, hesitant.

"Perhaps you could do a bit of investigation while we're in West Serafe," Theodor said. "The secrets are certainly buried well if they're there at all, but then again—I don't know that any foreign delegation has ever included a charm caster."

"One thing at a time," I told him. "There's a vote tomorrow, remember?"

"Indeed. I ought to go home and make the final edits to my grand, unifying speech." He paused. "I'd usually love your insight, but it might be best if…"

"No offense taken, I need to get these orders out for delivery, anyway." I shooed him out of the store, then wrapped packages in brown paper as the late summer evening fell.

16

I WOKE TO A GOLDEN HAZE OF HOT SUMMER SEEPING THROUGH my open windows and the immediacy of remembering—today was the vote. Our hopes hinged on the votes cast in the Council of Nobles today. Not only my hopes, I knew, but the hopes of a quiet populace, waiting, their patience nearly threadbare.

Despite the monumental importance of the vote, I intended to put in a full day at the shop. I skirted Fountain Square; a small crowd already gathered, red caps conspicuous in the throng, ready to hear the results of the vote. Ready—I took a shaky breath—to respond to it. I wondered what Niko was doing today; not staying idle, most likely.

But there was nothing for me to do. Not today. I had fulfilled my role in the tableau as it had unfolded, as well as I could. As I walked to work, I let myself settle into the comfortable monotony of a morning routine, trying to put the debates driving a rift through the city from my mind.

I caught the scent of smoke first, wending its way up Bridge Street and strengthening as I approached the commercial street that housed my shop. I quickened my pace—was the scent coming from my district, my street? Which of my neighbors was affected? I didn't allow the panicked thought to emerge fully formed—that it could be my shop—and instead dodged a street cart selling pastries and a woman balancing a load of strawberries as I continued with single-minded purpose.

The smoke grew thicker as I rounded the corner onto my street. I was shoved to the side as a wagon from the fire brigade careened toward the source of the gray cloud, water sloshing in fat barrels and the volunteer firefighters already prepping their pumps and hoses.

I used the wake the wagon created as best I could, though the pedestrian traffic in the street quickly meshed together again, their curiosity over the miniature disaster unfolding somewhere nearby less pressing than their daily business of hawking wares and buying what they needed for their larders.

My footfalls quickened along with my breath as I grew closer to my shop—the smoke was thicker here and, to my dismay, the fire brigade's wagon had stopped.

"Sophie!" I slowed and looked for the speaker. Emmi rushed out of the crowd and gripped my arm with bruising intensity. "I was early, it was already—your neighbor helped me call the alarm."

I let her pull me toward my shop, mute as I realized that smoke was pouring from two broken windows. The firefighters, volunteers from the district who had left their day's work for a small bonus, had already broken the lock from the door and ferried hoses and buckets inside, but I knew it didn't matter now. Everything inside could already be destroyed by smoke if not by flames themselves, and if not, most of my fine fabrics couldn't stand up to the water.

My neighbors gathered close behind, concerned, I was sure, about my losses, but also still worried that the flames could leap the walls separating our shops. There were no firebreaks in this part of the city—a blaze could get out of hand quickly. We all watched in silence.

Of course, I couldn't figure how it had started to begin with. I hadn't been in the shop early this morning; no one had, as far as I knew. Alice had a key, but she was nowhere to be seen yet, and Emmi and Heda couldn't have been inside. We hadn't even lit a candle or lamp the day before, and of course there were no fires in our stoves this time of year. A stray spark from outside? Had I slept through a thunderstorm in the night?

The buckets sloshed as the firefighters turned them, draining all the water into the hoses they had dragged inside. The smoke was growing less dense, and one of the men manning a pump motioned that they were done. The fire hadn't spread.

"Is the owner or the proprietor here?" a gruff voice called from the doorway.

My throat was gummy with dry smoke, but I managed to answer. Emmi let go of my arm, and I wove my way forward alone.

Then I saw it, scrawled in crude lettering with runny paint on the stones in front of my doorway. *Politicking Witch*, in an orange-leaning red, impossible to miss. I scuffed my toe on the stones, not believing what I was seeing.

"Miss?" The speaker who had called me to the doorway wasn't a volunteer firefighter but an officer in the city's garrison forces. "I need to take a statement and ask a few questions."

I nodded, still fighting the smoke in my throat and now a lump of angry tears that threatened to wash the smoke away.

"When were you here last?"

"Yesterday afternoon. Early evening. Six hours after noon." I had been wrapping and sending final packages, and by something just shy of a miracle, I had taken our paperwork home, to reconcile my income and expense accounts.

"Alone?"

"Yes."

"And were there any open flames—"

"No," I snapped. What a farcical question. "There weren't any broken windows, either," I added. Had the windows blown out from heat inside the building, I would have expected to see glass on the stone walk outside. There was none.

He sighed. "I have to ask." He glanced at the words splayed across the sidewalk with no change in emotion. "If you want to survey the damage, I can accompany you inside for a few minutes."

"It's safe?" I asked.

"No," he replied. "Not technically, until the Lord of Stones' office sends someone to certify it. You rent?"

"Yes," I replied. From a nameless owner who managed his assets through a countinghouse. "Do you notify him, or do I, or..."

"Doubtless he knows already. But yes, the Lord of Stones' office will notify him." He gestured toward the gaping doorway. "Do you want to take a look?"

I nodded. I had to know—were all my fabrics destroyed? They were an investment, a deeper investment than I knew how to recoup. They were the core of the assets I intended to pass on to Alice. My chest tightened as I stepped through the door.

The front room was a charred mess, but I had expected this. Fire had lapped up the sides of the counter and destroyed the finely upholstered chairs I had bought to outfit our consultation salon. The slate bearing the list of orders was cracked from the heat, and half of it lay in shards on the floor. Gathering the last resolve I had, I walked into the back room.

There had been one gown, draped on a mannequin, in the front of the room; I knew immediately it had to be sent to the trash bin. The silk was charred and the linen lining had burned clear through. The fire had licked up the sides of the room, consuming some cotton kerchiefs and caps, but these works in progress weren't my main concern. The bolts of fabric on the far side of the studio, shelved by type and color, were irreplaceable.

I turned slowly, afraid of what I would see.

The shelves were untouched.

The flames had gnawed away at the counters and work-tables on either side of the shelves, and had torn the bolts of fabric lying on the worktable in the center of the room to bits, but the dozens of silks and cottons stowed in the shelves appeared unharmed. I hurried across the room.

"Be careful—the floor may not be stable," the officer called. I ignored him and thrust my nose against the first bolt I found. A faint scent of smoke, but I was sure it could be salvaged.

The gold of the charm I had set into the wood glowed as I stood, shocked, in front of the minor miracle. I traced it with a timid finger, terrified and awed by what I had done.

I met Alice and Heda when they arrived for work and sent them home quickly with assurances that I would send a messenger soon. I had a few days' worth of wages in my pocket; I doled these out despite Alice's protests that they would be fine without the charity. I ignored her. The fire had quite possibly ruined my plans of passing the business on to her, and certainly put them all out of work for several weeks, at least.

I pushed fear and anger into a hollow place in my gut and forced myself to stand tall as my neighbors wandered back to their shops and their homes. Most offered me quiet condolences, more than one taking a long, uncomfortable look at the scrawled epithet on my doorstep. I held my chin up and purposefully avoided letting my eyes land on the crude writing. It wasn't the truth; there was no point in acknowledging it.

But it was unavoidable. Someone—probably a decent-size group of someones—had believed so strongly that I had overstepped my bounds, that my intentions were evil, that they had sought me out to harm me. They didn't set out to discredit the Reform Bill or to engage in some debate on its merits, but simply to strike at me. My shop, my sewing, my life's work for years; they knew where to aim their attack to hurt me. I wouldn't cry now, not in the street, not where someone who hoped to wound me could see it.

With no work to do and a thick red tape tied over the gaping hole of my shop's broken door, I walked back toward Fountain Square.

The bells in the cathedral tolled; it was barely midmorning. I didn't expect the vote for hours, so I settled quietly under the shade of the flaxwood poplar, still dropping seeds shrouded in minute clouds. I watched the ebb and flow of the people, how the crowd slowly grew in size. The sun crested at noon, and a ripple of excitement passed from the edge of the square toward the center.

The shouts could have been in celebration or anger; I couldn't tell from my corner under the tree. I leaned forward, craning my neck along with the others nearest me to hear what was being passed, person to person, a moving arc of voices across the square.

"Can you hear?" I asked a tall man next to me, his red cap perched at a jaunty angle.

He shook his head and elbowed his way forward; I was only pushed back farther. I stood stock-still, my heart hammering in my chest, the heat suddenly almost too much.

"It passed!"

The shouts finally reached our side of the square, and the tall man's cap was in his hand, thrust into the air, one of many miniature banners waving under the brilliant sunlight, and around me, the press of human bodies erupted into a unified cheer.

All of the air went out of me at once. My personal loss was a speck in the sea of triumph around me, one tear diluted into an ocean of laughter and shouts and broad, confident smiles. All the months of work, all the scorn I'd felt under the scrutinizing eyes of nobles, all of it paled and faded under the sun-soaked joy in the square.

I sat down, hard, on an unforgiving bench, trembling and, I realized as the tears coursed down my cheeks, sobbing. Someone handed me a faded purple-print kerchief; I thanked them, but they'd already moved on, toward the jubilation at the center of the square. Women and men climbed the fountain, waving and shouting and splashing diamond-bright streams of water into the crowd.

I had been willing to give up anything for Galitha, for reform, for the future of the country. And even if I had lost everything, even if the shop could never be salvaged, even if I could no longer give Alice and Emmi and Heda secure employment, even if the success I had built was erased—it was worth it. It had meaning.

I stood, still shaking, and watched for a long time, watched the work of months culminating in joy. Then I slipped away from the celebration.

17

BRILLIANT RED AND WHITE STARBURSTS EXPLODED ABOVE THE harbor, raining sparks amid cheers from the shore. I opened the curtain of Theodor's bedchamber wide, taking in the panorama of a dozen fishing boats and small merchant ships taking turns launching fireworks from their decks.

"You wish you were at the celebration?" Theodor asked.

"Not really," I replied. I didn't care for the press and heat of large crowds, and the assembly at the docks was certainly the largest Galitha City had seen in recent months. Elections for the committees replacing the Lords of Stones, Keys, and Coin were set to take place within the fortnight. Even more revolutionary, the Council of Country, to govern alongside the Council of Nobles, would be elected before autumn. Riders had been sent to every corner of Galitha with the procedures the moment the vote had passed, so I imagined that in other towns and villages, along the coast and in the river valleys, there were smaller but similar celebrations.

"I feel as though we ought to have done something," he continued. "A small party, a reception, something."

"I suppose I didn't want to jinx anything by planning a party," I said.

"I didn't want to consider the outcome of the vote at all," Theodor confided. "I didn't quite believe we could do it." He took my hand. "I do mean we. You—you're in that bill as much as I am."

"You mean law," I replied with a creeping, unbidden smile. "We ought to at least drink a toast."

"I could use a drink," Theodor replied with a wry smile. He rang for a maid. "I don't suppose either of us feel much like celebrating after what happened with your shop today. You do think..."

"It was written plainly. Arson, aimed at me." I held up my hands. "It's not what's important today. Or, frankly, tomorrow or any day after that." The victory today was not the end of our struggle. It was only a waypoint, still on the uphill climb. The revelers in the city's harbor and filling her taverns and streets were pouring beer and punch in celebration, but would the cheering crowds be disappointed as change rolled out slowly, faltering as nobles and commoners bickered and fought over legislation in their respective councils? I watched the fireworks stain the sky red; the colorful display, meant as celebration, seemed almost foreboding.

And though the streets rang with cheers, there were certainly common people at home tonight, upset at the turn of events. Counter-reformist protests had cropped up in Fountain Square, surprising even me with their varied participants. Fear of change motivated even dockworkers and bargehands, and something coarser, too. Some of the pamphlets circulating the city following the bill's passage suggested a subversive Pellian takeover, or at least an unhealthy level of influence by Pellians. It didn't matter that most of the participants had been Galatine born and bred; Niko Otni and Kristos Balstrade were still well-known names, and then of course there was the noxious Pellian enchantress marrying the prince.

The maid returned with a bottle of sparkling wine. "To the future," Theodor said as he raised a delicate cut-crystal coupe.

"Whatever it may be," I said.

"We know one thing," he said. "We're in it together."

As it turned out, Theodor didn't need to plan a party to celebrate the passage of the bill at all. Viola arranged, in her characteristic refined excess, a grand fete in a closed section of the public gardens. It was no surprise that most of the nobles and other guests sipping wine and sampling tiny iced cakes decorated with rose petals were the bill's proponents and members of Viola's salon. Much of the nobility were quietly sulking or openly complaining about the vote. Others had made quick retreats to their estates to spend the rest of the summer. Even though the bill had gained a majority, it was clear that the results disappointed many, and that even some of the nobles who had voted for the bill felt compelled by threats of another revolt rather than pure ideals.

"Lovely choice of location," I said to Viola as she greeted us.

"It was the closest I could get to throwing it specifically for Theodor," she said. "He doesn't want any attention on him, but faint mercy, it's his doing."

I agreed that Theodor deserved the largest share of the credit, though I deferred to the line we'd practiced earlier. "Everyone who petitioned, argued, and voted for the bill should be celebrated."

"Good gory offal, he's turned you into a councillor, too!" Viola laughed and plucked a glass of sweet honey-colored wine from a nearby table. "Are you quite ready for the summit?"

"I'm trying to finish a cotton gown or two before we leave, but I'm not sure I'll be successful." I didn't add that I was also scrambling to try to salvage the shop for Alice, though the fire commissioner had shaken his head and proclaimed the building a total loss. The likelihood of finding a new location so quickly was slim, and without one, I couldn't transfer my license to Alice.

"Quite wise of you," Viola said. "The climate there is much different from even Galitha in summer. The heat is beyond your reckoning, and the humidity. If you'd like to borrow a few things, I'd be glad to send some lightweight gowns along with you."

"It's a lovely offer," I said, "but you forget that I've done sewing for you. The shoulders in your gowns will be too narrow for me."

"Your build is so regal," Viola said.

"Or like a Pellian ox." I laughed. "I've been making over a few cotton gowns, and I have my chemise gown. That seems appropriate for summer anywhere."

"Indeed, and a bit of a comment on affairs here, besides. You aren't nervous, are you?" she asked.

"Of course I am! I have no idea how to behave at a Galatine function half the time, let alone an international summit. I'm just a plain Galatine seamstress with Pellian parents and the shoulders to match," I replied.

"You are far more than that," Viola said. "You're the betrothed of the Prince of Westland. If you want one bit of advice, remember that and act the part."

Annette and Theodor joined us. "I'm ever so pleased," Annette said, her voice dripping sarcasm, "to discover that Admiral Merhaven will be joining us at the summit."

"That old hay bale with legs attached?" Viola snorted.

"He said that Viola's portraits were inferior to the previous court painter," Annette confided. "That was three years ago and she's not forgiven him."

"My work is not inferior!" Viola set the glass down, the

wine inside churning toward a tsunami under her trembling hands. "He only said that because I paint in the new style, the natural style. And because..." She huffed instead of adding the second reason.

"Why?" Theodor asked, brow tightening. "I always thought it was just that he didn't agree with the less formal styling."

"I'm a woman!" Viola threw a pale blue linen napkin at Theodor, hitting him square in the face. "You are such an idiot sometimes."

"I had no idea," Theodor replied, setting the missile back on a nearby table.

Viola rolled her eyes. "I don't suppose you've addressed any of those particular injustices and inconsistencies in your blessed Reform Bill. Coverture. Inheritance. All the unfair property laws privileging anyone with extra flesh between their legs."

Annette laughed and brandished her wineglass. "Yes! We would write the laws differently, wouldn't we? Ladies inheriting estates and titles. Married women keeping their property."

"If only we could rewrite everything." Viola sighed, laying a hand on Annette's arm.

"Well, draft something for next fall's session," Theodor said. "The vote is final, we've prevailed, hurrah, and now on to the next thing." We had met with the foreign minister, Lord Crestmont, to discuss the travel arrangements and high points of the summit's agenda. It was clear that he was not particularly pleased that I was accompanying them, though he was mollified at the inclusion of the once-Princess Annette.

It was clear, as well, that the delegation had explicit designs on negotiating a marriage for Annette while we were abroad. From the pained glance Annette and Viola shared, it was clear they knew, too.

Suddenly overwhelmed, by the celebration of what we'd worked so long to accomplish, by the daunting tasks that lay ahead, by the prospect of an official role at an international summit, I excused myself. I moved away from the laughter and chatter at the center of the party toward the quiet avenues of green hedges that bordered the formal gardens. The public gardens closed at dusk, and the silence and shadows of a lingering summer evening gave me space to breathe.

"Well done, you."

I jumped, tripping over a bit of loose brick in the walkway. A steady hand caught my arm. I whirled, gripping the hand, and faced a laughing Niko. "Sweet hell, Niko. Are you on the guest list?"

He released my arm. "Don't be snippy. I was just...taking in the view."

"Did you climb a fence?"

"I take it even a great patron of the public gardens like the crown prince doesn't know about the water gate." He grinned. "Down where the fountain runoff drains into the river. It's a bit mucky, but—"

"You shouldn't be here, you prize idiot! If you were caught, I couldn't help you."

"What? I just think it a bit gauche that your party didn't include a slightly more stratified guest list."

"It's not my party."

"Figures." He scuffed his toe against the loose brick. "I wanted to see my allies up close."

"Allies."

"Don't make any mistake, Sophie. You got your bill passed. But they're going to fight you on keeping those laws. Every damn step. So I wanted to see—who have I got on the same side

as me? I also hoped I'd find someone I could pass this along to."
He pressed a letter into my hand. I moved to put it in my pocket,
but he stopped me. "It's not from me. It's intercepted. Read it."

"Intercepted?" I asked as I unfolded the paper. The seal was
already broken. I recognized the device—Pommerly.

"We do more than distribute pamphlets, you know."

I was primed to argue about his disregard for both privacy
and the legality of stealing mail when I scanned the opening
lines of the missive. It was brief, but directive. Wait until the
crown prince is gone, then hold up the election proceedings.
Levy new taxes before any new council can be convened. Garrison provincial fortifications with loyal troops. "Do you know
what this is?"

"Active treasonous writing, yes."

"Who was this addressed to?"

Niko shrugged. "Don't know. Coded envelope. That's how
I knew it was important, make sense?"

"Surely it's only that Pommerly idiot," I breathed. "And
surely—surely this isn't actually happening."

"Maybe. Maybe he's just upset and venting a few ill-
conceived ideas." Niko shook his head. "I wouldn't count on it."

Before I could ask anything more, about where the letter
came from, about what he intended to do, shadows and voices
echoed down the path. Niko cut through a gap in the hedge and
I was left alone, a damning writ of treason in my hands.

18

WITH THE VOTE FINALIZED AND THE REFORMS UNDER WAY, THEODOR had to shift swiftly into planning for the Five-Year Summit despite the enormous task of actually instituting the reforms. He entrusted setting elections to the Council of Nobles with the anxiety of a mother letting someone else hold her newborn baby for the first time. Given that any accusations against Pommerly would be made on the basis of a letter stolen by a fugitive, he hid the evidence in his study, showing only his brother Ambrose to confirm the legal implications of what was written.

I barely saw Theodor, as he spent the long summer days studying historical and current trade agreements and shipping routes, as fair use of trade ways and fishing grounds was the prime piece of negotiation at this year's summit. The Allied Equatorial States, a nation of islands, claimed that the West Serafans and Galatines in particular taxed trade routes and ports to their gain unfairly. The East Serafans, lacking extensive waterways of their own in the highly trafficked trade routes, were eager to curtail Galitha and West Serafe. Kvyset, with its uncontested near-arctic waters, was expected to remain circumspect in their opinions. It didn't escape me that Pellia, along with Fen, was not considered important enough to attend the summit at all, though both island nations certainly would be affected by any agreements on seafaring trade.

We shared a short and disappointing dinner in the garden days before our departure. It was almost too warm to eat, and Theodor's leather satchel bulged with papers, letters, and carefully folded maps. He pulled out one letter and sighed.

"From Lady Crestmont," Theodor said. "She says an attack of gout on poor old Lord Crestmont will prevent them from joining us."

I glanced at her warbling, shaky handwriting. "That's too bad, I certainly hope he'll feel better," I said.

Theodor snorted, and I started, appalled that he would be so callous. "Come now, I'm not so cruel as to wish gout on even him," he replied. "I saw him two days ago, as hale as a horse. I can't help but wonder if he's avoiding the trip." He paused. "He and Pommerly are great allies in the council."

Even in the thick heat that lingered in the summer evening, I felt a chill. "You think he's staying behind to cause trouble with Pommerly, or staying behind to avoid being affiliated with you?"

"Perhaps both, perhaps neither. Ah, it's no matter. We'll have Admiral and Lady Merhaven, and Annette. No more retinue needed, and frankly, it will make for better company anyway."

"But if he does intend to plan something with Pommerly, or others—"

"Plan all he likes, the law is final."

I picked at the crust of bread in my hand. The law may have been final, but the nobles who had opposed it didn't have to make the implementation easy. I opened my mouth, ready to ask if Theodor truly had to leave the country, if he couldn't stay to shepherd the law a little longer. But I knew the answer. I bit into my bread instead. It was dry and dissolved to crumbs.

While Theodor gained fluency in international trade, I had to finish my summer-weight clothes and, heavier work, shut up the shop. There was a symbolic finality to hanging a sign lettered in bold CLOSED, and cleaning out the inventory of fabric still piled in the back, a finality I had hoped to avoid in passing the store off to Alice.

The charmed shelves still glowed with the good fortune Theodor had spun from his melody and that I had embedded in the wood. The silks and cottons and wools stacked neatly by fiber and color waited to be carted to Theodor's, where he had agreed to store them until our return. I traced a particularly delicate yellow silk, fabric that I had hoped some demure brunette would choose for a ball gown, and picked up a bolt of fine blue Fenian wool that I had envisioned as a traveling suit for someone with a pink-and-white complexion.

"You're nearly done," a timid voice said from the doorway. Emmi.

"Yes—oh, don't come in. It's a dirty mess in here." I gestured to the soot already covering my checked apron. I had worn my oldest, simplest worsted wool gown and wished I had something I cared about even less to subject to the mess.

"I got a packet from a bank this morning," Emmi said. "It had—it had way too much money in it."

I smiled. "No, it didn't. That's a severance payment. It's..." I couldn't say it was purely standard, as it wasn't. Far from it, as Theodor had given me enough to pay my assistants the equivalent of a full year's wage. "It's the least I could do," I said.

"Thank him for me." Emmi scanned the room. "How was it that the fabric wasn't destroyed? This place looks like nothing could have survived."

"Luck," I replied honestly.

Emmi shook her head. "Even for a business dealing in luck,

that's luck." She turned back toward the street. "Good, she's here!"

Alice appeared in the doorway next to Emmi, crowding the frame.

"Outside, both of you," I said.

"I wanted to thank you," Alice said.

"Don't thank me for severance," I replied.

"Not only that," Alice said. "You've given me good work and better opportunity. That's something to be grateful for." My throat tightened—I wanted to give her much more than that. Not only had I failed Alice, I was failing Emmi and Heda and all the other women Alice might have one day employed. I bit back tears.

"Alice?" Emmi prodded.

"Right. I brought cake."

She produced a lumpy gingerbread loaf from her basket. I laughed. "Is this one of those bakery castoffs your cousin gives you?"

"Of course," Alice said.

"Heda didn't want to come," Emmi added, "but she sends her thanks as well." I could imagine the many reasons Heda had chosen to avoid an impromptu farewell gathering, but chose to ignore all the possibilities about associating with a "Politicking Witch" and instead chose to believe that she was still very new and hadn't been fully invested in the shop yet.

We settled on the curb and split the cake, not saying much at all as the bolts of fabric were loaded into the cart.

"Wait!"

I started—Viola trotted down the street in her chemise gown, a white beacon in the midday sun.

"The fabric—hold on." She laid a hand on her ballooning silk hat, keeping it from floating away as she hurried toward us.

Alice watched with a carefully neutral expression, while Emmi gaped with her mouth fully open. Though nobles took strolls in the finer districts in Galitha City, running over the cobblestones was far from typical.

"Vio—Lady Snowmont," I said, glancing at my employees.

"Sophie, I didn't want to say anything unless I could work something out." She laid a hand on the pile of fabric bolts, catching her breath. "Theodor told me your plans for the shop, for Alice, and how the fire caused a mess of things. I called in a favor with Lord Cherryvale—the Lord of Coin—and if you still wanted Alice to take over the business, he'll sign off on a new license."

"That's very kind, but I haven't a new location—"

"Oh, of course—no, that was part of the deal. The lease has been paid for a storefront on High Street. It's a bit smaller than your spot now, but—"

"High Street?" Alice gasped. "That's—" She snapped her mouth shut.

"I made sure that the rents were equivalent." Viola's brow tightened. "Did I make a mistake, is High Street—"

"No, it's—it's more than perfect. It's a...nicer area than this is, I had hoped to move there someday." I exhaled, overwhelmed by this. "I can't think of how to thank you, and I oughtn't to accept at all, but..."

"This only happened because of all you did for the reforms. And you won't be here to take advantage of those reforms to keep your shop going without a bit of a push so..." She waved a hand. "Cherryvale owed me. I introduced his pockmarked whelp of a son to the only woman in the world who shares his love of ornithology. I don't think they'd have gotten him out of the house otherwise."

"Then...thank you," I said, the chasm between the words

and the debt I felt I owed Viola wide and hollow. I had nothing to offer her, nothing of value. "I don't think I can repay a favor like this."

She gripped my arm with unexpected strength. "You can help Annette. In West Serafe, at the summit."

"I fear she's more likely to help me." I almost laughed. "She's far more likely to know what she's doing among all those dignitaries."

Viola's eyes leveled with mine in a grim line. "They'll be wanting her to come home with the beginnings of a marriage arrangement. Perhaps not a notarized betrothal contract yet, but something with good intentions for their alliances and a wretched end for her. Her mother knows her stock is slipping the longer she isn't a princess and the older she gets; she wants her to drive her stake in now, to claim something that will last. Crestmont and Merhaven both know she's still worth something at the negotiating table.

"Even Theodor..." She exhaled through her nose. "He'll put aside all sorts of tradition and expectation to marry you, and I don't deny it's politically advantageous to gain the trust of the people. But he won't be of any help when it comes to passing up the security marriages lend to international alliances. He won't shield Annette."

"How... Viola, I barely understand what I'm supposed to do at the summit, let alone how I can be of any help to anyone else."

"You don't need to work it out for yourself. But if Annette asks, please. Help her in whatever way she needs."

I nodded slowly, even though this was a favor with different stakes. Viola had expended money, perhaps some political capital, wasted a favor she likely didn't need. Whatever Annette might ask left me open to all sorts of possibilities. Still, I would have done what I could to help Annette even without favors owed to Viola, and it was a small price to pay for the security I knew Alice, Emmi, and Heda would have in a new, better shop on High Street. So I broke off a piece of my gingerbread cake and gave it to Viola. She accepted, letting go of my arm, and we watched as the last of the fabric was loaded into the wagon.

19

I STOOD NEXT TO ANNETTE BY THE RAIL OF THE *GYRFALCON*, the ship pointing her nose toward West Serafe as we left Galitha City's port to open water. She wasn't a huge vessel, not intended to impress foreign dignitaries or Galatine nobles, but Admiral Merhaven had chosen her himself, praising her "clean lines" and "right rigging," terms I didn't understand. Her speed, which he had also extolled, I did comprehend. We'd given ourselves scant extra time to make the journey to Isildi, the capital city of West Serafe, and relied on the *Gyrfalcon*'s purported ability to, per Merhaven, "carve the waves of even the Midway Sea like a pat of butter." Theodor's brother Ballantine, more properly Lieutenant Westland on this ship, tolerated Merhaven's excessive metaphors with taciturn deference, but I knew that Theodor appreciated his brother's presence, reliable albeit silent.

"You seem at home on board a ship," I said to Annette.

"Enough trips accompanying my father, I suppose. But I've always liked the water. The possibility in it—once you're on a ship, you could go anywhere," she explained with an impish smile. "If I'd been born a boy, I'd have joined the Royal Navy, I think."

"If you'd been born a boy, you'd have been heir to the

throne," I reminded her, then winced. She'd be king, not heir, and acknowledging that brushed up against the loss of her father, wounds still raw and painful.

Annette was kind enough to let my insensitivity pass without remark. "Even had I been first son, waiting on an inheritance to a crown, a naval career wouldn't be unheard of. But a girl—that would never do." She glanced at the sails unfurling over us. "They'd do well to let her out a bit if we're to take advantage of this wind."

I laughed. "And a fine sailor you'd make!"

"I used to follow the sailors around and watch them work until my mother caught on. She might not have minded the observing, but I was overhearing language that would have shocked my tutors." She laughed, then she looked back over the rail. "The city looks so pretty from the water," she mused.

"I've never seen it this way," I said. "In the midst of it, it doesn't look so deliberate, somehow. From here it looks like a painting, all the buildings in layers as though someone meant it."

"And in the middle of Fountain Square, it feels like a maze. Sometimes distance adds an artist's touch where none was ever intended."

"And so white and clean," I added. "You don't see the horse dung or the dingy alleys and even all that dark gray stone looks paler when the sun is hitting it, from here."

Annette smiled. "I confess I don't see much of the dung, myself."

"Am I interrupting state talks?" Theodor joined us at the rail.

"Yes, very important, height of secrecy," Annette said. "We're far too busy for you."

"Even if I'm here to brief you on agendas and itineraries?"

Annette groaned. "Especially that. Can't you just enjoy the

view and forget that we're duty bound into a fortnight of oblig-atory smiling and forced pleasantries?"

"You have today to enjoy the cruise, but we're docking at Havensport tomorrow to collect Admiral Merhaven's wife and will have to do a bit of waving and handshaking while we're there."

"What exactly does that mean?" I asked. "Waving and handshaking?" I had known we planned a couple of brief stops in Galatine ports on our way—nothing that would slow us down overmuch, but would satisfy everyone's insistence that we give some attention to our own people as we made our way to Serafe. I was less clear what, exactly, was expected of me.

"For you and Annette, fairly literal meaning. I anticipate that we'll be greeted at the dock by a fair-size crowd eager to glimpse royalty—yes, I'm sure they'll be disappointed by me—and you two ladies can disembark, make your way to the wait-ing carriage, and throw a few smiles into the crowd."

"Like acrobats and mummers in a parade. Lovely." Annette beamed a wholly insincere smile.

Theodor cracked a grin but didn't argue with her. "The carriage takes us to Merhaven's townhouse, where I will have a brief meeting with local dignitaries. Havensport's city lord, who's a Pommerly, for what that's worth. Unlikely to be pro-ductive, just a formality."

"And we sip tea with their wives?" Annette asked, clearly familiar with this standard protocol.

"Yes," Theodor said. "I'm sorry, is that going to be too burden-some? Did you have an appointment with your hairdresser?"

"I can rearrange it," Annette joked, sighing with feigned dismay, as though our close quarters on the little *Gyrfalcon* could have accommodated a retinue of hairdressers and manicurists. "Then back here and embarking by noon?"

"That's the idea." Theodor shrugged. "If they invite us to lunch, I'd suggest we accept—their seafood stews are legendary in Havensport."

"Hmm, lunch. I skipped breakfast—I'm going to scrounge something up," Annette said. She headed toward her cabin, and I had a feeling our steward would be the one to do the scrounging.

"Not too overwhelming yet, I take it?" Theodor said, moving closer to my side.

"I think I can handle waving. Smiling, though." I grimaced.

"Do your best." Theodor laughed. Galitha City lay behind us now, the imposing stone defensive wall stretching to the south and, no longer visible to us, the north giving way to a sheer cliff face and, high above, dense forests.

"It's hard to believe that most of Galitha is like this," I said, gesturing toward the untouched forests. "After living in the city, it's easy to forget that the city isn't all that Galitha is."

"That will be worth remembering for quite some time, going forward," Theodor said, eyes scanning deep into the forests. "The nobility in the south, in the agrarian regions, are not particularly satisfied at the moment."

"They don't like the changes," I ventured with a wry smile.

"Indeed not, most of the provincial nobles voted against reform."

"Rules are rules," I said with a sardonic shrug.

"And their response—you're not concerned?" he replied.

"Of course I am. They can make things difficult moving forward if they don't wish to cooperate, I'm sure. But they lost. By a slim margin, perhaps, but the law is the law now, as you keep saying."

"That it is. Regardless, what little time we spend in ports on this trip south will be smoothing their ruffled feathers. And I've a feeling they've gone into full-blown molt at this point."

I wrinkled my nose at that image—nobles shedding clumps of down like overgrown parrots. "And here I'd just discovered that I like sea travel after all. Too bad official business is going to put such a damper on it," I said.

"We'll have to take a trip then, for fun, sometime," he said, with a hollow smile that told me "for fun" was unlikely to happen for him anytime soon, if ever. "Speaking of official business—I brought some books along for you. I've left them in our cabin. On the other countries attending the summit, so you have some preparation on their customs, clothing, title nomenclature, the like."

I forced an even-keeled smile. This was, after all, the duty of a royal consort, even if it sounded utterly overwhelming. "So I have less than a week to memorize the customs of East and West Serafe, Kvyset, the Allied States—I assume their various differences, too?"

"Well, at least a study on Pellia and Fen won't be necessary."

"That's right, they're not important enough to invite. Or are you suggesting I'm allowed to offend them?"

"You can offend them another time. I'm sure we'll have some diplomatic visit with Pellia soon enough. Just not this time."

"Perfect," I said with forced cheer.

"You may want to give some attention to ports and trade routes," he said. "The largest point of contention for the summit is an agreement suggested by the East Serafans—the Open Seas Arrangement. You won't be in the official debates, of course, but they'll probably discuss them during the social events."

"The seas seem pretty open already," I said, glancing around us.

"Looks are deceiving. As it stands, nations can claim waters near them—prohibit shipping, tax merchant vessels, prohibit military vessels even if they're only en route up to fifty miles from their shores, with some special rules in place for shared waters. This puts East Serafe at a bit of a disadvantage compared to, say, West Serafe when it comes to throwing their weight around over shipping—they're barely on any oceanic trade routes at all."

"Compared to us as well," I said. "We levy a tax on foreign merchant ships utilizing our ports, don't we?"

"Yes," he said. "Quite good. The Open Seas Arrangement would prohibit claiming any waters. No prohibiting or taxing anyone passing through, no matter how close they get."

"It seems to only benefit East Serafe," I said. "Easy to vote down, no?"

"Except that the Allied States may be on board with it. They benefit from taxes and port fees, but they trade so widely that they lose more to Galitha and West Serafe than they gain. So—it's rather tied with Kvyset not laying her hand yet."

"Sounds terribly exciting," I said blandly.

Theodor clapped my shoulder, like an officer sending a private to do some sort of unpleasant task like digging out a latrine. "I'll quiz you later."

20

CLOUDS HAD ROLLED IN FROM THE EAST OVERNIGHT, AND THOUGH I welcomed the reprieve from the sun, the low gray sky made for a gloomy welcome into Havensport. The *Gyrfalcon* slid effortlessly into the harbor, and I braced myself for cheering crowds and the feigned smiles that I was sure would be expected of me.

Instead, the people gathered by the dock were quiet, not part of one undulating mass but sequestered into groups of ten or twelve at most. Bright scarlet peppered the browns and grays and indigos in the crowd, in red caps but also in sashes and cockades and kerchiefs. They hung back, and I found myself mimicking their reluctance and staying away from the rail of the deck. The only detail that had the look of a formal welcome party was the soldiers lining the perimeter of the docks. The garrison of Merhaven's naval station would have been present at any arrival of dignitaries, but in the presence of the stone-faced crowd, they appeared more of a necessity and less of a formality.

"I thought you expected a *small* crowd," I said as Theodor joined me, looking out over the knots of people waiting on the cobblestone square by the dock.

"We may require a change of plans," he replied, scanning the near silence with concern. "I've misread something, for certain." He walked rapidly toward the captain's quarters, where Admiral Merhaven waited, then turned back to me. "Go find Annette. Tell her—just tell her to wait. And not to wear anything too flashy."

I intercepted Annette before she left her cabin, dressed in a modest dove-gray worsted traveling suit. Not flashy at all, even with the pert tricorn hat perched atop her glossy dark hair.

"Theodor says to wait inside," I said.

"Whatever for?"

We could see the shore from her cabin's doorway, and I simply pointed. "Well." She pressed her lips together, turning them nearly white underneath her light coat of carmine rouge. "They look like they could use a colonic, don't they?"

I smiled, but it was an empty smile and we both knew it.

Then a bellow like thunder erupted on the cobblestones and I jumped back, into Annette. A thick plume of smoke accompanied a brief and unimpressive flash. As the sea breeze wafted the smoke aside, I saw the source—a pair of barrels lay in shards and the stones around them scorched. Gunpowder. Annette's audible gasp next to me mingled with shouts and a few screams from the docks. Not everyone on shore had anticipated this particular form of demonstration.

The soldiers moved like quicksilver, sliding into position and moving on the center of the square while maintaining some defensive positions nearer the docks. Then I saw something that hadn't been there before the explosion—a pair of figures, like crudely crafted rag dolls, slung with thick rope over a tree branch. Effigies, hung from miniature nooses.

My stomach clenched and I tasted sour fear at the back of my throat. "Is that Theodor?" I asked, voice tight and distant.

Annette stiffened beside me. "I don't know," she said. "I can't see well enough—there's no royal insignia."

"It's someone," I countered. "Two someones. The king and the first heir to the throne?"

Annette laid her hand on my trembling arm. "It's impossible to know from this far away." She edged backward, as though by instinct. "But that is a fair guess."

Lieutenant Westland stood by the railing near the bow of the ship, surveying the scene with a looking glass. "I imagine he could tell," I said.

"Perhaps," Annette said. "In any case, I assume we're not going ashore."

I leaned against the nearest wall, watching the effigies sway gently in the sea breeze as though they were merely toys, not threats. No one seemed to claim them or make a move toward them—or, I noticed, toward the quay or toward the soldiers.

Then the first bottle landed in the water.

"Down!" Ballantine shouted as more bottles rained into the sea, hurled by clutches of men and women on shore.

Annette gripped my arm and pulled me backward, into her cabin, but I strained to see. The bottles weren't doing anything—just floating. Floating with something stuffed into each one, something white and, to my first glances, something that looked like coarse fabric.

I let Annette pull me inside and she slammed the door. "We'll wait to see what Theodor wants us to do," she said, as much to herself as to me. "No one can reach us on the ship, not without launching boats—and we can be out of the harbor before they've cleared their docks."

"I didn't think—I thought we were past this," I said, shaking. "Past fighting and past division. The reforms—I thought—I thought—" To my surprise I was nearly crying, images of Red Cap protests six months old dredged up from my memory, the slick texture of fear coating every thought. My brother nearly shot at a protest. The scythes and guns in the streets the night of the coup. The wet stain of blood on the stairs of the palace. "It can't be," I whispered.

"It may not be anything of import," Annette said, but her voice was hollow and insincere. Long minutes passed in silence, the closeness of the cabin pressing in on me from all sides.

A sharp rap on the door made us both jump, but it was, perhaps predictably, Theodor.

"It's the city lord, Pommerly. And Merhaven." He ran a hand through already-disheveled hair. "The effigies."

"It's not you?" I gasped before I could think better of it.

"Are you disappointed?" Theodor cracked a strained smile. "No, it's not me. Those people are happy enough to see me. And you. And probably Annette, though, no offense, I don't know that they're worried much about dignitaries or royalty."

"What do you mean?"

"I mean that the crowd out there is unhappy with their local governance and wants to tell us about it." He pulled several scraps of canvas from his pocket and held them out to me. "These were in the bottles."

"Not explosives?" Annette managed a small smile. "My cousin the lieutenant seemed to think they were water-borne grenades."

"Explosive enough," I murmured. "*Traitors to the people, traitors to the Crown*," I read as I passed the rough canvas to Annette. "*More taxation without election, there will be men without heads*." I scanned several more. "They've refused to hold elections?"

"It appears so." Theodor shook his head. "Merhaven said there had been delays in enacting some of the reforms here, but this suggests deliberate avoidance—or, at least, that the populace interprets it as such."

"And how do you interpret it?" Annette said, squaring the stack of canvas as neatly in her hands as she could.

"I don't know. I hadn't seen Merhaven as an obstructionist, but then again, he's been in Galitha City for the past few months. It's entirely possible he's guilty only by association as the most powerful lord near Havensport."

Annette considered this, then looked toward the shore again. "But the city lord?"

"Yes, he should have, per the Reform Bill, been joined in governance by an elected committee. That has not happened. The people seem to think that their best recourse was to make me aware of this by a demonstration."

"My goodness, they could try writing a letter next time," Annette said.

"They learned from the revolt," I said quietly. Both watched me. "Words alone didn't suffice then, I imagine the people believe they can't suffice now. They had to show some force."

Theodor's face grew taut. "That interpretation doesn't bode well."

"I know."

"I imagine we're staying on board, then?" Annette said.

Theodor swallowed. "On the one side of it, yes, there's been a threat to safety and we ought to cancel our events on shore. At the same time—the people don't seem to be a threat to us. The soldiers will of course obey our royal person"—Theodor cracked a smile—"and there may be much to be gained in terms of the people's confidence by going ashore.

"At the very least, I do have to meet with Pommerly. There is no reason not to be moving ahead with the implementation of the reforms. In fact, there is nothing worse than not moving forward—it shows incompetence and weakness on the part of both the Crown and the local lords."

"If you're going," I said, raising my chin, "I am, too." I considered, then added, "But I'm not drinking tea with a gaggle of perfumed ladies. Why are these messages written on canvas?"

"Shipbuilding and fishing are predominant trades here—this is old sailcloth. I think they were establishing themselves as tradesmen."

"Then I want to see the fishing docks. Or the shipwrights. Something that tells them we're listening to them."

Theodor hesitated, weighing, I was sure, the dangers of sending me on a one-woman diplomatic visit to the working class of Havensport. "Merhaven will arrange something. You will be under guard, of course."

"Of course," I replied. "Annette, care for a short shore visit?"

Annette took a deep breath. "Why not?"

21

—◦〜◦—

THE FISHING DOCKS OF HAVENSPORT WERE SMALLER THAN GALITHA City's docks and far more specialized. While Galitha City welcomed droves of domestic and international trade, the Havensport docks seemed focused nearly solely on welcoming nets full of fish. Shadowed by soldiers, Annette and I toured the open space where loads of fish were hauled off boats and the low-eaved buildings where they were sorted and salted. Annette wrinkled her nose, deftly pulling a kerchief dosed with scent out of her pocket, but I inhaled the base, honest smell of work.

"The primary export from Havensport to the rest of Galitha and overseas is salted fish," the portly packinghouse owner said, wiping nervous sweat from his hands. Tasked last minute to allow a pair of ladies from the royal delegation to tour his facility, he was handling things surprisingly well, especially given how the soldiers insisted on examining every nook and corner of the building before allowing us to proceed. "Oceanic whitefish and silver cod, mostly." He paused, gauging our interest. I gave him an encouraging smile even though I didn't particularly care. "They take the salt well."

A flash of red caught my eye from across the building, the dim interior highlighting the interruption of color.

The packinghouse owner stiffened as he noticed the bright spot, as well. A cap—a cap in a style I knew all too well. "Hey! Put that thing away," he shouted, taking off at a surprisingly nimble clip toward the offending workman.

Several other workers flanked the first man, producing their own caps. "You know," the owner said in a huff, "that those are not allowed in my place of business."

"Why not?" I said, approaching him from behind and surprising both him and the workers with my question.

"They are—" He closed his mouth, reddening, unsure what to argue to a royal consort, even if she was a common-born seamstress. I raised an eyebrow, well aware that we were both navigating what, exactly, my sympathies were and happy to let him make the choice of what to say next, because I certainly didn't know what angle I ought to take. "They are disruptive," he finally decided.

"Disruptive," I repeated. "The cod don't take salt as well when they're packed by workers in red?" The men fought not to crack smiles, but the glare of their employer subdued any amusement at the comment.

"No, not—no." He flushed darker, right up to his balding crown. "I need my employees focused on their work, not on dissenting with the Crown and with one another."

I considered this. "Galitha has always welcomed a culture of open speech and has avoided hindering the printing presses. I suppose that I see wearing even such a noxiously bright cap as a part of that."

"Be that as it may," he replied with controlled politeness, "you haven't got a business to run."

"I did," I retorted before I could stop myself. The red-capped employees watched, tautly interested in the outcome of this exchange.

"And today, of all the times—I simply do not want you to feel threatened by this...demonstration."

I could have laughed—as though a few red caps could, after the Midwinter Revolt, after Pyord, after all I'd been through, make me feel threatened. Annette, beside me, merely smiled in bemusement.

"You'll find we are not so easily frightened," I reassured him. "But I am curious—why are you still wearing those caps? In Galitha City, they're a celebration, but you do not seem to be a very festive sort."

The man in the middle, the first to have put on the cap, hesitated before his neighbor nudged him to speak. "Things aren't so celebratory here," he said. "We got news of the reforms, same as everyone, but nothing has changed."

The packinghouse owner interjected himself quickly. "These things take time, it's unreasonable to—"

"What hasn't changed?" I asked, cutting him off. "We read the messages in the bottles."

"Then you know the bulk of it. Two days after the news of the reforms arrived here, the city lord enacted a new tax on fishmongers and others who peddle freelance. There was to be no new taxation, if the Reform Bill was followed, without a vote by elected council."

"That's true," I confirmed.

"And there's been no date set for the elections."

"I see."

"We know what happened at Midwinter—we all read the pamphlets then and we read them now. Seems we're of one mind with the folks up in Galitha City about what happens next, if the reforms aren't followed."

I glanced around me for the first time since engaging the

red-capped workers. The entire packinghouse was quiet, watching us. The soldiers' wary stances betrayed their discomfort with the turn our tour had taken, but I knew that there was no threat from these people. I had seen threat in the wordless language of a mob before; the crowd in this dim space wasn't interested in threatening Annette or me. They saw us as the ear of the king, as a vague form of hope.

And I had to say something that would affirm their rights without unleashing a tempest in the salt vats.

"Your concerns have been heard," I began, regretting instantly how weak those words were. "You are correct that the reforms are to be enforced without delay." I hedged back, not willing to discuss the legality of complex codes that the reforms addressed—without confirming with someone who knew more, I couldn't know for sure if the new tax or the delay in elections was truly illegal or merely outside the spirit of the law. "The Prince of Westland is distressed, as you are, that more progress has not been made."

They seemed heartened but not entirely reassured. I couldn't blame them—I had no authority to speak, and I could only hope that Theodor, in fact, was currently addressing reform implementation timelines with the city lord and the local nobility. I couldn't, however, promise that. "What is your name?" I asked the de facto speaker for the Red Caps.

"Byran Border," he replied, blanching with surprise that I should ask. "Miss. Ma'am. Your Ladyship." He nodded to both Annette and I, so pale his freckles stood out like block-printed spots on white cotton.

"I appreciate your willingness to speak, Mr. Border." I essayed a smile.

Border hesitated, then spoke again. "If I may—we're hearing

the same from all over southern Galitha." He swallowed, and his comrades encouraged him. "There's Red Caps in every town, every province. We write to one another—there's a few in each town and village what can read and write well enough, as it were."

"And?" I said. I hadn't realized that the laborers outside the city were organized enough to maintain a network of communication. If they already communicated with one another, what else might they be capable of?

"And it's like this in all the fishing towns. The agricultural regions are worse—plenty of nobles seem to have disregarded the orders for local elected regional councils entirely and some aren't paying wages for work." He shifted, his broad shoulders bearing the uncomfortable weight as speaker for his comrades. "We want no trouble, Your Ladyship, but if it comes to us, we'll return it in kind."

"I'm not a 'Ladyship,'" I interjected with a smile, which he shyly returned.

I nodded, taking this in, unsure of what to say, to promise, to reveal. We hadn't learned any of this in Galitha City—of course, news was slow to travel from the extreme south to the north, but I had a sinking feeling it was more problematic than that. The gaggle of nobles convened in Galitha City were certainly corresponding with their acquaintances and neighboring nobles at their ancestral holdings, but they had no interest in sharing this kind of news with the champions of the Reform Bill. The people in the streets of Galitha City were probably more well-informed than Theodor.

"Thank you," I said, addressing Border. "This tour has been very informative. If ever you wish to raise any more concerns, I—" I paused. What could I offer, who was I in the system of governance? An official consort and, someday, wife—but I would speak for my people. "You can write to me."

22

THE REMAINDER OF THE VOYAGE WAS QUIET. WE MADE BRIEF stops at two more port cities, each time greeted by quiet crowds in red caps, each time sending only Theodor and Merhaven ashore for meetings with local nobility. Theodor had swiftly changed course from meetings intended to exchange pleasantries and reaffirm the importance of the southern regions that royalty seldom visited to meetings intended to discern what delays were occurring with the reforms. Local nobles insisted that there were no delays; stone-faced commoners didn't have to speak to disagree.

The only change for Annette and I was the addition of Lady Merhaven, who insisted on maintaining the formality of dinner times on board ship, which Theodor, Annette, and I had gleefully abandoned in favor of charcuterie plates and baskets of fresh fruit eaten on deck.

"Thank the Galatine Divine we still have breakfast and lunch to ourselves," Theodor said as we left a particularly long dinner.

"I don't even have an appetite for all this food," I said. "It's too hot for roast anything—and the poor cook. She actually made him fix boiled puddings?"

"I know." Theodor sighed. "There are some things even a crown prince can't control. Lady Merhaven is, apparently, one of them. But I will say—she knows protocol and formalities like a first language. She'll be useful to both of us in Isildi."

"Well, bully for her," I grumbled. After our discoveries in the port cities we'd visited, my impression of the importance of the Five-Year Summit waned. It wasn't a fair comparison, of course—foreign affairs and international trade were still important—but I was personally invested in the Reform Bill and its success.

"My complaint is that it's impossible to discuss the problems I'm seeing on shore with Merhaven around."

"You don't trust him?" I asked, surprised. We were sailing into the uncharted waters of a foreign diplomacy mission, and Merhaven was setting our course.

"I trust him for what we're doing in Serafe. But he does little more than make excuses for the delays and shortcomings of the reform implementations. I asked each of the city lords to provide me their plans, with timetables. None could do more than sputter about change taking time."

Annette joined us at the bow of the ship. "I do like seeing where we're going rather than where we've been," she said with a wry smile. Admiral Merhaven had spent most of dinner reminiscing about battles he had witnessed that were otherwise relegated to history books.

Theodor laughed. "It helps if one can see both," he said. "I don't like this," he said, his pensive expression returning.

"You don't think they'll openly oppose the law, do you?" Annette drummed on the railing. "Open sedition—that's a lot of work for most of these dumplings."

"They're opposing it now, just quietly." He sighed. "I think they're hoping the Crown won't push, that we'll ignore them and let the laws lapse." Theodor watched the coastline moving past at a distance. "My father wants stability most of all. Instability can come from the nobles or the common people."

"Enough speculating," Annette said, waving her hand. "What? I know it's important, but don't look at me like a baleful sheep, Theo. We are on a boat."

"A ship," he corrected.

"A ship, in the middle of the ocean."

"We're less than a half mile from land."

"Surrounded by water, en route to a foreign nation. There is very little we can do," she said, with which Theodor couldn't argue. "I brought several new novels and I intend to have them finished before we're back—Viola and I plan to chat about them. Rather our way of keeping in touch, I suppose," she said. "I'll be reading."

"Does she know she's supposed to go shopping for a husband in Serafe?" I asked after Annette left.

"Yes," Theodor said. "She knows it's expected of her. Whether she'll cooperate is anyone's guess. Lady Merhaven is supposed to be playing matchmaker."

"What a horrid term," I said.

"The Serafans use them nearly exclusively," Theodor replied. "Most marriages in West Serafe are arranged."

"So they don't even know their spouse until—ugh."

"Hardly. The clan houses all know one another to some degree—well, like much of our nobility. They make one another's acquaintance with the assistance of the matchmaker. And they can typically refuse any match—though it's often ill-advised to do so."

"Still, it seems odd—to have some third party meddling with your marriage."

"Yes, we only have an entire nation meddling in ours," Theodor replied.

I wasn't sure if I should protest, laugh, or cry a little, so I chose to laugh.

"I hope you don't mind that I've let Mother begin making some arrangements—there's not much damage she can do while she's in Rock's Ford, but it's rather widely expected that the wedding will take place before winter."

"If you think that's best." I had never harbored any illusions that I could expect a modest wedding, but relinquishing control of the preliminary planning reinforced the tiny role my preferences would have.

Theodor's shoulders tensed. "It's not what I think, it's what's expected. And yes, I don't think delaying sends a particularly good message."

"I never said I wanted to delay," I shot back. "It's just that it's—"

"You aren't having second thoughts, are you?" His fingertips traced the gold at his wrist.

"I'm allowed," I said tersely, "to be less than thrilled with the prospect of a very public wedding planned by your mother, who is, shall we say, less than enthused about me."

"Yes"—he sighed—"you are." I pinched back more argument, that I didn't need him pouncing on every shred of frustration and reticence I felt as though they were attacks on our betrothal. They weren't—but I couldn't be expected to behave like a gleeful bride when I knew full well that this marriage would be read as a political statement by the entire country and resented by my groom's parents.

Evening was pulling darkness tighter around the ship, making the coastline appear murky and dreamlike, blurring the lines of the horizon in every direction but the pale gold where the sun had set.

"What is that?" I said, eyes trained to a brilliant speck of orange-red ahead of us, nestled in the coastline.

He squinted. "Looks like a fire," he replied.

"Is there a town or a port or—"

"Nothing for miles of that sort." He pressed his lips tightly closed. "Hard to tell—local farmers or fishermen having a bonfire for some celebration, or someone shipwrecked signaling for help?"

I shifted uneasily, fingers tracing the rail. "Wouldn't they go farther inland—if it was someone in trouble?"

"Most places, yes, but there are cliffs and thick forests along some of the southern coast. If you didn't know your way?" Theodor shrugged. "You might decide to take your chances on the coast and save your neck from a fall." He sighed. "I feel we're duty bound to investigate," he half grumbled as he trotted toward the captain's cabin.

He returned with Merhaven and a pair of spyglasses. "Well, they certainly aren't celebrating," Merhaven confirmed as he closed the glass. "More folks gathered than I would anticipate for a shipwreck or some other trouble, but they aren't having a social gathering unless it's a funeral."

"Drop a longboat and go ashore?" Theodor said. We were nearly alongside the fire now, and I could see dim figures gathered around it. Even at a distance, the scene appeared sober despite the bright firelight and swiftly emerging stars.

"I think that would be best," Merhaven agreed. "I'll send Lieutenant Westland and a small contingent."

Ballantine looked perfectly tailored as usual, despite having been fetched from off duty, and quickly assembled a half-dozen sailors. As the longboat dropped toward the water, Theodor watched the shore, trying to discern some kind of response from the group gathered there. The dark obscured his vision, and we waited.

The boat landed on shore, and neither Theodor nor I had any idea what was happening in the dark until the sharp crack of a gunshot echoed across the water.

"Whore's ass," Merhaven cursed as he whipped his spyglass out. I wasn't sure which shocked me more—the gunfire or Merhaven's choice of words.

"You should get inside," Theodor said, pushing me behind him, away from the rail.

"As should you," Merhaven interjected. "The last thing I need is the heir to the throne shot on a boat under my command." Theodor hesitated, craning to see the shore. "Now, Your Highness!" Merhaven bellowed as another shot was fired.

"They couldn't possibly hit us here," I insisted, to myself as well as Theodor, as we moved inside.

"They couldn't aim effectively, no. But the shot can certainly travel that far."

"What happened?" Annette cried, bursting into the captain's cabin where we waited.

"We don't know," Theodor said, leaning on the table that anchored the center of the room. "We sent a longboat to shore to investigate what we thought was a signal fire."

"And our sailors shot at them, or they shot at the sailors?"

"Don't know." Theodor bit his lip, impatient. "Either way, we didn't send them armed with much and they certainly don't have ammunition for a firefight."

"So they'll return to the ship?"

"Unless the longboat is overtaken, yes."

"But who could they be?" Annette pressed. "The people on shore?"

"Annette," Theodor said with barely controlled frustration, "I don't know."

Merhaven strode into the room. "The longboat is on the way back."

"Our men in it?"

"Unless one of them has the same beanpole silhouette as Lieutenant Westland, then yes." Merhaven heaved an agitated sigh. "No more shore excursions," he said to no one in particular. There hadn't been any more scheduled anyway.

Long minutes passed and the ship was strangely silent. There was always a quiet bustle of sailors working and cleaning, the cook and his mate in the galley, even, in the deepest reaches of the night, someone on watch. Now the only sound was the lap of water against the *Gyrfalcon*'s sides and, distant but growing closer, the rhythmic splashing of oars.

Finally the boat was hauled up—we could hear the orders and the jangle of iron and the hollow report of the boat as it met the deck. Ballantine came into the cabin a moment later, disheveled and, I saw immediately, spattered with a bit of red across his white waistcoat that could only be blood.

"It's not mine," he replied to the admiral's unasked question. "Brooks took a ricochet—he's fine. Will be fine."

"What happened?" Merhaven asked.

Ballantine glanced at Annette and I, and Theodor interjected before he could protest. "Go ahead. They've a stake in this, too, of course."

"It's not that I don't believe that. It's—" Ballantine stopped. "It might be upsetting."

I almost laughed at the absurdity of anything upsetting me, short of a cannibalistic feast on shore. "I'll take my chances," I replied instead.

"The gathering on shore wasn't a bunch of castaways—it was an organized meeting. The bonfire was serving as a sort of lighthouse to mark the meeting spot."

Merhaven nodded. "Yes, but who?"

Ballantine hesitated again.

"Spit it out," Theodor said.

"Minor nobles—I saw house crests. And some non-nobles, too, most likely. I can't say for certain—they didn't continue talking once we arrived—but their response at the king's navy arriving in the midst of their meeting? Reeked of sedition."

I sucked in air, not sure if it was fear or anger or a bitter sense of repetition that I felt.

"And they fired on you?"

Ballantine nodded at Merhaven's question. "Yes, they were armed—not well, not as though they were intending some kind of formal engagement," he supplied in answer to the question that would surely follow. "Pistols, mostly. A couple fowlers. Not military weapons."

"Well, that's some good news—they aren't lining up for war just yet," Theodor spat.

"When they saw the uniforms, some of them ran, a couple seemed to attempt some kind of cover—they spoke to us, tried to make nice—but a group of them primed and fired." He shook his head. "We returned fire, but of course most of them ran."

Theodor cocked his head. "Most of them?"

"That's right. One was injured—it looks to be a slash wound to the leg, which must have been an accident from one of his own people."

"What happened to him?" Theodor asked.

"We brought him on board. He continues to insist that there is no formalized collusion," Ballantine said with a slight twist of a smile that said he didn't believe the man at all.

Theodor sighed.

"So he and a dozen of his friends were simply having a beachside bonfire and Royal Navy target practice for a bit of fun?" I interjected.

Ballantine's smile faded. "No, he admits that they were having a meeting, discussing the troubles they're running into with the reforms. But nothing seditious, of course."

"Of course not. At night, at a secluded beach." I snorted. "People who meet in the dark can't be trusted."

"Typically a good rule." Theodor paced back and forth, only a few of his long strides taking him across the cabin with each pass.

I pressed. "People who fire upon the Royal Navy also can't be trusted."

"I don't disagree." Theodor shook his head. "What's his name? Who is he?"

"Lockwood," Ballantine said.

"I don't think—oh, right. I remember the Lockwoods. Very minor noble house. Small holdings, farmers. Barley, I think, or rye."

"Who else?" I asked. "At their 'meeting'?"

"He won't give me names, but he said they had some common folk joining them last night. He was forthcoming on that much."

"Forthcoming," Theodor repeated. "And no way to force more, I imagine."

His brother hesitated. "I'm not in the business of interrogation. My naval education failed me on that front."

Theodor shook his head. "And I doubt pressing would do us much good. If a lack of faith in the Crown is spurring these 'meetings,' stringing a noble up by his thumbs will only alienate the rest of them all the more."

"Fair point," Ballantine agreed. "Especially if the king's son is doing the stringing. So you put him off at the next port?"

"I don't think there's anything else we can do," Theodor said. "I'll remit him into the custody of the city lord of Southlea. I wish we had time to follow through on this, but we don't." He rapped the wall with his toe, as though just recognizing the constraints of the cabin on his pacing. "Southlea is the last Galatine port we'll pass before we cross the Midway Sea."

"I will write a formal report and make copies to distribute to the governance in Galitha City, as well." Ballantine saluted and left.

"A formal report. The last thing the council or my father is going to want to read—reports of resistance to the reforms and now something that brushes a bit too close to sedition."

Sedition. I tensed at the word, but Merhaven shrugged it off. I raised an eyebrow at his indifference, but he didn't so much as look at me. "These are difficult times, Highness. Your father understands that. It might behoove you to extend more understanding to the nobles who are most grossly inconvenienced by these reforms."

Theodor returned Merhaven's suggestion with a hard stare and stalked out of the cabin.

23

—ᴍ—

THE REMAINDER OF OUR VOYAGE WAS UNEVENTFUL, BUT WITH the eerie calm of a silence we all knew was imposed by wide swaths of water, not reflective of the reality in Galitha. There would be no news until after we reached the summit. Would reports of sedition wait for us? Red Caps recalled to action by the refusal of local nobles to implement reform? Chaos erupting once more in the capital city as debates broke into violence?

No pressing news awaited us when we docked in Isildi, and there was little time to search out any rumors of unrest from home. We were expected at welcome meetings within hours of docking, and I tried to block the uncertainty of Galatine affairs from my mind and focus, instead, on the dizzying prospect of maintaining a good face with dozens of delegates.

The summit was held in a diplomatic compound, once a large army fortress but repurposed and expanded. The reddish stone walls were built like the layers of a cake, with newer construction of brighter stone and at keener angles than the faded historic structure. We separated within minutes of arriving, Theodor and the admiral whisked off to the first of dozens of important gatherings, and Lady Merhaven, Annette, and I shuttled to a welcome reception for the retinues of the official delegates.

We were received on a wide loggia, well shaded with thick-trunked trees. A breeze swept across the gardens bearing a faint hint of salt and, fainter, some coolness. I was grateful for the lightweight cotton chemise gown I wore, decorated with a red silk sash. It was simpler than what some of the other women had chosen for this informal reception, but the Serafan women and the women from the Allied Equatorial States wore lightweight clothing suited to the heat. I tried not to stare at the women and their clothing, but I couldn't help but notice the elaborate draping of the Serafan gowns and the bright colors chosen by the Equatorial women. I wished I could understand everyone's position and motives as easily as I could mentally deconstruct their gowns, made plain into patterned grids and draped silk in my mind.

"I hope they serve something cold and liquid fairly soon," Lady Merhaven said, fanning herself slowly with a sandalwood fan. Perspiration dotted her forehead and made curls of her dark blond hair stick to her neck. "Once this is over, I'm looking forward to nothing more than a cool bath. I do hope the porters arrive soon with the trunks—I'll want my goat's milk soap."

Annette made a face that indicated what she thought of Lady Merhaven's soap, and I forced back a laugh that was half nerves.

"I hope I'll have a chance to explore a bit," I replied.

Lady Merhaven started and then regained her damp composure. "Don't get in the way, dear. The gardens are fine for strolls, and there are public areas inside, too, but keep out of the official business, hmm?" *Don't embarrass us,* she said as clearly as if she'd used the precise words.

I scanned the gardens, spreading out on all three open sides of the loggia like a controlled jungle. Galatine gardens tended to be formal, with carefully shaped hedges and long avenues paved in pale stone or bricks. These were wilder, giving themselves over to the natural spray and fan of the plants they featured. They also seemed to favor heavily scented flowers; occasionally the salt scent of the breeze was accompanied by something intoxicatingly heady.

"Ah, the Kvys," said Lady Merhaven with thinly veiled derision. The small group arrived quietly but somehow still obtrusive, dark wool gowns and starched veils out of place among the color and movement of the rest of the party.

"I believe we are all arrived." A Serafan woman stood by the center columns of the loggia, her brilliant orange gown fluttering in the breeze of her slightest movement. "While the delegates are in their discussions every day, there is a light schedule for the rest of the delegations." She distributed a stack of heavy ivory paper printed with a list of events that looked, for the most part, like social gatherings. I forced a pleasant expression onto my face, but if I had been nervous about Galatine social functions, the thought of the complexities here was unnerving. "The vast majority are, of course, optional," she continued, "but you should consult with the rest of your delegations on which require your attention."

Optional social gatherings requiring attention—I digested this quickly to mean that alliances and relationships were made here, as well as in the delegation chambers. Already I perceived the divisions and hierarchies, that each of the women here represented not merely herself but a host of other interests. What would they think I represented, I wondered? Galitha, its government, the reform? Given Pellia's clear absence, would I stand in some way for that ignored nation despite having never so much as seen its shores?

A servant in pure white wheeled a cart to the loggia laden

with fresh fruit, icy glasses full of various colored liquid, a dozen kinds of cheeses, and a creamy slush that Annette chose swiftly but looked like curdled milk to me.

"Traditional Serafan nooning meal," Annette said, handing me a glass. "Pureed goldenfruit. It's delightful. And try the cheese even if you don't want a butter pudding."

"That's what it's called?" I asked, pointing to the shallow dish of pale slurry Annette ate with a tiny spoon.

"Mmm-hmm." She nodded, mouth full. I selected a few cheeses. Modern Serafe was descended from nomadic herdsmen, unlike primarily agrarian Galitha. Its curve of coastline supported orchards and some farming, but inland the ground grew rocky and more suitable for goats than farms. Across the mountain ranges in East Serafe, the land was drier and more desolate, but, according to my books, still supported traditional Serafan herding practices. And, I discovered as I tasted a ball of fresh cheese sprinkled with fresh herbs, delectable cheese making.

Lady Merhaven drifted away, greeting the Serafan woman who had welcomed us. She was, I knew, a high-ranking woman from a high-ranking clan given the honor of serving as a hostess, not an official delegate to the negotiations. Those, from East and West Serafe, were all male, made up of Ainirs, clan heads, whose long-standing families were the nobility of Serafe. Lady Merhaven was swiftly impressing herself on the delegation as representative of Galitha; as the hostess moved away from her to give a coolly cordial greeting to the Kvys women, Lady Merhaven attached herself to a gray-haired Equatorial woman with enormous diamond earrings. I nibbled at a wafer coated in sesame seeds as I surveyed the crowd; Annette returned to the cart for a second dish of butter pudding and found herself face-to-face with our West Serafan hostess. The two conversed as I finished my wafer and immediately regretted the choice, as seeds had lodged themselves in my teeth.

"Well, ask her yourself," Annette said to the hostess, forcing cheer into her voice as she nudged me subtly with a foot. My fingers burned impressions into the frosted glass.

"You must be the prince's consort." The West Serafan hostess in her blinding orange silk assessed me. Next to her, a wisp-thin Equatorial woman in delicately tailored white cotton and with regal bearing subtly turned her shoulders away from a nearby table of fruit and cheese to join our conversation.

"I—yes, I am here with the Galatine delegation on the invitation of the Prince of Westland," I said.

The Serafan smiled knowingly, almost patronizing. "Is consort a term the Galatines do not use? I can admit my ignorance," the Equatorial woman said.

"No, it's a—we use the term," I confirmed. "We are betrothed," I added, showing them the gold bracelet as though they needed some kind of proof.

"I am Ainira Siovan ad Rhuina," the Serafan woman said, and I was grateful for the tutelage about titles present in the books I'd studied—Ainira meant the wife of a clan head, but she identified herself by her natal clan, Rhuina.

"Dira Mbtai-Joro," the other woman said. Her status was less clear—the Allied States did not have the defined orders of nobility that Galatines and Serafans did, but princes ruling each island and a spate of high-ranking families that were, in any given decade, favored or out of favor. The books I had been given had not, unfortunately, given me any indication on the current ranking families.

"It's a pleasure to meet both of you," I said politely, then remembered to add, "I'm Sophie Balstrade."

"Of course," Dira said coolly. She assessed me with a knowing, not entirely comfortable, scrutiny.

Siovan leaned in. "Now. Do tell—the story is that you were actually at the palace when the assassins broke into the ballroom."

"I—yes," I said, flushing.

"You should be warned, the whole revolt is the reigning topic of gossip currently. That, and the Ainir of the East Serafan Dar clan's bastard son," laughed Siovan before I could rush to explain that our attention in Galitha had turned to reform. Had she cut me off on purpose? Were political topics too heavy for an opening reception? Or did she simply not want to hear about weighty topics from me?

"Only among Serafans," Dira replied.

"He has a harelip and some say a tail."

"In truth?" Annette set her empty dish down. "Poor fellow if so."

Siovan shrugged. "At any rate, he isn't here, so we can't confirm either rumor."

"How would you confirm the tail? Follow him into the bathhouse?" Annette said.

"I can think of other methods," Dira replied. "I am given to understand that your...arrangement with Oban is off," she added.

Annette flushed at the implied connection—she had been in the final stages of marriage negotiations with Prince Oban of East Serafe before the Midwinter Revolt. Now that she was no longer of the royal family, and Prince Oban no longer an appropriate alliance, a bastard was still far below her station.

"You are correct," she replied. "I don't believe that anyone with a tail is on the rolls for consideration."

"Of course not," Dira demurred. A glimmer of something—humor or hostility?—passed in subtly narrowed eyes, but she turned and took a glass of pureed goldenfruit instead of speaking further.

"Miss?" A servant in white, a girl of perhaps twelve, waited at my elbow. "Your chambers have been prepared. Would you like me to show you?"

I glanced at Dira and Siovan. "Please excuse me," I said.

Dira bowed her head. "Of course, yes. We'll see more of you, I'm sure."

24

—⚭—

DESPITE LOOKING FORWARD TO EXPLORING THE GROUNDS OF THE
diplomatic compound, I, like Lady Merhaven, succumbed to a
bath as soon as I had been shown my room. Built in a more open
style than fine Galatine homes, with their specific rooms for
sleeping, dressing, receiving guests, and private study and reading, the chamber was a single, open room with curtained spaces
for study and dressing, a raised area with a curtained bed, and
an alcove with a bathing tub sunk into the floor. An ingenious
system of pipes ran water to each of the rooms, so filling the tub
was little trouble.

I had to admit that I did feel refreshed after bathing, and
took the time to comb and powder my hair while a breeze from
the open balcony danced into the room. The balcony looked out
over the gardens, but the architects who had drafted this place
had created a marvel of rooms, open to the fresh air outside,
that still maintained privacy. I could see the hedged paths below,
but the position of the trellised balcony ensured no one would
see me.

Someone could dance in the nude with the balcony doors flung wide,
and no one would be the wiser, I thought with a laugh. How Alice
would blush at that idea!

I sobered—and immediately searched the delicate marble-topped desk in one alcove of the room for paper and ink to pen letters to my employees. The shop, the fabrics, the permits—had everything fallen into place as it was supposed to? A letter was unlikely to reach them and their reply reach me before I was back in Galitha City in any case, and it was no longer truly my responsibility. It was Alice's shop. Even here, in a strange country, with flowers I couldn't name creeping over the desk from a vase crafted in Serafan rather than Galatine style, with voices floating up from the garden in a language I didn't speak, the strangest thing I could fathom was thinking of what was once my shop as Alice's.

A knock on the door interrupted me midway through the letter, and I had moved toward the main door of the room before the knock repeated and I realized it came from the door separating my room from Theodor's.

I cracked it and, seeing him on the other side already stripped down to his breeches and shirt and a banyan, opened it.

"Room to your liking?" he asked as he strode inside.

"It's certainly different, but it suits this place," I said. "It seems such an indulgence—this much space for one person."

"The whole estate is so large, I wouldn't worry over it. I'm sure there are still empty rooms, even now. And don't be offended, by the by—everyone gets their own room."

"I hadn't even thought to be offended." I laughed.

"I didn't think you had. But so you're not surprised. Married or consort or second wife or first husband—there are so many variations on marital and nonmarital but official relations in the leading houses of the countries here that it was decided years ago that everyone should just be assigned their own room."

"You say 'it was decided' as though it was a major point of negotiation."

"It was. It took longer than a trade pact, if I recall correctly," he said with a smile that I wasn't sure meant it wasn't true, or that he thought the truth a bit of a joke. "Say, who's this?"

I started, but Theodor was laughing. In the path of sunlight cutting through the room from the balcony opening lay a large black cat, his dark velvet fur punctuated only by white paws and, taming his fearsome face, incongruous pure white whiskers.

Theodor knelt and let him sniff his fingers, then scratched his huge head. "He's a funny little fellow, isn't he?"

"Are—are pet cats that common here?" I asked, watching the cat's claws emerge and then harmlessly scrape the floor.

"I wouldn't be surprised if they keep a phalanx of mouse police here," Theodor replied. "I wonder if this one prefers your balcony for his off-hours."

I approached the cat warily. My brother and I had never kept pet cats, or any pets—they were another mouth to feed. Cats might prowl the alleyways for rodents, and we tolerated them there, but I never befriended any. This sleek, well-fed house guardian, however, was far from a street cat.

He languidly stood up as I approached and trotted toward me, stropping my ankles with his thick neck before I could react.

"He likes you," Theodor said.

"Does he?"

"Of course! What do you want to call him?"

"You mean name him? I'm sure he has a name, if he's someone's cat," I answered lamely.

"Yes, but it's probably given him by a Serafan servant and we'll never learn it," Theodor replied. "Come now—if he hangs about, you'll want something to call him by."

I considered this, not sure if I wanted him hanging about. He had flopped by my feet and was gleefully pawing at nothing, yellow eyes half-shut.

"What about Mister Boots?" Theodor prodded. "Or Mister Whiskers? Mister Whiskerboots?"

I laughed, and the cat lolled on its side to give Theodor a look that would have convinced me, had I not known better, that he understood the effect such undignified names might have on his feline reputation.

"Perhaps Onyx," I said, feeling charitable. "He seems a gentleman cat, he deserves a respectable name." He scrabbled to his feet to resume rubbing his head on my leg, leaving black fur on my white stockings. "I don't suppose there's much of a good way to keep him out, not without closing the door, at any rate."

"Not particularly," Theodor replied. "Onyx it is, then. Your cat for the duration of our stay."

"I suppose," I said, unconvinced. Though plenty of the nobles and wealthy women who attended Viola's salon and bought clothing from me kept pets, the thought of an animal inside still felt markedly unusual.

"I was going to explore the gardens a bit if you wanted to dress and join me," Theodor said. I agreed and dressed quickly, tying a large silk-covered hat I had made for the trip over my simply dressed hair before Theodor returned. Onyx lounged on the balcony, uninterested.

The gardens were expansive, and as I had ascertained already, less formal than the Galatine style. Theodor was quickly absorbed mentally cataloging all the various types of roses and even decorative grasses. "This," he said, reverently running a finger up the length of a blue-tinged grass stalk, "was nearly extinct in West Serafe after the cycle of seven-year droughts. Scholars at the university found preserved seeds and reintroduced it. And—oh, you have to see this," he said, rounding a bend. A stately tree presided over a courtyard, the leaves edged an unusual shade of deep pink. "It's a Queen's Beech."

"It's lovely," I said, but I was more impressed with the intricate design of the garden. Each time I thought I was merely looking at a half-overgrown hedge or a copse of trees, I realized that there was an archway in the hedge to a private room made of greenery or a trellis festooned with flowering vines among the trees.

"They're exceptionally rare, very hard to grow," Theodor said. "I've always wanted to cultivate one in the greenhouse—they don't get much bigger than this—but I've been convinced I would just kill it."

"Maybe the gardeners here would share their secrets," I said. "Speaking of secrets." I smiled and pulled him after me through a narrow tunnel built from a climbing rose–covered trellis through a hedge and into one of the tiny rooms I had spotted. "Isn't this incredible?" Thick foliage surrounded a low-lying bench, and a thin brook snaked through the space, bordered by pavers.

Theodor bent next to the deep green leaves of a plant. "Do you know—all of the plants in here are night flowering. And this—this is Firewort. It attracts fireflies. Genius."

"We'll have to come back here at night," I said. "Would that be proper?"

"Hang proper—I have to see this under moonlight." He moved closer to me. "Our secret garden, you think?"

I nodded, turning my face toward his so he could kiss me. He gripped me around the waist, and I could sense he wanted more than the kiss. So did I.

Voices outside shook us from our focus on one another and back to the very public space our privacy bordered. "It is overly bold of the Kvys, I am confident the patricians will not attempt to meddle openly in the Galatine affair."

"That would prove problematic, though hardly something we couldn't manage."

Delegates, I surmised, glancing at Theodor, who listened with a raised eyebrow. "We have no proof that the patricians were involved at all—and mercenaries are legal in Kvyset." I listened more carefully and recognized the voice—Admiral Merhaven.

"Attempting to force the Kvys to delegitimize mercenary work would derail the more important discussions about the Open Seas Arrangement and, of course, Galatine grain trades." The other voice was Serafan, judging by the lightly lilting accent. "And the influence of some Kvys cavalry for hire—it will hardly affect our work."

Their work? He must, I guessed, mean the work of the summit itself. "It is true that the mercenaries have very little efficacy in full-scale war," Merhaven said. "And the Kvys won't formally martial their military for anything short of invasion." The two laughed politely.

"Those I represent remain invested in maintaining our good relationship," the Serafan man said. The voices faded as the speakers moved farther down the path.

"Remind me," said Theodor, "to brief the rest of our delegation on discretion in public spaces." He shook his head. "I'm not sure I like Merhaven taking private meetings. Though it's not as though he said anything of import, or committed us to anything."

I pulled him back toward me and gently kissed his cheek. "Don't we have some important dinner to dress for?"

"Of course we do. You're a natural at this princess consort thing. One of the requirements is reminding us about getting dressed, you know."

I playfully shoved him away, but I had a suspicion that dressing for dinner was bound to be the least challenging part of my role at the summit.

25

THE WELCOME DINNER WAS AN ELABORATE AFFAIR WITH SMALL plates of tiny delicacies, large, refreshing salads, and a finishing course of ices and complicated layered desserts made primarily from the whipped cream Galatines called *snow*. I was seated next to Theodor, but Annette and the Lord and Lady Merhaven were across the room. A series of speeches punctuated the meal, and I was pleased to discover that most of them were conducted in Galatine so I at least understood the language, if not some of the content.

Annette caught my eye from across the room midspeech and shot me a sympathetic smile. At the break in speeches, a flagon of wine was passed down the table. I smiled at the East Serafan woman next to me as I passed her the flagon; she seemed to look straight through me and half wrenched the wine from my hands. I turned away, sipping from my glass. The wine was cold and shockingly sweet.

Theodor hadn't noticed the reaction of the woman beside me, or the pair of West Serafans across the table from us who pointedly ignored me after whispering something that sounded suspiciously like my name and *Pellia*. I tried to pretend I hadn't heard.

"I suppose every delegation has to have a speaker, or someone would be offended?" I asked Theodor.

Theodor laughed. "You've caught on."

"Why are the formal speeches from other nations in Galatine?"

"Most of the delegates speak Galatine—it's a simple numbers game. We're right in the middle, of course, and historically, initiated trade earlier than Kvyset or Serafe."

"And no one is offended?" I smiled.

"If they are, they allow the expediency of not translating everything into four languages and a couple dozen dialects to prevail over pride. Most people here speak multiple languages, at any rate."

My ignorance, knowing common Galatine and nothing more, served as a reminder of how wide a rift existed between me and the world Theodor occupied. My competency in the fields of languages, political systems, and economics was, despite Theodor's inclusive tutelage, woefully underdeveloped for the prospective princess consort of Galitha. My inadequacy for this role bit me like a persistent horsefly.

As the speeches droned on, I scanned the room, observing the one thing I did understand completely—clothing. I knew the traditional clothing of East and West Serafe from the Silk Fair, but ordinary clothing had been modified into more formal gowns here. None of the East Serafans wore *kaffa*, but instead carefully pieced, tailored gowns that showed off their impressive embroidered and brocaded silks. The Kvys were, unsurprisingly, in simple clothing similar to Galatine style, the drab colors they favored punctuating the bright silks and cottons in the room. I knew better than to discount the value of those clothes, however—the deep blacks, featherweight wools, and heavy silk satins were expensive. The Kvys weren't ornate, but they still displayed their wealth. My favorites were the clothing worn by the Equatorial women, silk open robes over lightweight cotton undergowns, trained and delicately gathered to fullness in the back.

I had a thousand ideas beginning to baste together in my mind, and I could imagine long hours over coffee with Alice, sketching ideas. That perhaps eccentric but unobtrusive amusement would be left to me, wouldn't it? I sighed—the duties of the wife to the Prince of Westland might not allow such liberties of time or diversion, especially if the country was in chaos wrestling with reform.

We were invited to the loggia for refreshment after the meal and the series of speeches finally ended. Galatines considered outdoor spaces too informal for most events with the gravitas of a summit dinner, but the Serafans embraced the natural elegance of their gardens.

Theodor was quickly swept into conversation with a pair of Kvys patricians, and I found myself wandering to the edge of the loggia with my chilled wine, marveling at the sunset painting the sky over the gardens. The thick golden light and shadows transformed the pathways, turning them velvety and soft.

"My pardon, but you are Sophie Balstrade, yes?"

I turned, met by an Equatorial man with a regal bearing and an impish smile. "Yes?"

"Pleased to make your acquaintance. You were a friend of my sister Nia."

"Oh," I said, my stomach suddenly hollow. Nia—who no one knew had prevented the king's assassination with her translations, who had died because of her entanglement with me. "Yes, Nia was my friend" was all I could say. "And you're her brother?"

"Half brother, actually," he said, breaking again into an

honest grin. "I'm Jae Mbati-Horai; Nia is Mbtai-Joro." I noticed that he used the present tense—was it a slip, or did the Equatorials speak of the departed as though they were alive frequently? "We have the same mother."

"Oh," I said, unsure how to respond. "I—I didn't know much about her family."

Jae laughed at my discomfort. "It's common on our island— what is the technical term in Galatine? Polyandry. Many women have more than one husband." He shrugged. "Good for them, no?"

I flushed pink. "You grew up with Nia, then?"

"Of a sort, she lived in the main house. Her father, Magistrate Joro, he was the first husband. We lived in a villa on the plantation. But we played together as children, were good friends in adolescence. Her sister—Dira—she's less fun."

Dira—the woman who had been so cold earlier. Perhaps she blamed me—or simply blamed Galitha—for her sister's death. I silently forgave her chilly reception. "She was not terribly pleased to meet me."

"She's not pleased to meet anyone." He laughed. "But she doesn't like Galatines. She says you're all *b'taki*." He laughed— his easy manner was infectious, and I leaned in. "It's a treat we make for children, fried dough that puffs up all pretty and golden outside, but—poof!—hollow inside."

"That's not very flattering." I laughed.

"Certainly not," he agreed. "She thinks Galatines are all vanity and appearances."

I considered the expensive silks, ornate jewelry, and even perfume that covered most of our delegation. "She may not be completely wrong," I acknowledged.

"No, she's a little fool. She thinks if it doesn't come from Tharia—that's our island—that it's no good. She won't even try hazelnuts. Because they're not native to Tharia. Can you imagine? Not trying hazelnuts? Pecans, either." He shook his head in mock frustration. "And I have to share an adjoining door with her for the duration of our visit here. Interminable."

It was difficult to imagine Nia with a closed-minded sister. Nia's core was that of a scholar, intrepid in her curiosity.

"Nia was remarkable—her knowledge of languages," I said.

"Yes, she was always the brains of the family. But we were all tutored in language, to some degree, and even ancient derivatives. She and I continued in Pellian longer than the others, but she surpassed me long ago."

"You can read ancient Pellian?" I asked, rushed.

"A bit. There are scholars at the university here who surely know more than I." He leaned toward me, conspiratorial. "I had hoped to get down to the university to inquire about doing a bit of study."

"I had as well!" I said, a bit too familiar in my excitement to find someone else interested in what the famed Serafan university might offer.

Lady Merhaven managed to intervene at that precise moment. "I needn't remind you, dear, that wandering the streets alone is hardly proper for ladies in the prince's retinue." She laughed and patted my arm with her bony hand, but it was clear that it was hardly a joke.

Annette must have seen the involuntary tension bind my shoulders into a knot, because she swiftly joined us. Jae bowed to her, and she responded by offering her hand, a delicate gesture I had never managed without feeling an utter idiot. "Pleased to make the acquaintance of the famed Princess Annette," he said as he raised her pale fingers to his lips.

"Lady Annette only now," she reminded him.

"I am very sorry, my lady, for your unimaginable loss this winter," he said, bowing his head.

"My thanks," Annette replied. She retracted her hand. "Lady Merhaven, the admiral was in search of you."

She smiled broadly. "He always does like to stick to one another at events like these—ah, when we were young and danced all night at state balls! Delightful." I nearly choked, imagining the dry powdered Lady Merhaven as a young woman, or actually enjoying anything. Annette's eyes narrowed, though she held her composure. "Sophie is so lucky to be here with her prince, is she not?" Lady Merhaven added.

Annette exhaled as gently as she could. "Of course she is."

"Though of course, it's too bad that he hasn't time to serve as an escort for you," Jae chimed in. "If it would serve, I would be pleased to accompany you to the university. Or anywhere else you would require an attendant."

"That would be lovely," I answered quickly, before Lady Merhaven could interject. Annette suppressed a smile at my out-maneuvering of the overbearing older lady, and nodded gently, approving of this arrangement. I had a chance to see if the massive collection of the university had something to help me regain control over my casting, and I didn't intend to waste it on Lady Merhaven's overly proper sensibilities.

"Very well! Day after tomorrow, shall we?" We agreed, and soon Theodor found me to make our exit.

As I entered my chamber, the cat skittered out of the corner, narrowly missing a chair leg as he slid on the marble.

"Easy," I said, laughing. I assumed it was a normal feline antic—that he'd been chasing a shadow or a bit of thread across the floor. But as I glanced again, I saw that the fur along his back was bristled and that his tail had doubled in size.

I paused, taking a careful step backward. What could have frightened the cat, making him hide under the settee? The balcony door was slightly ajar, but I had left it that way before the dinner, hoping to invite some of the cooler evening air into the room. The sheer white curtains swirled slightly over the marble floor; nothing else in the room moved.

Including Onyx, who sat stoically on the settee, his yellow eyes wide and his ears at full attention.

I stepped hesitantly into the room, forcing myself to cross the floor to the balcony door and look outside. Nothing there except the night-blooming white flowers that lined the terrace. I closed the door, feeling slightly more secure. I sat at my dressing table, pulling my slippers off my feet with my toes while I wormed hairpins from my hair. I tossed one on the table and nearly fell off the chair in shock as the cat pounced on my bare feet. I gently scooped him up and deposited him outside.

But as I brushed my hair, I swore I heard footfalls below and voices lingering near my balcony. Though I tried to imagine that the noise was merely Onyx hunting the night-flying fruit bats or teal lizards on the balcony, I couldn't shake the feeling I was being watched. I didn't fall asleep for a long time, and was absurdly thankful that Onyx watched the balcony like a guard all night.

26

MY TEACUP, BALANCED ON A SAUCER SO THIN I COULD SEE THE shadow of my finger through its pearlescent porcelain, rattled almost imperceptibly. If someone had taken Viola's salon, its character as vibrant and warm as a summer morning, and sent a Kvys blizzard wind through it, it might have provided the only parallel I could imagine to the Summit Ladies' Tea. While the delegates opened their first session of negotiations on the Open Seas Arrangement, the ladies in the delegations' retinues gathered for one of the few scheduled events that was, in no uncertain terms, mandatory for all of us. I almost wished that I, like Annette, had developed a migraine from the thick humidity and taken to my bed. Sadly, I was as hale as a Pellian ox even in the heat.

"I understand, Ainira Duana, that the tea harvest in East Serafe is under siege by poor weather this year," Lady Merhaven said to the East Serafan woman seated near us.

She raised her cup to her lips, as though sipping the East Serafan tea we were all drinking would bolster her point. "The weather has been wet and less conducive to a highly flavored tea in our southernmost plantations," she said, "but we do not anticipate that this affects the market overmuch. Our tea is aged over a year, and we release only certain percentages of each year at a time."

"A wise strategy for a fine tea and to guard against fluctuations," Dira Mbtai-Joro chimed in from across the settee.

I smiled in agreement, but she simply stared at me and turned to the Ainira. "We would of course be most disappointed in any shortage of your best teas. Then again, we anticipate disruptions of trade of all kinds, given the current...climate."

Was the weather poor enough to affect agriculture in so many nations, I wondered? But no—Lady Merhaven shifted uncomfortably next to me, assuring me that the climate Dira alluded to was political, not meteorological.

"I certainly hope things aren't so bad as all that," Duana replied, but Siovan, lingering behind us, joined our conversation. As hostess of the summit, she pulled attention with her, dragging a dozen sets of ears into our conversation.

"If the unrest spurs a shortfall or even disruption of the labor working on the agriculture of the noble landholders, we can certainly expect shortages of grains and fruits this year, and of wines and ciders in the coming years," Siovan said, and I finally understood, my ears reddening as I struggled to keep my teacup from shaking—they were worried about Galitha.

Lady Merhaven shot me a look, her meaning clear—I shouldn't say anything. I didn't need the warning.

"Grain!" Dira shook her head. "Meaning no offense to the Serafans, we could live without tea but not without grain."

"Workers' riots shouldn't have been permitted to cause such a disturbance to begin with," Siovan said, then stopped herself. As hostess, she was probably required to remain as neutral and accommodating as possible.

Too late—another West Serafan woman, in blinding blue silk shot through with gold, agreed loudly. "No amount of protest ought to be worth interrupting vital trade."

A quiet snort drew everyone's attention to a slight Kvys woman, her hair completely covered by her white veil. "The rights of working people are worth a brief inconvenience to your wine cellar," she said, her piercing blue eyes pinning the Serafan woman. "This is not a mere question of a few ill-tempered men complaining, but of vital liberty and the right to govern."

"The right to govern!" Duana replied. "That right is well established in each of our nations, is it not?"

"Yet in each nation it is different," the Kvys woman replied. Her tone was even, deliberate, and disarmingly calm. "Any one of us could be mistaken in our self-granted rights and be in violation of those rights that ought to be held universal."

I felt, briefly, that I was in the middle of one of Kristos's books, one of the better ones that melded philosophy and governance and economics into a cogent theory.

"Universal rights—as the Kvys enjoy under the thumb of the Church?" Duana asked, raising a calculating eyebrow.

If she expected the Kvys woman to lash out, she was disappointed. "We articulate our rights as being borne out of the Creator's will," she replied. "That gives the Church the responsibility to uphold them."

"At any rate," Duana said, "East Serafe certainly cannot afford—for the sake of our people—to support any regime that does not hold up its trade responsibilities. We import most of our grain from Galitha, and I know that West Serafe does as well."

"There is no reason," Lady Merhaven said in a strained voice, "to anticipate any reductions in grain output from any estate I am acquainted with."

"You're acquainted with many?" Dira asked, the question barbed to wound.

"Yes, of course I am," Lady Merhaven replied, a bit too hurried.

"You could, of course," the Kvys woman replied, "import more barley from Fen."

"You know as well as I that the costs are greater for that," Ainira Duana replied crisply.

"Ah, yes. I know as well that the Ainirs control the imports and gain the profits from those imports in both East and West Serafe," the Kvys woman replied. The air felt thin in the room. I couldn't fathom the combination of polite tone and cutting commentary that the Kvys woman was managing to maintain. I thought, for a moment, that this might be normal for the Kvys—that they were a blunt, plain-speaking people—but the shock and even outrage on some of the faces surrounding me told me that she was pushing boundaries even if this were true.

Dira set her teacup down, elegant hands drawing no sound from porcelain that I rattled merely holding it. "Lady Merhaven, it seems that one of the Galatines is not here."

"Annette is not well this afternoon," Lady Merhaven replied.

"Too bad. I had hoped we might have some discussion that regards her." Dira leaned to pick up her teacup, then stopped, turning back to Lady Merhaven. "Unless, of course, you are able to speak to her prospects yourself?"

My stomach clenched, sour with too much tea. Prospects. Viola's charge came rushing back to me, that I should help Annette in whatever way I could, but she wasn't here to guide me, and I had no idea how to steer a conversation between powerful women away from a topic they were both determined to discuss.

Lady Merhaven smiled with little emotion. "I would be pleased to have a preliminary discussion," she said, smooth as a polished stone. Nearly rehearsed. Of course—she knew before setting sail that this would be part of her duties here.

"The Allied Equatorial States are eager to affirm our good relationship with Galitha," Dira said. Somehow diplomatic jargon sounded natural, comfortable as it rolled off her tongue. "Especially given recent events. We are now, and have always remained, neutral in the affairs of other nations." She inclined her head, pointed, toward where the Kvys woman and Siovan compared the embroidery on their respective pocketbooks, having retreated to safe conversation about needlework.

"And for that, Galitha has always respected the Allied States."

"In the interest of continuing our mutual respect, there are several young men from prominent houses who have expressed some interest."

"They would, of course, need to be from *quite* prominent houses," Lady Merhaven said, a subtle reminder folded into an agreement. Annette had been a princess and was still a cousin of the royal family, after all. I watched in horror as each woman silently assessed Annette's value like a pair of fishwives sizing up one another's mackerel.

"Of course. I imagine that any of our high-ranking families would be delighted. And the Lady Annette in turn," Dira said. "Even our lesser houses are of greater prominence than any prospect from Pellia or Fen," she said with a rehearsed laugh. I stared at my hands—was there an insult layered into her assessment, suggesting Theodor was marrying far under his station not only to a commoner but to an insignificant foreigner, as well?

She didn't elaborate, and I bit back an impulse to argue that I was not from Pellia, that I was as steeped in Galitha and as invested in her future as any noblewoman.

Siovan interrupted before the conversation could continue. "It seems that our menagerie keeper has arrived a bit early to

begin the tour of our collection," she said. "We have both Serafan native and imported animals on display, including a Serafan
mountain wildcat and the only leviathan salamander in captiv-
ity." She continued listing caged creatures like a menu as she
escorted a large clutch of women toward the door.

I set my teacup down on the cart laid out for that purpose,
spilling a bit of the deep brown liquid on the pure white cloth.
The walnut-hued stain spread quickly. I wavered between wanting to daub it up and knowing that this was work for the servants.
The Serafans probably wouldn't care about the ruined tablecloth
that would result if the stain wasn't treated immediately, I chided
myself. I wasn't in my leaky row house, scrupulously caring for
every dishrag and trencher, haunted by their replacement costs
every time I chipped or stained something.

Leaving the room, I slipped out onto a quiet balcony overlooking the fountains at the front of the gardens. The spray
caught the sunlight and bent it into rainbows.

"I am sorry." I turned, startled, to find the Kvys woman
already seated on the other end of the balcony. "I was careless
with my consideration of the Galatine attendees today."

"It's no matter now," I replied. "You've every right to speak,
and they've moved on to wildcats and salamanders."

"Wildcats and salamanders—now, that's a fair metaphor for
most of these delegates," she said. "Half of them bare their teeth
and snarl, the other half burrow into the mud until their quarry
comes close enough. And there I am again, forgetting I am not
in Kvyset." She smiled. It transformed her, the cold blue eyes
suddenly sparkling with suppressed laughter. "I am Sastra-set
Alba, a daughter of patrician house Preata, vowed to the Order
of the Golden Sphere."

"I—I am pleased to make your acquaintance," I replied.

She laughed in earnest now. "Silly titles, aren't they? Your word for Sastra-set—well, it wouldn't exist, you don't have religious orders in Galitha. But I'm a high sister. That may clarify things slightly."

"Like a priest?"

"Nothing like those perennial bores. I am the head of my house within my order—the closest parallel you have is akin to a noble with his estate. The religious orders are barred from formal discourse here, so I am part of my brother's retinue."

I nodded, then realized I hadn't introduced myself. "I am here as part of Prince Theodor's delegation, Sophie Ba—"

"I know, of course," she said, laugh lines crinkling at the corners of her eyes. "Everyone knows the Seamstress-Sorceress Sophie Balstrade."

I bit my lip and edged toward the balcony's white columns. I couldn't forget the strict bans on charm casting in Kvyset, the deep distrust most Kvys had for the practice. But Alba didn't pull away in revulsion or distrust. "You've pegged me fairly," I replied.

"And revolutionary?" Alba's smile was patient and kind, but I felt trapped by the question.

"Not terribly active," I hedged.

"Your prince is a reformist, your brother a leader of a revolt—you seem steeped in revolution," she said. *Your prince*—not meaning, merely, the prince of the country I resided in. "I should not speak so boldly, in a place so full of...wildcats and salamanders. But Kvyset—and my house—supports your reforms. We could not openly support treason and revolt, but your ideals are true."

I wasn't sure how to respond. This wasn't an official meeting, not part of the summit, but Alba spoke as though her words had great importance.

She wormed a finger under her starched veil, relieving an

itch. "To think, I'm missing the Kvys birch forests in summer to sweat in this hellhole," she said. "Let them plan the next summit for Midwinter in Kvyset and see how the Serafans like it. And serving us hot tea—bah. I'll order us some iced citronade, how does that sound?" she asked, and I agreed, wondering what kind of unlikely alliance I might be building.

27

Morning accosted my room with bright sunlight, pulling me awake earlier than I might have liked. Theodor had stayed up late, deep in discussion with two West Serafan Ainirs concerned with Galatine imports and Theodor's position on the Open Seas debates. I had been asleep before he'd come back, and even though he slept a few yards and an interior wall away, I felt more lonesome for him than I did when we were half a city apart at home.

I began to dress, choosing another of my cotton ensembles, anticipating a walk to the university library with Jae later that morning. The heat rose quickly, and though my silks were more impressive, they were stifling under the broad midday sun.

"I don't know how the Serafan women do it, wearing silk all summer here," I mused.

Onyx was the only one listening. His white whiskers perked when he heard me speak, and he trotted from the open balcony to my feet.

I knelt and scratched between his nicked ears—he had prevailed over a few rows in his day. "Yes, you're very sweet. Now don't get fur on my clothes."

The door between my room and Theodor's opened a crack. "You mind company?"

"Of course not," I called back. Theodor looked tired. "Long night of negotiations?"

"Hardly a problem," he said. "It's useful having the best supply of grain and a wine industry that fuels the intoxication of most of their parties." He flopped on my dressing table's petite bench. "No, it's this."

He tossed a letter onto the dressing table, and I picked it up. Viola's handwriting. "Dated just after we left," I noted. I scanned the letter, my throat tightening. Riots in Galitha City.

"Then it's not only in the southern provinces, the port towns." I recalled the stony faces and red caps, their resolve.

"The elections were canceled. The nobles are fleeing riots in the city in droves." Theodor paused. "Viola says riots, but what if it's not just rioting?"

The possibility hung between us, nearly tangible. Open revolution.

"It can't come to war," I said, not knowing how else to react. "It can't."

"We're a week behind news. Anything could happen and we'd be quite literally the last to know."

"You can set it right, as soon as you're back. And the king! He must have the situation in hand, yes?"

"I dearly hope the king is upholding the law and not acquiescing to the demands of Pommerly and Crestmont and the like. I'm more than a little curious why he hasn't contacted me about this at all." Theodor drummed my dressing table with his forefinger, sounding too close to the tattoo of a military drum for my taste. "We could leave," Theodor said. "I could empower Admiral Merhaven to act on my behalf, and I would trust him to do so. But that would signal serious trouble to the other nations here."

"Should we?"

"Not yet," Theodor said with a forced smile. "We will all go on pretending we have things well in hand, get the Open Seas Arrangement inked, and make haste out of here. For now, you're still dressed like a better-appointed harlot."

"Very funny," I said, though the image of myself in the mirror—hair dressed, jewelry in place, but wearing only my stays and a petticoat—was quite similar to a cartoon whore.

"No, if I had my way, you'd be in a dressing gown and I in a banyan, eating dates on your balcony." He wrapped an arm around my waist. "And we'd have long days with nothing to do but…"

"If only you were a rich noble who never had to work for a living." I sighed in mock despair.

"If only. Listen, I've a long session on the Open Seas issue, but the afternoon is a forum on naval defense and fortification agreements that, frankly, it would be absurd of me to even attend with Admiral Merhaven here. We can't do anything about the situation back home, and maybe we should go somewhere and clear our heads. What do you say we go to the coast for the afternoon? We could visit the famous bathing beaches of Serafe?"

"Bathing!" I said. "The one thing I didn't bring any clothes for."

Theodor laughed. "In Serafe, you don't need any clothes for bathing."

"No," I said, shocked laughter bubbling from my mouth. "This is some elaborate prank—you convince me to take off all my clothes and then I jump into a lagoon full of people in bathing costume."

"Now, would I do that?"

"Maybe," I said with a slow smile.

"No, it's true. But the bathing beaches are private—they

build little changing houses out in the water, and you use those. No one can see anything without a spyglass."

"Oh, lovely thought—some pervert with a glass, just waiting to catch a glimpse."

"If you don't want to see the shore…"

"I do!" I said. "And I especially want to get away with you for a while."

"No bathing, then?" Theodor pulled me onto his knee. "I'm shocked."

"I have to finish dressing," I said, planting a kiss on his cheek. "And so do you."

Viola's letter still rested by my hair powder. There was no questioning the fact that reform hung by a tenuous thread, and that there was nothing either one of us could do about it.

Jae waited for me in the grand marble hall of the diplomatic compound's main building, leaning against a fountain. "Looking a vision, Lady Sophie!" he said as he greeted me with a bow. "This weather agrees with you."

"I don't mind it, to a point," I said. "They certainly know how to live alongside the heat, don't they?" The buildings, the frequent baths, the light meals—all of Serafan culture had adapted itself to its thick weather.

"You ought to come to Tharia. Perhaps someday you will, if Lady Annette finds herself married to an Equatorial man."

"Indeed," I replied, the word stale in my mouth. We set out, Jae telling me about the wide loggias and sleeping porches of his home, the goldenfruit tree that grew right against a corner of the house and how he could wake up and pluck ripe fruit without leaving his bedchamber. Our walk wasn't long. Isildi's streets were laid out in neat grids and, though I couldn't read the street names, were neatly and clearly marked. This city had been planned with deliberate pen strokes, not added onto piecemeal like the patchwork that was Galitha City.

"It isn't every day one has access to *that*," I said as we came to the cross street where our wide avenue ended and the university blossomed ahead of us. "I had thought our Public Archive impressive, but this is—something else entirely."

"It is indeed. Now, forgive my inquisitiveness," Jae said as he escorted me across a street busy with pushcarts, wagons pulled by oxen and surreys pulled by horses, and occasionally, a palanquin borne on broad shoulders. "But I am unschooled in Galatine culture of...betrothal and marriage arrangements. You and the prince are—betrothed?"

I stepped from the stone-paved street onto the broad walkway that bordered the university. "Yes. We are formally betrothed." I showed him the slim gold chain around my wrist. "He wears one like it."

"Ah! The Kvys exchange rings at marriage, the Serafans give the parents gifts to formalize an engagement—this is lovely," he said, examining the fine links. "My father hoped that accompanying the delegation would provide good education for me in foreign affairs and cultures, but I find I have more questions than anything else."

"I know the feeling," I replied as we stepped inside the atrium of the university library.

I had expected a building like the Public Archive in Galitha City, a large structure, to be sure, and filled with shelves of books and manuscripts. This was beyond my imagining. Four three-story structures were joined around a central courtyard by covered pathways.

"Intimidating, no?" Jae said with a laugh. "They're quite well organized, not to worry."

"I can believe that," I said as I followed Jae through the main entrance. Unlike the cold gray stone of the archive at home, the Serafan university library was warm sandstone, with windows, domes, and skylights arranged to allow the most light into the space as possible. The main atrium bustled with students and professors in academic robes. The practice of wearing robes had been abandoned by Galatine academics ages ago, but it continued here. I was sure that the colors, styles, and regalia each person wore had particular significance, but all I could discern easily was that the students wore lighter shades of gray and tan while the professors wore deeper grays and browns.

"I'll ask about where to find what you're looking for," Jae said. "And then I'm going to get someone to show me the map archive."

I agreed, wandering slowly into the wide expanse, drinking in the excitement of hundreds of students each pursuing some niche of knowledge. Kristos would have loved this place, I thought with a pang of something between regret and hope. He had left Galitha City and me on a one-way passage to Fen, but I could believe that someday he would make his way here.

"*Lyat dharit*," someone said behind me, and I turned, surprised to hear the commonplace Pellian greeting—roughly, *to your good fortune*—here.

"I'm sorry," I said in Galatine to the Serafan man in storm-cloud gray academic robes. "*Y-na Pelli.*" *I don't speak Pellian.* Something I had repeated dozens of times in the Galitha City Pellian quarter.

"Oh, no, the apology is mine. I had forgotten how many Galatines are of Pellian ancestry. Your forgiveness?"

"None needed," I replied.

"Your friend—the Equatorial man?—inquired if anyone

could guide a young lady here toward some ancient Pellian materials, and I assumed she would be Pellian. It's my error."

"He's already headed toward the maps, then?" I asked, laughing. Jae hadn't wasted any time.

"Hmm? Oh, I didn't ask where he was going. I study ancient Pellian and have a free morning so—well, I volunteered immediately," he said.

"I don't want to take you from your studies," I said. "I have—rather complex questions, I'm afraid. And no real idea how to find the answers."

"And how is it you find yourself here, with questions, but no means of finding answers?"

What a question—its incisiveness nearly took my breath away. Yet it had not been intended or delivered rudely. "I'm here with the summit delegation from Galitha. I am no scholar, I'm afraid."

"It's not a problem at all," he answered. "It's an honor to assist one of the dignitaries of the summit with whatever may be needed."

I paused. "I—I don't want to mislead you," I cautioned. "This is my own personal business, not a summit matter."

"That is of no consequence," he replied with a smile.

"And I'm—I'm not a high-ranking dignitary," I added.

"It's a great honor for our city to host the delegation," he said. "And so it's an honor for any of us to assist you." I remembered Aioma's tent at the Silk Fair, the insistence she had for hospitality, that it would have disgraced her to be refused. I felt as though I was taking advantage of this man's generosity, but I had been as honest as possible.

"Then I thank you," I said. "I am Sophie Balstrade. Accompanying the Galatine delegation," I added as an afterthought, realizing he might expect some sort of title.

"Corvin ad Fira." He dipped a formal bow. "Fifth-year master understudy." I had no idea what that meant, so I simply nodded. "My specialty is ancient Pellian, particularly the language development in the century after the colonization of the East Serafan peninsulas."

"That sounds most impressive," I said. "I—" I squared my shoulders, deciding that a fair amount of pride in my particular field would earn more respect in this conversation than shame in it. "I am a charm caster. I'm sure you're familiar with the practice?"

His eyes grew wide. "Yes. The practice of curse casting and its attenuate theories are regularly mentioned in Pellian texts both ancient and modern. It's honest-faith true, then?"

I smiled at his near-boyish curiosity and what had to have been a slip into a Serafan expression that didn't translate into Galatine. "Completely true. There's been very little study done on the theory itself, and I'd like to take advantage of your resources while I am here to make some headway. If there is any compensation I might offer..." I added, unsure how finances and money worked in West Serafe, let alone its university.

"Of course, yes," he said. "I—my lady, I don't expect financial compensation for doing the work I am supported by this university to do. But if you would be willing to consider— that is, this may be presumptuous—if I am of assistance to you, would you consider making me a charm?" His tan face took on a reddish hue. "Unless, of course—it may be your trade is one that is not for sale. I apologize."

"No, no—it's very much a commodity," I said, almost laughing, wondering what Corvin would think of my atelier. "And I would be pleased to. My specialty is stitching charms into fabric goods. Let me know what you would like and I'd be pleased to oblige if it's within my skill."

"This, I have never heard of in the ancient texts—charmed

fabric." He grinned. "Then let's go to the Pellian section—it's in the east building—and find what we can," he said.

I followed him down the long halls, outdoors through the covered loggia, tiled with green-and-blue mosaics of oceans and shorelines. I had heard that the Serafan shore was one of the most beautiful landscapes in the world, but aside from its frequent depictions in artwork and mosaics and murals lining their interiors, I hadn't seen it aside from the busy port we arrived in.

"Now," Corvin said, settling us at a bleached wood table and benches. "Is there something in particular you're searching for?"

I hesitated. What I really wanted to know—what clawed at me—was why my magic had become muddled, dark refusing to separate from light. Why I couldn't control what had once flowed like breathing. I couldn't admit that here. "Theory," I said carefully. "The casting is done by...well, by harnessing a light...a good...something that exists all around us. Cursing is done by harnessing its opposite. I want to know more about those...elements? Can we call them elements?"

Corvin weighed this question with a tilted head. "Yes, I suppose so. Ah! I know where to begin. The *thirati*. This sounds related to ancient Pellian religious views on the thirati—the balance of the universe."

"That sounds promising," I said, and Corvin hurried to the shelves and returned with several books. I waited patiently, recalling from my time with Nia that Pellian texts were difficult to translate.

"Yes—here's a diagram," he said. "Allegorical, of course," he added, turning the book toward me. A sphere was divided into segments, four large quadrants bisected by arrows. "The thirati is the wholeness of all things, prefaced on the concept that there is nothing now that once wasn't, and nothing that will be that isn't now in existence in one form or another."

"That's not confusing at all," I replied blandly.

Corvin laughed. "Yes, well. I believe the most prominent physicists have a term for it—material conservation. Since the beginning of time, since the world came into being, it is finite. We may transform, but we may not create out of thin nothingness."

"I see," I said, squinting at the page. "And each of these sections is some form of material?"

"Not quite—they are the thirati that govern material. There is light and there is dark, which you say are familiar from casting, and related to light is mass, and related to dark is void. Running through all of them is energy."

I traced the image. There were combinations and permutations, surely, from the detail marked out in ink, but the basic concept felt intrinsically correct. No one who had not casted would understand it, I imagined, to the same degree I could—that the light and dark were real things, as real as the mass and void that one could see and feel.

"So these elements. Are they—linked? How do they exist, precisely—floating? Tied to things?"

Corvin pursed his lips. "They simply are, as matter and nothingness are. What I have never quite understood, and perhaps you can enlighten me, is that we can manipulate matter, and we can render matter into another form, and we can harness energy. The light and dark seem to merely float as some sort of balance, but you say you harness these as one does energy."

"Yes, that's accurate," I said. "It's not like molding clay, it's more like taking a piece of the light and impressing it upon something."

"So you do not change the light."

"No—the light, it simply is. I don't create it or change it, I just use it. That's all a charm caster does."

"And a curse caster, the same with the dark." He nodded. "Light and dark being, of course, not fully accurate terms."

"No," I said quickly. "I—I think I realize that now, that light and dark is how we perceive them, but they aren't physical light or dark—physical light is energy, correct?" Corvin nodded. "And dark like the dark in a closed barrel is the absence of light, or another way of thinking of void."

"So the light and dark, if they are thirati, they are their own entities. Not simply other names for the same thing on the sphere."

I wondered how I would define them, then, light and dark—good and bad? Positive and negative? Luck and misfortune? Each felt insufficient. "How do they relate to one another?" I asked. "Do they play nicely or repel each other?"

Corvin read on, turning pages and finally shaking his head. "We are thinking of this the wrong way. They simply are. They don't fight one another or supplement one another—the theory keeps coming back to balance."

"A charm caster, by definition, disrupts balance, doesn't she? By manipulating the light into something. Is that—is that something the theory does not believe is right to do?"

"It was certainly acceptable to them," Corvin said, gesturing to three other books on the table. "These are all religious works dealing with the theory and nature of casting. The ancients believed it to be a gift for working in a material, just as metallurgy or spinning or chemistry makes changes to matter."

I was fascinated, but also disappointed. There was nothing here indicating that something about the thirati itself, about the light I knew so innately or the dark I had come to understand, could be causing the disruption in my ability.

"I have a few ideas of where to look," Corvin said. "Any other hints?"

"There is one thing." I hesitated. "I only deal in charms. But I understand that the ancients dealt far more extensively with curses. We shouldn't limit ourselves to charms."

He nodded, comprehending, and disappeared for almost an hour. I watched the scholars and examined the mosaics on the walls, and Corvin found me squinting at the styling of an ancient Serafan robe as depicted in stones on one of the walls. "I found a few more books," he said. "Not all books, exactly—some scrolls. Older than the books," he said with a smile. "I love the scrolls. With the books, I sometimes forget they were penned centuries ago. But the scrolls—I cannot help but remember when I am unrolling them that someone wrote these words perhaps a thousand years ago."

"I've never seen writing that old," I admitted.

"And I have never seen the elements of charm and curse. Nor have I the skill to drape fabric into—well, what do you call what you're wearing?"

"A caraco," I replied, tracing the pinked trim on the printed cotton jacket, impressed at the insight that had revealed to Corvin so quickly my self-assigned inadequacy at being in the presence of so much knowledge, so much learning that I couldn't even begin to comprehend.

We spent the next hour poring over scrolls. Most were fascinating explanations of the craft of casting, relating it to the thirati Corvin had explained already, but never considered the light and dark as anything but separately controlled entities.

"This may be less than helpful," Corvin said, "but it's a rare narrative account of casting, by an individual caster, and it might be of some personal interest."

The scroll was simply a ledger of several years of casting work, likely kept, claimed Corvin, for personal education or business reasons. The vast majority of the work done was in curses, but this caster did work in charms, as well. Like modern and ancient casters alike, the caster worked solely in clay tablets, inscribing the curse or charm in wet clay and instructing the patron to wear, hang, or bury the piece depending on the intended result.

"This is the most unusual part of the work," Corvin said, scanning a section in the middle of the scroll. "Her house burned down, and she lost her daughter in the fire. I am not sure why she includes this here, aside from perhaps an explanation of her losses if she intended to use this as a business ledger."

He continued reading and translating in summary. "And here she says she is plagued by some difficulty in casting and must shut down for a few months, but she returns—"

"What difficulty?" I jumped at this lead, more loudly than I intended.

Corvin started at my sudden interest. "Perhaps you will follow better than I—she says the curse is unruly and the charm is tainted with dark. It takes too long to produce a single tablet."

My hands trembled as I tentatively touched the edge of the scroll. This woman—born perhaps a thousand years ago— described exactly what I was fighting. Yet my first assumption, that casting the curse had impacted my abilities, couldn't be the reason she had encountered the problem. She cast both curses and charms regularly in her work.

I let Corvin continue reading and summarizing for me, but nothing else stood out. She took a short hiatus, returned to her casting, and there was another year's worth of records before the scroll ended.

"And then what?" I asked. "Is that the end of her career, or her life?"

"Likely just the end of the scroll," Corvin said. "If she wrote anything else, it does not survive."

A glimpse into the ancient past, and then the door closed. This nameless woman had left me with something, however.

"She couldn't cast after a house fire that killed her daughter," I said. "Does it—does it say anything else, does she believe it was that loss or trauma that caused her to lose her ability to cast?"

Corvin reread the passage and shook his head. "It does not speculate so far. But it is unusual to include a merely personal anecdote in a business account, no?"

"Casting isn't merely business," I said, realizing the innate truth to that claim as I said it aloud. Casting wasn't work like digging a ditch or harvesting turnips. It demanded something of the self; it was deeply personal.

"And here you are!" Jae strode into our corner of the library, seeming to occupy more space than he actually did with his resonant voice and broad grin.

"We were just finishing, I believe," I said. "Would you give us just a moment?" Jae agreed and waited by a large window, observing a small flock of decorative coronet fowl pecking at the ground in a courtyard outside.

Corvin checked the time on a watch suspended from a belt in the folds of his robe. "Miss Balstrade, I am sorry, but I have a recitation to conduct this afternoon. I must beg your leave."

"Oh, you've been too kind, please, don't apologize. I've taken so much of your time. Your charm—what did you want me to make?"

"I could use some luck," he said. "My examinations, to advance to the next stage in my career here, are approaching soon and...I tend to get nervous. Anything—a little kerchief I could carry in my pocket."

"Luck alone?" I asked. "I could infuse it with—well, calm, success, other things besides simply good fortune."

"You can do that?" His eyes widened. "The ancient scrolls seem to discuss good and back luck almost exclusively. Maybe money, maybe love. Nothing so specific as you describe."

"If my clients can be believed, then yes—I can bring a bit of nuance into the charm. Perhaps it's the fine-tuning work of stitching," I said.

"Perhaps," he mused. "Yes, anything you think is helpful for combating anxiety when one's life hangs on a speech and a test."

"I'll get started right away," I promised. "How can I reach you?" I asked. "If we wanted to plan another session, and at least to get your kerchief to you."

"You may always leave me messages at the university mail service. Send a message to Corvin ad Fira, Mhuir Cai." He wrote it down. "That's just Cai Hall—my residence."

I pocketed the note and waved to Jae, who accompanied me home talking of maps and the architecture of Isildi and skirting, always, his intentions with Annette. I could barely answer him, my thoughts wrapped up in the struggles of a long-dead ancient Pellian woman whose grief at the loss of her family mirrored, perhaps, my own.

28

THEODOR WAITED WITH A HARNESSED SURREY, THE LIGHTER, open carriage suited to the heat of the Serafan summer far better than our closed Galatine carriages.

"I feel badly," I said, tying my hat a bit tighter at the nape of my neck, "that we didn't invite Annette. But I confess I wanted a bit of your time, uninterrupted."

"I'm of the same mind," he confided as our driver left the confines of the city and trotted down a broad avenue. The sea glittered in the distance. "And it's perhaps best if I allow Annette to take my place as the face of Galitha for a few hours at today's luncheon. She's ever so much more graceful than I." I raised an eyebrow in unspoken question, which Theodor answered. "It grew tense this morning. Bad news out of Galitha and I admit I almost lost my head."

"Has something happened?" I asked, startled. I glanced at the driver, nervous—should we discuss official proceedings in earshot of anyone?

Theodor followed my gaze and waved off my concern. "Hardly state secrets. Nothing more on any unrest, either. The news is economic in nature, by way of the Allied States. They claimed their usual midsummer shipments of last fall's fortified wines haven't arrived. It sent half the room into a mild panic that our unrest is already affecting our exports, and forecasting doom when we don't have enough grain available this fall."

"Based on one shipment of expensive wine?"

"The Serafans and some of the Equatorials are eager to exaggerate anything. Their alliances have long been with the nobility, and any unrest or even controlled change in Galitha means change for them, as well."

"All because they fear their imports will grow more expensive," I said.

"I think it may run deeper—if we reform our views on nobility and monarchy, on the distance between the common people and the ruling class, it may force similar changes on them."

"After all," I considered, "much of what Kristos used to write his pamphlets came out of ancient Pellian work and from studying other systems. We don't live in a closed world, do we?"

"I suppose not. Though I might prefer it at the moment."

I sighed, understanding what he meant, and clasped his hand.

The view of the sea was beautiful, emerald vegetation and bursts of sunset-hued flowers traipsing down easy hills to an ocean more blue than the most intense indigo that dye could ever produce. The shoreline itself varied—sometimes broad beaches of pale sand, sometimes narrow strands bordered by thick trees and vines.

The surrey slowed at a road hewn from sand and stone, and the driver pulled the horses to a stop. He spoke to Theodor, who nodded and helped me down. "He can't drive farther without sinking in the sand, but this is the place I was told we ought to see."

The driver stopped us and handed Theodor a plain canvas

bag, speaking a few sentences that made Theodor laugh. "For our shoes," he explained. "He suggests going barefoot lest we get stockings full of sand."

I laughed and agreed willingly, rucking up my skirts through the slits meant for my pockets to keep from trailing them in the sand.

"You look like one of the farm girls at harvest time," Theodor said. "Those skirts are quite fetching."

"Think I could make a fashion of it back in Galitha?" I asked.

"If anyone could, it's you." He slung the bag over his back and took my hand. The sand was exquisitely warm and surprisingly soft, my feet sinking in nearly to the ankle. The path wound between walls of thick green foliage. Thick, sweet floral scents wafted from the trees. Suddenly, the path curved and we spilled out onto a broad sand beach bordered by huge rock formations framing open water.

"Someone gave you a good tip," I breathed. I sank onto a low rock and took in the scene, more like a planned mural than anything I'd seen happen in nature by chance.

"I'm going in," Theodor announced.

"What?" I laughed.

"Don't tell me you don't want to see what that water feels like," he said. "I won't strip naked and dive in off the sea stacks, I promise."

"You're wading in with all your clothes on?"

"Just up to my ankles," he promised. "This place is fairly secluded, but it's well-known among the Serafans at the summit. I wouldn't be surprised if a few showed up—we ought to take advantage of the privacy while it lasts."

"Not too much advantage." I laughed. "Is it—is it safe? The water?"

"What could be dangerous about wading in up to your ankles?

"I don't know. Shallows-dwelling Serafan sharks?"

"The only sharks native to northern Serafan waters are half-fin moon sharks. They're nocturnal, and besides, they've only been known to eat reef bass and striped sunfish."

I hesitated but followed Theodor to the water. Galatine shorelines, at least near the city, didn't lend themselves to bathing, and I couldn't imagine dipping even a toe into the swift-moving, debris-swirled river that bordered the city. This was different—open, clear water.

Delicious, open, clear water, I amended as I stepped in, letting the cool water envelop my feet. The eddies tickled my ankles, and I wished we could wade in deeper. I wanted the pure blue to wash over my entire body, to give myself over to something natural and beautiful with no restraint.

Theodor moved closer to me, gently pulling me into him, and kissing me with such intensity that I almost fell into the water. I wouldn't have minded. "You know that I love you," he said, cupping my face in his hands.

I murmured assent and pressed my lips into his, craving, I knew, more than the envelopment of seawater, but submersion in him. My skirts grazed the surface of the water, but I didn't care. "I want you," I whispered, knowing I couldn't find the words to say what I meant—not just now, not just in stolen moments and private spaces, but a life fully entwined.

I knew he took one meaning as I felt him press against me. An impossibility here—exposed on all sides—but I didn't stop kissing him.

A sharp crack interrupted us, and I pulled away, gasping. "What was that?"

"It sounded like a gunshot," he said, brow constricting. "Perhaps a local hunter in the forest?"

I clambered toward dry land, letting the sand stick to my wet feet and my sodden hemline cling to my legs. "Perhaps."

Wordlessly, Theodor took my hand and we walked back toward the surrey. The delight I had felt in the sand turned to frustration as we stumbled in our haste, sand clinging to our wet feet and throwing clouds of grit over our legs. The driver met us halfway down the path.

"Safe?" he panted in Galatine.

Theodor answered in Serafan, and the two exchanged terse words while I warily looked around us.

"It's fine," Theodor said, realizing I had no idea what they had discussed. "There was a shot fired in the woods—the driver doesn't think it could have been a hunter, but no one has come out of the woods."

The driver added a few more details, and Theodor nodded as we headed back up the path.

When we arrived at the road, the surrey was gone.

"What in the world?" Theodor turned to the driver, whose face was drawn, the bronzed tan turned ashen. He repeated his question in Serafan.

The driver merely shook his head, and then began to speak very quickly.

"No, no, you're not—I'm not—stop!" Theodor said. He turned to me. "He thinks I'll punish him, have him sacked, that I think this is his fault."

"Someone stole the surrey," I said. "And I'm guessing they also fired that shot to get him away from it long enough to get away with it."

Theodor nodded and turned back to the driver. I stared down the wide avenue leading back to the diplomatic compound—our drive had taken enough time that, though I knew we could make the walk back, I didn't relish the thought. The sun was oppressive, and any refreshment from the sea was sucked into the humid fog of late afternoon heat. Worse, we were effectively alone and unguarded here.

Our driver seemed trustworthy enough, but it was entirely possible he'd been in on whatever scheme, whether random horse thievery or something more pointed at Theodor and I, was playing out. "There's little choice but to walk. Perhaps someone will meet us on the road and take pity," Theodor suggested with weak confidence.

The sand scratched inside my stockings, and the sun was hotter on the main road than in the shade of the thick forest on the small path we'd taken to the beach. "Damn it all," Theodor muttered. "There's no way we'll be back in time for dinner, and West Serafe was making a bid on the Open Seas Arrangement. It was rather important to attend."

I caught his arm. "Could someone have intended for you to miss that meeting?"

"Hang it all," Theodor said. "It's entirely possible. Though why, I haven't the faintest notion. Someone who thinks Merhaven would make a better representative of their interests. That's as far as I can get with it." We hiked in silence for another mile, then crested a short hill and a wide plantation lay before us—a low, sprawling stone house and wide swaths of tall trees and low shrubs.

"Oranges," I said as we grew closer. "And what are the shrubs?"

"Citrine berries, I believe. They don't transport well, so I've only ever encountered them in preserves." As we approached the house, the field hands tending the berry shrubs stopped to stare. They wore simple undyed linen trousers and most had bare chests, their heads wrapped against the sun in white linen scarves. I tried not to stare back, but I was curious—I knew how hiring day laborers in agricultural regions of Galitha worked, the nobles who owned the land making the work available first to the residents of the villages nearest them, then to itinerant workers who followed planting and harvest seasons in waves of migration across Galitha's fertile valleys. Did these workers live here, I wondered? How were they compensated? Or were they traveling specialists, like those in Galitha, here for a certain task and gone next week?

"Wait here," said Theodor in a low voice as we approached the main house. An arbor stretched in front of the house, laden with showy red vining flowers above and populated with benches below. "In case our hosts are not particularly friendly."

I waited as Theodor knocked on the door and then spoke in quick Serafan to the boy who answered. His white servant's garb was similar to that of the diplomatic compound's staff. While he waited on the doorstep, I watched the field hands work. They seemed to be pruning the bushes, snapping off shoots and pulling dead foliage from inside the bushes. Occasionally one glanced in my direction, still as curious about me as I was about them. Though only partially obscured behind the huge red flowers, I felt at a great distance from the workers who made up most of the population here. I had come to Serafe confident, and concerned, that learning the various cultures I would be surrounded by would be part of the journey. I saw how limited that education was bound to be, shut inside the diplomatic compound and speaking only to the elite leaders of these nations.

These men were, like the field-workers in Galitha, cut off from their capital and its politics. Yet the agrarian workers in Galitha had, according to Byran Border, organized themselves and joined the loose association of willing revolutionaries bound by letters and homemade red caps. These Serafan farmhands may have been invisible to the privileged Ainirs and Ainiras I had met at the summit, but I saw them. I saw their strength, their numbers, their potential.

Theodor returned. "The overseer is having a wagon hitched as quickly as he can to take us back to the compound."

"It seems curious that we haven't been invited inside," I said.

"The family isn't here; the overseer can use the family's farm equipment, but to invite us inside their home would be beyond his purview," he replied.

The overseer was a lithe man with pockmarks pitting dark skin made deeper brown by a lifetime under the sun. He and the driver exchanged words briefly, deciding the logistics of returning the wagon, the driver said.

"The workers," I whispered to Theodor. "Why not have one of them drive with us?"

He shook his head slightly. "Most of them are indentured, either to the plantation itself or to a labor exchange. Many were forced into indenture to pay debts or penalties, so they're not typically trusted with a responsibility like the family surrey." I glanced back at the linen-clad field hands, bound here in service. If every citrine berry and goldenfruit plantation in West Serafe relied on a supply of forced servitude, no wonder the nation felt threatened by populist rumblings out of Galitha.

"Will we get back in time for that meeting?"

"I'm not sure." He sighed. "Merhaven had better not say anything stupid."

29

We arrived back with a scant quarter hour to spare before dinner. It was enough time for Theodor to put on a fresh neck-cloth and comb his hair, making himself, almost by magic, presentable enough for the dinner still wearing his plain dove-gray suit. The fine worsted wool had survived the misadventure with barely a wrinkle. I, however, would never have enough time to change from my rumpled cotton caraco into formal silk and brush all the sand out of my hair, let alone powder and dress it, so Theodor went on without me.

I had food brought to the room, and indulged in a bath in my sunken tub, and then lay barely dressed on the bed with the refreshing breeze from the open balcony drying my hair. Onyx paced the bed, begging ear scratches and chin rubs, then flopped on his side and fell asleep.

When morning sunlight pierced the gauzy curtains by the balcony, I realized that I had fallen fast asleep, too. My legs were sore—city life had meant plenty of running errands on foot but little overland hiking—and my feet were rubbed raw in a few spots where I hadn't adequately cleaned off the sand before putting my stockings and shoes on. I rose, stiff, and padded to the door between my room and Theodor's. I rapped lightly, and it swung open.

"I didn't want to wake you," he said, striding into my room. He looked as though he hadn't slept at all, and given that he hadn't changed out of the clothes he had been wearing yesterday, I presumed he hadn't. His haggard shoulders slumped. "I saw something last night at the dinner."

He was harried, haunted as though he had seen a ghoul or a ghost. "Saw something?"

"Charm casting."

I sank onto the bed. "Casting?"

"With music. Like mine." He ran a hand through disheveled hair, his neat queue abandoned. "There were musicians playing during the dinner. When the Serafan delegate began to speak on their proposal for the Open Seas Arrangement, I expected them to stop. But they didn't, they kept playing. I started to feel strange, light, as though I'd had too much wine. The delegate kept talking, and I thought all of his ideas sounded wonderful." He paused, looking right past me, as though seeing the whole scene again. "Then I saw it, golden threads snaking around the room, licking at all of us, binding us together..."

I realized I had the coverlet clenched in my hand. "No one else would have seen," I whispered. "It's not you they wanted to prevent from being at the dinner last night!"

"You're right," he said. "It was you. They know you're a charm caster, you'd be able to see it..." He broke off, disgusted. "At any rate, the delegate called for a short vote, right there. Not entirely outside protocol, but unusual. I had the presence of mind to move for a stay on it, but—by the divine, Sophie, they could have coerced the whole summit into the deal."

"Would it have worked?" I thought of the ballad seller I had encountered in Galitha City, her untrained casting prompting me to fish a coin from my pocket, and of Theodor's casting, which I had easily bent to my designs, yet neither was schooled in whatever art of coercive casting was at play here.

"I'm not sure. I don't know how long it lasted, I was so shocked at the whole thing. And the delegate looked shocked, too, that I moved for a stay. I suppose the other delegates' reflexive caution outweighed whatever charms were used and they voted with me."

"Maybe they're not very strong charm casters."

"Or maybe they didn't use very strong charms." Theodor leaned, heavy, on the bedpost. "It doesn't really matter. This is...this is beyond the pale. It can't go on."

"What do you propose to do?"

His lips narrowed into a line. "I suppose I can't go about hurling accusations of magic that no one else can see, can I?" I shook my head. We hadn't even told anyone else that Theodor could cast. "And I certainly can't ignore my duties here to investigate, looking for magic in places I'm not supposed to be."

"No, you can't." Our position here was tenuous enough, with a new king on the throne in Galitha and unrest threatening disruption of trade and alliances. The rest of the delegates didn't, presumably, even know how badly things were deteriorating in Galitha. "But perhaps I can."

I dressed as quickly as I could, forgoing dressing my hair and hiding it under a large cap. When Theodor left for a renewed discussion of the Open Seas Arrangement, I hurried toward the common rooms of the compound, the library and game room and reception lounge with its perpetually refilled tables of fruits and candied nuts. Jae stood next to a samovar of tea, chatting amiably with Duana and an East Serafan gentleman. I waffled next to a table of tiny pastries, unsure how to interrupt, how to ask him to come with me to the university. Unsure of everything.

"Lady Sophie," he said. "I couldn't help but notice you, looking like the cat who ate the prize hamster." He mistook my breathless look for confusion at his expression. "We raise ornamental hamsters in Tharia. For fun?"

"Of course." I bit back laughter—of all the strange hobbies the Galatine nobility indulged in, fancy hamsters was something I'd not encountered. "I—I don't want to impose but, well, if you are not tied up, could I ask you to come to the library with me?"

"The university?" He grinned. "Of course! I'm free all day. And I wanted another look at those maps, anyway."

As we left the compound, Jae asked, "And what is your interest at the library today?"

I blanched, hiding my face under the brim of my hat. "It's such an impressive collection, I simply wanted to use it as much as I can, while I'm here," I said. It wasn't exactly a lie.

Still, I didn't want to elaborate, so I changed the subject. "Did you and Annette enjoy the garden tour the other day?"

He grinned. "The tame deer were something to see," he said. "They eat right from your hand, imagine! And of course Lady Annette was a lovely companion." My smile grew strained as he continued to extol her virtuous features, but Jae didn't notice.

When we arrived at the library, he peeled away and I began looking for Corvin, chiding myself for the fool's hope that he would be waiting as though expecting me. Scholars in their variegated shades of gray moved easily here, homing in on shelves and stacks of books, passing one another with rote greeting, gathering in clutches to compare work or debate. I watched for a few minutes, absorbed by the notion that a whole group of people, hundreds of them, could be as fulfilled by words and ideas as I was by fabric and thread.

"Miss Balstrade! I had not expected you today. Did I forget an appointment?"

I turned, finding, to my surprise and relief, Corvin. "No, I hadn't—no." I forced a smile. "I had hoped I might run into you and we might arrange an appointment." Or, I wished fervently, that he might have time to help me now.

"Ah, of course, yes." He fidgeted with the hem of his robe's voluminous sleeve. "I would be pleased to work with you right now, if you will only excuse me to rearrange another matter."

"No, I couldn't dream of interrupting your plans!"

"It is nothing, no. A...personal favor I can complete anytime. Do excuse me?" He almost ran away, leaving me to wonder what pressing matter I was pulling him away from. Who was I to command such attention—did Corvin think I was a higher-ranking Galatine than I really was? Or perhaps, I thought with sobering realization, I was regarded as high-ranking. I was going to have to adjust to an entirely new set of expectations, especially when it came to inconveniencing other people. No one would think of denying a favor to a princess.

He returned moments later, looking calmer. "Now then. You have the appearance of someone who may have some pressing matter to consider. Shall we sit down and begin?" He led me to the Pellian building, to the same sunny corner we had used on my previous visit. "One of the benefits of my rank in the system," he said with a smile, "is that I am permitted a cart to store my books." The cart still held the scrolls we had used before, along with a new pile of volumes.

"That's strange," murmured Corvin as he lifted a book. "I had these in order and—well, someone must have rifled through them. Curious initiates, no doubt," he said, but his smile seemed a bit forced. Someone meddling with his books—especially priceless ancient scrolls—was sure to annoy him as much as having someone paw my best silks would aggravate me. "Now. What did you wish to investigate?"

I hadn't considered how to frame this particular research topic. I was sure that the Serafan casting was a secret, and one that I couldn't risk myself, Theodor, or even Corvin by divulging. I took a breath, weighing carefully what to say. "There is temporary casting. Through music. At least, I know for certain it can be done with music..." I was rambling, realizing as I spoke how little I knew. "I want to know more about that."

"Temporary casting, with music." Corvin pursed his lips. "The Serafan court sorcerers are rumored to use true magic," he said. "Which I have interpreted to mean, possibly, the application of the thirati as you do with physical objects. Yet those who have seen their work indicate nothing to me of charms or curses."

"What is their...work?"

"As far as I can tell, entertainment," Corvin said. "The sort of display of illusion one might see from a street magician or a harlequin, but elevated in its artistry."

"Do they use music in their...entertainment?"

"So I understand. I have never been invited to court, personally," he added with a wry smile.

"Then that would be a good place to start," I said.

"I'm afraid it would lead to a dead end very quickly," he replied. "The secrets of the Serafan court and especially its sorcerers are closed even to the most highly ranked of our scholars."

"Doesn't that make anyone even a bit suspicious?" I asked. "That is, I can't imagine the Galatine nobles in the delegation being willing to subject themselves to magic."

"If anyone believed anything of it, surely. But it's old superstition wrapped in tradition. You must realize, Miss Balstrade, that very few people here believe in magic. Of any sort, even your charm casting. They would see it as a quaint novelty, if that."

"I suppose that's true in Galitha, as well. It's only the efficacy of my charms that convinces anyone. Even then..." I hesitated. Though my work had plenty of advocates, I also had the sense that some customers, especially more recent ones, didn't truly believe in the charm they were paying for, but that they saw owning one of my pieces as a faddish indulgence.

"So you see. The mystery of the Serafan sorcerers is understood by most as a tradition that must be maintained in order to avoid revealing the—how do you say it?—the charlatan's trick of the whole thing."

"Do you think—there might be something in the old Pellian texts on casting like this?"

Corvin considered this. "We have found nothing in our search thus far, have we?"

I stopped. Of course—we had already delved deeper than I ever had into Pellian theory. If the kind of casting I wanted to learn about had been explored by the ancients, we should have stumbled across some mention of it by now. And Pyord, who had spent at least some time investigating the practice of casting, had given no suggestion that he had known anything about the temporary, musical casting Theodor had witnessed. If he had, the temporary casting might have worked better for his means. A singer at a public appearance of the king, a musician hired to play at court?

My imagination's quick assessment of the sinister applications of musical casting made me shiver, and added urgency to

the question of why there had been casting in the compound
at all.

"I am, of course, willing to continue the search, but I do
wonder—" He stopped. "It's worth considering, of course,
that the ancient Pellians were not terribly musical. Their music
tended toward simple percussion for liturgical dance, and work
songs that were more like chants." His smile was slow, like opening a window to discover that flowers had bloomed overnight.
"But the ancient Serafan nomads were highly musical. Troves
of recorded songs, lyrics, treatises by later scholars on ancient
music, instruments on funeral pyres—oh, yes." His smile culmi-
nated in a grin. "This might be something."

Corvin took a few notes in a notebook suspended from the
belt of his robe, the tools of his trade close at hand in the same
way I carried a needle case and a pinball in my pocket. "I'm
afraid anything we need will be in the Serafan building, rather
than here. It will take me some time, but I can send you a message, I suppose?"

"Yes, of course!" I paused. "You've been of more help than
I can explain."

"It is my duty," he said with a bow. "Knowledge is meant to
be used, not hoarded."

I returned to the atrium, looking for Jae, but he was nowhere
to be found. I was ready to give up when a wiry woman with an
untidy kerchief tying back her dark curls found me. "The man
you came with is outside."

I thanked her and left to look for Jae on the loggia, but I saw
Dira first. She faced away from me and appeared to be talking
to a large potted palm, which I quickly realized hid Jae from my
view. Her Tharian was rapid and she was clearly upset.

"You do not disagree, do you, Duana?" she said, abruptly

switching to Galatine, the language they shared. I craned my neck to see the East Serafan woman standing next to Jae. "We should cease our interests in the Lady Annette and allow the East Serafans to pursue the match with Ainir Aidlo's son."

"But, sister," Jae said, anger wrangled into tenuous submission, "we had agreed that a favorable match would advance my fortunes—I appreciate our alliance with East Serafe, but I do not wish to let this opportunity pass."

Duana edged back. "This is a family matter, and not of my concern. But with your understanding, and the understanding of your family, Lady Dira, I will approach the Merhaven woman with our bid."

I bit my lip—Annette's future was being haggled over like any other negotiation here. Was this the sort of intercession Viola had asked me for? I couldn't very well interrupt this conversation without looking like an eavesdropper, and moreover, there wasn't much I could say that would change anyone's plans.

"Then I don't see a need to continue chaperoning her cousin's doxy," Jae muttered. My cheeks burned—how could I have thought he might have some interest in my company, not only access to Annette? I should have known better. In this perfectly manicured but ever-cold society, there were no alliances for friendship's sake alone.

"Very well," Dira said, waving him off. "I'll stay and find the poor girl." Dira's pitiful *poor girl* was almost worse than *doxy*. "Duana, thank you for your assistance in this matter, and I do apologize for dragging you all over the city—I felt we needed more privacy than the compound allows, yes?"

I slipped back inside before Duana could answer, evading Dira as she entered the front atrium by snaking through several aisles of scrolls. Her condescension was the last thing I needed at the moment, and there was no need for a chaperone, save

Lady Merhaven's sensibilities. Isildi was not only safe, but any idiot could navigate the carefully gridded streets. Dira made a perfunctory search for me, then left by the same way she'd entered. I was alone, and relieved that, for a scant couple of hours, I was beholden to no one's alliances—nations or scrabbling individuals.

30

I LEFT THE LIBRARY AND STROLLED EASILY THROUGH THE UNIVERSITY grounds. The jewel-colored coronet fowl skittered over the flagstones, pecking at insects and occasionally flapping their bright wings to lift themselves into perches in the palm trees. I watched their aerial dance, delighted, even if I looked like a gap-jawed tourist. I had little time to spend in Isildi and had barely explored the broad avenues and wide marketplaces of the city.

I walked past tea shops and hatters, drapers and cheesemongers, guessing at their names from the unique signs hung above each establishment. An angry ewe glared at passersby above a cheese shop, and dueling swordfish marked a fishmonger. A pair of silver shears signaled a draper's shop, and I ventured inside.

Bolts of fabric lined the walls. As in Galitha City, drapers sold cloth to buyers who took it to their seamstresses or tailors. I always kept a private selection of fabric, as well, mimicking the practice of the most elite, noble-catering seamstresses. I let my fingers wander to fine cottons and silk gauzes, delicate taffetas and the lightest weight wools, testing the hand of each. The familiar action of assessing fabric, considering its uses, and weighing its value as an investment was comforting. Even stranded in a foreign country, I could find where I belonged.

I owed Corvin a kerchief, and I fell into long-practiced confidence as I fingered featherlight silks and deftly block-printed cottons. I could command enough Serafan to purchase a small length of fabric. Something genteel but not stuffy, special but not foppish. I considered a vibrant saffron silk before questioning if academics, with their strictly graduated robe colors, were permitted to wear such hues. Something less showy, I decided. A fine cotton printed with simple gray diamonds caught my eye.

I found the shop owner and stumbled through the few Serafan phrases I knew—"So sorry, I am Galatine" and "I do not speak Serafan" established our limits, but "How much?" and a gesture to the cotton produced a swift transaction. I was sure that finagling over price was as common here as it was in the markets in Galitha, but I didn't have the language to attempt to haggle and simply counted out the silver Serafan chips of coin into the woman's waiting hand.

I put the fabric in my pocket and returned to the avenue. As I passed a milliner's shop, silk-covered hats displayed in the window not unlike ones I had recently made and infused with love charms and protection spells, I caught an image reflected in the window. I turned quickly, glimpsing before she ducked down an alleyway the figure of a rather familiar Kvys nun. Her deep gray gown faded almost immediately into the shadows of the narrow street.

I started. Had she followed me? Or was her presence here mere coincidence? Perhaps she hadn't seen me at all; if she had, her quick disappearance was suspicious, so I preferred to believe she had business of her own in the markets of Isildi. I didn't like the cloying misgivings settling into my thoughts, making the broad street feel too close, the bright city almost claustrophobic.

I left the market and wended my way through the careful grids of Isildi, back to the compound. It was quiet; meetings were still in progress in the large drawing rooms and the small parlors. I lingered outside open doorways and listened at closed ones, searching for a sign of the magic Theodor had spotted, but there were no musicians and no bright threads or stains of shadow.

A long day with no obligations stared at me, unflinching, but I had one tiny project I could fill the time with—Corvin's kerchief. The breeze outside was pleasant and the sun not too hot. I fetched my housewife from my room and found an open terrace, empty of guests but full of potted palms.

Tentatively, I pinned one edge up and began a rolled hem. I stitched a few uncharmed inches, interested in only the magic of the zigzagging stitch that rolled into a minute finished edge. Then I began to pull a charm into the fabric. I repeated the methodical steps of the tiny rolled hem—stitching and pulling the thread taut in turns, hiding the stitches in the roll of the hem itself. The golden light burrowed into the turned fabric, glowing faintly through the thin cotton.

I finished several inches before I saw the curse magic licking the edges of my work, testing the boundary of my will. I staved it off for a time, finishing one side of the kerchief and beginning another. It was easier to separate the two than it had been the last time I had cast, in Galitha City, though I felt my control beginning to weaken before I'd finished the second side. I set the fabric down and let my eyes and my thoughts wander.

I thought of the story buried in the scroll Corvin had found—that woman had struggled to cast in the grief of losing her child. That didn't help me much, I thought, toying with the threaded needle. I had begun to lose control of the ability I had always understood as innate only after the Midwinter Revolt— not right away or all at once, but in the spring months leading up to summer, I had struggled more and more. Unlike so many, none of my family or dearest friends had died.

I stopped myself—in a sense, my brother had died. I had lost him. He was gone, likely forever, an expatriate whether he wanted to be or not, and I would never see him again. And even before he had taken Theodor's deal of leaving the country, I had lost him. He betrayed me to his cause. I could have died because of him, and I had sacrificed my ideals because of him.

I was grieving.

It was grief, I realized with a start, grief that I shared with that ancient Pellian woman. I should have seen it when Lieta confided that she had struggled with casting after the loss of her husband, but I had been too focused on the intrusion of the curse magic to understand what was happening. Grief muddied the distinction between the light and dark magic in our perception; grief sapped our control over the casting. Lieta didn't know the curse magic, and so had merely felt the exhaustion of trying to control the light while grief welled inside her. I had been grieving for my brother, grieving for our friendship and our family and our future. I would never sew his bride a gown for her wedding, I would never hold my nieces and nephews. I wouldn't serve him a piece of Galatine wedding cake or a traditional Pellian *baka* at my own wedding.

Tears rolled down my cheeks and made fat circles on the cotton kerchief. In the months immediately following the revolt, I had been too overwhelmed with shock, tumbling along with most of the city, trying to reconfigure a world where this kind of violence was possible, plausible. Then I had been busy recouping my shop's losses, making sure that Alice and Emmi were all right, building the atelier back up. I hadn't stopped long enough to acknowledge my own loss, but it hovered, always, unseen and unspoken.

I folded the fabric, carefully weaving the needle, still threaded, through the layers. I felt strangely calm. Casting didn't matter, not for the moment. I simply sat still for the moment, sat with my loss.

As afternoon wore into evening, I finished the kerchief for Corvin, still drawing the curse magic away from my stitches but with a calm confidence that I understood my struggle better now. Perhaps my casting would never be quite the same, I acknowledged as I tied off my thread and snipped the loose end. Life was certainly never going to return to how it once was, sharing a row house with my brother, celebrating birthdays with sweet wine and plum cake, enjoying the summer horse races from the lawn.

I had to accept those changes and accept that they had changed me. Perhaps that was the process that would let me learn to cast easily again—learning as a changed person.

31

Lieutenant Westland found me on the terrace, my eyes red but face dried of tears and the kerchief finished. "Miss Balstrade, I came as quickly as I—" He halted as he noticed my tearstained face. "You must already know something?"

"No, I—" I coughed, clearing my throat and my thoughts. "What's going on?" I hadn't expected to see Theodor's brother again until our trip home, Merhaven having charged him with minding the *Gyrfalcon* in port.

He carried a packet of papers, bound loosely with red ribbon. "These were supposed to be sent to you," he said, pressing them into my hands. Letters, I realized, addressed to my attention first at Southlea and then at the summit. "I didn't open them," he added, unnecessarily, I thought, until I saw that the cheap red wax seal had been broken and was flaking away, leaving an orange stain on the paper.

"Someone did," I murmured, swiftly beginning to read the rudimentary printing spaced out as carefully as its untrained hand could write on the inexpensive, knobbled paper.

"They were open when I found them, but I must confess I did read the contents. May I ask—who is the writer?"

"Byran Border," I said. Theodor's brother waited for an

explanation. "A commoner from one of the cities we visited—Havensport." I thumbed through the other letters—four of them in total, all from Border. "I told him he could write to me."

I skimmed the first letter, Border's poor spelling slowing me down less than his poorly practiced handwriting. Galatine schools only taught common students through the age of twelve, and plenty of boys and girls left before that to start working. Despite any difficulty reading his letters, his message was clear.

I glanced at Ballantine. "We have to find Theodor," I said.

Less than a quarter hour later, we were holed up in Theodor's room, Annette perched on his desk and he and his brother poring over the letters by the window. "Where did you find these?"

Ballantine ducked his head. "I shouldn't have been in the admiral's desk," he began, "but I needed the tide charts we'd worked out and he forgot to give me a copy. I accept fully that it was a breach—"

"Of protocol, of courtesy, yes, but damn it all, Merhaven had stolen these!" Theodor managed to keep his voice contained below a yell. "I don't care what rules you broke."

"The Royal Navy might disagree," Ballantine said, shifting his weight.

"You idiot, there isn't going to be a Royal Navy anymore if this all goes to hell." Theodor threw the letters down and began to pace. I plucked them back up again. Annette silently took one at a time to read.

"One thing seems very clear to me," I finally said. Both men turned, waiting, expectant. "They were waiting until you were gone, Theodor. These nobles dallied until you were out of the country and then abandoned the reform, reversing it where they could. And the people don't blame you." I rifled through the paper and read aloud, "*If we can hold fast, we will. We will wait for the return of the prince and we will not give in.*"

"Sweet hell," Annette cursed gracefully. "Riots in Havensport and they've burned the city lord's offices."

"Keep reading," I said. "They tried to take the fortress along the seawall, but..." I shook my head—they'd failed, at the cost of many men.

"It seems, cousin, that they expect you to stand against the nobles," Annette added.

"As they rightly should," Theodor said. "The laws are clear. We followed the laws in bringing the Reform Bill, in debating it, in voting, and now the reform is the law." He paced back toward us and slammed his hand on the spindly desk that held the weight of Byran Border's letters. "They should stand against the nobles, and those of us with any shred of ethics left will stand for the law alongside the people!"

"I suppose this means heading home early?" I said.

Theodor drummed his fingers on the desk in rapid, martial tempo. "Yes. It's no use keeping our allies if the country burns while we delay. There's a final vote on the Open Seas Arrangement in two days. Will that give you time to prepare to go back?"

"Of course, but Merhaven commands the *Gyrfalcon*."

"Not any longer. I'll charge him with representing our interests for the remainder of the summit. No, it's not ideal," he argued with himself, "and he's bound to overpromise something, but we'll untangle those knots later."

Ballantine nodded. "The *Gyrfalcon* can be ready in two days' time. At least it's not open war. Not yet, anyway. We can make it back before the real fun begins."

I raised an eyebrow at Lieutenant Westland. "Were you born an optimist?"

"Optimism helps at sea," he replied. "Especially when you've no idea what you're up against."

32

Ballantine returned to ready the *Gyrfalcon* with provisions and comb her over with a final check for repairs, Theodor called on Merhaven to explain the sudden change in plans, and I folded and wrapped Corvin's kerchief in plain paper from the desk in my room, ready to send it on to the university first thing in the morning. I had accomplished at least one thing while I was here, and though the victory over my casting felt small compared to matters of state and the volatile powder keg that was Galitha, it was mine. I knew, now, that I could heal the rift between the light and dark within myself and cast again.

We dressed for dinner, thankful at least that we wouldn't have to spend much time discussing the politics at home or the issues at the summit, as Siovan had informed the delegates that entertainment had been planned for the evening.

Lady Merhaven sailed toward me as I waited for Theodor in the hallway outside our rooms, diaphanous pink silk thick like a haze around her. "I understand we're to go our separate ways sooner rather than later," she said, tautly cordial.

"It seems so," I hedged, falling silent as an East Serafan couple passed us.

"And with several prospects still in hand for Lady Annette's marriage. I suppose she shall stay with us?" Lady Merhaven raised a knowing eyebrow with a self-assuredness I didn't quite trust.

"That's up to her," I replied, acknowledging the tacit negotiation.

"You're not going to the dinner tonight, are you?" Lady Merhaven abruptly changed the subject.

"I had intended to." I almost laughed.

"I really don't think it's appropriate," Lady Merhaven said, sighing. "This evening—I've been given to understand that the entertainment is a demonstration of sorcery, and, well." The pained expression on her face was not sympathy for me. "It may be unwise for a purported witch to attend, no matter how… unfounded the rumors. I know it's impolite of the Serafans to not show complete courtesy to a member of a delegation, but you must understand how uncomfortable you've made so many of the other guests."

I clamped my jaw shut and exhaled hot anger, two thin, barely controlled streams. That feeling of control steadied me. "I can and do understand discomfort, Lady Merhaven." I understood the discomfort of being Pellian among Galatines, of being working class among nobles. I understood the fear of the other and the comfort of the familiar, and the myriad ways my very presence violated that comfort here.

"Besides, it's silly pageantry. We all know that." She smiled a terse smile as her knuckles turned white, silk bunched between them. She turned, her face brightening as she noticed the woman approaching us—Siovan, the Serafan official hostess. "Ainira Rhuina," Lady Merhaven called. I kept my expression neutral, but noted this with surprise. It was clear the two knew one another better than I would have assumed.

"Lady Merhaven," Siovan returned with a smile that was, I

thought instantly, silly pageantry of its own right. "And Prince Theodor's companion."

I couldn't manage even a forced smile.

"I was just discussing with Miss Balstrade the evening's social functions." She placed additional and unnecessary emphasis on the *miss*, highlighting my lack of title with dexterous venom. "We had quite nearly determined that it would not be in the best interests of the Galatine delegation, or of the summit as a whole, really, for her to attend."

Ainira Rhuina pretended she hadn't considered this before, wrinkling her brow delicately. "Yes, I can see the trouble. I hate to admit I agree—you really should stay back for this particular performance. It might upset the other guests, knowing that a real magician-artificer was in the audience."

"Of course," I demurred. As the two swept down the hall, cold suspicion overcame any instinct to avoid causing a stir. As I had speculated with Corvin, was there something to Serafan sorcery that they didn't want me to see? Was it possible that it was linked to the musical casting in some way?

After I gave a swift account of the interaction to Theodor, he paused. "You do realize that Lady Merhaven is either playing right into their hands, or she's in on it, too?"

"What a perfect beast," I spat in reply. I hadn't considered it, but did the informal alliance between the Galatine and Serafan nobility extend to sharing state secrets?

"Do you think I'll be able to tell again?" he wondered. "If there's casting?"

"I should hope so," I said. "I've been told in no uncertain terms I'm not expected."

"Yes, but—if you could, perhaps you could slip in unnoticed?"

I took a breath—a risk, perhaps, but of embarrassment to

myself more than anything. "All right." I took a private dinner in my room, sharing a bit of cold roasted chicken with Onyx before slipping back out into the deserted hallways.

Dinner had been served in the ballroom itself, so the rest of the audience merely needed to displace their napkins and adjust their chairs to watch the sorcerer. I found an alcove in the back, sliding between servants clearing the tables. The sorcerer had already taken the stage, so all attention was on him, not the movements of the waitstaff. The perpetual blindness of the nobility to the labor bustling about them worked, tonight, to my advantage.

This was no commonplace street magic, I gathered very quickly. Billowing sheer curtains shrouded the stage, and their twilight purples and blues washed dusk over the platform with every whisper of breeze from the open doors. Only low, dim candles illuminated the audience, with a few well-placed, mirrored sconces lending light to the stage. In the corner, a pair of musicians played a double-tuned harp and a stringed instrument not unlike a mandolin. The careful theatricality of it was street performers' illusion elevated to an art form.

After a brief musical prelude, Ainira Rhuina introduced the performer as a master sorcerer, and I buried my doubts under polite applause along with the rest of the audience. He was tall for a Serafan, robed in almost comically voluminous copper taffeta. All the more space to hide spare rings and balls and even doves, I thought to myself with a cynic's eye. After all, this was illusion, not real magic. Real magic didn't require the bells and whistles of stage setting and musicians. Still, I watched silently, and had to admit that, as an entertainer, he was quite good. He ran through elaborate versions of several tricks I was familiar with—the disappearing egg, the rent handkerchief reassembling itself. Unlike the streets of Galitha City, where these tricks were done with little fanfare and to the tune of a few copper coins thrown in the hat, this entertainer slowed his pace and incorporated the music into his timing. I glanced around the room; he had the audience eating out of his black-gloved hand.

He was in the midst of making a bird disappear when I noticed it—an odd cheerfulness tempered with focus on the tiny white southern dove in the sorcerer's hand. I started, and then I saw it. Emanating from the musicians' corner, a cloud of pale gold charm, cast over the performance.

I gaped, but recalled quickly enough where I was and kept my expression as neutral as possible. This was how the sorcerers could perform such stirring and elaborate stunts, I realized; they combined their illusions with charms that affected how the audience felt and what they focused on. The optimistic, light music from the instruments provoked a pleasant, whimsical joy—just the thing to make an audience not only ignore the tells of sleight of hand, but also to remember the feelings of amazement and delight.

That was all entertainment was, I conceded; it was manipulation of the emotions and responses of an audience. A play, a song, a dance, even sport—it was successful when it produced the desired emotion in the viewer. Joy, sorrow, triumph, defeat, even mild cheerfulness. I felt almost giddy at the discovery of the use of charm casting, surely a long-held secret of the Serafan court magicians, though I was quick to remind myself that the light-headed happiness was likely induced at least in part by the musical charm itself.

The music shifted, and he welcomed a young woman onto the stage with him. Dressed in an affectation mimicking Serafan court costume, she was a swath of pleated and draped silk. At his direction, she lay on the table in the middle of the platform. A levitation act, I realized, as he brandished silver rings and showed that there were no strings or pulleys attached to the petite Serafan woman.

Suddenly, I felt strange, anxiety mixing with distrust deep in the pit of my stomach. The charm had changed along with the music, and as I searched the room for it, I saw the dark sparkle I knew was a curse. I swallowed—could a musical curse produce more than just the emotional manipulation I was already experiencing? Could it harm or even kill? I shook the fears off—I knew that wasn't how casting worked. I knew, and yet the thought wormed its way into my mind and lodged there. Despite my rational refusals of it, it held fast, anchored by the effects of the casting in the music.

I turned my attention back to the performance itself. Through some visual manipulation, the woman appeared to levitate several inches off the platform. What surrounded her, however, brought all the artificial anxiety produced by the casting into immediate, jarring fear based in stark reality. The Serafan woman was accosted by silhouettes of peasants with scythes and pitchforks, shadows produced by ingenious puppetry in front of the largest of the sconces. The phantoms danced around her in an imitation of nightmare.

Then the pantomime took a strange twist. I had expected the levitation to continue for some time, and then for the woman to return to the platform. Instead, her billowing silk constricted and shrank. She appeared to be withering to nothing until the silk twisted a final time and she had disappeared.

The audience applauded in surprise, but the dread and suspense of the curse lingered. Worse, the woman didn't reappear. Servants bustled about the hall, lighting more lamps and repositioning sconces to cast a brighter glow. The sorcerer bowed, and the musicians packed their instruments in tidy boxes and left the stage. Still the aura of fear and mistrust hung over the room, not held back by the illumination or the forced, pleasant chatter as the audience rose and began to file out.

The pantomime's meaning was clear—at least, it was clear to me, having discerned the presence of the curse. Galitha's peasants would starve Serafe—and others as well. The influence of magically enhanced fear ensured that the anxiety over this would last, memorable and treacherously persuasive, into the next day's talks, perhaps beyond. Perhaps the audience had been inculcated into a lifelong prejudice against agrarian workers—who knew?

I slipped quietly into the corridor, now knowing why I had been intentionally discouraged from attending the performance by the Serafan hostess, who was likely in on the long-held secret of the court sorcerers. A polite member of the delegation would have acquiesced to the hostess's suggestion that she stay away; they had expected the typical social daintiness of the Galatine nobility and had gotten, instead, the shrewd discernment of a Galatine businesswoman. Now new worries blossomed—if anyone discovered that I had seen the performance, what would happen?

I was walking purposefully but, I hoped, not suspiciously back toward my quarters when I saw Lady Merhaven and Siovan. Lady Merhaven deliberately avoided looking at me, but the Serafan woman met my eyes, and I hurried away.

Just outside our rooms, I almost ran into Theodor. He was pale and I knew immediately that he, too, had seen the gold and black tendrils woven by the musicians.

"You saw—" he began, but I cut him off with a brusque wave.

"Inside," I said, following him into his room. "The sorcerer's tricks are ordinary illusions, as common as street hawkers', but he incorporates a casting to increase the impact on the audience."

Theodor sank onto an ottoman, unbuttoning his waistcoat

with trembling fingers. "And clearly intended to influence the audience about whatever is in the interests of West Serafe. Do you think it can even be undone? Does it fade, or is it permanent?"

I had inspected and assessed that very problem as if it were a new gown to be draped—picking at a thread here, tucking away loose material there. I knew how tangible casting was done, and that it could be undone. I knew that a charm or a curse could be lifted from the stitches I had imbued with my casting, and I knew that the true work of casting wasn't in the physical presence of stitches or carvings but that these acts helped the caster bind the magic to an item.

"I don't know," I said. "I know that the effects of your casting aren't permanent. But whether that's your inexperience, or that there's something additional these casters might be doing..." I sighed. We had been so surprised at Theodor's ability that I hadn't begun to question the range and strength of his ability. I knew that casters like me had differing aptitudes. Testing our questions against inexperienced Theodor wasn't likely to yield substantive answers. "It's only that you're rather untrained, and I know so little about it that I'm not a very good teacher."

"You've been an excellent teacher, and you needn't spare my feelings. Compared to these Serafans, I'm a mere novice." He stood and began to brush his coat, a pale gray wool with matching silk thread buttons. It was beautifully tailored, but understated and subdued compared to the sunset-hued silks and embroidered pieces he often wore.

"I don't hate Galatine peasants," I said suddenly.

"What?"

"The effects of the casting. I don't hate Galatine peasants. Do you?"

Theodor considered this. "No. So it's either very temporary, or knowing about the casting ruins the effect."

"Or it merely intensifies feelings you already had," I mused. "I suppose the future king of Galitha oughtn't to admit if he hates Galatine peasants. But you didn't before, I imagine."

Theodor raised an eyebrow. "I have not now, nor have I ever, harbored ill feelings toward the agrarian workers of Galitha."

I rewarded his politic speech with a terse smile. "I certainly didn't, either. Well, more questions than answers, I'm afraid, in either case. For one," I said, ticking the count on my finger as though I could keep track of all of the unknowns by mere numbers, "how long has this been going on? I imagine that the inclusion of real magic started innocently enough, just something to enhance their sorcerers' tricks."

"Maybe," Theodor said. "Or not so innocently—people used to believe and fear the sorcerers' magic far more than now, and the Ainirs relied on that in matters of governance. Don't cross the Ainir, don't rebel, he's got a sorcerer on his side." He unbuttoned the last delicate death's-head button and shucked his waistcoat. "The question is, what do we do now?"

"Do?" I almost laughed. "It doesn't seem we can do much of anything—the damage is done from tonight. I don't think you want to out yourself as a charm-casting prince here, or now. And I oughtn't to even admit to being there. Even if I did, it's my word against the entire Serafan court, and who will be believed?"

Theodor sighed. "I suppose you're correct, but—it's not right. They've used this to influence how many decisions over the years?"

"And now they're trying to turn the entirety of the summit against the reforms, against Galatine law." I began to unpin my gown, the heat of the day combining with overwhelming exhaustion.

He flopped back, his shirt sticking to his skin. "Damned Serafans." He picked up his waistcoat again, rebuttoning it. "Well, we know in no uncertain terms whose side they're on in this civil war. And whose side they hope everyone else takes, as well."

33

ANNETTE, THEODOR, AND I STAYED UP LATE INTO THE NIGHT making our plans to return to Galitha. Admiral and Lady Merhaven would stay behind so that a delegate from Galitha could represent our interests at the summit, though that seemed pitifully unimportant to me now. The important thing was to get Theodor back to Galitha, where he was confident that, with his father's backing, he could reconvene the Council of Nobles and begin to enforce the reforms, forestalling a complete descent into civil war.

Morning came too soon. I gathered what little courage I had, wearing my favorite deep teal jacket, cut a bit like a military coat. There was a battle here I barely understood, but I had to muster up to fight as best I could. My chest constricted tighter than a badly laced corset, thinking of the ways that charm or curse influence might serve as diplomatic subterfuge, thinking of the ways it would be all too easy to dispatch anyone who threatened its secrecy.

I slipped into the hall, quiet on silk slippers instead of hard-soled shoes, and padded toward the rooms used for meeting and negotiations. I was intercepted before I could reach them by a clutch of ladies in the echoing atrium. Lady Merhaven, Annette, and Duana were among them, along with a dozen other Serafan, Galatine, and Allied Equatorial ladies. Eyes darted away from me, and low whispers echoed in the high corridor. Annette's face was set in a stoic, cold mask, her fists bunched into her skirts, visibly angry. My eyes narrowed—what was there to gossip about, aside from the fact that I hadn't cared to accompany them on a walking tour that morning?

"...with curses," I heard, the whisper amplified louder than the speaker intended by the curved marble walls. She was tall for a Serafan, and wore a delicate open robe over a white cotton gown, a meld of Galatine and West Serafan sensibility in dress. Annette hadn't yet seen me, and shook her head, ready to protest.

"And Pellian, at that." An East Serafan woman sniffed. "Born in Galitha, they say, but honestly, does it matter? She really has no place here. It's not proper."

"It's downright unseemly. And to think that the future king of Galitha is marrying a lowborn immigrant girl instead of shoring up an alliance with—well, with any of our nations," the tall woman said.

I let my slippers slap the marble floor, and Lady Merhaven looked toward me, surprised, and then averted her eyes. "Now, then, we should continue to the solarium for tea, shouldn't we?" she said, a little too loudly.

"Will your...countrywoman be joining us?" the West Serafan woman asked in a tone that made it clear that this would not be well received.

"That's her choice, Eife," Lady Merhaven replied coolly.

"I am busy anyway," I said quietly. I hesitated, then added, "I don't know what sort of rumors you've heard about me, but I don't do curses."

Eife pulled her shoulders back. "That isn't what I understand.

I understand that you've even gone so far as to research curse casting at the library here."

I tried to smother my surprise. Who had reported on my work at the library? Had I been trailed by Alba to the university, when I had seen her in the streets of Isildi? Or was someone else monitoring my movements?

There was, of course, no use in denying my trips to the library. "I took advantage of your extensive library and the availability of scholars, yes. But my interest was not in curses."

"Then why," asked Duana, brow furrowing and reticent as though she didn't want to believe anything bad of anyone, "did you read works on curse casting?"

"Because ancient Pellian texts don't talk about anything else!" I snapped, then composed myself. "I'm interested in the theory of magic. Ancient Pellians cast curses. I don't."

"So you say," Eife sniffed. "It's a wonder, allowing common folk and known conjurers to an official summit. You could easily curse all of us."

"I assure you—I'm not here to wield curses. I'm only here because..." I swallowed, hard. "At the invitation of Prince Theodor." Someone had been casting, I wanted to shout, and I didn't know why or how.

"I'll take my leave, as well," Annette said, joining me and pointedly linking her arm through mine.

The group of ladies filed past me. Duana gave me a sympathetic look, but Lady Merhaven sailed past without a glance. Distancing herself, I assumed, from the newly minted pariah of the Five-Year Summit. In any case, the path toward the official negotiations was blocked now, and I didn't need to rouse more suspicion as to why I was poking around where I had no invitation.

"I could use a walk," she said. "I've been listening to those vipers long enough that I've a wretched headache."

"This is bad," I sighed.

"We could almost thank the noble mutiny for sending us back early," Annette said with a pained smile. "Let's go hide until luncheon."

I couldn't argue. We wandered away from the public rooms and meeting chambers, past verandas and open loggias linking our building to a lesser-used wing of the compound.

"You've done beautifully, you know," Annette said, tracing the fragrant petals of a huge white gardenia. "They're bitter old hags, most of them, and you've given them nothing but grace. It makes them even more spiteful, but it's not your fault."

"It doesn't feel that way," I replied, inhaling the heady gardenia scent.

"Lady Merhaven was trying to begin arrangements for a courtship with an East Serafan man before we leave," she said abruptly. "Duana's cousin, the delegate with the long queue and the scar on his left...never mind, you haven't seen him."

"How do you get out of it?" I asked.

Annette smiled. "See, this is why I like you. Pragmatic. No dithering over who might be offended." In truth, I hadn't thought of it. "I won't be going to the meeting, and I won't return the formal letters of invitation to visit him, either." She shrugged. "I shouldn't even drag you into it, but I wanted you to know that...I appreciate that you didn't let them manipulate you into helping them. And...if anyone asks where I am, let me make myself scarce."

"Of course," I said. That was a simple enough fulfillment of Viola's request, and I would have done it anyway. "We leave soon enough, anyway."

She squeezed my hand, cleared her throat, and changed the subject. "I believe," she said as we passed open windows covered with intricate trellises, "that these are residences of the West Serafan diplomatic corps."

"Perhaps we oughtn't to be here," I said. It felt a bit like trespassing, especially as I smelled tea through the windows and heard a faint strain of music, scales being practiced under unsteady hands.

"The gardens are still public," she replied. "And I wasn't going to suggest we drop in uninvited for tea." She took my arm to lead me toward a silver-trunked beech tree shading a reflecting pool, but I stopped her.

A strain of music, a light patter of notes I would usually ignore, caught my attention. I didn't only hear them. I felt them, pulling at the sinews of emotion, a gentle pull like the nostalgia of a happy memory. I followed the sound to one of the low-eaved houses. A slim window allowed some light inside, but was certainly intended to maintain privacy. I ignored that clear directive and peered inside.

Three teenage girls gathered around one older woman, who demonstrated scales on a delicate, pale Serafan mandolin. I didn't know much about mandolin technique, but the elegant precision she brought to the simple scales told me she was an expert. The three girls, in turn, repeated the scale. One was more proficient than the others; a pink ribbon fluttered on the neck of her instrument.

The teacher repeated the scale again, this time more fluidly, and the girls repeated. This time, however, a light sparkle grew around the strings of the girl with the pink ribbon. Casting. The other two girls watched the girl with the pink ribbon as she repeated the exercise. They could see it, too, could see it but either could not create the casting yet, or were not permitted to.

My heartbeat quickened, the gently pleasant emotions stirred by the first strain of music dissipating into cold panic.

"Now that might be construed as rude." I jumped, but the voice was only Annette. "There are koi in the pond, you should see—" She stopped, seeing my face. "What on earth?"

I pulled her arm and hurried away, putting as much distance as possible between the damning chords trickling from the music lesson and us. My slippers scuffed on the pebbled path, biting my toes, but I didn't care; I didn't even care that I was likely ruining the slippers.

"Sophie," Annette whispered. "I know something's wrong, but try not to look like you've just been witness to a murder. They're watching."

I slowed and resumed a ladylike pace, then looked up. Lady Merhaven, Siovan, Eife, and the other high-ranking ladies of the summit watched me from the veranda of the main building.

34

‑‑m‑‑

I FOUND THEODOR AS SOON AS HIS BREAKFAST MEETING WAS OVER, pulling him onto a small terrace and away from Admiral Merhaven, who watched with badly disguised contempt.

"Some witness gave them ammunition against you." Theodor sighed as I told him what I'd heard the ladies gossiping about and seen in the mandolin lesson. "You did read work on curses, though?"

"Of course! Pellians didn't write about anything else. What was I supposed to do? You suggested..."

"I know! I know I suggested we look into it, but now it seems a wretched mess that we can't begin to understand, let alone do anything about. You're quite sure the music lesson you saw was casting?"

"I'm positive. They're training these musicians here. What we've seen so far is still bad, of course, but this... it's an entire program of influence by casting."

He ran a hand through his hair, mussing his carefully pomaded queue. "The sooner we leave here, the better. No one watching your every move, believing you're the only one here who can expose them."

"I need to clear my head," I said.

"Not alone," he replied. "If they've started spreading rumors about you—I don't trust them." I acquiesced, less than convinced that his presence or the flimsy ceremonial sword he wore would do much good against the attacks on my reputation.

We wandered, quiet, through the garden as the sun's rays brightened the shell path to a warm gold and tied the shadows of the trees together.

I pulled us away from the center of the garden as tears spiked behind my eyes. I tried to force them down, but the anger that spurred them remained, and their heat spilled over my cheeks. Our allies were manipulating us with casting, Galitha was on the verge of civil war if it hadn't erupted already, and I couldn't do anything to stop it. The future I had sacrificed my shop for could dissolve into smoke and ruin. I could almost capture again the feeling the music lesson's casting had pulled from me, a deep-seated and gentle happiness. It was my own emotion, drawn forth by the casting, and I recognized it—the optimism of accepting Theodor's proposal, the confidence of the reform passing. A fragrant flower in full bloom that I hadn't realized was one strong breath of air from dropping all its petals and becoming nothing more than a stalk stripped bare by harsh reality.

I hiccupped back a sob and then stopped, turning my attention to voices on the other side of the hedge. Theodor laid a hand on my arm, knowing I wanted the sliver of dignity that privacy could afford. I recalled where I was—right by the Queen's Beech tree and the space in the hedges secreted away by tangled rose vines. We slipped inside the sweetly scented chamber, and I sat on a bench to compose myself as the conversation continued outside.

"Let me see you—I can hardly believe you're really here!"

The female voice was muted, but nothing could erase the excitement in even its whisper. And faintly familiar, despite being muffled. "I could devour you, you know that?"

I flushed and wiped my eyes—if I had expected to overhear something in the garden, I had anticipated political intrigue. Instead, it seemed I had blundered into a lovers' reunion.

"It wouldn't do at all to be seen here." Another female voice. And it was familiar, too—but I couldn't quite be sure, nor could I believe it.

"I know, I know. The villa is arranged—but who did you bribe to get you in here?" It was, I realized with a start: Annette and Viola. I grabbed Theodor's hand, and one look at his face told me he already knew.

We stepped out from the hidden room, and I hadn't decided whether to speak to them or try to pull Theodor away when a bright clatter of stones erupted behind me and both figures jumped to attention.

My skirt trailed a clump of weeds whose tendrils had straggled through the rocks beside the path. I raised a hand in weak greeting.

"Sophie?" Viola swept forward. She was dressed in an outdated and plainly cut dark blue traveling suit, impractical in the heat but not betraying her identity, either. I jerked the weeds from my skirt hem and hurried toward them. "And Theodor. I admit I hoped to see you both at some point, but not quite yet."

"What are you doing here?" I hissed. Whatever their reason, it was clearly clandestine. Otherwise, Theodor and I would have known to expect Viola's arrival, and certainly they wouldn't be stealing about the gardens like a pair of besotted thieves. Annette hadn't breathed a word of this when we had spoken mere hours earlier, spoken what I now recognized were words of farewell.

Viola grimaced at my tone, but Annette squared her shoulders. "Running away," she said. "We're hounded no matter what we do in Galitha."

"We were going to tell everyone, you and Theodor included," Viola added. "As soon as we figured everything out. But things have changed so much in the past few weeks." She unbuttoned the top of her traveling jacket and loosened the kerchief wrapped around her neck. "No scolding, not now, Theo," Viola said. "There isn't the time and you won't change anything anyway."

"Then start explaining," Theodor said. "So help me if this gets out." He didn't need to say it—there was enough scandal surrounding the Galatine delegation without a lovers' elopement added like so much grist to the mill.

"Yes, Annette and I had planned, since she was invited on the delegation, to make use of the trip. It's not running away, precisely," Viola pleaded. "Yes, I know how selfish that would be. But we wanted a place we could retreat to. Out of Galitha."

"Out of Galitha." Theodor maintained an impressively placid face.

"Plenty of people do it! Have homes in the Allied States or here."

"For diplomatic or trade purposes, typically. With, typically, the blessing of the Crown."

Viola matched his iron stare. "Typically, perhaps. But not always. And sometimes for far more questionable practices than having somewhere to live unmolested by constant rumor and political machinations. Ever since those sketches were stolen, it's been one ugly cartoon or satire or falsified gossip rag after another. We wanted to get away from that, from all the infernal gossip and cruel marriage schemes, so Annette found us a villa while she was here."

"Is that where you were when you begged off for head-aches?" I demanded.

"I'm sorry, Sophie, I did feel badly leaving you to fend off the old buzzards and their gossip on your own."

Viola continued. "We planned to spend the better part of the year here—regardless, that part isn't important."

"It's not?" Theodor shook his head. "You running off on your family, your obligations—Vivi, what would your father say?"

"After the past fortnight, he'd tell me to go!" Viola bit her lip, fighting to keep her voice low. "In fact, he did tell me to go. Galitha is collapsing on itself. It won't be safe for nobles or commoners much longer."

Theodor nodded. "So I'm to understand. Lucky you arrived when you did," he added caustically, "given that we're returning."

"If you insist," Viola said, eyebrow raised. "You might consider staying here. Lord Pommerly, in Havensport, even called up the army against his own people." She exhaled. "I barely got out of Galitha City. There are those among the common people who have taken to violence against the nobles and those common folk they see as colluding with the anti-reformists. Shops attacked, effigies burned. Most of the nobility who hadn't already headed for their estates have done so now, but…" Her shaky breath made her petal-pink lips tremble. "I know that several didn't make it, and there are more unaccounted for."

"How do you know they didn't make it?"

She returned his stare with misery flooding her deep brown eyes. "I recognized some of them, strung up from the ramparts of the wall just outside the city."

Nausea hit my stomach like a hammer, and I had to sit. It was happening again, but worse, much worse, than Midwinter. "What now?"

"But to go back—Theo, there's no telling what might meet

you at the docks in Galitha City. What if the rebels have taken the port?"

"They're not rebels, Viola—the damned nobles who refuse to obey the law are." Theodor heaved a sigh. "I have to go back. There's no other way to clean this up than to rally those nobles who will uphold the law to unite with the reformists among the common people."

"You're determined to go back, then," Viola said.

"Was there some question about that?" Theodor barked. "Of course."

"It's only—if anyone isn't willing to return, perhaps we could organize a bit of an expatriates' community here. Just for the time being," Annette added in a rush. "I'm not keen to cause any more problems by returning."

"I'm not going to condone your stunt here by encouraging others to join you," Theodor said.

"I thought, Theo, of all people, you would understand," Viola said softly. She glanced at me, and hesitated before adding, "I know you justified your betrothal as beneficial to the political situation, but it very well may be that it pushed some of the nobles over the edge."

Theodor huffed, then glanced at me before answering. I deciphered the ingredients of that look in an instant—remorse, hope, conviction. "I never ran away from my duties."

"Your duties didn't involve having a marriage thrown at you," Annette snapped. "Or being dragged along on a diplomatic envoy for the sole purpose of being paraded about like a horse before a race."

"Please," Viola said. "What's done is done. Theodor, you have no more power to force Annette and me to go back to Galitha than we do to keep you here. And there are things far greater than where we're living to worry about, in any case."

"I should say so," I said. My voice, silent for much of the conversation, had the effect of a tolling bell ending a service at the cathedral.

"We should leave," Annette said quietly. She pressed a paper into my hands. "We were going to send this to you after we'd left, but since we had the good luck to happen into you, take it now."

Names I didn't know tripped in Annette's neat handwriting across the page. "The location of our villa," Viola said. "Province, town, name of the property."

I embraced them both, wishing them well in the same hushed whispers our conversation had been conducted in, hollowly unconvinced this trick of theirs would work yet fervently hoping it would. Theodor wavered but eventually kissed each of them on their cheeks.

"And if things ever degenerate to the point that you can't go home," Viola added, "you'll know where you can find us."

35

WHILE THEODOR TOOK EXTRA MEETINGS LATE INTO THE EVENING and tried to push the work of a week or more into our last remaining day and a half, I returned to my room. I was surprised to find a tray waiting on my table. I lifted the cover and found fruit, cheeses, and the thin bread the Serafans favored. Theodor must have taken the liberty of ordering something for me, I thought, and appreciated his thoughtfulness.

I untied my hat and kicked off my shoes, and decided as I peeled off my stockings that there was no reason I couldn't change into my dressing gown and take my hair down. I wasn't expected at dinner; I upset, Lady Merhaven was clear, too many other guests. Very well. I was tired, wilting like a plant left out too long in the sun. I sat at my dressing table and extracted pins from my hair, rubbing sore spots where my hair had been pulled taut and shaking freedom back into the pomaded sections.

Rattling silverware interrupted me. "Onyx!" I shouted as he wrestled a cube of cheese to the ground and mawed it. "You thief." I hurried to the table and covered the tray again, not before realizing that the cat had already devoured another piece of cheese.

I nudged him with my toe, annoyed, and returned to my

dressing table. A round of cold cream and I felt refreshed, just in time to hear a horrid coughing sound coming from under the table.

Onyx was in the process of vomiting on the carpet. "Shit," I muttered, not sure how to extricate the cat from under the table before he stained the fine—and pale-colored—wool carpet. A thin drizzle of bile trailed from his mouth, but then he began to shake.

I backed away. I didn't know cats well, but I knew they hacked up the occasional hairball. This seemed different, as though he were truly sick.

I glanced back at the tray. Cheese couldn't make a cat ill, could it? Cats, I knew, famously drank milk. "The cat is the milkmaid's friend while her bucket is full" was a Galatine proverb. Nothing else on the tray had been touched, including the fruit, which I supposed could be poison to cats.

Poison. Impossible, I insisted, as Onyx finally finished vomiting on the floor, leaving a pile of what had very recently been neatly cubed cheese. He backed away from it and mewed at me piteously.

What to do for a poisoned cat? One of my neighbors in Galitha City had told me a story about her niece, who drank half a bottle of laundry bluing. They had made her throw up, I recalled—very well, that was already done. But then? I couldn't remember. Gave her water? Kept her warm?

Shaking, I poured water into a shallow jewelry dish and set it next to Onyx. He lapped a few sips and lay down tentatively before beginning to shake.

I exhaled—what was I doing? Fussing over a stupid stray cat while I was, I slowly began to appreciate, in real danger. Someone had brought this tray here, bidden by Theodor or not. What was I supposed to do? I closed the balcony doors, latching them securely and setting the lock, and checked the rest of the locks. It couldn't do much good, I knew, if someone had a key to the room—and if someone had delivered the food here, I had to assume they did.

Onyx vomited again. I retreated to the other side of the room and clambered to the far side of my bed, as though I could distance myself from the danger.

Then I realized that, if I left the room, whoever had tried to poison me would know they had not succeeded. Perhaps it was better to wait, listen for Theodor's return, and emerge unscathed in the morning.

Sleeping was, of course, not an option. I stared into the darkness pressing against the door, filling the balcony. What else lurked outside, or, worse, inside the compound? I felt cold, the evening cool washing over my clammy sweat in waves.

I waited in silence long into the middle of the night until I heard Theodor return, the clack of his shoes and the scraping of the door audible through the wall separating our rooms. I lit the candle next to the bed. Surprising even myself, I checked first on the cat, still curled by the carpet, which had taken on a distinctly foul odor. He looked as though he was sleeping, paws curled under him, but as I approached I saw that he wasn't breathing. I laid a trembling hand on his soft fur, the body beneath already cool.

Then I pounded on Theodor's door until he woke and let me in, and burrowed next to him for the rest of the night. I could almost pretend nothing was amiss, the cool breeze filtering in through the screens in the balcony door, the sheer bed curtains breathing in and out with its movements. Sunlight punctured any illusions I might have laid out in the night—I could no better hide a dead cat than try to pretend I hadn't been the target of an attempt at murder. I showed Theodor Onyx's silent form and the tray, which Theodor confirmed he had never ordered.

"But what can we do?" I whispered against Theodor's rightful rage. "Accusations might only make things worse—and we haven't anyone to accuse."

"Too many to accuse, I imagine," Theodor said, already well entrenched in his pacing, following the edge of a richly colored rug. He trod methodically on the fringed edge.

"Lovely to imagine that so many people want me dead."

"What's changed in the past days?"

"News of the breakdown in Galitha. Or…" I sucked in a breath. "If anyone knew I'd discovered that Serafan sorcery is, well. Real."

"Who might know?"

"Lady Merhaven and Siovan saw me in the hall, after the sorcery exhibition. And in the garden after I saw the music lesson."

"Lady Siovan is the highest Ainir's wife. If anyone would know how Serafans use casting, it would be her." He shook his head. "And that's a grave accusation—that our hosts might try to kill a guest."

"I don't imagine we can do anything about that," I said, "certainly not throwing accusations at anyone. So what do we do? Do I skip on down to breakfast and pretend nothing happened? Join a tour of the water gardens or the museum of antiquities or whatever is on the schedule for today?"

"That's not a terrible idea. Isolation is a threat here—we can't truly keep anyone out if they've keys to our rooms. And clearly someone does."

My brow creased. "Not only do I have to playact that no one tried to poison me, it's entirely possible that whoever did—or was involved—is two feet from me the whole time."

"I hope your acting skills are up to the task."

"You're the one who told me that—what was it? 'Never gamble for real money, you have a face that doesn't lie well'?"

"I hate to contradict myself, but you did manage to lie about the whole business with Pyord, rather effectively."

"That's not exactly a compliment," I said, surprised by how much it stung.

"I know. It's not what I want to remember, either, but—I know you can hold out. Less than one day left," Theodor said. "I'll have our trunks taken to the *Gyrfalcon*. We can spend the night on board ship.

"Perhaps," he said, almost an afterthought, but I could tell he'd considered it carefully, "would you at least consider that you might benefit from a charm now?"

I had all of my old retorts ready, but I was shaken enough to admit I could question even the strictest prohibition on casters, even my mother's strongest exhortations. "I haven't time to make anything in any case," I said weakly. Then I remembered the kerchief, wrapped in plain paper and ready to be sent to Corvin. I pulled it from the desk drawer.

Theodor picked it up, examining the glistening strands of light that clung to the minutely rolled hem. "It's lovely," he said blandly.

"I made it for the scholar who helped me at the university. And it's not charmed for safety. Just luck and calm and success. For his examinations."

"Better than nothing. Consider it out for delivery, on your person, if it makes you feel better."

I hesitated, knowing that skirting a rule on purpose was as bad as breaking it, but I tucked the kerchief into my pocket anyway.

Theodor nodded. "Stick to large groups, and..." He paused, weighing his words. "Be careful around food."

36

EVEN WITH A SUN OBSCURED BY HAZY CLOUDS, THE AFTERNOON was still relentlessly hot. I surreptitiously daubed sweat from my brow. My straw hat was already damp on the inside brim. The acres of channels, pools, and waterfalls making up the water gardens had been remarkably engineered and particularly striking given its location on a high plateau overlooking the sea. From some angles it looked as though the gardens meshed with the ocean, one continuous display of water, perhaps all created, perhaps all part of the natural landscape.

I kept to myself, never too far from the group, never quite in the middle of it, either. For once the distance I had been treated to by many of the delegations' women worked to my advantage. I tried to at least look as though I were enjoying the scenery and the scent of water lilies and flowering trees punctuated by the salt of the breeze, tried to look as normal as possible.

But I found myself starting at each sound, whipping my head around at each flicker of movement in my peripheral vision.

As our tour guide began a lengthy lecture on the history and architectural significance of the water gardens, I settled on a bench next to a pond teeming with multihued fish.

Alba, still wearing her Kvys religious order's plain gray

clothing, joined me. She hadn't been with the tour group. I edged away, instinct driving me from sharing space too closely with anyone. "Variegated carp," she said.

"What?" I asked, cautious. She could be hiding a dagger in her skirts, a vial of poison in her pocket. She could be a distraction, drawing my attention so someone else could stalk me. She might have been the informant who spread the half truth of my curse research at the library, after all.

Or she could be a harmless Kvys nun.

"The fish. They're variegated carp."

"You didn't come here with the group," I said. There was a question there, hanging over the still water of the fishpond.

"I did not. I had some business at the compound, and it brought me here." She traced a finger in the pool. The fish, contrary to my expectation, flocked around it, some aqua and blue, others peach and orange, and a few flecked with black, like pepper flakes. "They're used to being fed, I think."

"Giving a new meaning to 'spoiled fish,' I suppose," I said, watching one royal-blue carp circle Alba's fingers. "They won't bite, will they?"

"If they do, they haven't much in the way of teeth." She glanced around us. "That's more than can be said of plenty in Isildi."

I started, but Alba had gone back to swirling the water with a fingertip. Was she voicing a threat, solidarity, or was her comment unrelated to what had happened to me?

"Why did you come here?" I asked quietly.

"I needed to find you."

She couldn't know. No one knew. Everything around me continued as though nothing was amiss. The man giving the lecture, a short Serafan with tufts of white hair over his ears, continued speaking, now explaining the use of pipes and siphons in creating the ever-flowing water in the gardens. The ladies in attendance listened, eyes trained on him politely. I scanned past them, around the gardens.

"It was Merhaven," she said quietly. "The poison."

I edged away from her.

"Not directly, he paid one of the servants, of course."

"How—" I clamped my mouth around my questions. She couldn't know. She could be trying to pit me against my own countrymen for some Kvys gain.

"I would advise returning to the compound as soon as you can," she added in an impossibly gentle voice, "because my inquiries also revealed that he was leaving. Today. Your ship is called the *Gyrfalcon*, yes?"

"Impossible," I breathed. "Suppose you're telling the truth— why?"

"Not here. You look like you've seen a *jimji*—that's a wicked little Kvys water sprite," she said with a placid laugh and a pointed glance at two Serafan ladies passing us. "Now. We can go back to the compound quietly, unobtrusively."

"I can't—" I swallowed. "I shouldn't trust you."

"Very good. You shouldn't trust anyone you don't know well. But we're in a terrible bind, and we haven't time to rectify our lack of friendship at the moment. You're not in danger from me, or even, really, the Serafans, though they'll gladly help. It's your own people you should fear."

"That's what you'd say if you were trying to kill me," I replied, trying to sound clever and failing as a tremor passed through my voice.

"Fine. He said you'd be suspicious." Alba pressed a piece of fabric into my hand.

Not plain fabric—a cap. Red wool. Hands shaking, I turned

the edge up and traced the initials stitched into it—and saw the faint glow of a charm in the seams.

"How did you get this?"

"You know what I'll say. That he's here, that he gave me this as a way to make you believe me. You'll doubt that reason, too. Make your decision."

I had no reason to trust Alba, and she could have come by Kristos's cap in myriad unsavory and ugly ways. My fingers worried the wool, finding the charmed seams and wishing I had some other gift—the fantastical divination of storybooks or even the commonplace ability to discern when someone was lying. I had neither.

At the moment, however, Alba seemed like my best option. From my limited understanding of the international tangle of trade and policy I was now bound up in, a Kvys stood the most to gain by protecting me. And there was the cap, a flimsy and unsubstantiated tie to my brother, but a tie nonetheless. He had betrayed me once, but I still trusted him more than I trusted the strangers I was surrounded by.

I stood, arranging my skirts as though nothing was wrong. "Very well," I said with a forced smile.

37

—⁓—

No one seemed to notice when we slipped away from the tour; I doubted they would have cared anyway. The Galatine commoner and the Kvys nun were no one's favorite delegation members. We strolled toward an empty section of the water gardens, where rows of southern cypress flanked a long, narrow reflecting pool.

My breath hitched in my throat, but I evened my pace to match Alba's unhurried gait. She glanced at the reflecting pools and white-petaled lily ponds, strolling as though enjoying the scent of the cypress and the tranquil water whose quiet now felt like a threat.

One of the gates leading out of the idyllic gardens and back into the hot, dusty streets of Isildi was just ahead; Alba nodded almost imperceptibly to indicate we would be leaving. We passed between carved sandstone columns and Isildi spread out below us, the sea to our right, the verdant green forests outside the city to our left, and the sunbaked roads and buildings straight ahead.

I let Alba lead as we descended into the city proper. When we turned corners or passed taller walls, I wondered if I caught a glance of a shadow behind me, if there were threats stalking us.

We entered an open square, one of Isildi's many small specialty marketplaces. This accosted us with scents of bright pepper, heady rosemary, and thickly sweet cinnamon—a spice market.

"We're not near the compound," I protested as Alba slowed to inhale a jar of ruddy ground peppers.

"No? Oh, I hadn't realized," she said with dry sarcasm, capping the jar. "I wanted to make sure we weren't followed."

Stray pepper dust accosted my nose and I coughed. "Followed?"

"One never can know for sure"—she shrugged—"but I think we're safe enough."

"Safe enough?" I choked on the words, embarrassed by the panic in my voice even as Alba remained calm. "You think?"

"I recognize that this is unfamiliar for you—"

"It's familiar for you?" I whispered.

She ignored the question. "—but it's at this point important to return quickly to the compound. I know you can do little to stop Merhaven's leaving, but your prince may."

"Why didn't you go to him?"

"Because I told your brother I would protect you. Now. Step lively, there we are." She led us at a quick clip past storefronts and countinghouses and onto the broad avenue leading toward the compound. "Merhaven intends to dash away back to Galitha and leave you and Prince Theodor behind. He's put a price on your head—"

"What?"

"Don't fret, we'll watch out for you. But he's made a payment to one of those underbelly demons in Isildi's assassin market—didn't mention those on our tours, did they? Quite the local specialty. He's bought himself insurance that you won't sail out of the main ports because, well, you'd have a terrible accident if you tried."

"He wouldn't dare assassinate his crown prince," I argued.

"Oh, certainly not! But you? You've been nothing but a hassle." I picked up our pace and Alba didn't argue. We nearly flew through the main gate of the compound.

"How in the world do you even know this?"

"Rich people don't carry their own bags. Anyone coming or going hires porters. So I paid the head porter here to tell me what came in and out. Galatine trunks with Merhaven's seal left this morning. I might believe he'd need nothing but his hair pomatum and tooth powder for the next few days, but his wife? No, she wouldn't go without her wardrobe."

"I meant the hiring assassins bit."

She winced. "More commonplace. Picked the lock of your room, there was a threatening note. I left it there, you can have it if you want."

We had reached the main colonnade and so slowed our steps, conscious not to draw attention, gossip, more danger. "You investigate your own apartments if you wish, find the letter, see that I'm in earnest."

"And you?"

Her face closed, neutral. "I have a few quick messages to send. For, shall we say, the next phase of this little adventure." She clasped my hand quickly, tightly. "Find your prince and see if it's not too late for him to sail for Galitha instead of Merhaven."

I walked on pins toward my room, forcing my feet to be slow and gentle on the marble halls but wanting nothing more than to sprint. My hands trembled as I unlocked the door, and sure enough, a fresh piece of good white paper lay on my dressing table, sealed with a pretty flourish of deep red wax. Like an invitation, like a social note. I read it quickly—Merhaven's usual formality was missing from the letter, as though he assumed I couldn't be trusted to read more than a six-year-old's vocabulary.

*I will sail for Galitha without you and the prince. You will stay
behind until I send for you. Do not attempt to leave. You will be killed,
as I have hired local mercenaries, the a'Mavha, to watch you like guard
dogs. Of course this arrangement must be kept secret.*

That damning bit of evidence in hand, I went to the adjoining door between our rooms. It cracked on its hinges as I flung it
open, confronting, to my shock, Merhaven.

"You know then?" I asked Theodor, looking dumbfounded
at his desk, a pile of freshly inked papers in front of him.

"Know what?" Theodor asked, eyebrow ratcheting upward
in mild irritation. I went still—Alba had misled me, fed me false
information. Merhaven wasn't leaving. He was right here, going
over some final bit of paperwork, some last notes on the Open
Seas Arrangement or grain exports with Theodor. The letter
was a plant. I chastised myself in stunned fear that I didn't know
Merhaven's handwriting well enough to spot a forgery.

But Merhaven edged away from me, eyes narrowing ever so
slightly.

There was one way to find out for certain.

I steadied my breath. "You're leaving. Attempting to leave
us stranded here."

For a long, painful moment, no one spoke. My stomach constricted. I could still be wrong, and have made a fool of myself.
Theodor rose halfway from his chair, watching me as though
watching a cornered cat, unsure if it would run or bite. Then he
turned his eyes to Merhaven, who was growing red.

He unclenched his jaw and spoke. "So you discovered a bit
too early. You were supposed to be on a tour of the water gardens, not returning for hours."

"What does she mean?" Theodor asked quietly, and when
Merhaven didn't answer, he roared, "Answer me!"

"I'm leaving, and you are staying here. I will return to Galitha to restore the country. To drag it out from the mess it's in. You'll stay here past the conclusion of the summit."

"What mess? The country is moving forward, and you haven't the authority to stop it!"

"You weren't supposed to succeed!" Merhaven exclaimed. "Your Reform Bill—it was supposed to fail entirely, or pass in a much weaker version. So we have to correct that mistake. We've already begun—as soon as you left, we began."

"You planned this? From the start, when we introduced the bill?"

"The Reform Bill was never supposed to pass, so your time here was merely supposed to be a bit of a...break. From this talk of revolt and reform, for the common folk to go back to worrying about coal prices and bickering over when to plant the winter rye. But when that wretched bill passed, we had to take charge a bit more. We decided that once you were out of the country, we'd reinforce the nobility's control over Galitha City and the provincial regions."

Theodor gripped the table. "It was all organized. All the trouble we've been hearing about—it's not a malcontent noble here and there, but a damned formal insurrection. Fomented by—who? You and Pommerly and how many others?"

"Dozens. And I thought we would have matters well in hand, but you got word somehow of the bit of unrest we've had—I was quite careful not to bother you with all of this, you know—and were ready to storm off like a toddler having a tantrum. We can't have that."

"I was ready to return to my country and defend its law."

"Law! You're like a child, playing at a game you don't understand. Knocking all the wickets to the ground with a croquet mallet in a fit of pique. Enough now. The senior nobility of Galitha will set it right."

"They'll fight," I said quietly. Merhaven looked to me, surprised I had spoken. "The people. They won't give it up now. Not when reform was fairly won, not if you take it away."

"You can stop with that now," Merhaven snapped. "Your racket about the common people rising up again. I thought it an ugly tactic before and it's entirely useless now."

My eyes widened at his terrible miscalculation borne out of aloof and distant separation from the people whom he had made into his enemy. "But they are fighting back. We both know that."

"In pockets here and there, perhaps. But not the grand revolt you sold half the nobility on."

I pressed my shaking teeth together. Merhaven couldn't read the truth when it stared him straight in the face. I looked desperately at Theodor, who had turned a horrible shade of white.

"Just go along with the plan," Merhaven said, almost wheedling, "and we'll be back to rights soon. You'll still be crown prince, you can pretend this never happened. You can even have your wedding, and I imagine everyone will be more amenable to *her* now that the trouble is nearly over."

"Not on your life," Theodor returned. "I could have you arrested."

"You won't." Merhaven took a breath, and before I could think to warn Theodor, he had drawn a small silver pistol from his pocket. He trained it on me. "I didn't want it to come to this."

"Then put that away!" Theodor began to step away from the desk, but Merhaven's hand stayed steady on the pistol. With deft and calm precision, as though adjusting his sextet, he cocked it.

"You held the council hostage with your threats of violence

and staged riots! With your rumors and pamphlets promising revolt, and your sorceress doxy holding her magic over our heads!" The pistol was still aimed at me, even though he faced Theodor. I shook as I looked down the small black barrel.

"None of it," Theodor said, enunciating each word with palpable anger, "was staged. The threats are not empty—you know as well as I do that they're resisting you all over Galitha."

"They will quickly stop when there is firm leadership back in control. That's what has been missing—firm, just leadership."

"It's insurrection." Theodor trembled.

Merhaven sighed with nearly paternal regret. "It's not insurrection, it's reinstituting the law. The proper law, the natural law. Crestmont and Pommerly and your father have things well in hand at home."

"My father." The bottom dropped out from Theodor's voice, leaving it a hollow echo.

"Yes, your father. He's not going to allow a wayward son to grind the nation into dust. He's convinced that your reforms will be a disaster for the country and has given us license to rectify them."

"License. He told you to maroon his son in West Serafe? To point a gun at his son's betrothed?"

"He told me to do what had to be done. For Galitha." He heaved another sigh. "I am sorry it came to this. But you understand now, what must be done. I'll leave you two here—door locked, I'm sorry for that—and you'll make your way back to Galitha when I send for you. Not before."

He strode to the door, plucking Theodor's key from a dainty marble-topped table on the way. The room was so silent I could hear the tumblers of the lock clack into place. Then I sank into a pile of sweat-soaked cotton on the floor.

38

"What now?" I said, still shaking. "They'll believe—oh, sweet hell, Theodor, back home they'll believe we abandoned them!"

"There's nothing to stop us, as soon as he's gone, from hiring our own ship," Theodor said firmly. He shoved his chair away from the desk and it fell with a sharp crack.

"There is," I said, fishing Merhaven's letter from my pocket. "He's hired—I don't know this word in Serafan, but some assassins. If we show up in the ports, they'll kill us. Or, rather, me."

"Dirty old shark," Theodor said, dropping to the floor next to me. "We'll find a way." He rocked back on his heels. "We never could have anticipated this," he said, though whether to console himself or mollify me, I wasn't sure.

It didn't matter. The flood of anger that had been suppressed under the terror of Merhaven's pistol pointed at my head surged forward. "We could have," I said, the words bitter as they spilled out, "and I did. And I said we couldn't trust the nobility to be held in check by something as fragile as a law."

"I was supposed to consider treason a suitable response to losing a vote in the council?" Theodor nearly shouted. "To assume insurrection as a logical outcome?"

"Yes!" I twisted my skirts in my fists, wanting to wring some sense into Theodor. "Yes. They've never been humbled, not like this. They've never shared their authority."

"But to turn against their own country's laws—what's a country without laws? They're raised with that sense of duty, never to turn their backs on their country—"

"How blind are you?" I shouted. "You were counting on some arcane sense of honor preventing them from doing what they've always done—take what they want. They'll tidy it up with rhetoric about another manufactured version of honor— duty to their country, to the 'true' Galitha." I swallowed the thick sour taste of this truth. "Their honor has always been a convenient excuse for what benefits them."

"Not," Theodor said, "all of them."

I closed my eyes and exhaled anger. "No, not you. Not your brothers or Viola or Annette—I know. But you still can't look past that, beyond what you wanted so desperately to be true."

"Then the nobility—all of us, me included, are just scavengers taking from the rest of the country? Always have been, always will be."

"I didn't say that." I stopped. "No, I won't apologize. You know damn well that you and plenty of others have been trying to rectify the injustices Galitha is built on. I don't need to coddle you on that point. But do you see—do you finally see—that what the nobles grant, the nobles can take away?"

Theodor's hands shook. "You want me to tell you that you were right? Fine. You were right. Does that feel better?"

"Of course not! But do you understand now?"

He slumped on the floor next to me. "If I didn't already, I'm afraid that the lesson will be administered far more harshly by what we find back in Galitha."

"It's not too late," I said. "We know that the people are far more determined than Merhaven and his allies believe. They won't give in without a long fight."

"And we'll join them, somehow." Theodor's hand grazed his coat, and his fingers found the family crest pinned to the left side. Then his hand fell away. Joining the fight against the nobles meant joining a fight against his father. "First we have to figure out a way out of here."

"Do you know how to pick a lock?" I asked.

"Sadly, no, lock picking wasn't part of my education." He stood up. "Shit. This is—someone will eventually find us."

We both started as a sharp rap on the door echoed through the room. "Have you out in a moment."

"Who's—"

"Alba," I answered. "The Kvys nun."

"Of course." He swept a few loose tendrils of hair behind his ears. "The Kvys nun. Of course the Kvys nun is picking our lock."

"I'll explain later."

The lock clicked and the door opened. Alba slid a bent hair-pin under her veil. "No, I will." She paused. "I'll explain to him while you pack a few necessities. I'm taking you to your brother—Creator knows you aren't safe here."

"Not on your life you're taking her somewhere else—her brother?" Theodor asked, slowly comprehending what Alba had said. "Her brother is here?"

"Where else, the Fenian coal mines?"

"And we have to make haste, to the harbor, to stop the ship—"

"They'll be gone before you reach port," Alba countered. She turned to me. "Just a few necessities. What you can fit in your pockets."

The space around me seemed to constrict and then I met

Theodor's eyes, finding some anchor there. He was still lost, sifting through his broken trust, searching for meaning in the shattered pieces of the past months' work, in the fragments of the system he thought he'd understood. I reached out, offering him the same foundation I held firm to. "We still have each other. We still have friends who are loyal to us and the cause. And we have the Galatine people, ready and able to fight for themselves."

He wavered a moment, and then nodded, once, nearly imperceptible. "Pack your things," he said quietly. I dashed into my room and shoved a few necessities—what little coin I had on hand, a comb and hair pomade and hairpins, tooth powder, my sewing kit, spare stockings—into my pockets. My cotton gown was practical enough, and there certainly wasn't room for a change of clothing. I heard Alba's calm, commanding voice through the open doorway. There was still a wrapped packet in my pocket, too—Corvin's kerchief. I hesitated, then tucked my comb and hairpins into the packet. I needed luck enough to bend my own rule; after all, I hadn't deliberately made it for myself.

"Now we go," Alba said when I returned. "Prince Theodor will stay here, to allow Merhaven's Serafan allies to believe, for now, that everything is going to plan. He'll join us later."

"No, I don't want to separate," I argued. I saw my anchor in Theodor's steady eyes, and I knew he saw his in mine. "We can't," I added, taking his hand.

"She's right." Theodor pulled me close, his face buried in my hair. I relaxed slightly, under the spell of his familiar scent and heavy hands on my shoulders. "If we go on as Merhaven's plans dictated, his allies here will believe the charade. As long as we don't try to leave, we ought to be safe. So I won't leave, and you're merely doing as you've done all along—touring the city. If I go running off with you, I put you in danger." He lowered his voice so that Alba couldn't hear. "Remember—the Serafans have as much reason to want you dead as Merhaven. They don't want their secret exposed." He pulled away, swallowing hard. "So we play this game for now and I'll find you as soon as I can."

My throat was nearly pinched shut by suppressed tears, but I managed to agree.

"Let's go." Alba's decisive yet patient command gave me direction—toward the door, down the long hallway, through the colonnade, and into this unexpected and unwelcome detour.

We turned up one of the wide avenues that formed the main grid of Isildi's center. I was surprised to recognize the university quarter—but of course, if there was a place my brother could have been expected to settle on in Isildi it was the university. He had all but vowed to find somewhere to study when he had left Galitha, and the large and remarkably egalitarian Serafan university was one of the few places I might have expected to find him. We passed the imposing structures that housed the libraries and archives, lecture halls, and theaters, and entered a shabby but clean street populated with low-eaved bookstores and wineshops. Alba steered me toward the crumbling doorway of a bar. I couldn't read the name on the sign swinging overhead, but the sigil—a dark arch punctuated with candles—was recognizable. The Grotto.

The place was empty, though it took me a moment in the dark room to realize that. A single barmaid with her dark hair bound in an emerald-green wrap noted our entrance. She simply nodded in greeting to Alba and then stared at me, eyes widening, as though recognizing something she'd only heard about. She slipped behind the bar, her lithe figure disappearing behind ceramic carafes.

"He's in here," Alba said quietly. "Your brother."

39

I WAVERED BEFORE THE DOORWAY, ARCHED PLASTER COVERED with layers of thin net. My brother? The thought of seeing him again—rich and full and yet bitter. We had not left on good terms—I could forgive his betrayal in an abstract sense, knowing I would never see him again. Now that he was just past this flimsy curtain, what would I feel? The last time I saw him, there was relief he was alive; with that assurance long established as a comfortable fact in my mind, would the hurt and anger surpass anything else?

I pushed aside the curtain and strode into the room with more confidence than I felt.

It was brightly lit, unlike the bar it hid behind, and open above and with only partial walls that made it more of a courtyard than a proper room. Several people sat or reclined on cushions. There were books stacked in tidy corners and an abandoned game of cards on a table. I swallowed, taking another step, forcing myself to scan faces instead of objects.

The first face I saw was Penny's.

"Sophie!" She leapt up, her brilliant smile illuminating her face and then quickly fading. Our last meeting had not been on good terms, and I saw her face transposed, not on the sunlit

Serafan courtyard in front of me, but in my shop on a wintry afternoon, collecting her final wages and leaving. The expression was the same—regret and loss, pride and conviction.

I hesitated, but Penny didn't. "You look well," she said. "We read about you in the Galatine gossip pages of the magazines," she added with a laugh.

I couldn't help but smile in return. "I can't be so well-known as all that," I said.

"Well, they don't always use your name," Penny replied with an impish grin.

And then Kristos strode into the courtyard and I found myself short of breath.

He had grown a beard, common enough in Serafe if terribly gauche in Galitha, and his hair was longer, clubbed in a queue. Instead of the Galatine workman's clothing I was used to, he wore loose Serafan trousers and no waistcoat under his linen coat. He hardly looked like Kristos at all, older and foreign. It made it easier, somehow. He had left his old life behind, the life we shared in a drafty row house, and had made himself into a new person, a new actor in a new life.

"Sophie." He didn't move toward me, or I toward him. "I'm sorry this is how we had to meet."

"How long have you known I was here?" I asked. Pragmatism felt easier than addressing everything unsaid between us.

"Since before you arrived."

Penny cracked a smile. "Like I said, gossip pages."

"Please," Kristos said, as though remembering himself, "sit." He gestured toward a quartet of chairs huddled around a fat ottoman. I obliged.

"How long have you been here?" I asked. "The beard is new."

His smile was thin. "Not so new—I started growing it as

soon as I left Galitha City. Turns out I'm terrible at shaving on shipboard. I only stayed in Fen long enough to save up some money, working for a small foundry. Then I came here. I've been studying at the university under a professor of politics and ethics for four months now."

"Where are your novice robes?" I joked. He flicked his hand toward a rumpled pile in the corner—pale gray robes. "Fair enough. Your professor knows who you are?"

"Not quite," he admitted. "But he knows I was involved in the revolt and doesn't care." He tilted his head, considering his words. "Or at least doesn't allow it to interfere with his sponsorship. The revolt wasn't exactly popular in Serafe."

"So I gather." I watched a beetle with jade-green wings traverse the tufted ottoman, falling into the divots and struggling to right itself. "Why didn't you reach out to me?"

"When I arrived here?" He shot me one of his smiles, the rakish, uneven grin I recognized, even half-hidden by his beard. "I was given fair warning by your intended not to give the Galatine authorities any hints on my whereabouts. Extradition from Serafe is a real thing, you know."

"I meant when *I* arrived."

"It seemed more prudent to wait." Kristos sighed. "In case you hadn't noticed, your delegation is as full of rats as the wharfs on the far side of Galitha City."

"I hadn't, in fact, until quite recently," I replied. "How do you know more than I do about all of this? And how—" I stopped myself from finishing. *How do you know at all? How can I trust you?*

"That's where I enter this conversation," Alba replied.

"You're not really a nun, are you?" I said. "You're some—some kind of Kvys spy."

To my surprise, Alba laughed riotously, and even Kristos

joined with a badly concealed chuckle. "I really am a sister of the order," she said, wiping a tear from the corner of her eye, "and no one has ever suggested that I was anything but a meddlesome one, at that. But yes, I have been, shall we say, placing myself at the summit to be of service for you when the time came."

"But why?" I asked, growing a bit exasperated. Fighting back the resurgence of loss and pain over my brother had left me with little patience.

"The Kvys are sympathetic to the aims of reform in Galitha. Unlike our friends in Serafe. The reasons for this are, as I'm sure you've discovered already, complicated and include plenty of practical economic concerns and machinations for beneficial alliances. And as for me, I am an egalitarian, personally. Motivated by a fool's dream, perhaps." I assessed her as she spoke; she sounded like she was telling the truth, but a truth almost too neatly packaged. "I have been in contact with Kristos since I first read his work, last autumn."

Kristos nodded. "And I've built a small network here. Including some contacts within the diplomatic compound. I've kept an eye on you."

"Well, that isn't disturbing at all," I shot back, resorting to the kind of jokes I was used to lobbing at my brother.

Kristos shrugged. "What can I say? At least I'm not using my reach and influence to become a first-rate Peeping Tom."

Alba shook her head at both of us. "Our...shall we call it monitoring? It is not nearly as disturbing as the fact that your own countrymen have attempted to dispatch you."

I eyed them both warily. I had underestimated Kristos before, but was I to believe that a Kvys nun and an expat scholar were more capable of protecting me than the security in the diplomatic compound? Yet, here I was, a near victim of poisoning and stalked through the city by the thin shadow of a promised assassin.

I threw my hands in the air. "This is absurd! All of it. I'm a common seamstress. Why do away with me?"

"It's a very widely held belief that Prince Theodor's insistence on reform is at your behest," Kristos said. "I know reading isn't your favorite pastime, but you've at least seen the cartoons?"

"The Witch Consort? The Rebellious Curse Caster? The Prince's Commoner Whore? Doxy of the Pellian Cabal?" Kristos received my best icy stare. "Yes, I'm aware of what's said about me. Theodor would have pushed for reform without me, too."

"If you say so." Kristos shrugged, unimpressed. "But something doesn't have to be true for it to gain traction and push people to act. A little destabilization—and knocking off the so-called witch holding the prince's puppet strings will thoroughly destabilize things, along with the obstruction in Galitha—and the nobles get their way."

"And Serafe will support them," Alba added.

I slouched into my cushion as much as my stays would allow. The Serafans had their reasons to dispatch me, too, but merely knowing about Serafan music-based casting could be a death sentence. I wasn't sure who, or when, or how much to tell. "And now what?"

"Now it isn't safe for you to go back to the diplomatic compound," Kristos said. "We've a fair network of folks here in the university quarter who are happy to put you up. For now. You know one already—Corvin."

"How?"

"I confess he may have been planted," Kristos said with a grin. "He's one of my good friends here. When I heard you were arranging a tour of the archives, I guessed what you might be after, and I made sure he stayed within earshot."

"And how did you hear I was arranging a tour?"

"Dira Mbtai-Joro." Alba smiled. "She and I are acquaintances of a sort—I brought her into our fold. Mutual distrust of Serafan maneuvering, you see."

"Dira!" I suppressed a shocked laugh. "Dira hated me."

"Ah, dear, no. Dira is cold, I'll grant you, but the Allied States are keen to see the old guard of Galatine nobles shaken up a bit." I recalled what Theodor had said about the Open Seas Arrangement, and that all of these nations had their own complicated plans in which I was only a footnote.

"I have the most helpful friends." Kristos grinned.

"You are a devious snake, Kristos Balstrade."

"Good thing I'm on your side, isn't it?"

"Well, snake? What next? And what about Theodor—does he know where I am?"

"I'll make sure he gets a message." His voice was gentle; in fact, he was quieter, more staid than how I remembered him. There were worry lines around his eyes that hadn't been there before the revolt, and he seemed less poised to speak or act and more inclined to contemplation.

"We were leaving as soon as we could," I said. "Returning to Galitha."

Penny hovered just beyond our earshot, waiting for us to finish. "I was thinking—Kristos, your sister is probably hungry. Maybe Mairti has something? One of her hand plates?"

Kristos nodded. "And bring wine," he said with half a grin.

40

THE WINESHOP OWNER, MAIRTI, SERVED US SEVERAL LARGE platters of what she called hand plates—though the phrase was far prettier in Serafan than translated. They were what we called appetizers in Galitha, what finer houses served guests before they were seated for dinner. Kristos explained that it was the fashion in the student district to make a meal of them, ordering plates and sharing them, passing them hand to hand. "Hence the name," he said.

"You speak enough Serafan to get by?" I asked, only half-surprised. He was always quick with languages.

"His Serafan is awful," Mairti said, handing me a weighty plate of thick pottery. "Those are—what is it in Galatine?"

"Tomatoes," Kristos supplied. "Mairti's Galatine vocabulary is nonexistent," he added.

"That's hardly true! When do I have to say *tomatoes* in Galatine?" She plucked one of the thumb-size orange tomatoes, their hollowed stem ends studded with herbs and what I guessed was some kind of cheese. "Don't let him have any," she teased me.

Penny sat between me and Kristos, uncharacteristically quiet, but she kept glancing at me and then back to Kristos.

She grappled, I was sure, with the same thorny barrier between us I did. Even Mairti's cheerful interruptions didn't loosen the tightly wound tension that pushed us apart by reminding us how we had once been drawn together. What could we say to one another that didn't dredge up all of the ugliness of our all-too-recent past? In the wake of the failed revolt, could we all believe that we had ever really known one another to begin with? I worked with Penny every day, but she had surprised me, choosing supporting the revolt over her livelihood. I was taken aback again to find her here, in a foreign country, following the uncertainty that was Kristos. She was braver than I was, in many ways, I conceded.

"Do you like red wine or white, Lady Sophie?" Mairti asked, the deep emerald wrap in her hair bringing out her startling green eyes.

"I'm not a lady," I corrected her.

"They haven't given you a title of some kind?" Penny asked. "I figured they'd add some string of impressive words to your name."

"No, I'm still just plain old Sophie." I stopped, remembering snide whispers at parties. "They're trying to kill me, remember?"

A shy smile broke through Penny's somber face. "Right."

"What have you been doing here in Isildi? I mean, to keep busy?" I asked.

"Keep busy? I'm up to my chin in work," Penny said. "I'm sewing."

"She's one of the most in-demand seamstresses in the university district," Kristos said with pride I had once wished he'd bestow on my work. "She hung out her shingle when she arrived that she sews 'in the Galatine style' and hasn't had a break since. Keeps the roof over our heads."

"And pays for wine and your expensive book habit," Penny

replied. That, at least, sounded familiar—Kristos chasing world-shattering knowledge while someone else paid the rent.

"It's not that impressive," Penny said, turning to me. "The Galatine thing—Galitha is kind of seen as the height of fashionable clothes, so being Galatine, well, I could turn out rags and they'd still buy them."

"Most of the delegates' wives are wearing Serafan clothing," I said. "Who's buying Galatine styles?"

"Plenty of women. I modify them, for the heat," Penny explained. "Lots of cotton, looser sleeves sometimes. But the higher-ranking scholars and the students with money like the tailored jackets and gowns. Some merchants' wives and shop owners are coming to me now, too."

"For official events, everyone wears Serafan styles," Kristos added. "But if you visited those delegates' wives at a ladies' luncheon, half of them would be showing off Galatine jackets."

"I'd rather not," I replied. "I've had enough of social events with delegates' wives, thank you."

"I thought you liked that kind of thing," Kristos said. "All that time spent with the Lady Viola—wasn't just for measurements, was it?" There was an old edge to his voice, familiar disapproval that surfaced and chided even though it didn't matter any longer.

"I liked Lady Viola, and her friends." I recalled Pauline's quick questions, Annette's kindness, Nia's intense curiosity, Marguerite's artistic talent. "You probably would have, too."

The snort and eye roll, so much like the ones that had responded to requests to clean our kitchen many times, should have angered me, but I felt a comfortable rapport returning. "These women at the summit? Most of them are a gaggle of—"

"Say no more," Alba interjected, holding up her hand. "There is a saying in Kvyset—words fly like birds and peck only the speaker's eyes."

"That's pleasant," Kristos said with a laugh. "You don't tell the truth in Kvyset if it isn't nice?"

Alba shrugged. "We find other ways to say what we mean. But most of the time, it needn't be said. Everyone already knows. To state the obvious, and the obvious being unflattering, is seen as mean-spirited. And so reflects on the speaker."

"The upshot is that Alba agrees and wants to say something mean but her Kvys nun vows won't let her," Kristos said to me.

"My vows say nothing about—that was a joke, wasn't it?" Alba said. She shook her head and poured herself another glass of wine.

"I'd love to see you work," I said to Penny, pulling the conversation away from Kvys social custom and back to my brother's life in Isildi.

"Normally I would suggest that posing as Penny's assistant would be a fine cover for a Galatine woman in Isildi. But given that it's well-known you're a seamstress, maybe stay away from needle and thread for a while."

I was about to retort that, without needle and thread, there wasn't much I was qualified to do when the curtain blew aside as though propelled by strong winds. Not winds, but Corvin entered, his gray robes dusty at the hem and rumpled.

"Please tell me you aren't drunk," he said to Kristos in greeting.

"Not yet, just enjoying this delightful company."

"Don't enjoy it too much," Corvin said. "Mairti tells me they threatened her with assassins."

"Only if I misbehave," I joked weakly. I fished out the letter from Merhaven, still stashed in my pocket, and handed it to him.

"We should probably start to figure out when we will get you back to Galitha—what's wrong?" Kristos's tone changed instantly as he read Corvin's face.

"You could have mentioned we're dealing with the *a'Mavha*."

"The what?" I had set my wineglass down as soon as Corvin arrived, but my fingers hadn't left its blown-glass bowl. I slowly uncurled them, sensing danger in the word even though I had never heard it.

"They aren't even real. Supposedly," Mairti said.

"They're real," Corvin replied. "Just ignored by the Serafan authorities because they find them useful too often." He turned to me. "Assassins. Professionals, for hire, highest bidder sort of thing. All underground."

"We already knew that Merhaven had a contract." I tested the new term, a'Mavha, not stopping to be surprised that I was suddenly living a life where knowing the Serafan word for *assassin* might be useful. "The a'maftha? It means *assassin*?"

"Your pronunciation is close," Corvin said, as though tutoring a student. "It's a'Mavha. The soft *v* in Serafan is difficult. And it's not *assassin*; it's the name of their operation. Technically the word means *salamander*."

"Salamander?" I tried not to laugh. "This deadly assassin guild is named after a cute little lizard?"

"They're not lizards; they're amphibians," Corvin said, unable to resist an explanation. "And the river salamanders of West Serafe can grow up to twelve feet long. They linger in the deepest parts of the riverbed, barely moving, until their prey comes close enough, then they strike like lightning. The a'Mavha are not dissimilar in their tactics."

"They sound absolutely disgusting," Penny said, recoiling.

"Which one?" I asked. "The river salamanders or the assassins?"

"Both," she said. "Ugh, I want to go back to Galitha. We don't have giant river lizards."

"Amphibians. Your mountains have silver-crested eagles that can take a man's head off, though," Corvin said. "I have nightmares about those."

"Not important right now," Kristos snapped. "The a'Mavha have a contract on my sister."

"Which we already knew," I protested again.

"We didn't know it was the a'Mavha," Kristos hissed. "You didn't think that was worth sharing?" he demanded, turning to Alba.

"Forgive me, but the letter—" She gestured to me, with an open hand, asking for the paper. I plucked it from Corvin and handed it to her. "The letter mentions the ports, assassins, waiting to get word from Merhaven—oh, yes, it does say a'Mavha." She set it down. "What? I didn't know what that meant. Forgive a single misstep in a complicated dance of delivering your sister alive."

"As long as they don't believe I'm attempting to return to Galitha, they aren't supposed to do anything."

Everyone's expressions convinced me quickly that I had underestimated the threat. "The a'Mavha will track you," Corvin said. "Ordinary hired thugs would just wait in the harbor for you to try to leave, but the a'Mavha are not ordinary hired thugs. They won't wait for you to try to leave before finding you, and once they find you . . ." He shook his head.

"And anyone in the way is in danger, too," Mairti said gently.

"We can't stay here," Kristos said, as though I had no say in the proceedings. I shot him a pointed look that he ignored. "The a'Mavha know about plenty of things, but I'm fairly sure they don't know much about the Warren."

41

I LET MAIRTI BUSTLE ME INTO HER ROOM AND DIG THROUGH
her trunk, searching for clothes that would fit me. "No offense,
but you stick out like—in Serafe we say 'a drunk's nose.'"

"Sore thumb," I whispered, shaken by all I'd just heard. I
was doubtful Mairti would find anything in her wardrobe to
fit me—Serafans tended to be petite compared to Pellians, but
Mairti was slighter and shorter than most. She produced a loose-
fitting shift in pale yellow and a belted green over-robe.

"It's not perfect," she said. "It will be too short, and I haven't
slippers to fit you. And it's the sort of thing no one would wear
out of the house unless she was ill and going to the apothecary."

"Then she can be ill and going to the apothecary," Alba said,
appearing in the doorway behind us. "Just get changed. Leave
the clothes here," she added.

"I'll try to get them back to you." Penny slipped inside after
Alba.

"No, make them over and sell them," I said. "I don't even
know where to tell you to send them." I laughed as though it
were a joke, but the uncertainty opened like a pit before me—I
didn't know where I was going tonight, or how I was going to
leave Isildi, or where I would find safe haven in Galitha. I felt ill,

and regretted having drunk any wine at all as I stepped behind the carved screen bisecting Mairti's room.

"It's a very pretty print," Penny said, picking up the sleeve of my gown with its ruched trim. "It suits you well. The clothes, your betrothal, your place beside the prince—it all suits you well," she added with a shy smile.

I returned it, and wished we had more time to talk about clothes and weddings and sewing—how Penny would have loved debating what color wedding gown I should make! But there wasn't time for that now. "Where are we going?"

"The Warren," Alba said with a wry smile. "I will not be accompanying you. It is not the sort of place considered proper for a sister of a Kvys order."

Mairti rolled her eyes, handing me the shift. It was of light-weight linen, and I blushed as I realized it was nearly transparent. "It's not proper for a princess, either, but we're sending her."

"I'm not a princess," I said, rote.

"It's a brothel," Alba said abruptly, holding up her hands as though absolving herself of the decision. "Prostitution is illegal in Serafe, but the Warren survives."

Before I could protest, Mairti explained, "It's ideal for hiding someone. It's not merely a—a brothel. It's a sort of traveling party. It moves, nearly every night. But the students always know where to find it—and Kristos is well connected, even if he's only been here a few months."

"Sounds about right for Kristos." I sighed.

"We've a friend there," Penny said. "Sianh. One of the men in the employ of the Warren." I tried to keep a disapproving frown from pulling at my mouth; surely I was in no position to judge the friends Penny and Kristos kept here.

"He and Kristos argue like a pair of drunk barristers, but he's a trustworthy man," Penny said.

"How can you be sure?" I asked. "Not that I don't trust you, it's just..."

"The stakes are rather high, I understand." Penny tugged at my sleeve and tied a loose drawstring. "When I first came here, I didn't know the neighborhood well. There are...some wine-shops it's better to stay away from when the fellows are deep in their cups. I didn't know, and went looking for Kristos in the wrong one. Sianh knocked the man's teeth loose before I'd thought to call for help."

"And then," said Mairti, "he walked home with her. That is something, in Serafe—to stand up for a woman and then to walk with her like an equal. Not expecting compensation."

I nodded. If Penny trusted him, so did I. "But surely the a'Mavha would know where to find it, too?"

"It's possible, but the Warren is very judicious in who they let in on the secret. High-ranking scholars and advanced students, mostly."

"I can't imagine the prostitutes are so judicious," I retorted.

"Of course they are—they don't want to be arrested," Kristos said from the other side of the door. "But more importantly, it's not the sort of place one can just stumble into. The Warren is usually in someone's private home, or gardens, or a hidden corner of the university. They'll be looking for you, likely, in slightly more traditional accommodations. Inns, the diplomatic compound, near the harbor. They won't think to look in a moveable coven of courtesans."

Mairti adjusted the belt on the over-robe, grimaced, and dug a length of yellow silk from the trunk. "I'll wrap your hair. I can't say you look nice. Or Serafan, if that's what we were aiming for."

"She wouldn't look Serafan even if we costumed her perfectly," Alba said. "But at least she won't be wearing Galatine finery. That's the first thing the a'Mavha would ask about, and the first thing someone would notice. This"—Alba shrugged—"this is a foreign woman wearing an unfortunate housedress."

"I'm sure it looks much better on Mairti," I added hastily, but Mairti merely snorted.

"Hardly. I bought it at a rag sale."

I finished adjusting my stockings, and then Alba allowed Kristos inside. "She's decent. Well"—she shrugged again—"she's clothed." I dipped my hand into my pocket, which I had kept on, with my shift, under the Serafan clothing. Corvin's kerchief, still wrapped in the paper, met my fingers. Guilt stabbed me—I should have given it to him while he was here, but I had forgotten. And, I admitted, I liked the additional luck it gave me. Luck that, perhaps, shielded me from the assassin, calm that perhaps reduced my anxiety and helped my judgment. I left the kerchief in my pocket. Alba sidled into the hallway as Kristos entered, and Mairti followed, leaving us alone in the cramped, low-ceilinged room.

Kristos took one look at me and laughed. "Far cry from what you made in your atelier," he explained. "It's kind of nice seeing you like this. Like when we were kids."

I had to smile. "When we wore castoffs that Mother tried to make over? I recall a particular orange coat you wore for years; it was half patchwork."

"I loved that thing," Kristos admitted. "It was probably hideous, wasn't it?"

"Absolutely," I said. It was so long ago, but I could see both of us as children, wearing oversize coats with breeches too short, gowns that gaped in the back and whose skirts had been let out as many times as they could. Now he was finally a scholar, and I, the crown prince's betrothed and, at a faded and hazy distance, an uncertain future queen. We had come so far, but the costs had been high, far higher than any cost we paid as poor Pellian ragamuffins scrounging the streets of Galitha City. They weren't diminishing, the costs of these new lives, I acknowledged. They were only mounting, the stakes rising higher and higher, and I wasn't sure how long I could keep playing. I sank onto Mairti's neatly made bed.

"A few things before we go," Kristos said, sitting next to me. "The Warren is not dangerous, not in and of itself. The patrons are respectful, because they know the madam is the law there, not the authorities. They won't bother you. The madam might put you to work—" He laughed as I jerked away in shock. "Washing dishes or doing some cleaning," he amended. "To further your cover. Sweet mercy, Sophie, I wouldn't whore out my own sister."

In an uncharacteristically compassionate gesture, he took my hand. "I wish we could stay here longer. I—I'm happy here. I wish you could meet my patron at the university, his wife, his children. She'd want to fatten you up like she's done me."

"It sounds as though they've adopted you," I said with a twinge of jealousy. My only family had left me and found another.

"It's customary for the student to be somewhat integrated into his sponsor's family. I just got lucky that Thain's wife is such an excellent cook." He smiled. "I'm learning so much, refining so much of what I thought I knew. Discovering that for all he knew, Pyord didn't have any sort of monopoly on political theory." He snorted.

I searched his face. "You discussed him here?"

"Not in so many words, no. I don't acknowledge the role I played at Midwinter and they don't ask. But Pyord—it's no mistake he settled at the Galatine university, as a lecturer, instead of pursuing tenure here. He's not exactly well-liked or respected.

He came here, briefly, years and years ago. Threw a fit that he'd have to begin as an apprentice-level scholar—not even a lowly novice—and when no one acknowledged his genius or acquiesced to his tantrums, he left."

"That's not the image he would have had us believe, is it?" I could almost laugh at arrogant, self-righteous Pyord, unacknowledged and unappreciated in the great Serafan university. But I didn't laugh; his rejection here had spurred him on to Galitha, and his unsated ambition turned to something else.

"No," Kristos said, "it's not. I fell for him, Sophie. I fell for his lines like a hooked fish because I...I was like him, in a way. I wanted more than Galitha as she stood could give me. I only hope it's not too late."

"And you were right all along." I sighed. "That those in power won't yield it without a fight."

"I don't relish being right. And I wasn't, not completely. Plenty of nobles yielded power, willingly. Your...friend Theodor, for one." I couldn't resist laughing as he awkwardly sidestepped calling Theodor by what we both knew he was—my betrothed, my future husband.

"Plenty yielded it grudgingly, too, and are all too willing to take it back."

"Yes, well, that I would have expected. I didn't expect a crown prince to fight for his own people. I believed we would be alone in any struggle to rise up. But we have allies." The creases between his brows deepened and knotted as he spoke. "That was your way, not my revolt and demands. Maybe...maybe I should have thought about the whole thing differently."

I shook my head. "When I have a length of fabric, I can cut it dozens of different ways. A large piece for a pleated back, narrow curves for a bodice, flared skirts of a jacket, panels for a petticoat—it's a dozen things at once. But put the scissors to the cloth, and it's one thing. We've cut the cloth, Kristos. Now we have to work with it as it stands."

"And we will. We will get back to Galitha, and soon, and make a stand."

I smiled faintly; the spark was coming back into Kristos's eyes, that fire fueled by philosophy and dogged belief.

"Any time you're ready," Alba said, fingers drumming the door frame.

"Patience is a virtue," Kristos replied, though he got to his feet quickly. "I thought nuns tried to exemplify all forms of virtue."

"Discernment is also a virtue," Alba replied, adjusting her coif as she led us down the hallway. "And when the a'Mavha is sniffing at your scent, patience ceases to be a virtue and becomes a liability."

42

THE WARREN WASN'T AT ALL WHAT I HAD EXPECTED. I HAD NOT
known, of course, what to expect at all, but my understanding
of houses of a similar nature in Galitha City led me to envision
smoke-filled rooms, grimy walls, and sparse, broken-down furniture in seldom-used common rooms. Kristos did his best to
disabuse me of my assumptions before we arrived.

"The Warren employs courtesans, not common whores,"
Kristos said, voice low as we moved as discreetly as possible up
a narrow, winding street. I felt as though every footfall echoed
tenfold on the stones, but no one glanced at us. "They consider
it a profession, not merely their day's pay."

"I'm not sure I see the difference," I replied, sidestepping a
pothole.

"There are games, music, food. The men and women entertain the guests, not just...you know," he said, reddening. "Not
just...service them." It didn't matter how old the two of us got,
or how clear it was that we were both well versed in physical
"service," Kristos would never be comfortable admitting as
much to me. "Some are apprentice-level scholars at the university, even. Their primary talent is engaging patrons in intelligent
conversation."

"Scholars hired to talk." I smirked. "Is *that* how you found the place?"

"I haven't been employed there, if that's what you're asking. But yes, I've enjoyed conversations over a cup of tea at the Warren. As a guest, for the social hours, not a patron of a particular courtesan."

"You're that well connected? Wanted at elite society parties?"

"My patron is quite well-known, yes. And I've been told I have a certain charm." I rolled my eyes, but Kristos persisted. "No, really. They collect acquaintances here like souvenir handkerchiefs. Scholars, foreign visitors, artists—people who make them feel like they're well versed, worldly. Conversation is a currency here, and one in which I'm fairly affluent." He paused, and added, "And that is a large part of the Warren's cover, making it look like an upscale party, and part is Serafan culture. Hospitality and conversation, first and foremost."

"So a nice cup of tea is like foreplay?"

"Sophie!" he hissed, ears on fire. "Is this how they teach princesses to speak in Galitha now?"

"New protocol," I replied with a cool smile. Mairti, who had until now watched our conversation play out with an amused smile, choked on a laugh, trying not to draw any attention to us. It was absurd, joking and laughing while we were, quite plausibly, stalked by assassins, but I was buoyed by a strange nervous optimism.

"At any rate. If you're seen in the common areas at all, just try not to react like..."

"Like a Galatine prude?"

Kristos grinned. "Or a Kvys nun."

We stopped at the crest of the hill, the city center behind us and a residential quarter opening up before us on a plateau. "This is it," Mairti said, gesturing toward a walled villa.

"It's...someone's house?" I stared in unabashed awe at the sprawling pale stone main house, the treetops that hinted at courtyards and gardens from behind the wall, the faint spray from a fountain escaping in the breeze. Not just a house, I acknowledged, but a fine villa.

"Tonight it is," Kristos replied. "Once it was in the catacombs underneath the oldest university buildings, and the amount of wine—of course, I was only there for the conversation," he added with a crooked grin. He caught my hand and squeezed it. "Good luck. I'll see you soon." He stayed behind, and I realized I was sad to see his silhouette fade into the shadows.

Mairti took my arm and steered me toward the alley that bordered the villa's wall. "People don't only come for the professionals," she said. "The Warren is also the best party in Isildi."

"Whose house is this?" I asked as we entered through a gate behind the house. A service entrance, most likely, I surmised by the lack of decoration and the kitchen smells wafting from an open door.

"A high-ranking scholar at the university," Mairti answered. I gaped at a residence that would have put Viola's townhouse in Galitha City to shame. "The elite scholars are well paid by the Serafan government as well as the university, so that they want to stay in Serafe. It makes the Ainirs happy, to know they hire the smartest people in the world." She motioned for me to wait. "Let me make the introductions."

She slipped inside, slim figure disappearing into what I could now clearly see was a bustling kitchen. I wavered between a twisted fig tree and an herb garden, unease reappearing as soon as I was alone. The breeze animated the branches of the tree, and I started at every shadow. I thought of nightmares I had woken from, terrified and gasping, as a child, the realness of the terror of those dreams following me into morning though I couldn't place what, in the dream, had forced me to feel so strongly. The threat was undefined and only the fear was real. I felt none of that terror now; the fear felt abstract, distant, as though it was happening to someone else. This was the deadly opposite of a nightmare, in which the danger was real but my fear bland and out of my grasp.

"All right," Mairti called. I followed her through the kitchen and into a small anteroom, clean and simply appointed. "This is the Mistress."

The woman who greeted me was taller than the average Serafan, and plump, with cheerful dimples. She wore her dark hair in a tidy bun, like a grandmother might, but her robes were the brilliant hues of a garden in bloom.

"You, my dear, are very lucky your brother has such an influential network. He's a charming goose," she clucked with a laugh, taking my hand, businesslike and maternal at once. "You look a fright."

She ushered me farther into the house, talking the entire time as Mairti trailed us. "I could set you up in the kitchen, washing dishes, but servants talk. They might already talk, but at least they've no idea yet that you're, well, unusual. Not local. You know." She gestured to an arched doorway. "I could also dress you up like a little doll and have you just sit in the front room, but that wouldn't do, either; you'd out yourself the moment someone tried to talk to you."

She followed me into what I realized was a makeshift dressing room. "My employees know better than to talk, but just the littlest serving of a strong tonic and lime and a few of the guests..." She shook her head. "So you'll be entertained by a particular employee of mine in the private dining room."

She handed me an intricately pleated and draped robe of the finest, lightest silk I'd ever handled, pink and diaphanous as a sunset cloud. I balked. "I don't think I can manage pretending to be one of your...guests."

"It's a cover, dear. He's in on the whole thing, don't fret. He's a friend of your brother's—Sianh." She rustled through a bag, producing a lightly boned Serafan corset and petticoat in sunset hues that matched the robe. "He wouldn't impress any services on you that you don't want," she said with a smile.

"But—" I protested as she laid the clothes out with dainty, precise movements. "I shouldn't be seen, really."

"You'll be seen regardless. This way you're seen by a lot of people who have no idea who you are." She paused, and added with a dimpled smile, "Think about it—it's far easier to go somewhere unquestioned if you walk out your door in broad daylight rather than if you crawl out of a window at midnight."

"I suppose that's true," I admitted.

"And this is the same. If I tried to hide you in the back, and you were found? Questions. If I put you right up front, no questions. A finely dressed woman conversing with one of my best— quite in keeping with the ordinary. And of course, no one asks what anyone else is doing here, because they have no interest in revealing what they are doing here themselves."

Her logic made sense. I picked up the corset, examining its deft construction. Aside from a pair of steel bones reinforcing the front and back lacing, it was stiffened with intricate cording, almost like embroidery, the soft orange silk crisscrossed with yellow stitching. It was meant to be seen, unlike Galatine corsets. I let the Mistress, whose name I neither knew nor asked, help me to dress in the evening clothes of an upper-class Serafan plantation owner or merchant's wife.

"This is the best plan we could manage," Mairti assured me. "Kristos will have the rest arranged soon."

"And Theodor?" I asked. We were supposed to leave, together, soon.

"We'll arrange it," Mairti said. I had to trust her; there was no other option save take to the streets myself and hope that the a'Mavha didn't find me before I found Theodor. I took a deep breath, then nodded my agreement. Worry built like the pressure of the corded corset against my ribs, but I sighed, shaky, and resolved that I only needed to get through one evening. Even that felt daunting, so I made a pact with myself: one hour at a time.

"Now, you ought to get back to your shop," the Mistress said to Mairti. "Go out the back. If anyone sees you, you're trying to sell me your wine."

Mairti grasped my hand in farewell and slipped back out through the kitchens. I was alone.

I took stock of the house as I followed the Mistress to the stage she had set for me. It was a sprawling villa, one story, with rooms branching off one another like tributaries of a stream, double doors and archways connecting separate rooms. The scholar who owned this house must have been very high-ranking, I thought as I spied marble statues, silk wall hangings, and thickly woven carpets strewn, haphazard, through the house.

In each, small groups and couples gathered on cushions dotting the floor, low settees, and couches. I couldn't tell who was the guest and who was the courtesan in most cases. In one room, a lively game of dice was orchestrated by a Serafan girl with a mischievous smirk; in another, an Equatorial man with pockmarks played an instrument not unlike a large mandolin.

"I had to find someone who spoke Galatine well enough," the Mistress said as she showed me my place for the evening, a quiet antechamber of one of the main rooms, partially hidden by a screen. "I hope you find him as charming as most of my clients do." She straightened, reciting my instructions in a manner not unlike a military leader assigning duties. "You will be served drinks, food if you like. You will converse, pleasantly, quietly. You will drink, but not too much. At the end of the evening, you will retire to the room appointed for you."

"And then?" I asked.

"I would highly encourage a nap," she said.

She left me alone, and I finally thought to take a deep breath, clearing my head. This was not so different, I considered, than the game I had played at Theodor's side as his betrothed—the game of pretending to fit in among nobles, to have a nice time while I fretted and worried over doing something uncouth or unusual, saying something that would give me away. The stakes were different; we'd changed the wager. But the way the cards were dealt, the order of play—these hadn't changed.

I sat, grateful that someone had already left a carafe of cold water and glasses on the table. The water tasted faintly of lime and mint, refreshing and bracing.

"Miss?"

We ought to have agreed upon an assumed name to use, I fretted as I turned to greet my companion for the evening. "Yes, I—good evening," I finally sputtered.

"And to you," a tall, lithe Serafan replied. He was exceptionally handsome, though I had expected that, given what I had seen thus far of the Warren. What I had not expected was the scar meandering from his temple to his chin, a white line tracing some old story across his clean-shaven cheek.

"I am..." I began to introduce myself but second-guessed my impulse. Did he know my name? Was he supposed to know my name?

"I have been made aware of certain...biographical details,"

he said with a faint laugh. The scar on his cheek creased when he smiled. "You may call me Sianh."

"Is that your name?" The question was bold, but I wanted to test this new territory, stamping my inquiry on it like a boot on uncertain ice.

My companion didn't crack. "It is my given first name, and what I am known as here. I wouldn't want to embarrass my parents with my clan designation. Can I send a server for something stronger than water to drink?"

I hesitated; I had no taste for strong drink and certainly wanted to keep my wits about me. However, the Mistress had suggested it, and as I caught glimpses of others at the Warren past our carved screen, I saw that most sipped from flutes sparkling with wine or etched glasses of clear liquor. Following the way my glance darted around the room, my companion laughed. "You will want me to have a bottle brought if you want to fit in. I would make a wine recommendation, but a Galatine like you must surely have a better appreciation for vintage than I do."

I managed a smile. "Something light," I said. "An early harvest Lienghine, if there is one."

"You do know your wine," Sianh said. I wasn't nearly as well versed as the nobles I knew, who would have requested a particular year and estate if given the opportunity. He waved to a white-uniformed servant and relayed the order in a soft voice.

"And now." He leveled his gaze at me, reminding me more of the intelligent, demanding eye contact of a business partner than the softness of a paramour. For that I was grateful. "We are supposed to converse pleasantly. What do you wish to speak of?"

"I'm not sure I can think of anything pleasant to talk about," I answered, my voice breaking slightly.

"Fair enough given your circumstances. But still. We must at least appear to be making conversation."

"Who is paying you to keep me company?" I asked bluntly, but with a delicate flick of my wrist and a coy smile that, to anyone out of earshot, transformed my impertinent question into a flirtation.

Sianh returned the charade with a lilting smirk. "I believe I was paid my usual fee by your brother." By Penny, then, and it probably wiped out their savings. "A most charming conversationalist, by the by. He and I have spent many evenings engaged in the great classic ethical debates. A Serafan pastime, you see." Our wine arrived, well chilled and resting in crushed ice. When the server retreated, Sianh continued, "And I've been promised a substantial bonus from the Galatine prince provided you take leave of my charge unharmed."

My breath skipped and I remembered to maintain a pleasant, neutral expression. "He knows where I am?"

"I doubt so. You see, he didn't personally agree to the terms. Your friend the Kvys made the assurance that he would be most grateful. And that if he was not, she would make up the difference from her own house's coffers."

I didn't know if Alba meant her personal assets or that of her religious order, but the thought was somewhat unsettling. What value did I have that she would leverage her finances for me? Still, I nodded as though I had expected this. There was no reason to trust Sianh, a courtesan hired with some silver who could doubtless be bought by someone else with more. He was a professional, carefully trained and practiced in the art of making men and women comfortable in his confidence.

Nonetheless, my next question startled him. "Where did you get that scar?"

Given the fashion in Serafe, he could have worn a beard, but he bore the mark openly. Even so, his hand flew to the ridged skin as though by instinct. He traced it near his chin, letting his hand fall into his lap as he replied, slowly, "I was in the army. Ten years' service."

"That hardly answers the question," I replied, this time with a genuine smile.

He shifted, lifting his wineglass and staring at the pale gold liquid for a long moment before downing half of it. "Ten years is a long time," he said. "Near half of my adult life. Yet I rarely have cause to discuss it." I waited. "The very first years of my service we were in the midst of the—I believe the Galatines term it the 'Oriole Uprising.'"

The name was familiar, but all I recalled of the conflict was something having to do with an island south of the Serafan mainland. "I confess that I am as educated as your average Galatine seamstress in the conflicts of foreign nations," I replied.

"Your honesty is refreshing," Sianh said. "Most pretend to know things they do not in order to impress even a whore. The Orioles—Bhani in Serafan—are a religious minority in most of Serafe, but not on the islands in the southern sea. They asserted that they ought to have their independence."

"And West Serafe was disinclined to give it?"

"To put it mildly. It was put down very quickly. It doesn't help their cause that the Orioles' convictions demand a nomadic existence nearly devoid of property. It is the way all the clans in Serafe used to live, but only the Bhani cling to it completely today, and it's very difficult to match a large nation's military without fortresses and cannon. They had excellent cavalry, though. Which brings me to this," he said, mirroring the curve of the scar with his little finger. "Bhani saber."

"I see," I said. "These Orioles—they are still there?"

"Of course." He refilled his wineglass. "And they pay their taxes and are included in the draft and have the protection of the Serafan Navy—citizens like they've always been."

"Their grievances were addressed? Or they've given them up?" I pressed my fingers into the mother-of-pearl inlaid in vines and flowers on the table. "You must understand, Galitha is in the midst of some unrest, and I cannot imagine the calm ten years might bring."

Sianh sighed. "The uprising was devastating to the Orioles, and their acceptance of defeat therefore necessary to their survival. But the situation—it was much different from yours. Their beliefs were driven by religious zealotry, and their defeat taken as the will of their gods. I cannot see the same patterns in the uprising of your people."

I didn't stop to dissect what he might mean by *your people*. Galatines, merely, or common Galatines, or reform-minded Galatines? Pellian-Galatines, even. I might be any or none of these to an outsider. "I suppose not." I hadn't touched my wine, but now I lifted the glass and inhaled the flower-and-herb scent Lienghine was known for.

"If we are being so bold as to inquire after personal histories, I must confess that I am intrigued by yours," Sianh said.

"There's not much to know," I replied honestly.

"No, nothing of import at all." Sianh laughed. "However did you manage to meet a prince? Do Galatine commoners frequent the same circles as nobles?"

"Not overmuch," I said. "Wealthy merchants, elite tradesmen— to some degree, they are acquainted with nobles. I was only acquainted with the nobility, and very minor nobility at that, professionally."

"You made them clothing," Sianh supplied.

"Yes. Until I met Lady Viola Snowmont, and she invited me to spend time in her salon..." I remembered those first visits, the beautifully appointed salon, the delicacies laid out on fine china, the foreboding hanging over the city. There was too much to explain, too much I couldn't translate into words. "Theodor also regularly visited her salon."

"And yet, at the same time, your brother was planning his death. You must see how it reads like the plot of an overdramatic opera." He paused. "The Serafans love their opera."

"Kristos..." I searched for words to excuse him, but of course there were none. Even if he didn't, initially, include Theodor's death in the mechanics of revolt, that potential eventuality was implicit all along. "Yes, it does sound like a ridiculous melodrama, doesn't it?"

"Yet the best operas are thus." He shrugged. "It is too bad you are not staying longer in Isildi. You might have gone to the opera house. It is beautiful, of course—the marble colonnade, the mosaics, the stage itself like a great, jeweled oyster revealing its pearl—but it all pales to nothing when the singers begin to tell their stories."

"I've never seen an opera," I said.

"I am not surprised—they are not often staged in your country. Galatines do not seem to care for them," Sianh said. "Nor the Fenians, nor the Pellians. I'm not sure if they truly like them in the Allied States, or if they are merely being polite."

"And the Kvys?"

Sianh laughed. "The Kvys—they don't like anything civilized, let alone the high arts like opera. A whole country of tundra-oafs."

From what I had seen, this was far from true—Pyord, for all his faults, was the furthest thing from an oaf I could imagine. Alba, too, was intelligent and quick. "I wonder what the Kvys say of the Serafans."

Sianh shrugged. "It's not my business what petty names rats have for the cats," he said. "Come, now. Your glass is nearly empty."

"And ought to stay that way," I replied.

"If you wish." Sianh sighed. "I know you have no reason to trust me or, truly, anyone else in this city." He hesitated, and added, "Even your brother. If what I know of that particular history is correct—if he wished, truly, the death of those you knew personally? Of friends?"

He didn't know the half of why my trust in my brother was cracked and broken like so much fragile glass. "He did truly wish that. But he did not know their relationship to me, not with any real understanding."

"Even so. I know him now—he is a remorseful man. We have a word in Serafan, for one who has seen and done much he now wishes to undo and cannot. It means, roughly, a river turning against its own current." Sianh met my eyes, demanding I do the same. "You needn't trust me, but know that he is fighting, always, the current of his own history."

I nodded, slowly, wanting very badly to believe him. "And should I trust you?"

"A trustworthy man need not be asked," he said ruefully. "Here, a man who has seen and done what I have in the service cannot be trusted. He knows violence and it is part of him now. Part of the undercurrent that guides his life. He cannot resist it forever."

"That cannot be true," I scoffed.

"It may not be true that it is part of a man. But it is very true that Serafans see it as such."

"Rather hard on all of you who give them protection and serve their interests, if you return and aren't trusted, isn't it?"

"Better to not return," Sianh replied with a wry smile. "But you ask if I can be trusted. I can't answer you. I am paid for an illusion of trust. Every day."

Sianh, for all his elegant speech, didn't strike me as a clever, conniving sort. It could all have been an act, but the hesitation in his fingers as they traced his scar, the long-established ache in his voice as he described the current of a man's history—I didn't think that these could be counterfeited.

The room was emptier than it had been when I had joined it. Couples and groups had retired to other rooms. The candles were burning low, and half the lamps had been extinguished.

"If you are tired, we need not sit up any longer," Sianh said gently.

I drank the last of my wine. "I am very tired."

43

When I woke I felt as though I had been asleep for days, but the morning had only begun to press against the windows, painting strips of light across the bed. I blinked sleep from my eyes, and I found Sianh, standing next to the door.

He shifted, and the early sunlight from the window glinted off something in his hand. A blade, thick and heavy. I stiffened.

The bedclothes rustled lightly, and Sianh turned. He pressed a hand to his mouth, and then slowly, clearly, pointed to the door. He was not threatening me.

Someone was outside.

I forced my breath as quiet as possible, training my ears to the sounds outside of the room. The soft creaks and sighs of the breeze rearranging the branches of trees in the garden, a night bird of some sort speaking a low, mournful language to its partner. And then, as distinct as the report of a cannon in the silent house, a footfall in the corridor.

I suppressed a shake. It could be anything, a patron of the Warren in search of some necessity or pleasure, a courtesan on official business for the Mistress. Sianh was merely taking precautions. Perhaps something of the military did flow through him, prompting action when others would roll over and go back to sleep.

The footsteps resumed, slow and methodical, and I heard a creak like a door opening. Someone searching, I thought, and the way Sianh poised himself beside the door's hinge, his hand confirming its purchase on the long knife in his hand, told me he discerned the same.

My door inched open. A shaft of brighter light pierced the room, sunrise's pink and gold. I didn't move. I didn't even make a sound, and neither did Sianh, but it was clear that whoever was searching had discovered what they were looking for. The door swung wide, and the figure in the fresh wash of light was tall, male, and armed with a slim blade.

Sianh was on him in a moment, the gentle curve of his knife pressed firmly into the throat of our intruder. I tumbled off the bed, and before my feet hit the floor I recognized the figure.

Sianh had already loosened his grip. "Idiot," he said, shoving my brother back and swiftly closing the door. Kristos still held his knife, and his hand rubbed his neck with his free hand.

"You actually tried to kill me," he said with half a grin.

"If I had actually tried, I would have killed you," Sianh answered, simmering anger.

Kristos didn't answer him. "It's morning, time to get out of here. Before the other patrons are up—we don't need you wandering the halls."

"You're wandering the halls," I muttered.

"I've arranged with the Mistress for you to remain with the Warren another evening," he replied. "I wasn't wandering the halls like some peeping pervert."

I smiled indulgently, which always infuriated him when we were younger. "Of course you weren't."

"You're exhausting." Kristos rolled his eyes. "I'd almost

forgotten that." He glanced at Sianh, who watched us both with detached amusement. "Time to leave. I can't go with you, so he'll take you," Kristos said, jerking a thumb at Sianh.

"Very well." I hesitated. "Are you—do you know if Theodor is all right?"

Kristos softened. "Haven't checked in at the compound. We're trying to lie low and avoid any suspicion. But I've heard nothing, so I'm sure he's fine."

I swallowed against the hollowness in my throat. "I wish you could come with me," I said impulsively. "No offense meant," I added to Sianh, "but a familiar face, his stupid jokes." I sighed. Even much of that familiarity was pale and hard to grasp, blurred by all that had happened between us.

The clothes I had worn the previous night were not conducive to slipping quietly through the streets, but Kristos just laughed as I picked up the sunset-hued petticoat. "The Mistress left this for you," he said, handing me a pale pink Serafan sulta, cut simply and decorated only with white embroidery along the collar. "It will do for a short surrey ride. Take the evening clothing with you, you'll need it tonight."

"I need to change," I said, pointedly.

"By all means," Kristos answered, showing himself and Sianh to the door with an exaggerated flourish. When I opened the door, Kristos was gone.

I dutifully followed Sianh through the maze of hallways to the service entrance. There was little activity here now, the servants having cleared the remnants of last night's party and one bored scullery maid left in charge of preparing a light midday meal for the house's owners. I was ravenous; I hadn't eaten since Mairti's stuffed tomatoes the day before, but I didn't dare interrupt Sianh's purposeful stride.

"It is not impossible we could be followed. I will see to

protection. And it's highly unusual for a patron to . . . accompany her hire after the evening has ended. But the Mistress will see to discretion."

"How much did my brother pay her to help me?" I said, the question coarser than I had intended.

"I don't know, but it must be a goodly sum." The surrey was waiting outside the gate. "Or perhaps she took no payment at all. As I said, it's like an opera. The Mistress likes the romance and intrigue of the stage; you would surely see it in the Warren if you knew your operas. It is sometimes, for people like her, worth a bit of risk and inconvenience to feel themselves a part of the stage, the story, a thing bigger than themselves."

"And for you?"

He stiffened. "I have been too much a part of the theater of the world's operas already. I've been promised a payment, and I've my orders."

The horses trotted merrily through the upper-class Serafan neighborhood, past villas and walled gardens, and though the sun brightened the cleanly manicured vistas to brilliant hues, I couldn't throw off shadows.

We descended from the hills and into the city's gridded streets, and came to a stop in a quarter I recognized—the university. The back of the great library stood in front of us, its sandstone edifice nearly glowing in the height of the sunlight. "Inside," Sianh said, offering me a perfunctory hand. "We are to entertain our guests this evening in the music archive. The curator is a particularly good client."

Beneath broad rooms hosting lines of shelves like the ones I had used alongside Corvin were archives, repositories for even more books and scrolls and, in this case, reams and reams of sheet music. It was after midday already, and space had been cleared in the long, narrow room for tables and chairs and a low platform where a Serafan harp stood ready. Cold rushed to my stomach; could there be a casting planned? Could this be a trap? Sianh ushered me from the main room to an antechamber stacked high with thick-bound books; I couldn't read a single one, as they were all Kvys liturgical music.

I changed into the evening clothes Sianh had given me, and had resigned myself for a very long, very dull wait when Corvin appeared in the doorway. "I thought you might appreciate some company," he said. "And some flatbread."

I accepted the food eagerly. "I certainly won't be doing any reading," I replied.

"Even if you could read Kvys, it would still be dull. 'O magnanimous Creator, the world is the will of your pinky finger.'" He flicked one of the texts with a satisfying thunk. "Very repetitive. But, I will allow, the polyphony of the sung versions is quite beautiful."

I cracked a smile. "I can't imagine Pellian charm-casting theory is any more exciting, but you were keen to read enough of it for me."

"I've already admitted I was planted," Corvin said, holding up his hands. "And yes, Pellian casting is more exciting than 'Bountiful Loins of the Creator.'"

"That is not a real song," I laughed between bites.

"Ask Alba." He hesitated. "Tell me, did you find what you were looking for? In the research we did? I sensed it might be more than mere curiosity."

"I did," I said, measured. How much to admit, and to whom? It was a game I was growing weary of playing. "I came in with questions about my own casting. It had grown...blurred. I understand now what happened," I said, clipped, unwilling to examine grief with a man who was still too close to a stranger. "And my second set of inquiries . . . I admit those were of a more pressing nature."

"Serafan casting," Corvin guessed. "You believe it's real?"

I nodded. He waited. I didn't reveal anything beyond that. He drummed his fingers on the book next to him. "I wonder . . ." He paused. "I always was given to understand that the Pellians weren't invited to the summit solely because it is intended for the largest countries, but even Fen has sent unofficial delegates." He breathed through his nose. "Too many charm casters. They must have tried very hard to keep you away from the truth."

I didn't want to tell him too much; if knowing about the casting had been enough to warrant killing me, I didn't want to drag anyone else down alongside me. "It seems that the interests of the Serafans and those of the Galatine nobility align."

Voices and the constant hum of activity from the main archive room had increased as we'd talked. Sianh returned for me. "It would be best if the other guests did not see you arrive from a dusty book bin. Please, join me."

"Wait," I said. I dug into my pocket, the large bag still holding my personal effects despite multiple wardrobe changes. Including Corvin's kerchief. "This is yours," I said.

"It should bring luck?" he asked.

"Yes," I replied. "Luck, calm, success in your studies."

"If it offers luck, perhaps you should keep it," he said.

"No," I replied. "I made it for you, and it is yours. Thank you," I added, hoping he knew I meant to thank him for the many hours with the Pellian books as well as his help more recently. He bowed slightly and left.

Sianh had reserved a table for us, half-hidden by one of the arches that ran from floor to high, peaked ceiling. We didn't speak much, instead watching the arrival of other guests joining courtesans at tables and in knots of chairs. I watched with curiosity, drinking in the riot of color and personality as Serafan scholars and patrons flooded the dim archive with silk robes and laughter and conversation. Oil lamps bobbed and blazed above us, and candles floated in shallow dishes on each table. I glanced at Sianh. He wasn't watching with idle curiosity, but intense calculation. He would see to protection, he had said, and he took his charge faithfully.

Courtesans greeted the guests who arrived, ushering them to seats already prepared for them. Riotous laughter and loud greetings gave way to quieter conversation and flirtations around the room. Courtesans passed bottles of wine, filling glasses and raising them in quiet toasts with their patrons.

A woman took the stage and, without an announcement or introduction, began to sing. I swallowed—could this be a Serafan trick of casting? I let that concern fall quickly; no threads of gold or dark appeared around her, and I found myself, instead, in awe of the music itself. I wasn't sure that I liked it, precisely; the sound filled the space and echoed from the arches, but I couldn't understand the words, and the pitch and flow of dynamics seemed to matter more than the delicate melodies of Galatine ballads and chamber music. I could tell that the song was rife with emotional resonance, however, a piece about love and loss and, perhaps, grief.

"This is Serafan opera," Sianh whispered as the singer's voice crescendoed into the ceiling. "A famous aria from *The Goldenberry Tree*." The other patrons seemed well aware of this, anticipating the trickle and fall of the melody before it shot into soaring high notes. She concluded the piece to polite applause, and began another selection, this time more lighthearted. Something comedic, I guessed, confirmed with the laughter of the patrons at certain rhymes and intonations.

Everyone was so intent on the vocalist that few noticed the Equatorial woman sweep into the room in a long mantelet of dusky charcoal silk, but I did. She threw the drab cloak to an attendant, revealing an open robe of scarlet silk, and sailed toward me. Dira.

She settled at our table, draping her arms languidly over the back of her chair and greeting Sianh with a minute nod. No one turned to us or noticed as she spoke, in low tones, to me. "You've left quite a mess back at the summit."

"I couldn't precisely help it," I replied crisply.

"Not you, in all fairness. But the Galatine delegation was like the proverbial cat trapped in the china cupboard." She glanced at Sianh, assessing his presence, and then continued. "Word reached the rest of the summit about what you've known about for some time—open civil war in Galitha?"

"We weren't aware one could call it open," I hedged.

Dira's smile was cold. "In any case. Shall we say that the situation has deteriorated to an untenable point? Merhaven left, your crown prince has spent the remaining hours of yesterday and today in answering a hundred questions about the decline of Galitha, so the summit is, in effect, hung. To our advantage, at least—the Open Seas Arrangement was not finalized—and it was turning toward West Serafan interests, not ours."

The singer had finished the piece and retired from stage; the quiet hum of conversation around us masked our discussion well enough, but I felt exposed, a hunted deer caught in the open. "Then the summit is concluded and a war is begun."

Dira nodded. "And you should know that Merhaven and Ainir Rhuina have come to certain agreements about an alliance between West Serafe and the nobles on one side of your conflict."

"Alliance?" I felt cold, seeing again Lady Merhaven and Ainira Rhuina assessing me, dismissive and aloof. It hadn't merely been the frosty reception of an outsider, but of allied factions facing their enemy.

"West Serafan martial support for those you and your prince oppose in your civil war."

My civil war. I nodded. Perhaps martial support inclusive, I grew curious as I thought about it, of some form of Serafan casting. Invisible, influential, and clandestine. "That can't have been an official item on the summit agenda."

"Much that is discussed is never on any agenda." Dira leaned forward. "Economics dictates the interests of the Allied States. We are not large. Our resources are not unlimited. But there is power in retaining some control over import and export and trade routes." She narrowed her eyes. "Do you understand?"

"The Open Seas Arrangement."

"Your Galatine chaos was to our benefit. I came here to protect the interests of Equatorial trade against West Serafan machinations, on behalf of my country and of my family. Nia's family," she added.

I inhaled without meaning to, sharp and painful.

"I have my assumptions about her death. That it was not happenstance. She wrote to me of the unrest in the city, of helping a charm caster of whom she was quite fond, and of her tutor. She did not name him, or you, but how many charm-casting seamstresses, and how many Kvys scholars of Pellian are there?"

"Then you know who Pyord was. In the revolt."

"I do. I know she must have discovered something about his workings that he didn't want known. And I know who you were in the revolt." Her eyes were inescapable—had she discovered my part in the plot? Did she blame me for it? She could easily lure me to my own not-quite-happenstance death if she so chose. "You helped stop him from achieving his aims. So I owed you some debt."

Tears spiked behind my eyes. "You owe me nothing." I couldn't admit to my part in Nia's death, as much as the remorse bit into me, carving away the edges of my resolve.

"Whether I do or do not, I consider it paid. And this disorder, your Galatine war dividing the loyalties of the nations at the summit, it benefited my own mission here, so. Do not feel overly sentimental over it. He knows where you are," Dira added casually, snatching a crystal tumbler of something dosed liberally with mint and lemon rind. "Theodor."

I exhaled the breath I hadn't realized I was holding. "He's here?"

"Not here," Dira said, breaking into a terse smile. "He's still at the compound. You may be a wanted woman, but even the highest Ainirs wouldn't dare threaten the crown prince of Galitha. No, but he knows you're here, and that you're safe, and you're to leave together. Tonight."

44

DIRA LED US OUT OF THE ARCHIVE. "DO NOT CONCERN YOURSELF," she said. "This, too, was planned well—the library lacks the proper...facilities for what many patrons partake of at the Warren, so they will be scattering to finer inns and bathhouses with their hirelings." She glanced at Sianh. "Am I not correct?"

"Quite right," he said, clipped. He kept a hand on his hip as we walked down the wide avenue in front of the library—over a hidden knife, I knew.

"And here is your transportation," Dira said. "Mine is waiting elsewhere." She nodded to me, a slight but deliberate gesture of farewell, the most I was going to get from her.

Kristos waited with a hired surrey. "Against my better judgment," Kristos said as we settled next to him, out of earshot of the driver, "I had Dira tell him where to meet us. I figured you would need to see him. Would insist on it. I didn't feel like picking you up kicking and screaming the way Mother did that one time at the fruit seller's."

"Honestly, you're bringing that up now?" I shook my head.

"Seemed appropriate." Kristos shrugged. "Now. Silence is better until we reach our destination. Streets have ears."

We had approached the outskirts of the city by now, and the

first faint gray light of morning was shading the horizon. Kristos led us to a low building—a stables, I saw, or, rather, smelled. The honest scent of horses and leather and manure was oddly reassuring in its familiarity.

And inside, between a few stalls and sitting on a disintegrating bale of hay, Theodor waited for me.

"Sophie!" He caught me in his arms. Kristos and Sianh both turned away, whether embarrassed or honoring some intuited need for privacy, I couldn't say. "I was so worried—I can't even begin to explain."

I nodded, my face pressed into his coat. My cheek was damp with sweat and the fine wool fibers stuck to it. "I didn't want to leave you."

"I know." He stroked my hair, an increasingly tangled mess of dark curls under the Serafan wrap. "We're together now. I won't leave your side."

"But what now?"

"What we already intended. We return to Galitha. Somehow. Merhaven—that bastard left us stranded here. The *Gyrfalcon* left port, most likely with my brother along under some well-placed lies, and he's not one to disobey orders without good reason." Theodor began to plan, out loud, fairly ignoring Kristos and Sianh as though they were of no more import than the horses. "We'll return to Galitha by sea, to Galitha City, and shore up our support."

Kristos held up his hand. "Hold on, Niko has been fighting in the city already."

"Niko! Niko Otni?" Theodor started.

"One and the same," Kristos said with a lopsided grin. "He's kept the home fires burning, so to speak, so that if anything went awry with your attempt at peaceful reform, the people would be ready again, and quickly."

"How long have you been laying your plans?" Theodor snapped.

"Clearly it was a wise choice," Kristos returned fire.

"Enough," I said. "Niko did what he could to keep the people mollified, waiting on reform. He didn't undermine us. Right?" I said with a pointed look at my brother.

"Precisely correct. He didn't believe reform could happen, but he waited to try it your way. He doesn't want bloodshed; he just recognizes it's inevitable at this point," Kristos said.

"Not all of the nobles will be against us," Theodor mused, pacing between stalls as the horses chewed their alfalfa. "I'm not sure how much of the army we can count on, but surely not all of them will remain loyal to their noble officers. And if we can organize the common people who are willing to fight, we'll have a large force to work with."

"You're forgetting one piece on the board, perhaps the most important one. The king." Kristos faced Theodor with crossed arms. "Is he for us or against us?"

The question cut through Theodor's pacing. He sank onto a hay bale next to me, his hands falling into his lap, useless and weary. "He's against us."

"And you'll stand against him?" Kristos raised an eyebrow. "Forgive me, but I want it in no uncertain terms that noble blood doesn't run so thick that it will choke our efforts."

"Don't be a prick, Kristos," I said, sitting next to Theodor and pulling his hand into mine.

"I'm not. The king's position changes what we can do. We can't count on the full army—though mutiny is a very real thing and we can use it to our advantage. Even some of the common people will be reticent to stand against a king—squabbling nobles are one thing, but a king?" He held his hands open as though letting some heavy weight drop.

"But it doesn't change what we should do," Theodor countered. "We return to Galitha. My father surrounds himself with nobles he's familiar with. He's been convinced that the shortest route to resolve this is to cater to the noble majority. He would believe it is the right thing to do, and the only thing for a new king with little authority save what is in the title itself to do. He would do it for the right reasons, not because he doesn't care about his people. Perhaps I can convince him otherwise."

"You'll end open sedition by the nobility with a chat over tea?" Kristos snorted.

"What am I supposed to do?" Theodor returned. "The nobility are not all a passel of fools like Pommerly and Crestmont." Theodor slammed his hand against the nearest wall. A horse stared at him reproachfully. "Undoing our work as soon as I was gone."

"Planning—so it's not mere stubbornness but most assuredly sedition, then," Kristos clarified with a snide grin.

"We're on the same side," Theodor growled. "I know full well that they're seditious, that they're pissing on our laws. We'll rein them in, we'll—"

"It's too late for that," I said. Both my brother and my betrothed looked at me, surprised, as though they had forgotten I was there. "Theodor, all you've thought of is how the nobility is reacting, what is the king going to do—and isn't that precisely the problem all along? The common people's stake is barely discussed. But we know that they will fight now. More than the riot during the debates. More than at Midwinter. Something was lawfully given and is being taken away. They're already fighting."

"I know." Theodor's hands shook in mine. "And they have justice on their side."

"Indeed," Kristos said. "And when your father refuses to curtail them, refuses to uphold the laws of his own damn country? He's had ample chance already."

Theodor straightened. "Well, that's the answer, isn't it? If the king refuses to yield to the law, I must stand against the king."

45

THE STABLE FLOOR SEEMED TO TILT, AND THE COLORS BLED INTO one another, and even the sounds of horses shifting their weight and chewing their breakfasts sounded as loud and clear as Theodor's voice next to my ear. "You realize what you've just said?" I whispered.

"I do."

I barely breathed the question. "You'd face your father across the battlefield?"

"I'd sooner face my father than butcher my countrymen for demanding justice under their own laws. Yes."

"And can anyone give me any reason we need a noble on our side?" Kristos asked. The pragmatism was coarse and needle-sharp.

And warranted an answer. "Perhaps not, but if he's not the face of your efforts, who is?" I asked.

Kristos's ears grew red. "I think Niko and I can have that covered quite well," he said. "We did before."

"You did along with Jack. How much Galatine propaganda have you been reading?" He sputtered, and I continued. "It's rich stuff. Along with me being an interloping witch, and Theodor being a cuckold weakling, you should be aware that the entire revolution is a hostile Pellian takeover."

"That's nonsense!"

"But people believe it," I retorted quietly. I let that sit for a moment, the ugly reality of people's malleable fears and prejudices. "If the leadership is just you and Niko, there are Galatines—maybe quite a few—who may reject the movement. The people already consider Theodor the champion of reform. They'll accept him as a leader quite naturally, I think."

"I would never," Theodor said, "presume to take sole control of the leadership. You and Niko are at the heart of this whole endeavor."

Kristos snorted. "That goes without saying. Concessions like that aren't yours to give," he said.

"Fair enough."

"Then we go back to Galitha as brothers in arms, you and I."

Throughout the exchange, Sianh had remained silent, watching. "And how will you reach Galitha, without the a'Mavha reaching Sophie first?" he finally said.

"You're released from your contract now that she's under my protection," Kristos answered.

"That's not what I asked. Unless she is expendable to one or both of you?"

Kristos bristled, fully aware of the insult, but didn't counter it. Theodor considered the problem. "We can't sail out of Isildi. We know that the docks are watched. But despite that, we have to reach Galitha soon, to raise the army that will hold the rest of the country. Galitha City may be secure, but it can't stand alone. We need to move."

"It may be of use to know that the a'Mavha are not strong outside Isildi," Sianh added. "Their network is here, their numbers are here. Leave the city, sail from another port—it's not only less likely they would guess at your movements, but they are less able to counter you."

"Wait," I said. "Where is this?" I fished Annette's note from my pocket, still carefully folded and intact despite having changed clothes so many times. At least, in the rush of the past two days, I hadn't left my prettily embroidered pocket with my other clothes.

Kristos squinted at the names, but Sianh took one glance and nodded. "It's just outside Port Triumph, in the grove country. Estates, citrus plantations, sugar fields." He gave me half a smile. "I've told you where, now you can tell us what it is."

"A villa," I hedged, knowing Kristos was not likely to trust nobility at the moment. "It belongs to a friend. I would suggest making it our first destination," I added boldly.

"It makes sense. You'll be close to Port Triumph and we can likely secure passage there," Sianh confirmed. "In any case, it's a wise direction to take out of the city. Countryside, few people to ask questions."

"Wait," Kristos said. "You're talking as though you're coming with us. You've been paid, and your bonus will arrive soon."

"I have very little guarantee of that," Sianh countered. "And you clearly have use of my services."

"We won't," Kristos insisted.

"Kristos," I said softly. "I think...I mean...perhaps we could."

He turned to me, surprise lifting his brows. "Really?"

"He had you under the knife before you could even get both boots in the room. That seems like a useful skill to have on our side, doesn't it? Especially if the a'Mavha are still contracted to prevent us from leaving?"

Kristos hesitated. "I didn't budget for a sellsword," he finally replied.

"I have the coffers of the Prince of Westland at my disposal," I said, faintly imperious and actually enjoying the power that a bit of money granted me. Then I blanched, disgusted with myself for falling so easily into the same snare in which the nobles had tangled and knotted the country. I turned to Sianh. "We can negotiate your rate later, I presume?"

"You make quite the effective princess," he said in reply. "But I have something in mind more substantial than merely escorting you out of the country. I would propose you hire me on a longer-term contract."

Theodor held up a hand. "What do we have going for us that makes you want to join in? We're walking into a war."

"Precisely." His smile was cordial, as though we were entering into negotiations over a bottle of cherry brandy instead of his role in the Galatine Civil War. "And I've on good authority that you are unsure of your...military situation. Yes?"

"Fair enough, we've covered that," Kristos barked.

"And who will fight your war if the professional soldiers are under the thumb of the nobles?" He lifted a single finger. "And make no mistake, they will be. The nobility has the money, I imagine. And soldiers like to be paid. Don't count on that ceasing to matter. Some will desert, perhaps, a few might mutiny. Still. I pose the question: Who do you expect to fight this war?"

"The common people who stand to lose the most," Kristos said. "We did it once."

"You failed once," Sianh countered, earning a glare from Kristos. "Yes, there were other issues at hand, but can you deny that, as soon as the soldiers in Galitha City responded, the revolt was put down quite quickly? What makes you think a large-scale war would be any different?"

"It has to be!" he shouted at the same time Theodor slammed his hand against the nearest post and cursed.

"It can be," Sianh interrupted before Kristos or Theodor could launch into a tirade. "If you are correct in the scope of the resistance to the nobles, you have bought some time. Even the force of the Galatine army cannot put down every rebellion in every corner of Galitha at once."

Kristos nodded. "And to the best of our knowledge, they put much of their focus on Galitha City. And are held at bay."

"Good. Then you need an army to fight for and hold the rest of the country. Not a rabble of peasants with pitchforks. The Galatine army will know how to fight properly—tactics, musket drill, field formation. You need an army that won't run at the first sight of a bayonet charge."

"And where do we find an army?" Theodor asked. "Our alliances with our neighbors are a bit strained at the moment."

"I can make an army for you," Sianh said. "From your common people. I can turn them from farmers and dockworkers into an army. I was an officer, fairly high ranking. It's true, I have been...underemployed in recent years. But I know what you need and how to deliver it."

"For a price?" I said.

"For a price. All things considered, a low one. Pay equal to your highest-ranking officer, a commission in your army, a pension when it's over."

"And a spot on the gallows alongside us if we fail," Kristos countered.

"Understood," Sianh replied.

"Why would you risk that?"

"Great gain involves great risk. If I stay here, I have no prospects beyond my employment now. Someday I will grow too old for that, and then what?" The haunted shadow behind his eyes told me what that meant to him—not only financial hardship but uselessness, the promise of life as a spent man, wrung out and discarded. I met Theodor's eyes and nodded.

Theodor understood my approval and didn't question it

further. "That can all be arranged. And if we prevail," he said, "a pension won't be hard to manage. But if we don't—"

"If we don't, I have failed you." Sianh straightened his shoulders. "Do we have a deal? I'll accompany you back to Galitha, continuing to provide what protection I can along the journey. Once there, I will turn your people into an army."

"You have a deal," Theodor said.

Kristos grudgingly offered his hand as well. "Then let's get going."

46

<hr/>

IT TOOK LITTLE TO OUTFIT SIANH TO ACCOMPANY US. I WAS surprised to discover, as I took stock of the pack and the second-hand gray Serafan riding habit Kristos handed me, that Alba was joining us, as well. "The delegates are all leaving early, given the situation in Galitha. It seems my work continues past the summit."

"Accompanying the disgraced former consort of the prince seems an odd responsibility," I pressed. I had never been sure of Alba's motivations, nor of her connection to my brother.

"It is odd, isn't it? That a prince's consort could become so important to the fates of nations. Ah, well." She smiled, maddeningly complacent, and turned her attention to her stirrups.

"If your friends in Port Triumph can't assist us in securing passage," Kristos said to me, with uncomfortable emphasis on *your friends* as though already blaming me for their predicted failure, "we'll need to consider other options."

"I had wondered if we'd have better luck in East Serafe," Alba said. "And of course, jumping into Galitha blind may not be the wisest option."

Kristos nodded. "We could consider waiting for news. Or stopping over in Pellia, or even heading for southern Kvyset."

"No one said anything about not simply returning to Galitha,"

I said. "And as much as I appreciate the assistance, I have to be clear—I'm not going to Pellia or Kvyset or anywhere else. I'm going to Galitha."

Theodor stood beside me. "Same here. And I can't imagine Sianh would appreciate delays in training up an army. Sounds a daunting task already."

"I don't want to delay, either. But getting news from Galitha isn't exactly easy at the moment." Kristos wrestled with his pack as though it could absorb his frustrations. He nicked his finger on the buckle of his pack and thrust it into his mouth. "You could try accepting that, in this particular instance, I've a bit more experience," he mumbled around the wounded finger.

"Being forced into exile? Yes, I'm less than experienced."

"None of this need be decided now," Sianh interjected. We both snapped to attention, having, clearly, forgotten that our spat had an audience. "The thing now is to leave Isildi. Yes?"

"Agreed," muttered Alba.

I held up my hands in surrender. "Sianh is right. We have days, at least, before we need to decide anything, yes?"

"Fine. Truce," Kristos agreed, grudgingly. "But you'll promise to be reasonable." He turned back to his horse, absorbed in studying the straps and buckles on the saddle.

I burst out laughing. "You're going to demand reasonable behavior? From me? And this coming from you? After last winter?"

His back stiffened and he whirled on me. "Yes, even after that. How many ways can I apologize? I was mistaken in the details of that particular endeavor—"

"The details?"

"Yes! Who I trusted, what specific steps we took—"

"The entire mess, then? Who was involved, what you did? The entire spectacular failure of your armed revolt?" I lowered my voice. "You almost ruined me in more ways than one. You don't get to tell me to be reasonable."

"I could leave you here." He threw his hands up. "I don't have to risk my neck for you. Neither does she, or him." He jerked a thumb at Alba and Sianh, both waiting a respectful distance from us, pretending they didn't hear. "I won't speak for your besotted prince." Theodor began to argue, but I silenced him with one look. This was between me and my brother.

"No, you don't have to risk anything for me. You don't owe me anything." I felt tears spring hot and fierce into my eyes. "You made that perfectly clear last winter."

"I made mistakes!" he shouted. "You can't let me try to atone for those now? Try to make it up, at least, to you?"

I stopped the quick retort that burned to be set free—there was no making up what he had caused in Galitha City, to me or anyone else. No making up the wasted life or the broken trust. But the tears threatening to fall freely told me I still cared enough for my brother that I didn't want to wound him, even with the truth.

"We should leave. It's almost broad daylight," I said instead.

We passed easily out of the city gates and onto a broad highway like the one Theodor and I had taken to the shore. It felt like months had passed since I had dipped my bare toes in the cerulean surf. We rode single file, with Sianh taking the lead early and confidently, our self-appointed guide. Kristos took the rear, pacing himself far enough back that conversation was impossible.

None of us voiced the fear that stalked us, that the a'Mavha had already tracked us and would strike as we left the city. I hoped that, if it came to it, retaining Sianh would prove a wise investment. Theodor was no great swordsman, and though my brother had gotten into fisticuffs a fair number of times in taverns, he wasn't a skilled fighter.

My riding lessons with Theodor had prepared me well enough to know how to mount and direct and maintain my balance on the horse. I didn't anticipate our travels requiring more skill than I had—none of the jumps or caracole that festooned experienced nobles' riding. By midmorning, however, the saddle was wearing on me as much as the silence. I'd taken my share of spills in the training yard and on the park trail with Theodor, but I hadn't considered that the mere act of riding could induce such misery. By the time we broke at midday, I had made the acquaintance of several muscles I didn't know I had, let alone that they could scream at me in protest of the abuse I was inflicting on them.

"It gets better," Sianh said, suppressing a laugh at my stiff dismount.

"I have a feeling it's one of those things that gets worse before it gets better," I replied.

"I won't contradict you." He glanced at Kristos and Alba, who conferred over a map. "If it's any consolation, your brother's seat is worse than yours."

"That helps, actually." Kristos shifted uncomfortably, and I laughed. "Though I doubt he has the benefit of lessons. I shouldn't admit I've ever been on a horse before, I imagine."

"There's a great difference between learning to trot around an arena and spending days on the road." There was some faint condescension in the comment, but I wasn't offended at the truth. He nodded toward Alba. "What I want to know is why the Kvys nun is so experienced in the saddle."

I had no idea, either, but she seemed to match Sianh's endurance, and I noticed as we remounted her energetic grace in the movements that felt awkward to me. She and Kristos rode next to one another as we continued into the afternoon, and Sianh reined his horse beside mine as Theodor took the rear.

"I served in the light horse," he said, unprompted. "Elite troops, I suppose, compared to the infantry, but certainly no easier. In Galitha, your cavalry has pages, grooms to care for the horses. Not so in Serafe—we care for our own horses. Like children." He laughed. "It's believed in Serafe that the bond between horse and man, if strong enough, makes both better fighters."

"And does it?" I asked, cautious, not sure what memories I might be scraping against.

"As much as the bond between men makes them fight for one another, yes." He scratched his horse's mane absently. "This is the first I've ridden a horse that wasn't mine in many years. She's a dull thing compared to my old comrade."

I considered my own mount, a dappled gray mare. I had thought she'd a sullen sort of face and seemed slow and resistant to my commands but had dismissed the thought as foolish. Horses, I figured, couldn't have personalities. They were beasts of burden, creatures good for drawing wagons and working ferries. "I've never been around animals much," I confessed, hesitantly scratching the roots of my horse's mane in the same way Sianh did.

"City living," he said with a dismissive snort. "I despise it. I'll take the honest smell of horseshit over the stench of sewers any day. And horses, for all their faults, don't lie or cheat. People—people are another matter entirely."

"You seem to be in an odd line of work for someone who dislikes people," I said with a laugh that quickly faded at the fatigue in his face.

"Yes, I am." He stopped himself. "I *was*. Making a living off of people's lonely desires and corrupted needs is no way to live."

"I've always made my living off of people," I said. "Off of their needs, their wants."

"There is no comparison there," he said. "You're gifted with a rare talent. It would be abhorrent to waste it."

I didn't answer. That rare talent had caused more heartache than good in the past months, and I was only beginning to regain any control of it. Corvin's kerchief was the first thing in ages I hadn't struggled with, though I expected that facing my grief over my brother would allow my casting to continue to improve. I was still grappling with that loss, the loss of our family and our life together even if I had, at least temporarily, regained him. In any case, what was I now—a seamstress without a shop, a charm caster without clients? I confronted again the exhaustion in Sianh's face. I hadn't seen it in the candlelight the night before, but the sunlight betrayed the subtle scars of weariness. I felt that weariness creeping over me, settling into my face, my motions, my thoughts.

Perhaps this was why he had wanted to accompany us, I guessed, more than the money. This was closer to what he felt his purpose was, further from the warped version of himself he had lived for so long in Isildi. Here he wasn't a cavalryman without a horse, a soldier without a set of orders. It was imperfect, but it was closer to who he felt himself at his core to be.

We stopped for the night in a small town nestled in the curves formed by low hills. The sun's height above the hills still promised hours of good daylight, but Sianh noted that we would not reach another town large enough to guarantee an inn and stables if we pressed on. He didn't say so, but he also gave both Kristos and me long, assessing looks that told me he didn't think we were capable of dragging much more from our beaten, tired bodies. He was right.

The outskirts of the town, which Sianh said was named Croya Fai, or Twin Valleys, boasted several large plantations like the one Theodor and I had visited after the theft of our carriage. Workers in plain unbleached linen trousers stacked crates filled to spilling over with green fruits, and there were more crates listing dangerously by the door of the inn. We shared a wall with them, leaning against the sturdy stone while Sianh negotiated a night's lodging.

"Spiny apples," Kristos provided when he noticed me looking. "They're harvested unripe but turn a lovely gold in storage." He sighed. "Delicious."

He moved with such ease into Serafan life, I thought with another tinge of jealousy, or loss, or both. His new home, adopted and embraced, without any signs of grief for the one he left behind. I fought to find something to say, to begin to build the foundation for a bridge if not the bridge itself, but I found only trite small talk and obtuse observations. I could find nothing to say to my own brother? If I was honest, I had to admit that I hadn't had much to say to him before, as he built his rebellion, in the long, tense fall and winter leading up to the Midwinter Revolt. With a wash of guilt, I acknowledged that the distance had started before that. I couldn't pin the erosion of our close bond on him alone. I had poured myself into my atelier and, as I climbed the ranks of Galatine commoners from day laborer to business owner, I had created and then widened a rift between us.

Finally, the silence became untenable. "You seem to like the food here," I said. It was a poor excuse for a conversation, but it was something.

"Well enough. It suits life here, if that makes any sense. The pace is slower and yet more steady than in Galitha. No rush to finish anything before winter, no rush to wrap up a day's work before dark." He shifted, wincing as his muscles protested the same abuse that mine squawked about. Several paces away, Alba sat easily on a bench. Who was she, that the day's ride hadn't affected her, I asked myself for what seemed like the hundredth time. "And Penny likes it, too, likes having her own work and making her own name for herself. That wasn't going to happen in Galitha. She misses her family, her friends, but I never asked her to leave. She did that on her own."

"She found you?"

"She found me before I left Galitha City. And didn't let me out of her sight."

"I should have guessed." I smiled faintly; if the Lord of Keys had wanted to find Kristos, he ought to have tracked Penny.

"I'll send for her, once we have a safe place in Galitha. If we ever do. I promised her we'd go back if ever we could, but now—I wish I hadn't made that promise. Life here is what I'd always hoped for."

"It sounds like a scholar's life," I ventured.

"It is. Oh, it is. It's not perfect, not by a long shot. The amount of grunt work I have to do as an underling—sometimes I miss toting bricks when I'm deep in the weeds of a filing project." He ran a hand through his hair, snarls lurking in his dark waves catching his fingers. "But the books. So many books. And lectures from even the more advanced students that put the university in Galitha City to shame."

"What are you doing with it all?" The question sounded like an accusation, and perhaps it was. He had vowed that the revolt wasn't the end of his aspirations to change the Galatine political system.

"You didn't read my work?" He laughed. "Not that you ever

did, fair enough. I send manuscripts by way of Niko to a printer in Galitha City. I assume they're being printed regularly—I get the occasional final copy."

"I read them," I whispered. "I read them all. We both did, Theodor and I."

Kristos paused. "So you did take them into consideration, then."

"Yes. Not solely. We had other considerations. Your suggestion of tax code was refused outright—"

"I guessed that it would be."

"But the councils proved an easier compromise than we had anticipated. At least, I thought they had." My lips kinked into a painful smile. "It should have been you, talking with Theodor all those nights in his study and his garden, developing strategy for negotiation and compromise."

"I'm terrible at compromise," Kristos said with a shake of his head. "But it seems you've become as adept a student of politics as I ever was."

47

SIANH HAD SECURED ONE OF THE PRIVATE ROOMS AT THE INN FOR us, but the five of us still had to share the small, bare space. Eight pallets lined the floor, and a pair of crude benches served as the only furniture in the room.

"The ladies can each stack two pallets," Kristos said generously.

"And we'll still wake up bruised from the knots in the floorboards," Alba said with a laugh. "Very well. And shall we make use of the dining room here?"

To call the common space used for food service a "dining room" was a liberal treatment of the term, and I couldn't help an immediate comparison to the colonnade in the diplomatic compound or the formal spaces in Viola's or Theodor's homes. I stopped myself—I wasn't a spoiled noble, able to afford turning her nose up at an unassuming inn.

Still, even Kristos pulled a face as his hand hit the sticky tabletop, and Sianh quietly advised against ordering the vaguely named "meat pot."

While we waited for our meals, Sianh glanced around the room, avoiding conversation with Alba and Kristos, who chatted about a book of theological exposition they had both read.

"We are followed here," Sianh finally said, quietly and lacking any alarm. Still, the low ceiling and cramped walls of the inn's common room felt suddenly closer, and I saw only shadow around us. "That man in the corner, perhaps another."

"How do you know?" scoffed Kristos.

"It's his job to know," Alba whispered back.

Kristos clamped his mouth shut, but I knew what he was thinking—he still didn't trust Sianh completely. There was something more, some unanswered rivalry in which Kristos wanted to best Sianh and Sianh refused to engage.

"I know because I saw him three times in the village, and he didn't seem to decide where in the hell he wanted to go until we came here. Then he made up his mind. He hasn't ordered anything, and he's looking at everything but us."

"Fine. What now? We sneak out and—"

"No." Sianh stood up. "Stay here. The a'Mavha are men like any men. And this is likely some hired scout, not one of their best. We will want to act before their best arrive."

Prickles ran up and down my back, but I stayed perfectly still. Theodor paled, but Alba pursed her lips and leaned back.

"Where is that boy with the bread?" she complained.

Kristos leaned toward her, hissing, "Have you heard a word—"

"Of course, you idiot. But until Sianh bashes that fellow's head in or whatever he's planning to do, we're ordinary patrons here. Besides, I don't want that gangly boy tripping Sianh up or getting himself hurt. So where is he, exactly?"

I pointed—the innkeeper's son was scouring a table at the far side of the room. Alba nodded. "Fine."

Sianh didn't say anything as he left the table, and I didn't realize he had decided on the moment to confront our stalker until he had him by the throat, pinned against the wall. He shouted at him in resonant, commanding Serafan, and though I had no idea what he had said, the man blanched and the rest of the patrons deferred to Sianh as he lowered the man to the ground and dragged him by the arm to the back of the inn.

I gaped, expecting the innkeeper to intervene, but he didn't. Instead, he watched with mild amusement as Sianh shouldered a door open and forced the far shorter spy inside what I assumed was a storeroom. Then he limped over to us. Glancing at us, he said, in broken market Pellian that I barely understood, "If he breaks, you buy."

Kristos swiftly replied in Serafan. I heard a muffled thud from the storeroom; the innkeeper ignored it and asked Kristos a series of short, pointed questions, which Kristos answered. At one point the innkeep held up his hand, shaking his head and speaking loudly over Kristos's answer. Theodor and I edged closer to one another, finding each other's hands under the table.

Sianh reappeared, the other man nowhere to be seen. He hailed the innkeeper, who scurried away as quickly as he could with his bad leg.

"What did he say?" I asked Kristos as soon as he was gone.

"Sianh? Said to call the local constabulary."

"No, the innkeeper. Why didn't he throw us all out?"

"He could tell that our friend there was in the service. They're spooky about veterans, Serafans. So he wasn't going to cross him. But even more so, he doesn't want trouble. If we're willing to handle our own matters, all the better for him. I tried telling him that the man was probably a'Mavha and that's when he told me he didn't want to know. The less he knows, the better."

"Doesn't want his inn to get a bad reputation," Alba said. "And more, doesn't want to be known by the a'Mavha."

Sianh strode across the room, the other patrons backing

away in his wake, and dropped heavily onto his empty place on our bench. "He confessed immediately to everything. Or nearly so. We will not be bothered again, I do not think."

"What did he say?" Theodor demanded. "Is it true that Merhaven hired him? Is there—"

"Not here, I don't think it's wise. Out of respect for the inn-keep if nothing else."

By the time our lentils and sausage arrived, we had all, even Alba, transformed into antsy children in chapel, fidgeting and biting lips and fingernails. I barely tasted the stew—though what there was to taste, I wasn't sure, as the cook wasn't wasting any resources on spices.

"Do you think," Alba said as she mopped up the weak gravy from the lentils with a hunk of oatmeal bread, "that it's safe to stay here? Or ought we to move on for the night?"

"No less safe than before, and better than the road, I'd say. Don't forget that catamounts and nightsbane snakes are as real a danger as men with knives." Sianh had cleaned his plate efficiently and waited for the rest of us to finish. It became clear that none of the rest of us were hungry enough to polish off what passed for stew, so he gestured for us to leave, but not before pocketing all of our leftover bread. "It keeps well," he replied simply to my questioning look.

It was too early to go to the cramped, low-ceilinged room we'd booked for the evening, so we gathered in the stables instead. "I don't see a need to change our horses," Sianh said. I was about to interrupt and press for details about what the a'Mavha had said, but then I realized that Sianh was purposely diverting our conversation elsewhere.

"Agreed," Kristos said. "I'd rather not change them at all, if our pace doesn't overtire them. You never know when you'll get an old crank."

Alba shrugged. "Shared horses are shared horses."

"On that, Sastra-set, we can agree," Sianh said with a slightly deferential nod. "I, too, hope our pace does not warrant changing them."

"Changing them?" I had just, barely, gotten used to the plodding mount I'd used thus far.

"The Serafan stable system—one of the things you don't realize you're getting by without in Galitha," Kristos said. I swallowed any response to the perceived insult. Yes, as usual, among this group as handily as among nobles, I was uneducated and narrowly experienced. "It's a public service, allows for travel by anyone with the money to pay. One needn't maintain a stable and pasture to have access to road travel. Actually, I ought to draft a plan for a similar system for Galitha and send it—" He stopped abruptly as he recalled that Galitha had more pressing issues than public stables.

"So at any waypost we may exchange our horses. If you are dissatisfied with yours, of course, we can make a trade," Sianh supplied.

"It didn't throw me off, so I suppose I'm satisfied," I said. Might as well embrace my ignorance. "Now. What did he say?"

Sianh glanced around us. No one was here, loitering outside the horse stalls, though several grooms shared a plate of roasted vegetables near a shingled building I took to be an office. "I think we may speak openly," he said. "That man, with several of his associates, was hired to kill you. That is all he knows. The motivations of his clients didn't interest him. In fact, the job was arranged through their superior, their handler, and he maintains he doesn't know who the hire was. Only that you were the target."

"He's the only one?" Kristos said.

"The only one who left Isildi. Our gamble was well laid—they didn't presume she would leave the city unless by ship to

Galitha, and so continued their search within it and monitored the harbor. He will not bother us again." Sianh allowed himself a small smile. I didn't ask what he had done to ensure that, but I had a fairly good guess. "So we should be able to continue, unmolested, to Port Triumph."

"That's good enough for me," I said. "No offense meant, Sianh, but the sooner I'm out of Serafe, the better."

Alba tilted her head as though considering this, but decided against speaking. Kristos shrugged. "If you think you're safe in Galitha, think again."

"Safety isn't why I'm going to Galitha," I countered.

Sianh interrupted the argument before it could begin. "One more thing—you may wish to know that the a'Mavha, and their client before them, had an informant inside the diplomatic compound keeping them apprised of your movements."

I tasted the unpleasantness of that thought like sour wine, unwelcome yet lingering. "I suppose I shouldn't be surprised. One of the servants?" I hadn't managed to learn the names of most of the white-uniformed attendants in our wing.

"Your, shall we say, 'friend' Jae."

"What?" A servant, I had believed. But Jae? Even after I'd realized he wasn't being kind to me for friendship's sake alone, I would never have pegged him for a snake. His quick smile and easy manner weren't a complete façade, and he didn't seem calculating enough to be a spy. "But Jae hoped to be considered for a marriage contract with Annette."

"That may be precisely why he turned to working with Merhaven," Alba said thoughtfully. "He is part of the underlings of the upper class of the States—related by blood but not in line to inherit anything but a name. He was not in the running for a marriage contract, and it was foolish of him to attempt to work his way into your confidences to reach one. He looked for another way to advance himself." I recalled what Jae had said—the son of a second husband, not of the main house. Not like Dira, who I would have expected from her coldly aristocratic bearing to be in alliance with nobles like Merhaven. I had thoroughly misread both, to my detriment. I had unwittingly allowed Jae access to my research at the library, and he was likely the one who had fomented rumors that I was studying curse magic there.

"It is good to know who it was," Sianh confirmed. "If it were a nameless servant, we might be followed still and never know."

I wished I could have argued that I would have recognized every quiet presence I had encountered, but I had to admit that I hadn't. Kristos watched me, perhaps waiting for such an admission, a confirmation that I had slipped away from our modest upbringing and now took the servants of a noble for granted. In truth, I was disappointed in myself, but also defended my inattention—I had been preoccupied, overwhelmed, and their job was to fade into the background.

Precisely what a spoiled noble would say, I scolded myself, chagrined. As though their quiet lives meant less than mine, that I could ignore them when I was tired or busy as if they were furniture. "I ought to have paid more attention," I admitted. "To Jae and everyone else." Kristos gave me an encouraging smile, and it felt almost like being home again.

"In any case," Alba interjected, "we can sleep well tonight, and a good thing. I'm tired and it's getting dark enough to warrant finding my bed."

48

THOUGH ALBA HAD SAID SHE WOULD SLEEP WELL KNOWING THAT we'd thrown off the a'Mavha, I noticed when I woke in our spare rented room midway through the night that Sianh was sitting by the door instead of sleeping on his pallet. I didn't say anything, but drifted back to sleep vaguely unsettled by his wakeful presence.

The pallets were, if not outright hostile to sleeping, not conducive to a restful night even though I was grateful to have Theodor beside me again, and I woke sore from the bed as well as from the previous day on the road. Even so, I was the last one to wake. I limped toward the common room in search of some coffee or at the least some strong tea, and was welcomed by only a traditional Serafan breakfast done poorly—weak mint tea, bread only half-toasted, and bruised fruit. I plucked the few figs from the bowl that weren't oozing overripe juice and found Alba spreading what may, once, have been fruit compote onto a piece of toast.

"You look like something peeled off a tavern floor," she said as she nibbled her toast. "And how fitting. This tastes like something peeled off a floor, too."

I pulled a face and approached the figs with even greater caution.

"Sianh and Kristos are having an argument about whether to change the horses," Alba continued, as though this were just a bit of news and not anything to attach any emotion to. I had a hard time taking it as such; Sianh and Kristos snipped and tussled like a pair of alley cats. "Theodor is trying to appease both of them. And I'm going to go to the greengrocers to see if we can't get some provisions that look less like compost." She stood, brushed off her dark skirts, and dropped the half-eaten toast into a bucket by the door.

Kristos and Theodor were nowhere to be found, but Sianh was refolding his pack in the rambling, overgrown patch that passed for a garden between the inn and the stable.

"Thank you," I said, approaching him. "For…handling things yesterday."

"It's what I was hired for, no?" He buckled his pack. "Though I have strange companions in this job, I admit. A nun who rides like a soldier, a scholar who acts like he's itching for a brawl, and a princess who snores."

"I don't snore!" I laughed. "And I'm not a princess."

"I don't know anything about your titles," he said, "but last night you—well, as we put it in Serafan, you were like an otter singing an aria."

"An otter, really?"

"Yes, they make little barking sounds—oh, you think you don't bark in your sleep like an otter?" He slung his pack up on his shoulder. "Perhaps the Serafan air doesn't agree with you."

"I'll have to let you know if I'm still snoring in Galitha."

"I'll expect a report."

Kristos and Theodor joined us, having reviewed the horses

at the stables and determined we were better with our current mounts. Alba wended her way back from the greengrocer's with a bag of plums that she doled out like a mother with candied fruit peel at the Galatine Threshing Market. "Now," she said, "I should very much like to know where we are going."

"Our good friends," Theodor said. "The former Princess Annette and Lady Viola Snowmont."

"Nobles! Will a pair of fainting flowers like that take us in?" Kristos demanded.

"What, a title makes someone incapable of helping their friends?" I shot back. "Of course they will."

"You are sure they can be trusted?" Alba murmured. Sianh didn't speak, but his rigid face asked the same question.

"Yes! Of course." Theodor huffed. "Sophie would never have suggested it otherwise."

"I don't like it," Kristos said. "You sure they won't turn on me the second I walk in the door?"

"I'm sure," Theodor half shouted.

"Well enough for you to say," Kristos rebuffed him, muttering under his breath, "powdered prig."

"And you would be a dead man if it weren't for me!" Theodor replied. "Yes, we'll be safe with Viola and Annette. Yes, they'll help us. What do you want from me, a notarized guarantee?"

"Is there a solicitor present?" Kristos mocked him.

"Enough!" I interrupted. "You don't have to like each other, but we're going to have to at least try to trust one another!" I heaved a sigh. "That means all of us—nuns and former soldiers included. There is a damned civil war on, and unless I'm mistaken, the right side of it stands to lose unless we can muster up something resembling leadership to scrape together a proper army. That leadership, as much as it pains me to admit it, seems to be my idiot brother and my horse's ass of a betrothed."

Alba hid a smile, and Sianh nodded approvingly. "Horse's ass?" Theodor said.

"When you lower yourself to squabbling like a child, yes."

"I already knew you thought I was an idiot," Kristos said with a shrug. It was the closest I'd see to an apology from him.

"Then we've wasted enough time arguing over silly trifles—the road isn't short and we should make haste," Sianh said.

Despite feeling as stiff as new buckram, I was grateful that Sianh didn't slow our pace. I wanted to get to Viola and Annette as quickly as possible, to leave Serafe behind and return to Galitha, even if Galitha was not the home I'd left but a swiftly swelling battlefield. Theodor rode next to Sianh, questioning him on tactics, bayonet drill, methods for encamping an army, and more that I could barely follow. Midway through the morning, Kristos fell in step beside me.

"Not used to traveling on horseback either, are you?" he said with a laugh. I was struck again by how much older he looked, his beard softening his hard jawline and buffering his quick smile. Or, I considered, his smile might not be as easy or broad as it once was.

"That obvious, is it?" I leaned painfully in the saddle, aching to stretch muscles that I couldn't engage.

"You aren't one of them completely, then, if you can't ride well." I wasn't sure if I heard relief or bitterness as the underlayment of his joke.

"Hardly," I said simply. "I kept my shop until this month." I didn't elaborate on the possibility that it might be gone. "I still live in our old row house. Well, I did."

"You slept there?" Kristos said, suddenly harsh.

"Where I sleep really isn't your business. I never asked where you were, who you were with."

"I never shared a bed with a noble," he replied. "I'm sorry, but I can't understand it. What do you see in some powdered dandy that you didn't see in our neighbors, our friends? When you didn't marry, didn't even want to take a walk with any of the boys—and then men—we knew, I assumed you didn't want to marry at all. I even thought maybe you didn't like men."

"I couldn't marry and keep my shop." My reasoning had always been so simple, yet few people seemed inclined to listen to it.

"And now? You can marry the future king of Galitha and keep your shop?"

"Of course not!" I nearly shouted. "But I can still create, can still sew. And I've found something else, something more— being an advocate. A voice."

"The gossip rags had other words for you."

"I know. I don't even know if I'm very good at it, but it's important, and I feel...called to it, I suppose. I thought you might understand, after studying here. That you might know what it's like to have a vocation."

"I'm leaving it now," he answered. Kristos's gaze was focused, down the narrow highway and resting in the far-distant hills we rode toward. "We are at a great crossroads, Sophie." My name sounded so sweetly familiar coming from him, an echo of a lost yesterday. "The fight in Galitha—it's for more than the reforms. It's for the future."

That sounded like Kristos. Ideals and theory and belief colliding into an insistent demand for action. "And what part will you play in it?" I asked, afraid to know.

"I don't know. I've lived well in exile," he said. "I've loved the life I've been given, the life of a scholar. Long days in the library, reading and translating and discovering worlds I never knew existed. And then long evenings in the wineshops debating and playing charades and snapdragon when things grew too serious."

"It sounds not terribly unlike Lady Viola Snowmont's salon," I said, "not that you want to hear that."

"I suppose I'm more open to hearing it now than a year ago. There is potential in the nobility, in some of the nobility, to move Galitha where she must go." His gaze rested on Theodor's back, the easy way he took to the saddle, his intense conversation with Sianh.

"They can't do it alone," I ventured.

"Very well," he said, a bit of his old smile creeping into the corners of his eyes. "I can do some good. I started something last year. I didn't intend much of what happened, but I did intend change." He regarded me with more understanding than I'd felt from him in a long time. "I finally saw what you were afraid of. Change is a bird that, once loosed from its cage, may not fly in the direction you desired."

"Sometimes it flies right back and pecks you in the face."

"Or shits on your shoe." Kristos laughed. "But it's loosed from its cage now. I turned the key. I should do what I can to shepherd its path."

49

WE REACHED THE ESTATE VIOLA AND ANNETTE HAD BOUGHT just before nightfall, the thick scents of flowers seeping into the street like a fog. "White gardens," Kristos said, nodding toward the walled grounds of the estate. "Common here. The night-blooming flowers are almost all white and smell like a puddle of mixed perfumes." I wasn't sure if this was a good thing or not.

Theodor presented himself to the Serafan maid who answered the door, and she blanched as if she were a night-blooming flower herself and ran for her mistress.

"Our reputation precedes us," I joked weakly. The others didn't laugh. Any complacence we had begun to indulge in on the road, moving farther from Isildi and from the danger at the inn, faded now.

Viola hurried to the door after her maid. "When I said you should come to see me, I hadn't meant quite this soon," she said, embracing Theodor and glancing past me at my strange traveling companions. "Come inside."

Theodor and I followed Viola into the open hall of her new home. The doors were open to courtyards and gardens outside, and faintly cool breezes moved through the house. Alba moved after us with the possessed confidence of a highborn woman, but Kristos and Sianh hung back, moving gingerly as though afraid their boots would mar the mosaic floors.

"I'm sorry to intrude on you," I said, and explained the reasons for my unexpected flight from Isildi as quickly as possible. "But where is Annette?"

"An acquaintance called and asked if she could help with a bit of Galatine translation in a business matter." Viola watched Kristos and Sianh, both of whom were acting as though they had forgotten what to do with one's arms. Alba stood poised as a statue. "You did collect quite the entourage. The one with the beard is your brother? The great incendiary writer of the Midwinter Revolt?"

I nodded. "One and the same."

"I rather want to slap him and sit him down with a bottle of port for a long talk, all at the same time."

"He has that effect," I answered. "The Serafan is Sianh and the Kvys nun is Sastra-set Alba."

"Indeed," Viola replied with a twitch of a smile. "We'll arrange your passage tomorrow. Port Triumph is an hour's ride, at most, but the captains are deep in their cups by now." She hesitated. "That is—if you still want to return. You're welcome with me."

"I know," I said. Viola began to say more but stopped herself. Instead she called to the maid and arranged sleeping accommodations for all of us, in her swift and subtle way. She was at home here, speaking in low voices to maids in Serafan and wearing a loose Serafan housedress, pale lavender cotton enveloping her the way a cloud cushions a setting sun. I wondered if Viola had the rare gift of seeming at home anywhere, in a Galatine ballroom or a Serafan garden. Would she seem as comfortable in a Kvys convent, I wondered? In a cold and hard-bitten Fenian countinghouse?

Alba slid close to me and took my hand. "Your friend is a thorough hostess," she said, nodding toward a tray of lime tonics that had appeared. "And she is trustworthy." I began to answer before realizing that it wasn't, for once, a question. Alba had ascertained this for herself.

"Can I ask," I said, hesitating, "how is it that you can ride so well?"

Sastra-set Alba laughed. "We are not born nuns, Sophie Balstrade." She stepped lightly away to inspect several paintings hung along the hall—Viola's work, I knew.

The door swung wide and Annette hurried inside. I held back from greeting her; worry consumed her face and she was not nearly as surprised to see us as I had anticipated. Behind her, mirroring her worry, was the last person I had expected to see near Port Triumph.

"You were supposed to be halfway to Galitha on the *Gyrfalcon* by now," Theodor said, striding forward to embrace his brother.

"Merhaven left without me." Ballantine nodded in greeting to me and Viola, politely letting his gaze skim over Sianh and Kristos.

"That seafaring rat." Viola caught Annette's hand. "And the lovely Lady Merhaven, too, I imagine."

"Both rats," Theodor said with a wry laugh.

"I won't disagree," Ballantine said. "I waited at the docks for you and Sophie, but Merhaven came instead. He sent me ashore for provisions and sailed without me. Quite deliberately, of course."

"It was an entire plot, to prevent my return to Galitha," Theodor said. "And you were too close to me to be trusted."

Ballantine held up a hand. "I know, you needn't rehash the whole thing. I think they'd prefer you out of the game entirely.

The anti-reformists have begun calling themselves Royalists. Because they've got Father on their side, you see, and that makes them ever so official. It tarnishes their maker's mark if the royal house is, in fact, divided."

"Royalists? That's rich," Kristos snorted. "What ought we to call those in favor of the rightful, lawful governance?"

"I believe the common folk out of Havensport and Hazelwhite and the other places have that covered, as well; they've adopted the name 'Reformists' from the bill, and it's taken off—more palatable to the moderate common folk than the old Red Cap designation."

"I imagine," Alba said quietly to Theodor, "that even with your father siding with the Royalists, many among them fear your influence on the common people."

Theodor glanced at Alba blankly, then shook his head. "There is a Kvys nun lecturing me on the power dynamics of my own nation."

"Yes," I said, "there is. But Sastra-set Alba has been insightful thus far. And she's been a great help in rescuing me from underbelly assassins."

"The a'Mavha aren't underbelly assassins," Kristos interjected. "Only the finest quality assassins for offing foreign dignitaries."

"It seems I've missed some good stories. At any rate," Ballantine said, "we're going to need a new ship."

"This is all quite too much to arrange on a poor night's sleep and an empty stomach," Alba said gently. "As it is too late to do anything about arranging passage for anyone, perhaps we ought to retire for the night and hold our own summit tomorrow?"

"I think that's the best thing for everyone," Viola said hastily. "No use making any drastic decisions on no sleep." She swiftly ushered everyone to their rooms, still sparsely furnished as she and Annette had only so recently acquired the house. Yet each piece of furniture and each framed painting was carefully selected and positioned to show it to its best advantage. I sighed. I hadn't wanted to drag trouble onto Annette and Viola's doorstep before they had even had a chance to enjoy their life together.

Theodor was asleep before he even took his breeches off, his stockings and boots in a messy pile on the floor, but I couldn't fall asleep. Despite an aching weariness that settled deep in my bones and eyes as dry as the dust in Isildi, my thoughts fought sleep like a drowning man, flailing in a current of exhaustion and refusing to be swept away. When I did fall into fitful rest, I woke with a start, time and again. I finally rose and padded down the hallways of the grand house, feet hot on cool tile, until I found the door to the white garden.

I wasn't alone in my insomnia. Sianh sat cross-legged beneath a sprawling double-blooming magnolia, his arms above his head as though reaching for some invisible fruit caught in a high branch. The creamy white blossoms brushed his dark hair when the wind moved, and I caught their thick scent mingling with the sweet hair oil Sianh used. His eyes were closed.

I turned to leave, but he must have heard the faint rustle my bare feet made on the path. "Sophie. If you can't sleep, come sit."

"I don't want to disturb you," I said. "Or keep you up."

"I already slept. It's nearly morning." He unkinked his long legs. "And what I'm doing—passing time, nothing more."

"Meditation?" I ventured.

He laughed, a faint snort of derision. "That makes me sound mystical, divine. Is that what you think of Serafans, that we're some sort of mystics?" He shook his head. "I have a knot in my shoulder the size of a spiny apple. I was only stretching."

I flushed. "I didn't mean anything by it."

"I know." He pulled an arm across his chest and winced. "I

should not have made fun. You, I am sure, know full well the frustration of bearing the assumptions of others."

"Then let's leave assumptions aside. I still can't quite understand why you would come with us, why you would take on a charge that doesn't concern you." If it wasn't my country, I would have stayed as far from the bloody turmoil in Galitha as possible.

"Did you forget how much you agreed to pay me?"

"No, and it seems a low amount to risk your life for."

"What in life isn't a risk? It was only a matter of time until a jealous wife or angry brother came after me in my current position." He shrugged. "Or until I aged ungracefully out of my ability to serve in the Warren. It is time for me to turn to another way to earn my bread. But what I cannot quite understand is why you are not inclined to believe someone when he tells the truth."

I started. "The truth sounds too simple the way you tell it."

He shook his head. "I think it is because you saw ideals corrupted and now you don't recognize the truth."

I clenched my teeth, biting back a retort. He didn't have a right to speak to me as though he knew me, as though he understood what the Midwinter Revolt had done to me. He didn't have a right to understand, I amended, acknowledging that he had hit on the truth. My brother's ideals, corrupted into regicide and murder of innocents, my ideals, abandoned to craft curses. Even Pyord, I admitted, corrupt idealism personified. What could I trust? I struggled to answer.

"My brother would have let me die," I finally said. "For ideals. Ideals are not such noble things as you would believe."

"You ought to forgive him."

Now the anger flared into bitter laughter. "Forgive him? Didn't you hear me—he would have let me die. Plenty of people did die, but he would have let me die. His sister. He cared more about his ideals and his vision than about me," I said, my voice rising thin and harsh.

Sianh nodded. And waited.

"I've never said that before," I whispered. "He cared more about his revolution than he did about me. He chose it over me." *He loved it more than me*, I added silently, the impact of those words too great to say aloud.

"And for that, you must forgive him if you are to go forward. He is remorseful—why do you think he circles me for a fight, like a rangy hound? He has never behaved thus before. He wants to be the one to protect you, to save you. To make up for the past."

"So you say." I took a shaky breath. "And where do I go from here?"

Sianh smiled. "Back where you began, but entirely different, no?"

I blinked slowly, tension seeping from me. The sun was rimming the horizon, pale orange. Sianh had been right—while I had seen only night, it had been nearly morning. "True enough. I'm not sure what place a charm caster has in this." The thought struck me. "Sianh, does the Serafan army use . . . music?" I asked awkwardly.

"Drums and pipes on the field, yes. Not dissimilar to your own army's drums, for relaying orders." His eyes narrowed. "Why?"

"I'm not sure you want to know," I replied.

"I think you're telling me that I must know."

I hesitated, but there was no avoiding letting him in on the Serafan court's great, deadly secret, not if I wanted to have any way of countering it if it came to that. "The Serafan court uses charm and curse casting, executed through music. At least, only music as far as I know." Too much I didn't know, yet I had to press forward. "It influences the listener. They were using it to sway opinion on issues at the summit, but it could be used…" I shook my head, overwhelmed with possibilities.

Sianh considered this carefully, impassively, and finally nodded. "I can see how that could be effected."

"Was it?" I asked. "That you saw?"

"It's difficult to be certain," he replied. "No—I will tell you what I experienced. And you tell me if that is casting." He closed his eyes, centering a memory. "We were facing the Bhani; they had built several small redoubts and were defending them fiercely. The pipes retreated a short distance and played a song I'd never heard before—a march, but with a snake of a melody, twisting and fast. I felt—I am no coward, understand, but I felt invincible." He opened his eyes. "My horse didn't care for it. We took the nearest redoubts far more quickly than I could have anticipated, and—this was strange—the pipes played the entire time."

"And you felt different while they played?"

"Bright, fast, brave—yes. I thought I was simply fighting exceptionally well," he apologized with a wry grin.

"I've no doubt you were"—I smiled—"but it certainly sounds as though there was casting. A charm, for all those things you felt and needed to be. And, damn it all, but clever—so that they can use the charm without even the soldiers knowing, let alone the enemy."

"I suppose you have your answers. The knot in my shoulder is better," Sianh excused himself, "but I fear I've new ones in my head, now." He stood, sinewy muscle unfolding and engaging. A warrior's stance even as he walked through the garden. He was joining us out of a sort of ambition borne out of who he was, who he had fashioned himself to be.

And what was I? I was a charm caster. I was a seamstress. I had been born with the ability to cast and with nimble fingers, and I had fashioned them into what I was. Sianh could serve his ideals with a sword or a rifle. He saw redemption and a new life in doing so. I had put myself in service to corrupted ideals once. Could I redeem myself by serving something I believed in? If I could, what use was a charm-casting seamstress to the war raging in Galitha?

50

By the time I had dressed and combed the worst of the snarls from my hair, everyone was gathered in the dining room, papers and maps spread in haphazard layers. Sianh was already making notes on a map in fine graphite.

"I'm ever so glad you picked up a military tactician in your detour to the brothel," Theodor said to me with a wan smile. "Yes, you're right. We can't return without some plan to shore up our forces and our assets."

"Are those Merhaven's?"

"They're not Merhaven's any longer," Ballantine replied. "I took a few maps and charts. After I realized he'd withheld those letters from you, Sophie, I started going through his papers. Merhaven relied too far on either my ignorance or loyalty. Those," he said, gesturing to the largest two, "are not his usual seafaring maps. They're marked with the areas that the Royalists currently occupy, including, it seems, some of their storehouses, and they arrived less than a week ago."

"The Royalists appear to hold the majority of territory south of the Greenbow River, or at least have a significant presence there." Sianh pointed to notations made in a stranger's handwriting on the map.

Theodor waited a long moment before he allowed himself to ask the question I knew weighed most heavily on him. "And the king?"

"The map doesn't note his location," Ballantine said. "I don't wish to speak disrespectfully, but—"

"Hang it, Ballantine. If we're to get anywhere with this, we'll speak openly. Our father has turned on his people. So." Theodor swallowed hard.

Sianh scrutinized the map. "Then the Royalists hold much of the south, between these two rivers. Rock and Greenbow. And you say that Galitha City is held by the Reformists, under Niko, at least tenuously. Yes?"

"That's what I said," Kristos said.

"If it were me," Sianh said, meeting first Theodor's and then Kristos's eyes, "I would land in this region, in the center, and consolidate an army there."

Viola hugged her arms around her thin cotton housedress, even though the sun was already heating the room through its wide windows. "Consolidate an army? Living hell, Theodor, you're quite serious!"

Annette slipped next to Viola and took her hand as Theodor straightened his shoulders. "Yes, I'm serious. It's already begun—we make a stand now or forever forfeit our place on the ethical side of this war."

"What about the military?" Sianh asked Ballantine. "To whom does their loyalty sway?"

"That gets sticky. The soldiers in the City Guard and Royal Guard have always stuck close to the king—they'll side with the Royalists as long as there's a king to side with. From these letters, it appears most left with the king when he ran from the capital like a beaten alley cat." Ballantine cleared his throat. "Meaning no disrespect to His Majesty, of course."

"What of the army? The navy?"

"By and large, both naval and army officers are noble-born. A few will stand with Galitha and the law, but most will follow wherever their fathers and uncles and cousins go, and most will go to the Royalists. Their sailors—most will remain loyal to their officers and their ships. It's just their way," he said, shaking his head as though apologizing for them. "The army is, as I understand it, much the same. There may be some mutinies, but as it stands, we can't count on that."

"So most of your army's soldiers will not be soldiers at all," Sianh said, "as we had guessed. Not all is lost," he said with a faint smile, "provided they have leaders they trust. I presume this is the role of the Prince of Westland?"

"Not exactly," Theodor said. "Yes, the people will likely rally behind the Prince of Westland if he sides with them. But the Prince of Westland cannot and should not assume leadership by himself. He is nothing without the common people, and they need to be treated on equal footing in this endeavor." He looked at me, and I nodded with a slow, gentle smile. He understood.

"Stop talking in the third person," Viola said. "You sound affected."

"I mean it in the third person," Theodor said. "I'm not earning my place by anything aside from this title. But if this title can serve us, very well. They don't truly need *me*."

Viola glanced around the room. She slid her back against the wall, her gown like a delicate blossom against the dark, vining wallpaper. She had, I saw, only just realized that she was superfluous here. Her title, her money, her talents—they were secondary in a new game of influence and ability.

"And let's not forget that you're next in line for the throne," I said.

"Could we?" Kristos asked with a caustic laugh.

"You can try, but it's a fact. And Theodor can't play the role of returning prince, ready to take the throne from a corrupt despot."

Kristos leaned forward. "What are you saying?"

"If we let the common people elevate Theodor too much, the story very, very quickly becomes that he should take the throne for himself. Suddenly, the fight is recast, isn't it? It's not about the reforms. It's not about the law. It's about a young pretender to the throne mounting a coup." I let that sink in. "At least, that's how the Royalists can tell it. Any hope we have of securing any of the army will be gone, I think, and many of the people, as well, if this ceases to be about the ideals we are holding to."

"You're right. Damn, Sophie." Kristos gave me a faint half smile. "You've been around these politicking nobles so long you've learned their language."

"That's hardly a compliment."

"I'm not great at compliments."

"But what you are good at," I said, seizing the opportunity, "is writing the story. You did it once before. You can do it again, making sure to diminish Theodor's importance in relation to how important the people are. Delegitimize any propaganda emphasizing a claim to the throne. Especially if you're there alongside him."

"We have to tell the story before it happens," he mused. "I can't argue with your logic, Sophie, you're right." He let his fingers tangle themselves in his hair, absently tugging at knots buried in his thick waves.

"Then we have something like a plan," Alba said. I started— I had forgotten that she was in the room. "We travel north, land in this—what, central region?" Sianh nodded. "And we have to raise an army."

"Talking about it is easy," Viola cautioned. "But actually doing it?" She shook her head. "You should all eat something. There's fruit and pastries in the parlor."

Everyone else filed out, but Kristos stayed behind. "I didn't think you would want me to join your beloved's glorious cause," he admitted. "Thank you for—well, for cementing my place alongside your prince." He hesitated. "I'm not sure I deserved it."

"I admit it, Kristos, I hated every bit of every treatise and broadside you wrote last fall. I didn't want to let that promise of change you loved so much risk what we had. Your writing was a threat, and I hated it because it was good. Because it was effective."

"It *was*," he said. "But I—I failed. In quite a few ways. I failed to trust my own judgment. I should have known that Venko could tear our movement apart from the inside. I went ahead and blindly let him—you know the rest. I don't need to tell you."

I let the silence grow between us, thick and cloying. "Do you know," I finally said, "that for months now, I have struggled to charm cast?"

He started. "No. Why?"

"I didn't know," I said. "I could see the light—the charm— but the dark curse magic hung around it, blighting it. I thought it was from casting that curse on the queen's shawl. I thought maybe I had ruined my ability to cast."

He let his head sink into his hands. "Did you? Did I take that from you, too?"

"No. I did, without realizing it. I had to work through the doubts and the grief I had after last winter." I had to grapple with loss just as that ancient Pellian woman had, to accept change and to acknowledge that I couldn't go back. "I couldn't cast cleanly again until I had confronted what I had lost. I thought, at first, it was only losing you." He started, the realization that I had grieved for him smacking him almost physically. "And it was, but it was also…purpose, and drive, and direction. It was a whole tangled mess of grief."

"I think your grief is a bit different from mine," he said. "What you had was taken from you. What I lost I took from myself."

"Then all the more reason you have to do something—anything—to work for good."

"And if I don't know what that is?" he nearly shouted. "I don't trust myself! Why do you think I studied, buried myself in books? In theories? I thought maybe books and theories and brilliant professors could give me something to trust."

I took a steadying breath. "I can't tell you what to trust, and neither can they. But eventually you have to choose something. If it's wrong, it's wrong, but the right choice is most certainly not wallowing in your own self-pity."

He wanted to argue, I knew—his mouth contorted under his beard, holding back an angry retort. But my words had found a target, buried deep in his self-doubt and misery.

"It's your decision," I said. "But indecision is still a choice. I learned that too late. It's a mired mess of light and dark, and it can't effect anything at all." I left without another word, lest Kristos corner me into admitting my own indecision about what role I would play next.

51

VIOLA MET ME IN THE HALLWAY, PRESSING A PASTRY INTO MY HAND. "Ballantine's gone to see about the ship," she said. "And I suppose it's time to say goodbye."

She didn't seem happy, but of course her carefully planned and planted life had been uprooted before it had even begun to grow. We joined Theodor and Annette in the garden, the heady, spicy perfume of the flowers at odds with Viola's solemn face.

Viola and Annette stood close to one another but not quite touching. I smiled privately; I knew that there was comfort in mere proximity. "Let's sit a moment—the morning is so warm already." Our visit might have been a social call, an early breakfast before a boating party or a hunt, from the quiet grace with which she showed us to a dainty table and chairs under a shaded arbor. "I've started working on getting some of my funds from the Galatine banks transferred here," Viola said as she arranged her skirts in the narrow wrought-iron chair. "I'll be able to send some aid, I hope, when that's done."

"You hope?" Theodor's brow knotted. "I was sure you'd be coming with us."

Annette's eyes grew wide, and I was as surprised as Annette. Viola screwed her mouth into a hard line.

"Theo," Annette said quietly, "you're asking too much. For us to return with you? What good will that do? There's nowhere to go."

"You forget," Viola said, "that I saw nobles killed when I fled Galitha City. The Red Caps turned running to Annette into something else entirely, running from execution on the basis of my bloodline."

"But I was sure—you were happy to discuss theoretical ideals and proposed reforms in your salon. You were a leader in Galitha City. Plenty of the nobles who eventually drafted the Reform Bill began to think—really think—for themselves in your gatherings."

"Don't flatter me now, Theo." Viola sighed. "I am not opposed to the changes. I'm in favor of most of them."

"It's not flattery. It's misplaced confidence."

"Theo!" Annette interjected. "That isn't fair. You never asked—"

"No, I didn't ask. I expected. I expected everyone to be willing, once the time came, to stand for the ideals they enjoyed discussing so much. To come with me as a sort of Reformist leader. There are many people, nobles especially, who would listen to you."

"I can't do that," Viola protested.

"Then don't come back. Just—just a letter. A pamphlet. You can write to those who might still be unsure, who might decide to follow the law."

"If you're in earnest that I was influential," Viola said slowly, "then I have done my part. Let me fade into obscurity here."

"Obscurity? That's not life for you and you know it. Help us. Anything to encourage the intelligent among the nobles to make an intelligent choice."

"And risk ourselves here? Sophie was nearly killed, I won't

put Annette at that sort of risk with a few poor words on paper. What is worth that kind of risk?"

"The law, Viola!" Theodor slammed the table with his hand, so hard I feared the marble could crack. "With the law. We wrote the law. We debated the law. We voted on the law. It passed. What is a country without laws? It's anarchy."

"This is too much, too much too quickly!" Viola cried. I knew she was talking about more than the risks—she was thinking of the losses. She didn't want to admit that the happiness she believed she had finally found, the peace and comfort of an uncontested future with Annette, long denied them, could be taken so suddenly. "You do realize how difficult all of this is?" She clamped her mouth shut. "I'm sorry, that was—"

"Yes, you know damn well I know how difficult this is. He is my own father. I will be accused of attempting to usurp the throne for my own gain. I very well may die before this is over, and even if I don't, I will likely be driven from my own country. But the law will be upheld if I can do anything to secure it."

Viola hung her head. "No one ever asked you to die for anything," she said, to my surprise beginning to cry. "I certainly never did, and I never expected anyone to demand it of me."

Theodor shook his head. "I'm sorry. I can't wait any longer." He stood up sharply and left the table.

"Sophie," Viola said quietly. "I am sorry, I can't—" She choked. "I can't let anything happen to Annette, and I don't relish the thought of being murdered myself, either. My words don't matter any longer."

I began to argue but found I couldn't. "Perhaps you're right. About your role, your voice in all of this."

She nodded. "If I had known a salon could overturn a country, I would have stuck to card parties," she said with a bitter laugh.

"That isn't true and you know it," Annette whispered.

"I do, too," I said. I watched Viola, her eyes red and her carefully rouged cheeks tearstained. She needed to mourn, to let go of what she had carefully built. "I know you'll help us when you can."

Viola wiped away an errant tear. "I'll do what I can." She assessed me. "You're still wearing that Serafan thing because you haven't anything else, aren't you? I'll have a trunk of clothes packed. Who knows when you'll see the inside of your own closet again," she said.

"I—thank you," I said.

"If things...don't go well," Annette said, swallowing that thorny reality, "you are welcome here. Always."

I nodded, even though I knew returning to West Serafe was the least plausible scenario in my future, and embraced both of them. Then I found Theodor pacing the garden near the far wall and hidden from Viola and Annette by a trellis of trumpet vine. "Really, Theodor. You can't expect them to—"

"If I can't expect them to, Sophie, I am afraid how few I can expect it from." He leveled his hazel eyes on me, gripping my hands as though I could buoy him up and prevent him from drowning in the morass of uncertainty opening before us. "If even Viola and Annette are not willing to risk everything, is anyone?"

I withdrew my hands slowly. "The rest of the country, Theodor. This can't be a fight between nobles. It's not a fight between nobles and it never truly was."

He sank onto a stone bench. Knots of trumpet vine climbed behind him, and he absently plucked a sticky blossom. I sat beside him. "If you're going to take this on, you can't do it on behalf of Reformist nobles. That's over now."

He raised his head. "I am on the side of the law. Whatever else."

"And in being on the side of the law, you must accept that your allies are now the common people who have been fighting for their reforms longer than you have. Not your fellow nobles who finally listened. Yes, some of them will side with you." I closed my hand over his, the trumpet vine blossom trapped between our fingers. "But most will not. The king has not, and so those loyal to tradition over law will not. We have to look forward, not back."

"What frightens me, what I can't fathom—what comes out of this? I am fighting to uphold the law, to retain the reforms for the people. Not to overthrow our law, not to rout the nobility."

"There's no way to know for sure," I said softly. "Between you and my brother, I have confidence you will guide the ideals of this fight well. But you have to let go of the reins, at least a little. This isn't your revolution."

52

ALBA'S WHITE VEIL WAS FRESHLY STARCHED AND NEARLY GLOWED in the sunlight. If the purpose of the veil was to encourage modesty or to stifle beauty, it didn't work in her case, the stiff folds providing a contrast to her soft features and round cheeks. Keeping her hair covered only highlighted the sparkle of her pale blue eyes. The stiff sea breeze scoured some pink into her pale cheeks.

Ballantine had arranged the ship, a brig whose owner had a reputation of gambling debts, and would captain the ship himself, with a crew of Serafans paid well enough through the ship's owner not to ask questions. Kristos and Sianh jockeyed over who should direct the crew in loading our scant luggage, and Theodor wisely kept out of their scuffle, charting various courses with his brother, debating which was preferable, direct routes or routes that skirted Pellia or the islands that dotted the sea to hide our trail.

Though I perhaps should have stayed inside with Theodor, I needed the stiff breeze and bright sunlight to clear my head. Our leave-taking from Viola and Annette had felt stilted and pained; I knew that Theodor grieved what he saw as the loss of his cousin and his dear friend. I felt stretched thin, understanding their reticence but unable to sympathize with avoidance any longer. I had tried that route and failed.

Alba turned to me with a pale smile. "There is something we ought to discuss," she said quietly.

"Of course," I replied, though I was not ready for more conversations about strategy or my ultimate destination.

"I have not been perhaps entirely honest with you." She gripped the rail as my eyes widened. "And I should tell you before we leave port. You can run back to your friends' estate if you so wish."

"Very little could convince me to do that," I said.

She laughed. "Don't speak so hastily. You see, I was truthful that I have been in contact with your brother since last fall. I had read his work and I did wish to correspond with him." She broke eye contact with me and turned her gaze toward the deep aquamarine of the ocean. "But he was not the first in the movement with whom I had contact. Pyord Venko wrote to me first."

"Venko," I breathed. I should have known—I knew that he drummed up support from Kvys patrician houses. "That's past now," I said.

"It is," she said. "But you must understand. Pyord was not merely a contact, and my house not merely one he hoped to add to his bankroll. He was my cousin. On my mother's side."

I blinked, the sun reflecting on the waves suddenly too bright. "We...we don't choose our family," I stammered.

"For many years, I would have chosen Pyord every time," she said staunchly. "We were friends as children, playing games of make believe in the birchwood in summer and telling stories at the fireside during the long winter months. He—" Her voice caught and I thought I saw tears glimmer in her eyes. "He was a brilliant child. He taught himself to read before his parents hired him a tutor. He taught me to read. I suppose, in the end, he trusted his own brilliance too far."

I found I couldn't answer.

"When he asked my house to support him, I agreed. It seemed a wise investment, from the way he sold it—the government of Galitha was bound to change, and my house would shift from one of average consequence to highly influential if it was one of those that had been a friend and ally of the new government from the first." I understood this—the same reason Kvyset would tacitly support us now, the gamble that a new government would be a better ally.

Alba stared out into the water for several breaths before she continued. "I sent money. I even—and this is what I find I have difficulty admitting—I even promised him our cavalry." She turned back to me. "I am sorry. I didn't realize that his ambition had overtaken his ethics, or that his intellect had overtaken his compassion. I still saw him as a brilliant boy, a visionary."

I withdrew from the railing. Alba was right—part of me wanted to bolt from her, to run from the ship and up the gangplank and into Port Triumph. But another part of me understood. A part of me that had trusted Kristos, loved him, and been betrayed for that love. I had the tenuous, brittle chance of rebuilding that trust with my brother, something Alba would never have with Pyord.

"I wish," I said, with deliberate control, "that I had the chance to know the brilliant boy you did. I only saw the ambitious man he became."

"I wish you had, too," Alba whispered.

"Kristos knew, of course. That you and Pyord were close, were related. He didn't tell me."

"I asked him to let me tell you in my own time. I presumed that you wouldn't trust me if you knew. And I needed you to trust me enough so that I could help you and, in turn, help your country."

I hesitated. I had been lied to and manipulated in worse ways than Alba keeping a secret about her relationship to Pyord. Yet those lies had turned me into a pawn, and that had recast me in a new mold that didn't trust as easily, that didn't forgive lies. Alba had saved my skin, of course—but Pyord would have done the same if it benefited him. She had my brother's trust, but that inspired little confidence. She had sought me out at the summit, and that could have been a ploy from the beginning.

"I'm not going to abandon our plans," I said finally. "But I—please excuse me." I retreated toward the other side of the ship, facing the open water, and saw Sianh standing near the prow of the ship.

"How much of that did you hear?" I asked.

"Enough," he replied with a faint smile. "It's a small ship. We should likely get used to a certain lack of confidentiality." He turned his gaze back toward the low waves lapping the docks.

His distance was maddening. I didn't know or trust him any more than Alba, but I expected some response, either outrage at her deception or consolation that she was still trustworthy.

"And?" I finally asked.

"And she was close with a man who used you poorly."

"Perhaps you don't know the entire story—"

"I know enough." He shrugged. "What are you asking? Do I think you should be her friend, confide all your secrets in her?" He shook his head with a laugh. "I do not care. And neither should you, not any longer."

"If I can't trust her—"

"What is trust? What are you trusting her with, precisely? She is your ally, not your friend. You want the same thing, you are useful to one another to obtain it." Sianh didn't take his eyes off the water, so he didn't see my stunned face as I fell silent. I had layered the two, ally and friend, and stitched them up together with trust like a seam lapped over itself.

"Your friends may not be on your side, and those on your side may not be your friends," he continued. "You see that when you look to the Lady Viola and the Lady Annette, yes? Untangle the two, friendship and alliance, and you will be happier."

"I doubt I'll be happier," I replied.

"Wrong word. You will stop driving yourself to distraction, fretting over who is your friend. The meaning of trust with an ally is utilitarian, not emotional."

"I don't know if I'm ready for that."

He softened. "You're likely not. It is a strange thing, to stop seeing yourself as merely a self, and to see yourself as representing many others. Acting for many others."

Sianh was right. I understood, as a shop owner, that my choices were for others and not only for myself. I had to translate that into this new world I found myself floundering in. I wasn't acting on my behalf, but on the behalf of an entire nation. Sobered by that thought, I put aside the question of trust as a friend would think of it, and accepted, faltering, the reality that continuing a partnership with Alba was best for those I represented.

"It gets easier," he said. "I knew the men serving under me were not my friends. They had friends among one another. They were permitted that luxury. Those of the same rank as I, by and large, were not my friends. Peers, perhaps, not friends. It goes without saying that my superiors were not my friends."

"I don't think we quite have that sort of rank structure here," I cautioned him.

"We will. And you are among the leaders. And leaders have very, very few friends." He grinned. I didn't return the smile. "Come now. You will have fame and a place in history."

"At the price of being lonely and friendless, constantly embroiled in a game of 'who is my ally' with everyone I meet?"

Sianh laughed. "Hardly. Be patient. And don't look for your friends among those with whom you must work."

I nodded and left him looking out over the water. I wondered if he intended to spend the entire voyage that way, eyes fixed on some point in the churning waves.

53

I RETREATED TO THE TINY, SPARE CABIN I SHARED WITH THEODOR. The pale wood of the walls reflected the sunlight burrowing through a small porthole. On a gray day the cabin would be a gloomy place, but now sunlight danced on the walls, reflected from the water into warped, fanciful luminosity. Someone had placed a trio of water lilies in a low, footed bowl, an unnecessary affectation, but I inhaled their spicy scent anyway.

I sank onto the straw tick that would serve as a mattress. This is who I was now, then. A leader of the Reformists. A founder, perhaps, of a new era for Galitha. Just as likely—perhaps more likely—a footnote in history, one of the executed or exiled rebels to the Crown swiftly annihilated in the Galatine Civil War.

And what could I do, anyway? Theodor was an inspiring leader, Kristos was a visionary and writer, Sianh was a military strategist, and Niko had dredged together a resistance and held the capital already. I was no one. A seamstress with a business that was likely a casualty of war. A consort to a prince who was unlikely to ever inherit a crown. A charm caster whose magic, which once seemed so potent and full of possibility, now seemed insignificant.

I returned to the deck, where the coast of Serafe was beginning to recede and the salt spray to whip across the deck.

"We've a direct course mapped out," Ballantine said, noting points on the map in front of him with his forefinger and thumb, turning them like a pair of pincers. "Niko Otni has an army, of a sort, raised to hold the capital. We need to establish a base of operations south of the city—and here is a good place to make landfall." He pointed to a mark on the map—Hazelwhite, a small town I had never heard of.

"We'll be outmatched, at least at first, in manpower as well as supplies and funds." Theodor traced the sharp black dot on the map. I reached for his hand.

"Yes. But as you say, the Royalists are spread far and wide there, too, despite their money and their supplies. You will need to strategize, you see, to even the field." Sianh ticked off points on his thin fingers. "Capture what supplies you can, what arms offer the most advantage. Cannon, most likely. Render what supplies you cannot capture useless. Fight as foxes."

Kristos laughed. "That sounds like one of my bad metaphors."

"In the Serafan army, there are light forces—the word is similar in Serafan to *fox*, so they are often called the foxes. Small raiding parties, ambush attacks."

"Guerilla warfare." Ballantine exhaled through his nose. I felt Theodor's hand tighten.

"No, it's not dignified," Kristos said. "You'll notice you're the only one of us here in a fine uniform."

"We have little choice," Theodor conceded. "So we shore up at Hazelwhite."

"We should consider the map again," Sianh said. "There is much to discuss."

I slipped away. Sailors went about their tasks, experience showing in the quick, effortless movements. I wondered what they thought of us, a strange group paying more than the job was worth. Would they get a cut of the extraordinary bonus

Theodor had offered the brig's owner? One scrawny sailor in threadbare slops glanced at me; I doubted it.

Theodor found me leaning on the rail, watching a distant island slip farther into the horizon. The country already appeared as a low, green smudge punctuated by black peaks.

"Even from this distance, the outer Serafan islands look so very different from Galitha's islands."

"Perhaps not so different," I mused as a sailor hauled a rope past us, tugging his trousers up by the waistband. "Are you all right?"

"I will be." His strained smile torqued an immobile face. "What Sianh describes—quite frankly, it terrifies me. My only military training is book knowledge and some archaic swordplay, not this ragged business in the dirt."

"You mean actual war?"

"Yes, actual war." There was grief in that lopsided smile. "I never wanted war to come to Galitha. We tried to avoid it. And then . . . I'm not quite sure how to be a leader in this movement and not a usurper to the throne, how to ally with those who would have overthrown the government last winter when my goal is to institute rule of law today."

"Crown Prince of Contradiction," I said with a mock bow.

"Not a title I ever wanted." He lifted his head, watching a bird soaring high overhead. It dipped its broad wings and hovered lower, lower, and then dove into the waves, emerging with a fish already half-swallowed. "An albatross," he mused. We watched it bob on the surface, its long wings tucked delicately alongside its body as it finished its meal.

"It's huge," I said, the statement absurdly obvious. I didn't know what else to say—our lives were shifting with almost unbearable speed. I could be parted from Theodor and, in my greatest fears, never see him again. The chain around my wrist, promising marriage, promising future, might be nothing more than dead, cold gold. So there was a large bird preening just off the starboard bow; it was the only thing I could find words for.

"One of the largest wingspans in the known world. They must have a rookery on one of these islands—summer is their mating season."

"How did you come to know so much about albatrosses?" I asked.

"One of the more useless things my tutors insisted I learn was ornithology."

"And botany was so very useful?"

"If I need to, I could identify edible plants from all the major regions of Galitha and most of Kvyset, thank you very much." He laughed. "But I did like the bit about the albatrosses. They mate for life, and one of our books had illustrations of the dance they do when the pairs reunite. You see, they spend most of their time at sea, separated. They return to the same island every year and raise their young, then leave one another again, for months, and don't set foot on the ground again until they reach their island and greet one another with their dance."

"They...dance?"

"It's called a dance, at any rate. The book said they bob their heads and twine their necks and pat their feet—it sounds ridiculous, I know, but the idea of those two birds finding one another, across all that distance, and remembering their dance? I liked that idea." He covered his hand with mine. Our matching chains clinked gently. "I like it now."

"I don't think I can learn a dance." I smiled softly.

"I think we already have," Theodor replied. "I think we've started to learn to live alongside one another. We know one another, what makes us happy. What grieves us. What shaped us, what we hope for tomorrow. What makes each other smile, what makes you angry."

"What makes *me* angry!" I laughed.

He pulled an arm around me. "What makes the other laugh, when she needs it. When to stop laughing and simply be still." I held his arm close around my waist. The quiet bustle of seafaring work surrounding us faded, and there was, for a few brief moments, only us. "All the minute intricacies that make a life together.

"It's very possible we will have to separate at some point," he added abruptly. "I have to believe that if albatrosses can find each other and fall into their dance after months at sea, apart, we will, too. We might hit the wrong rhythms at first, or step off beat. But we'll remember." With a spray of water and rush of wings, the albatross lifted off from the waves, soaring quickly out of sight.

"Was any of that true? About the albatross?" I asked.

"Every word," Theodor said, pulling me into a swift kiss.

I closed my eyes, relishing this moment, perhaps the last one for a long time. The outbreak of war erased the need to shoehorn myself into acceptance with the nobility, and the uncertainty of our futures blotted out any reticence about marriage I stubbornly held to. I had fashioned myself by what I had made—a shop, a career, closetfuls of beautiful creations—and had likely lost it all. I was still Sophie, still a seamstress, still a charm caster, even without a sign over a door in Galitha City.

I didn't have to give anything up to accept a future with Theodor. He sought me, stayed with me, danced with me for who I was. As he held me, past and future melted away and for a moment we simply were, together, in the present.

54

WE HAD SEVERAL DAYS AT SEA BEFORE WE WOULD REACH THE Galatine coast near Hazelwhite, and we put them to good use. Theodor and Kristos spent long hours in discussion with Sianh, determining military strategy and, implicitly, solidifying their roles as leaders of an army.

"I've begun work on some...shall we say, 'inspiring' pamphlets to encourage participation in our cause from the people," Kristos said. "Not to boast, but the Pen of the Midwinter Revolt never had any trouble pulling support." I gave him an encouraging smile, but the question nagged me—what was I going to do of use? Theodor, Kristos, and Niko made a veritable trio of leadership, though I very much anticipated they would fight like cats. Sianh would train an army. I was marching to war with no direction.

Theodor drummed his fingers on the table, a marching beat of his own. "Even with manpower, we need supplies. We need cannon and shot and powder and—damn it, we even need wool and linen for uniforms. We don't have many noble coffers at our disposal, and the Royalists can outspend us ten to one."

"We have the majority of the country on our side, in terms of people, but the nobles have the money," I agreed.

"You won't get Kvyset on your side, not fully." Alba folded her hands neatly, prim as a pin. "Some houses will offer support, either financial or sending a troop of hired horse." A pert smile snuck through. "My house will certainly do so. It did once before. But overall—yes, the Royalists have West Serafe backing them, and you have no one."

"What of the Allied States?" Kristos asked.

Theodor shook his head and Alba laughed, adding, "They won't take a side. They don't have to. They're so secure in their neutrality, so assured that neither side would cut trade ties, that they will ride this out and befriend the winner."

"What about Fen?" I knew before I finished speaking that it was a stupid question—Fen was practically powerless, a neutered island nation.

Theodor began to argue, but Alba stopped him. "It's worth considering. Fen—and Pellia, for that matter—have little to lose and much to gain in an alliance with a new Galatine government. Not unlike Kvyset, but perhaps even more—a friend in a high place, perhaps, where there was no friend before."

"If they help us now, they can be assured of favoritism later," Kristos mused. "Are we in a position to offer anything concrete? Trade monopolies or assistance or lifting tariffs?"

Theodor nodded slowly. "Yes, we could do any of those things. But I'm loath to overcommit ourselves for—what? Bolts of wool and blankets?"

"We will need blankets, most likely. Unless you want soldiers to freeze this winter." Alba shrugged.

"Besides," Kristos said, "you've forgotten Fen's other resource."

"Rocks?" Theodor said.

"Coal. They're even now more fully industrialized than Galitha, and even in the short time I was there I saw the beginnings of a boom. Each factory and foundry owner racing to outpace his competition." He narrowed his eyes, as though squinting at a page of very small writing he couldn't quite make out. "If it's cannon and shot we need, muskets and bayonets, then we need Fen. We don't have many noble coffers, but we have some. Fen's foundries are hungry for investment, to grow. They would take our business; our money is just as good as anyone else's. And they could outfit a fleet by winter."

Theodor considered this. "We need cannon, and shot, and muskets—Galatine Divine, we need a damned navy. If an alliance with Fen can give us that, it's well worth pursuing." He glanced at me, ready to say something else, but stopped.

"And Pellia?" Alba asked, tickled by my brother's suggestion. "What is Pellia hiding?"

"Pellia produces salted redfin and fish oil." Kristos looked right at me. "And charm casters."

Theodor's eyes on me became almost too much to bear. "Iron and wool," he said, "and charm casting."

"Theodor," I said, voice low.

He pressed on despite the warning in my voice. "Remember the night of the Midwinter Revolt? You gave the soldiers charms then. What if we could give our army charmed uniforms?"

"Yes, but—" I shook my head. "I just wanted to keep them from being hurt. I wanted to keep everyone from being hurt." It hadn't felt like a military strategy at the time, like I was throwing my abilities on one side of a conflict. I saw clearly now that it was. I had, in a sense, militarized my own gift. "But I couldn't possibly outfit an entire army with charms."

"We both know there are other ways to embed your charms. Perhaps it could be done on a larger scale," he said, meaning implicit and unspoken, his own part in our experiments still secret.

"No," I whispered. "Theodor, no. If I could—and I don't

know that I could—what would that mean?" I imagined it, iron forged with luck, wool loomed with health. My ability turned commodity on a mass scale. The industrialization of the art of my grandmothers—it was a perversion, wasn't it?

"It could mean the turning point for an army that, at this point, will be outgunned and outmanned."

I trembled, though whether with anger or bitter guilt, I couldn't tell. I had always held fast to my ethics. I had broken them only once, to craft the curse in the queen's shawl, and that still haunted me. This felt like abandonment of the core ethics of casting, even if no one had ever warned me against this particular use. Still, Theodor was right. We needed far more luck than I could dole out piecemeal.

"I won't press you," Theodor said, disappointment thick and gray in his voice.

"I will," Kristos said.

"Damn it, Balstrade." Theodor whirled.

"No, Kristos, you don't get to argue with me about this," I said. "Not you. Of all people."

"I know. I—"

"If you know then you won't say anything to me. Not now, not ever. Not about this."

Kristos bit his lip. I knew that face, knew it better than even he did, perhaps—the burning impatience he felt when he wanted, very badly, to say something. He made it a dozen times a day when we were children, wisely restraining himself from talking back to our mother.

"I can never make up for what I did," Kristos finally said. "I coerced you. I promise I will never do so again."

I nodded, once. Terse acceptance of that earnest and yet impossibly inadequate apology.

"I will say this." He held up a hand to my protest. "This

is your choice. My life, Theodor's life, the lives of thousands may hang on it. Your life may eventually hang on it. The fate of nations may hang on it. But it is your choice. Yours alone. No one will force your choice. No one."

I fell into a morose silence. None of them would force me, but the war already had. My rules were, perhaps, good ones, guiding principles for ordinary times, but I had outpaced them. If I could do something, I was bound to try. Besides, I argued to myself, feeling the weakness of the ethics even as I considered it, someone would eventually discover what I had discovered. Someone else would find that charms could be pulled from the ether and embedded without a clay tablet or a needle and thread. Someone would put it to use for their country or their army.

The ethics were weak, but the pragmatism was inarguable. "All right. I'll try."

55

ALBA PRODUCED A SMALL LEATHER NOTEBOOK AND A GRAPHITE stick. She made a few hasty marks, concentration tightening the furrow between her eyes. "There. I've calculated the percentage of my house's coffers that we can put, immediately, toward infrastructure in Fen. I daresay we'll have little difficulty finding at least one foundry, perhaps two, able to turn these funds into cannons within months, and woolen and linen mills who will make contracts with us when they see what we're able to invest."

"Months." I shook my head. "It seems a long time."

"But it's worth it to establish our own supply line." Alba watched me carefully. "And you believe we can imbue those supplies with additional...fortification?"

"That's a puzzle I'm still working out," I hedged. "I certainly can't sew all the garments myself. I couldn't even sew cockades for a quarter of their hats. I'm not sure that there's any other method I could use." I met Theodor's eyes—the one method I did have was his violin, and we both knew that he couldn't come with me, fiddling at a factory to charm the fibers of the flax and wool they wove. "Worst case, I can...I don't know. Sew a few buttons on as many coats as I can...or make pieces for elite forces." This felt pitifully inadequate, but everyone was kind enough not to say so.

"I'll write to Annette and Viola," Theodor said. "I'm sure they'll be willing to put some money toward supplies. So don't finalize those calculations quite yet," he said to Alba.

"I won't." She looked at me again. "It seems to me that investing in wool and linen is only worthwhile if they can be charmed. So that, shall we say, puzzle must be solved rather quickly."

I nodded soberly and began to pace the deck. The sea reflected the sun in its rich, ever-varying blue. Watching the gentle swell and dip of the waves calmed my racing thoughts, so I stared into the depths and took a few breaths.

I stopped. Did I need the violin to cast directly? Surely, I had learned by now that the casting methodology was only the way a practitioner reached to the light and drew it out. The method was either literal and crude, like the folk practice of carving tablets, or utilized someone's talents, like my sewing or Theodor's violin playing.

But what if I could draw it from the ether itself, without the aid of a sewing needle or music?

I had always begun with sewing, starting with the needle and thread until the light appeared around my action. I struggled to even put myself in the right frame of mind—of being, really—to see past the visible and into the place where the charms and curses came from. Without my needle in hand, it felt impossible. I threw myself back in memory, to first drawing the light as a child under my mother's tutelage. Had it been easy, hard? Had she guided me? The first lessons blurred in memory, wrapped up with the scent of simmering spinach and the feel of our dusty packed-dirt floor beneath my bare toes.

I couldn't remember, and the invocation of the light was so tied with the action of sewing. I fished out my housewife from my pocket and began to sew, trying to locate within myself the moment where I sensed the light, the moment I could grasp it and draw it into my work. It was like staring into a bright candle flame—the closer I looked, the less I could see. The intrusion of thought over rote practice drove the light away and swiftly built a headache out of the tension in my temples.

I returned to my cabin. I tried mimicking sewing, then stopping the motions; I tried imagining music; I tried closing my eyes and slipping into a half daydream. Nothing worked, except pretending to sew, which only worked as long as I kept up the motions, and even then the trail of light was thin and recalcitrant, trying to follow the motions of an imaginary needle rather than my wishes for it.

I threw myself on the bed and stared at the pale wood of the cabin's ceiling, the water reflections playing on the slats above me. Not so unlike the charm light. The thirati, Corvin had said they were called. As real as matter and space, as real as heat and cold.

Real. Of course—I was trying to pull the magic from the air in order to see it. I had to reverse my tactic. My gift wasn't solely for manipulating the thirati—it was for *seeing* it to begin with. If I could see it, perhaps I could work with it. But how to sense something beyond my sight, feel something hidden behind the screen that cuts the invisible world off from the visible? It was like asking to see love, or grief, or joy, I thought with a pang of defeat.

Except it was, in fact, very much like seeing an emotion. I felt a certain kind of contentment while I cast charms, and a dark heaviness when I cast curses; I had always assumed this was an effect of the casting. But what if it was tied to its source, what if

I was "seeing" the magic with my intuition? I tried to find that emotion in myself, that feeling of unshakable comfort, of patient joy that accompanied strong charm casting. It was elusive, like trying to force a smile from a stubborn child, but the stirrings of it blossomed in my chest, warmed my limbs, tingled in my fingers as I pressed my thoughts toward the greenhouse with Theodor mere weeks earlier, or splitting a sticky nut roll with my mother, long ago. I traced the chain on my wrist and freed the unbound imaginings of future happiness.

Finally, I saw as well as felt the magic—a thin golden stream of light, distinct from the sunlight and the reflection of the water. I pulled the strand of gold from the air, twining it into a thin circle. It hung suspended in the air before me, a perfect golden ring. What to do with it now? I wondered, toying with it, moving it between my fingers, letting it bounce between my hands. I laid it on the bedspread and imagined it a part of the fibers, embedding it into the fabric. A little golden ring, now as much a part of the woven wool as if I had embroidered it with needle and thread.

I played at it for another hour or more, feeling lighter, feeling more joyful as I worked. I pulled light and twisted it, spread it, manipulated it like fibers and like clay, let it dance and swell and pulse in its own state, held but unchanged by me. I could work the light into cloth easily, into wood with some difficulty, even, awkwardly, etched into glass. I laughed, imagining the owner of this ship never knowing about the invaluable, invisible decorations in one of his cabins. I was still clumsy, and slow, but confidence welled in me—I could do this. I could charm cloth on the looms or shot in the molds.

Reticently, I allowed the light to fade away, slipping back into the ether. I swallowed—I had to know if I could, if it was possible, so I sought and finally found the heavy feeling of curse casting, buried deep yet too willing to rise to the surface. I drew the glittering black from the ether like a thick stroke of ink from a pen, wrapping it into a delicate spiral. I could manipulate it, move it, hold it just as the charm thread, though when I brought it too close to the golden ring in the coverlet it seemed to pull away, repelled by the presence of its opposite. I didn't want to embed it here, but letting it sink back into the air didn't prove anything to me about whether I could manipulate it as I could the charms. Eventually, I hovered it over the bowl of water with the floating lilies, and submerged the ring. Imagining it dissolving, I pressed it into the water.

The water took on a faint murkiness, still clear but now a dim, transparent gray. The thought unsettled me—what, precisely, had I done? Could I draw the curse from the water as I knew I could from fabric? Or would it linger here forever?

I lay down, closing my eyes. I felt the familiar exhaustion of casting, intensified without the crutch of sewing. I didn't mean to, but I fell asleep, rocked by the boat. When I woke, I heard the bustle of feet and clank of chains that told me the decks were busy with the sailors' work.

I glanced at the bowl of lilies, and my stomach clenched.

The lilies had withered. Their green leaves and stems were brown and brittle, and the petals aged to crackling parchment. Even the scent, a luminous, heady perfume before, had decomposed and become curdled, thick.

I scooped the flowers out with shaking hands and threw them away in a rusted waste bin, then turned back to the water. The distortions I had caused caught the light and glittered faintly, darkly. My questions were suddenly urgent instead of hypothetical, and I suppressed my panic and began to pull the curse from the water. Painfully, the disintegrated sparkle coalesced, first into a blot of dark in the bowl, and then pulled like stormy taffy into a thick thread. I drew it into the air, then dispersed it, pushing it back into the ether.

I sat shaking. This was far beyond the influence of curse or charm. This was life and death in a thin thread of dark sparkle, and no one could know that I could control it.

Theodor found me staring at the water in the otherwise empty vase. "Aren't you hungry?" he asked. "It's nearly supper and you skipped the midday meal."

I shook my head—hunger was the furthest thing from my mind, even though casting usually left me more than ready for a meal. I explained what I'd done, and Theodor's pride over my achievement shifted as swiftly as mine had when I described the effect of pure curse magic on the flowers. We agreed that experimenting further was not only unwise but impractical. After all, I wasn't going to try to soak a living person, or even creature, in curse magic.

"Don't tell the others about it," I almost begged. "The charm casting, of course, I'll tell them first thing tomorrow, but the curse..." I swallowed. "They might want it used, and I can't even begin to think how I'd control it. If I even wanted to."

"No, of course not. When we began to try out more methods and uses for casting, I confess even I hadn't thought of that." He sighed, creases between his eyebrows deepening.

"It's not your fault," I said. "At least...at least we know the Serafans can't do this, right? Or they probably would have tried on me." I tried for a joke and mostly failed.

"Are you sure you aren't hungry? I could bring a tray, or—"

"I'm really not. I'd rather go to bed," I said, holding out an arm to him, beckoning. He understood. With the weight of wielding death on my shoulders, I craved closeness, warmth, life. He slipped into the narrow bed beside me and pulled me close, his lips tracing the curve of my ear, the hollow of my cheek. My hands explored all the familiar lines of his body, his narrow shoulders, arms still lined with dexterous muscle from pulling weeds and digging in the dirt. Fingers tipped with callouses from his violin. All of him, expressed in the subtleties of his skin.

It was still light when we curled against one another and slipped into sleep.

56

As soon as we'd eaten a bland breakfast of porridge with dried fruit and weak tea, I cleared my throat. "I think I've figured out a...method to charm cast over larger quantities," I said. I wasn't sure how to explain it to anyone who couldn't cast, but no one seemed particularly keen on asking as they congratulated me.

"You could put it in cloth being woven?" Alba asked eagerly.

Before I could reply, Kristos added, "And cannon? Shot? What about cursed bayonets?"

"Wait," I said. "I'm not sure what effects curses would have." Not to mention, I didn't need to admit that I knew how to cast curses to a wider audience than already knew.

"Cannons with curses might be more accurate, might fire truer—"

"Or curses might cause the artillery pieces to blow up more frequently," Sianh replied. "Would the curse be directed at the enemy or no?"

"I couldn't say," I said. "So I think it's best if we work within the parameters of charm magic, for the time being."

Alba smiled. "Regardless. This will be a secret weapon

the Royalists can't even imagine. You'll return to Kvyset with me and from there, we will negotiate trade deals with Fenian businesses."

"There's one problem," I said quietly.

Alba met my eyes. "What is that?"

"Casting is illegal in Fen. Anything resembling magic— even illusion like Serafan magicians employ," I said. "Even card tricks."

Alba heaved a breath. "Illegal, yes. But this kind of money will convince any smart foundry owner to ignore what you're doing. If they even have reason to notice to begin with."

"Why is it illegal?" Ballantine asked. "I confess, for all my knowledge of the currents and winds, to know little enough of Fenian taboos."

"That's hardly important information at the moment," Alba said, sinking her forehead into her hands in a pantomime of weariness.

"It may be important," Sianh said, "to understanding how we can get around it."

"It is illegal because it simply...is," Alba said. "The Fenians have very little sense of humor. Less than the Kvys. They're the Kvys for whom Kvyset wasn't humorless enough, remember?"

I shook my head. "I'm afraid I don't."

Alba conceded. "I'm sorry, I assumed. Fen was colonized by Kvyset centuries ago. Before that, it was an island inhabited by...oh, seals, mostly. And terns. Bandyneck deer, I suppose. At any rate, there was a schism in the Kvys Church, and the outcasts scurried off to Fen. After they got there, some investors pulled their heads from their logbooks long enough to realize that the fishing and the logging out of a fresh country like Fen would make good money."

"So Fen is a nation of religious zealots and businessmen?"

Kristos shrugged. "Could be useful. To know a people, to get their aid, to see how they might be helpful."

"*They're* not helpful people at all," Alba replied. "The religious zealotry died away long ago, but it did leave quite a mark on their social norms regarding magic, marriage, music, general joy... don't try to tell them dirty jokes, they don't even understand them. But money, money they understand." She took a breath. "Fair enough, it is helpful to know where they come from. Fen is a hard place, difficult to carve a living from. They have to be focused on their profits, or else they won't eat."

"I know the feeling," I said quietly. "Very well. We find a Fenian mill and foundry who will take the alliance and turn a blind eye to anything unusual."

A sudden increase in the flurry of sailors around us wrenched our attention away from future strategies toward the immediate. Ballantine ran past, spyglass in hand. He posted himself at the stern, searching the waves intently.

"She's a frigate, no doubt, but is she Galatine?" He scrutinized through the glass further. "I can't tell yet."

"Does it matter?" Kristos appeared from the other side of the ship. "If she's Galatine or Serafan, that is. We don't want to be apprehended by either."

"If she's Serafan, she might not be after us. It might be coincidence." Ballantine lowered the glass. "If she's Galatine, there's no reason for her to be here save belligerence."

"Lovely," Alba murmured, joining us. "Just when I had in mind we'd manage a bit of a lull before we all had to chin up and fight."

"Never so lucky," Theodor replied. "We should likely assume she's foe and keep ahead of her, yes?"

"Of course," his brother replied. He called orders to the mate, who deferred with a grumpy nod. "They didn't sign on for this," he added, to himself more than anything. We had reticent sailors and a captain who had only served under other officers, but I quelled the rising panic. We were far ahead of the frigate, and it might be only a Serafan navy vessel on regular maneuvers.

"You all right?" Theodor whispered to me. He slipped his hand in mine. I gripped tightly.

"As much as any of us," I tried to joke. We waited, stiff and sweating under a mounting sun, to know if we were about to be sunk by one of our own ships.

Ballantine snapped his glass shut. "She's Galatine."

57

Nothing changed at Ballantine's announcement; the sailors still moved as though fixed pieces in the mechanics of the ship, the sails still billowed and strained against the wind, and we still stood rooted to the deck.

"Shouldn't they ready the guns, or have some sort of battle stations, or—"

Ballantine answered his brother's questions with a single look. "That frigate is fitted out with enough twenty-four-pound guns to make matchsticks of this vessel if it came to a proper broadside. Not to mention she's manned by His Majesty's sailors and officers, and likely a complement of His Majesty's marines, and you've got Serafan sea rats who have no skin in this game past their pay, and, might I add, a rather green commanding officer."

"Can we outrun them?" Theodor asked. "We don't have to fight, that isn't why we're out here. We just need to make port."

Ballantine pressed his lips together, running quick calculations he didn't verbalize. "It's possible. Not plausible, mind you."

"What choice do we have?" Kristos asked.

"We don't know what they want," Theodor cautioned.

"That is—we know they want us out of the fight. But that doesn't mean…"

"Even if it doesn't mean execution. Yes, I'll say it even if you won't." Kristos turned his face back toward the frigate's bright sails. "It means the war is over before it's under way, if you're correct in your assessments that what's needed is centralized leadership. If you're right that we can give the Reformists that leadership."

"I'm not going to sacrifice this crew fighting for me," Theodor answered.

"Very gallant of you," Kristos answered. "I'm willing to sacrifice anything for Galitha."

I swallowed. I knew Kristos believed he would—he'd been willing to sacrifice me once. "Whose decision is it?" I said. Both of them looked at me, confused. "It's the captain's decision, isn't it? And our captain is currently Lieutenant Westland."

"I'm hardly qualified—"

"You're the only one even close to qualified to decide what this ship does. You say she might be able to outrun them. You say she can't win in a fight. We all know that we could surrender."

He sighed. "It's a long way to Hazelwhite."

"Do we have to get all the way to this Hazelwhite?" Alba interjected with calm confidence.

"We could go overland," Kristos said. "If we can outrun them far enough to get us safely ashore somewhere." The imposing gray cliffs of southern Galitha seemed to mock us.

Ballantine considered this, glancing from Alba to Kristos, assessing both the idea and the speakers. "There's a cove perhaps twelve miles ahead. If we can outrun them that far, we could lower the longboat and you could make your way from there. If we're particularly good about it, we could have you out of sight before they can see, and continue on as a decoy."

"That could actually work," Kristos said with a wry grin.

"Just a moment. What if this ship were caught, what would they do with Sophie? And you?" Theodor asked.

"I'd be court martialed, most likely," Ballantine said. He held up a hand at my protest. "No, I knew it was a possibility. It's conceivable my father would intervene, but it's also likely that, out of principle, he won't. The foreigners—they wouldn't, if they were wise, harm them. They'd give parole and send them on their way."

"And Sophie?" Theodor asked again.

"I don't know," he said softly, glancing at me. "Truly. I don't know if she would be considered worth taking prisoner, or if she'd be let go, or..."

"Then we can't worry about that now," I said, as boldly as I could. My voice still wavered, but the salt wind blew hard enough that I didn't think anyone heard.

"Do you think," Theodor said, glancing at the billowing sails, "that there's anything you can do to assist?"

I felt the pitch and roll of the ship around me, the salt spray peppering us, the steady wind. I didn't understand how any of it worked. I would have to trust Ballantine to capture that wind and use it to our advantage even as the frigate on our trail would be doing their damnedest to utilize it, as well. "If I knew what would help, I—"

The report of a cannon interrupted me, its hollow echo amplified over the water and resounding in my chest. Behind us, the shot plunged into the ocean with a plume of white spray. Ballantine snapped to attention, watching our pursuer through his glass.

"We're still out of range," he said, "but I'm needed to direct the sailors."

"What can I do?" I asked, catching his sleeve before he could leave.

"You mean, with your...?"

"Yes. With charms."

"You can't curse them to a watery hell?"

"No," I answered, not interested in explaining that I wouldn't curse them even if I could, and that of course I had no idea how to cast anything on a far-distant ship in any case.

"Can you protect things?"

No time for complicated explanations of the limits of casting or the difficulties with my abilities. "Yes."

"The rigging. The sails. Unless I miss my guess, they will not want to sink us. So they'll fire chain shot at the rigging to disable us."

"The sails," I confirmed, letting the silver-braided sleeve of his coat go. He disappeared. I swallowed, forming a plan quickly. Charm magic, embedded into the weave of the sails and the twist of the ropes. As swiftly as I could, I began to tease grudging light from the ether, summoning more and more of it under my control.

"Do you need my violin?"

I almost lost control of the threads but held them steady as I answered Theodor. "I don't." It sounded almost like an apology. This was faster, if I could manage it, but I realized as well that I missed our tandem casting. I didn't need him in this tangible, immediate way.

But I didn't have time to explain that to him. Instead, I turned my attention back to the protection charm, pulling it from the ether and twining the light into the fibers of the ropes that made a web of the masts. Sailors moved past them, through them, moved the ropes themselves, but if the length of hemp twist I was working on moved away, I simply cut off the charm and moved on to another. Soon the ropes were awash with light, visible to me and Theodor alone, glittering unevenly due to my hasty work.

I continued on to the sails, this time attempting to craft a webbing from the light, imagining it becoming loosely woven swaths like nets. I wove and threw, wove and threw, settling the nets over the sails, and then pressing the charm into the fibers of the sails, messy crosshatches sinking into the fabric itself. Where it crossed the seasoned wood of the masts, I didn't bother trying to embed the charm—it took too much effort, too much time to work with the solid, hard grain of wood.

I began to weave another net from the charm magic, but an echoing cannon report broke my concentration.

"They're still out of range," Ballantine said. I glanced at him. He was pale, but no hint of panic breached his voice. "For now. I think they know we're not up for the fight and are trying to outpace them."

I worked another layer of protection charm into the sails. They fairly glowed with a web of charm. If we survived this, if the ship wasn't sunk or smashed to bits, I wondered how long the tangled charms would last in the ropes and canvas, if the salt spray and sea wind would corrode the magic from them as it wore away the fibers themselves.

A confident pessimism settled deep in the pit of my stomach, assuring me that my theory would likely remain untested. Out of my sight but in Ballantine's glass, the frigate's guns were readying charges for us.

"So that's what you can do, now." Theodor stood beside me, scanning the sails with wonder and, I thought, a bit of fear. Fear of me, or of the swiftly approaching frigate?

"The inlet is just ahead. Ballantine says there's space to land a small vessel easily enough, a longboat or the like."

"The longboat." I could try a charm on it—even though embedding charms in wood was more difficult, any bit of luck was better than none. And we needed luck. "Where is it?"

Theodor led me to the wooden vessel, intended for small landing parties, outfitted with several rows of oars. I hastily wove a charm, a weak, messy one, and pressed it into the wood with all my will. I repeated the process, beginning to sweat, my stomach knotting. The work of casting from the ether, without my needle and thread, was more taxing, and solid wood less pliable to the inclusion of the charm. I pushed through it, layering light on the small boat, willing luck on it as though my hope alone could ferry it to safety.

"There," I said shakily. "I wish . . . I wish I could do more."

"It's more luck than the Galatines behind us have," Theodor replied with a small smile. "I have the best kind of luck on my side."

"And then this is farewell." It didn't feel like a proper goodbye, hastily said on the deck of a ship now keening a bit to starboard as Ballantine pushed us toward the cove. But what romantic fantasy had I concocted without meaning to? A winsome private moment on the deck of a bustling ship? Being swept into arms that were holding too much already, gazed upon by a man who was focused on far bigger things than me?

"Only for a while. You'll be safe in Kvyset with Alba," he added, reassuring himself, perhaps, but not me.

A while—who knew how long? It was pointless to ask now. "I care less about being safe than about being useful," I said.

"You've done more than you know," Theodor whispered into my hair. I closed my eyes, briefly, and took in the scent of his clove pomade and his finely milled soap, let my fingers close over his.

Kristos joined us. "Readying the longboat now. I hope these Serafans can row."

"They can," Sianh said with a grim smile, striding toward us. "I've a feeling half of these fellows were prison galley fodder before this." A passing sailor gave him a wide berth.

"Good luck, Sophie," Kristos said, pushing Theodor aside and wrapping me in a hug that, once, would have felt familiar. "Good luck with the Fenians."

"I'll need good luck getting there first," I said.

"I figured you had that in the bag," he said with a grin. "Aren't you wearing a charm?"

"You know I don't wear my own charms."

Kristos shook his head, admiration beaming in his cockeyed smile. "You haven't changed a bit."

"It's time," Ballantine called. We passed a rocky outcropping, heavily forested, that would hide our maneuvers from the frigate, but only for a few minutes. If we were lucky, the Galatines pursuing us wouldn't realize that we had dropped a longboat into the waters of the cove, and if we continued to be lucky—very lucky—the boat could be ashore and hidden before they passed the cove. The former was likely enough; the latter, I knew, would push even the best charms, and mine had been a sloppy one.

I would blame myself, I knew, if they didn't make it. I would blame the charm's weak potency and messy casting, not the impossibility of the plan, not the superior manpower and strength of the ship behind us. My head swam, and I fought the feebleness that rapid casting had left in me.

Kristos took his seat in the longboat first, followed by Sianh and a complement of sailors who were ordered to remain hidden in the forest until the frigate had passed and rendezvous in the nearest town with any Serafan vessel that would take them home. Ballantine doled out pay equal to three times what they had been promised. Their mood lifted tangibly.

Theodor pulled me toward him in one final embrace, hurried and painful. I bit back sobs and saw that tears sprang into his eyes, too. "I love you," he whispered.

"And I love you. Albatross," I added with a laugh.

"Now, Princeling," Kristos called.

"Please," I called back, "don't you two kill each other."

Kristos forced a grin, Theodor took a seat and an oar, and the sailors lowered the boat over the side. We were well hidden by the outcropping, but the process was too slow for my liking. I gripped the rail, wishing I had either Galatine faith in the Sacred Natures or Pellian faith in my ancestors to cling to, to beg for succor, to believe would aid me. Instead, I had to rely on the strong arms of the Serafan sailors and the luck I had cast myself.

The moment the boat was lowered, Ballantine began shouting orders to move us quickly toward the open water. As they rowed away, I forced myself to watch, to show both Theodor and Kristos that I was there for them, that I wouldn't turn my back on them. They grew smaller, closer to the shore as we moved farther from it. I couldn't yet see the frigate; she couldn't yet see us. Just a few more minutes, I wished silently.

"They'll be fine," Alba said. I hadn't seen her approach. She had given us the dignity of our farewells with what small amount of privacy her absence offered. "Regardless of when the Galatines realize they've landed, they'll have a head start. And with only three of them, they'll move quickly through the forest. It isn't easy to track men through wild country like that."

"And have little chance in a fight," I said.

"It won't come to that." She placed a hand gently over mine. I let her. "Come now, a woman who bids luck and controls fortune is a pessimist at a moment like this?"

The white sails of the frigate emerged from behind the trees, their thick green foliage dark like spilled ink where the ship passed behind them. "No," I said, straightening my slumped shoulders. "For whatever good it might do."

58

As the frigate rounded the rocks blocking the cove, I essayed one final look at the longboat. It was beached, and the sailors had disappeared into the forest along with Kristos, Sianh, and Theodor.

"I told them, if they couldn't hide the boat before the frigate rounded the curve, to just leave it on the shore until the frigate was well away." Ballantine stood beside me. "It might—with a grain of luck—look abandoned."

"It has some luck," I replied. "She looks closer."

"I think we may have sent the last of our luck with the longboat," Ballantine agreed. "She's not lowering her own boats. She's following us, which means, thank the Divine Sea, she isn't investigating the boat on the beach." He lowered the glass. His hand shook slightly. "But she's gaining on us, finally."

I turned away. I knew what being intercepted by the frigate might mean for Ballantine, if his father wasn't willing to grant him clemency, and so did he, though his stoic posture didn't belie the fears that must have been coursing through him.

And to me?

"Ladies," Ballantine said quietly. "I would suggest we begin discussing strategy."

Alba nodded crisply. "Indeed. Sophie, with me."

"With you, where?" Ballantine said.

Alba cut him off with a flick of her wrist. "She can't stand here looking like a Galatine lady any longer, for one. They'll be close enough to see her soon, and then all's lost."

"All is lost?" I asked. "Cheerful."

"Lost, if we're to pass you off as anything but Sophie Balstrade, consort of the crown prince and charm caster extraordinaire."

"You want me to disguise myself."

Alba bowed slightly. "You've figured me out."

"But won't they know her—simply as herself? Whatever she is wearing?" Ballantine asked.

"Hardly. Most Galatines wouldn't know her on sight, not like the crown prince who has portraits all over and is known by every Galatine naval officer from here to the Fenian frontier." She pulled me toward her cabin. "And I will assure you. Most people do not look overlong at a nun."

Once inside the cabin, she pulled a second gray wool gown from her pack, nearly identical to the one she was wearing, and a length of fine linen. A veil.

"Be quick, arranging the wimple is a bit tricky," she said, politely turning her back to let me change.

"I haven't agreed to this," I protested. "I'm not sure I even know how to pretend to be a nun."

"You have a better idea?" she asked, her gentle tone taking an edge.

"I could dress as a sailor," I suggested, hesitantly unpinning the front of my gown and then unlacing the panel behind it.

"If I had good binding bands, maybe. But not with that ample endowment," she said with a nod toward my chest. "Leave your underthings on. The stays—sweet Creator, those are nicely made." She sniffed. "I hope no one has cause to see them, or we're sunk. Our underwear in the house is never nearly so nice."

I stripped my cotton gown and donned the gray wool, the lightweight fabric settling over my shift and petticoats as I shook out the skirts. It was a bit too long and a bit too narrow in the shoulders; Alba was built like a birch tree.

"At least your hair isn't dolled up into one of those ridiculous towers," she said, swiftly brushing it out, braiding it, and binding it. She then arranged the stiff, sheer linen veil and pinned it in place. I hardly recognized the woman staring back at me from the warped mirror hanging from Alba's wall.

"The shoes—well, leave them off. Plenty of us go barefoot." I kicked my fine silk slippers under her bed. "No, that won't do. They might look there." She bundled my clothes up and ferried them to my trunk in my cabin. Then, despite my protests, hailed a sailor.

"What are you doing?"

"I wish I could have them dumped overboard, but that would attract attention. I'll have them taken to cargo. I do hope they don't search too thoroughly."

I sank against the wall, still light-headed from too much charm casting, and overwhelmed.

A deafening report shook the ship.

I looked up as chain shot hurtled through the outermost rigging, ripping several ropes asunder.

"Their aim is off," Alba said with a sly look at me. "Or might the rigging have had some help?"

"It won't hold them off forever. It's a luck charm, not some all-powerful warding."

Ballantine joined us. "Well, were I looking for a runaway Galatine consort, I would not recognize you, Sophie."

"Stop calling her that," Alba said. "Sastra—Sastra what? Quick, pick a name."

"Pick a name?" Another cannon shot rippled through the air. It missed us entirely. "What, a Pellian name? A Galatine name? Kvys?" I gripped the gown so tightly I thought it might tear. "Who's going to buy a Pellian-Kvys nun anyway?"

"We have many of many nations in my house," Alba said with forced calm. "But it's best if we don't introduce ourselves as 'Sister Sophie the former consort of the crown prince,' I would think."

"Lieta," I said quickly. For my friend in Galitha City, for the gentle wisdom I hoped I could embody.

"Good, Sastra Lieta."

"Sophie," Ballantine said.

"It's Sastra Lieta now," I said.

He assessed me, unconvinced. "Very well. We can't hold them. We can't outrun them any farther. I'm going to run up the pennants to surrender."

"Ballantine," I began, but he stopped me.

"I know what it means."

"I will intercede as I am able," Alba promised.

The surrender moved swiftly. The signal flags run up, the sailors, standing at attention and unarmed, banked against the wind so our progress slowed, and the frigate approached us. I stood beside Alba, sweat dripping down my back and dampening my hair under the veil. Ballantine stood ready, ever so slightly canted in front of us, as though protecting us with his presence alone. I couldn't even begin to count the rows of cannons leering at us through gunports. There was no protection against that black iron.

The boarding party arrived quickly, a captain in the Galatine naval uniform.

"Lieutenant Westland," he said with faint surprise. "We had suspected, of course."

He inclined his head. "Captain Forsithe."

"What cargo is this?"

Alba stepped forward, perfectly poised with folded hands and impassive face. "I am Sastra-set Alba of the Order of the Golden Sphere. I am returning home."

"Home," the captain replied. "In a ship commanded by a deserter officer of the Galatine Crown? And with—a Serafan crew?"

Alba nodded. "We were unable to secure our own vessel to return home after the summit. Given the uncertainties in these waters of late."

"Ah." Captain Forsithe looked us over, barely glancing at me. It was true, what Alba said—most people didn't look long on a nun. "Kvys nun hires Serafan ship to take her back to her convent. That's almost understandable." He turned back to Ballantine. "Why are you commanding this ship? What business have you here?"

"I was hired. This woman paid well." I detected the lie in the stiff shoulders, the way his hand clenched into a fist. But these looked like fear, too, and of course Ballantine had much to fear.

"You're not, then, attached to the Reformist army?"

Ballantine saw the opportunity to cement his lie by mixing in one small truth, a truth that could condemn him but continue to provide a cover for the rest of us. "I intended to rejoin the Reformists in Galitha, yes. I needed a way to come back; my father wasn't going to pay passage for one wayward son to join the other in fighting a war against him. Captaining a ship for hire gave me a way to return."

Captain Forsithe sighed. "I had hoped you'd simply gone

missing, made some stupid, rash mistake, Westland. I might have found some way to be lenient."

"I've made no mistakes, sir."

"Very well." Forsithe nodded, and a pair of marines in sea green stepped forward to escort him back to the frigate. "I shall have to take you under arrest. Given the...circumstance, and your parentage, we will delay court martial until we come into port and word can be sent to your father."

Ballantine didn't respond, and I wasn't sure if it was relief at a short reprieve or grief at Forsithe speaking of his father.

"If it please you, sir." Alba stepped forward next to me, and I started.

"Yes?"

"You would leave this ship without a captain, sir. And leave us stranded at sea."

He glanced at the three of us, and at the sailors on board. "I would gladly escort you to the nearest port."

Alba blanched. "I appreciate your consideration. Will we, do you believe, be able to find passage back to Kvyset from such a port?"

He sighed. "I can guarantee no such thing. Not now, not this far south."

Alba didn't speak. She simply looked at him, large eyes searching him under that starched white veil. Forsithe squirmed. Alba stayed quiet.

"I could grant him parole." Forsithe shook his head. "I mean that it would be legal, under my jurisdiction, to do so, for pressing circumstances."

He was on the verge of refusing. I expected Alba to argue.

She just watched, lifting her chin in graceful, dutiful resignation, ever so slightly sighing.

"You could find alternative arrangements in Galitha City, I

am sure. The port is still open. Lieutenant Westland, I grant you parole to escort the high sister and her retinue as far as Galitha City. Our vessels will remain in sight of one another until arrival in port. If you attempt any escape, I will be forced to apprehend you by any means necessary, regardless of your parentage."

"I thank you for your compassion, sir," Alba said as Ballantine's face drained of color and he looked, for a moment, as though he might be sick.

"One final question," Forsithe said. I stared at my bare toes, avoiding Forsithe's eyes. "There was a woman with the Galatine delegation in Isildi. A Sophie Balstrade. With the prince."

"Yes," Alba said. My stomach lurched. "I made her acquaintance. A bit of a—what is the term in Galatine? A country relation, you would call her."

"A commoner, yes. Aligned with the Reformists. And quite likely a witch."

"Now that sounds like a fairy story," Alba said, properly aghast. I kept my eyes on my feet, even as they began to waver in my vision as I tried to betray no emotion, no reaction to Forsithe's question.

"Be that as it may. Do you have any indication where she might have gone? We believe she may harbor some power within the Reformist cause." He looked straight at me. I stared back as though I didn't understand his language, as though the terror I was sure painted in broad strokes across my face was merely the response to the confusion around me.

"No, sir," Ballantine said.

Forsithe waited for a reply that didn't come from Alba. "Very well. I leave you to your parole, Westland."

I breathed with relief, but only for a moment. "I'll leave a complement of marines on board with you," Forsithe added. "To ensure your compliance and to protect these women."

My breath hitched in my throat. The uniformed marines stepped forward, sunlight glinting on their fixed bayonets. I was Sastra Lieta of the Order of the Golden Sphere until we made port.

And after that, who knew?

59

ALBA ADJUSTED MY VEIL AS THE FRIGATE SAILED ONWARD. "PROBABLY ought to have considered a bit of costuming subterfuge from the outset," she whispered in my ear. "Just stay quiet. I'll tell them you've taken a vow of penitent silence."

I pulled away, shaking and watching the marines as though I could do anything to avoid them on this small ship. Ballantine held the rail, still sporting all the pallor of a corpse. He directed his mate to take charge of the vessel and keep her at a more leisurely pace, allowing the frigate to move ahead of us. I had seen her name and the brightly painted lady at her prow—the *Hopeful Wayfarer*. Hopeful, indeed.

I leaned against the rough sides of the ship, snagging the plain gray wool and not caring. If it had been my own good silk or expensive printed cotton, I would have cared. Sastra Lieta wouldn't care about clothing. She had dedicated her life to the worshipful contemplation of the Creator.

How long was I Sastra Lieta? My head thrummed with confusion—how to playact something I didn't understand? I shook my sleeve free and a wave of dizziness swept over me. Too much casting. I knew the feeling well, the bone-deep exhaustion reminding me that I was not Sastra Lieta, but Sophie Balstrade.

I nearly slipped as I tried to step away from the wall. Ballantine shot away from the rail and caught my arm.

"What's the matter?"

I stared balefully back at him, remembering myself and refusing to speak.

"Overtired," Alba said. She studied me carefully—did she guess that my weakness was from casting? She couldn't say in either case; the marines still stood watch not ten yards away. "She has a delicate sensibility for shocks, you see," Alba said, taking my hand. "I'll have food brought to you."

I didn't stay awake long enough for it. Sustained charm casting pulling directly from the ether, attempting to protect both the ship and the longboat, had exhausted me. Despite my best efforts to keep myself awake fretting over Theodor and Kristos, sleep washed over me within minutes of lying down.

I didn't wake until late in the night, already used to the steady wash of the waves on the sides of the ship and the movements of the crew keeping their watch. I sat up, still a bit shaky, and completely ravenous. I didn't want to intrude on the galley, but my empty stomach pitched and rolled with the ship and I knew I'd be sick if I didn't eat soon.

I tiptoed onto the deck, acutely aware that I knew nothing of the workings of the ship and crew, fearful I would get in someone's way. Rationally, I knew that the likelihood of a misstep from me causing any great harm was about as high as a wrongly turned seam ruining a gown; pick out the stitches and start over, no harm done. Still, the foreign movements and terms I didn't understand frightened me a little. I was an outsider here, no question.

I was growing tired of having to trust that those around me were working in my best interests. I was growing tired of having allies instead of friends. I missed Galitha City, missed my shop and Alice and Emmi. I missed my Pellian friends, and our lively talks about charm casting that, at their heart, were truly about family and community and tradition.

The moon bathed the deck in pale light, softening the hard edges and painting the unfamiliar tools and riggings with shadows. The ship looked friendlier with fewer people swarming it, as though, in the quiet, I could begin to understand how sail and rope and rigging worked together like fabric and thread and seams.

"It's late—past midnight," Ballantine said. I hadn't seen him until he spoke, but he didn't startle me. His voice was as pale and melancholy as the moonlight. "They're asleep," he added.

The marines, of course. I spoke quietly, in a single low breath. "I was hungry."

He didn't reply, but strode past me toward the galley, indicating I should follow. Inside, he produced a hunk of brown bread and some cheese, which he presented to me on a crude wooden trencher.

"If it's not enough, I—" He stopped with a wan smile as I tucked into the leftovers as though they were a fine feast.

I swallowed and nodded my appreciation.

"You missed supper." He shrugged, thin shoulders straining the uniform he hadn't taken off since we left port.

I felt I owed him some explanation. "Casting—it's more physically taxing than it looks," I apologized in a bare whisper.

"And it worked?" He coughed. "That is, both this ship and the longboat escaped unscathed, or nearly so. It took barely two shakes to repair the slight bit of damage we sustained."

"It's hard to say if it worked, exactly, or not." I always floundered in explanations of charm casting's efficacy. "It wouldn't have saved us from a direct broadside. But a bit of luck—it helped us. I'm sure your captaining of the ship helped more."

"That, I doubt sincerely." He sighed. "And my parole—it's temporary amnesty at any rate. You don't think—were your charms part of that, too?"

I set down the wedge of cheese I had been gnawing. "It's possible," I said, "but I think that was more Alba's doing than mine."

Ballantine considered this, unconvinced. In contemplation, his face looked much like Theodor's, more so now that both wore a drawn, tired mask of worry. "We'll make it through, one way or another. Now—back to your penitent vows," he said with a smile.

The days passed in sickening silence, the marines patrolling the deck like cats prowling for mice. Their uniforms, a washed-out green, made them easy to spot against the dark wood of the ship, but I didn't risk speaking or even leaving my cabin much. Instead, I hid inside and practiced the delicate work of controlling the casting I pulled from the ether. What I had done before had been crude, and I didn't trust that it was sufficient for the work that everyone expected of me. Already I noticed a weakening in the charms laid over the salt spray–scrubbed ropes and sails, the light scoured dimmer by the harsh conditions. My needle and thread would have secured a more lasting charm, but if I was to infuse good fortune in molten iron or the warp and weft of wool on the loom, I would have to refine this new mode of casting.

Alba slipped quietly into my cabin in the middle of a practice session. I had several threads of light held aloft, slowly spinning them into one another as I drove them into a bowl of water. I let them drop as the door opened.

"We're nearly to the port outside Galitha City," she said. I nodded. "When we come into port, I will do my damnedest to move us quickly to another ship. The less time we spend in port, the better."

I questioned her with a silent raised eyebrow.

"The port remains open, tenuously held by the Royal Navy. Tenuous, yes," she said in response to my unspoken question, "because the city, everything within the walls, is held by the Reformists."

"How do you know?" I mouthed silently.

"Those marines talk. This is, of course, news that's half a week stale. So it might be outdated. Regardless—the capital port is not a safe place to linger."

There was much I wanted to say, and Alba's fidgeting told me that she, too, wished to discuss more but couldn't. The cabin walls weren't thick, and nothing we might say now was worth being discovered.

Instead, I walked onto the deck, looking out over the rail, straining to see the coastline. The green tangle of forests gave way to the high cliffs and the stone walls of the city. My heart leapt at the sight of home, and I almost began to cry at the immediate demand to leave it. Was my shop still there? It hardly mattered any longer, with a city broken down the fault lines of civil war. What of Alice, and Emmi? My neighbors, the shop owners in my quarter? What of the Pellians who had chosen Galitha City for its opportunities, who were now folded into its crisis?

I turned away, my eyes swimming with tears. I loved my city. Everything I had done in the past months had been a sad, doomed love song to her, in a way. Despite everything I had done, everything Theodor had tried, war had cracked Galitha City open and her people were bleeding for her.

"My home port," Ballantine said quietly. I wasn't sure how long he'd been behind me—likely long enough to watch the city spires and rooflines come into focus as we drew closer. "You can see the palace from here. I used to watch for it, when we came into port, knowing my uncle was there, and later my father, that my family might well be gathered in the private dining room or the gardens. It was as though all was right with the world, when I saw the line of the palace roof. It doesn't mean the same thing anymore, does it?"

I shook my head, wanting very badly to embrace Ballantine or at least lay a comforting hand on his arm but knowing that Sastra Lieta would not do so.

The marines strode onto the deck. "As soon as the ship is secure, you'll be with us," the taller of the two said. He had the dark hair of a southerner and the creased, tan skin of someone who'd spent more time in sunlight than indoors. Ballantine nodded and took his leave of me.

The *Hopeful Wayfarer* already stood in port, her sails tucked like birds' wings waiting for flight. Alba stood nearby while we maneuvered close to her. I couldn't bring myself to look for Theodor's brother, to watch him taken away, to trial and possible execution.

Before we could depart, Forsithe was on the deck, flanked by more marines. I lowered my eyes, staring at my still-bare feet, as he passed, but I listened as he directed Ballantine's arrest. I met Ballantine's eyes as they escorted him from the ship and he gave me a small smile. I closed off the cries that threatened to erupt from my throat. He was led with little ceremony down the gangplank and I saw him, briefly, looking up at the city before he was taken to the *Wayfarer*.

"And her, too." A firm hand gripped my arm. The sea-green uniform of a marine brushed my gray habit. I gasped, looking to Alba, who watched with shock. She shook her head, confused and frightened, as another marine flanked me.

"Sophie Balstrade, you are under arrest, as well." Forsithe strode toward me, his boots echoing on the deck.

Alba forced herself between us. "I don't know what manner of jest this is, but—"

"I can't arrest you, Sastra. It would threaten an international incident if we arrested the high sister of a convent, and a member of a patrician house at that. But you will keep out of this."

"I will do no such thing with a member of my order."

"I've known since I set foot on this ship that this woman is no member of your order. I knew we were pursuing a ship with three fugitives we very much wished to apprehend. The crown prince, the revolutionary leader Kristos Balstrade, and this witch."

"You..." My knees felt like water and I could hardly breathe. "You knew? Why did you let us come all this way?"

He rested a hand on his sword. "For one, I had hoped you might lead us to the others. That there would be some rendezvous or rescue attempt. That gambit didn't work, and so you are now of little use. But further, I don't know what witchcraft you're capable of. If you'd bewitched this crew or some such dark arts."

"I have no such powers." I struggled to speak.

He raised a brow as though wagering a sporting guess at whether I was telling the truth. Of course, now it didn't matter. "You are under arrest for conspiracy against the king. Remove her," he ordered the marines.

The hand on my arm forced me forward. I nearly fell on the gangplank, my balance canted with the weight on my arm, and foolishly, briefly, considered flinging myself and the marine into the oily water below. It would do no good; they'd either let me drown or fish me out quickly enough.

As we stepped from gangplank to dock, I glanced at the man charged with my keeping; he avoided my eyes. Frightened of me.

Could I harm this man, if I wanted to? I could almost sense the dark curse magic throbbing around me, waiting to be drawn out. Could I drive it into him as I'd driven it into the water, crumple him as I'd wilted the lilies? Was that even how it would work?

No, I screamed at myself. It was wrong, despicably wrong. And even if I could control it for this one man, there was no way I could wrangle enough curse magic under my control to dispatch every marine, sailor, and soldier bustling around the port under Forsithe's control. Even if I killed Forsithe first, I acknowledged, hating myself for both identifying this best tactical move and for being too frightened to attempt it.

The bright crack of a rifle broke the low murmur of voices around me, and the hand on my arm first tightened, then fell away. I backed away from the marine, assuming he was readying his musket, but then felt the wet slick on my arm and saw the blood spatter on my skirt. He lay gasping on the dock beside me.

Someone screamed. Another rifle report, and another marine dropped. Forsithe shouted behind me, but I couldn't make out the words. I tried to blend into the crowd that pulsed and quivered on the dock, but it pulled away from me.

A strong hand gripped my arm; I wrenched away from it. "Quit it!" The voice hissing at me was familiar, and I realized with a start that the arm holding mine was clothed in rough brown linsey-woolsey, not the seafoam color of the marine uniform.

I met Niko Otni's eyes. "Come quick," he said.

"Alba, too. And Lieutenant Westland."

"We've got the nun already. Westland—" He shook his head. Westland had already been on board the *Wayfarer*. "Put this on." He handed me an oversize brown linen smock, something like a laundress would wear to protect her clothes from soap and steam.

I let Niko push me through the crowd on the dock. He ripped the veil from my head and threw it into the water between the docks, the filthy water soaking the white cloth quickly and muddying it, disguising that we had ever passed by. The sheer linen was now just more refuse in the thick water of the port.

We ducked down an alley and snaked quickly upward, the steep incline shortening my breath. Only a few avenues led from the port to the rest of the city, secured behind cliff face and wall. A red cap greeted us at the entrance to a fortified staircase. The symbol that once spelled danger to me now meant safety. More guards closed behind us, and we began to climb. "They know they're in for a fight if they try to search for you in the city proper."

"No one's following," one of the red-capped guards said.

"Good. They didn't see us leave the docks." He offered me a hand. "Well met, Miss Balstrade."

60

THE CITY WAS SIMULTANEOUSLY EXACTLY AS I KNEW IT—EACH shop and street and cobblestone familiar—and overturned completely. On a bright, sunny day that should have been bustling with street criers and market women and children playing hopscotch and the game of graces, the streets were silent. The pallor of war washed over deserted street carts and the broken glass of windows. Scorch marks and the remains of barricades marred the streets.

"We set those up right away, when the king declared a stay on the reforms," Niko said, pointing to crude but effective barricades as we walked, "and we drove them out of the city, block by block."

We rejoined Alba and several more of Niko's crew in what had once been a butcher shop in the narrow storefronts near Fountain Square. The butcher's blades were absent from the wall, but I felt sure they had been quite recently put to use. Most of the men in Niko's retinue wore red caps; some of the women had their hair wrapped in red kerchiefs. There was no other uniform demarcating what I presumed were members of the Reformist army. Several of the nearby buildings were festooned with red banners. "We tried to take the king out as he left the city, but we missed our chance."

Cold snaked through me. Niko hadn't changed—still distant, still directed by goals too simple and direct to consider the king anything but an obstacle.

"We knew he went south," I said.

"Royalist strongholds are down south. The only thing keeping us from taking the city completely is that the navy has the port."

"Completely blockaded, then?" Alba said. A door served as a large table, with a hodgepodge of chairs drawn up to it, and Niko settled on a rickety stool.

"From the port side, yes." Niko unfurled a map, drawn by hand on the back of a broadside. "The river is still open."

"Good. We'll find a way out of the city as soon as possible, likely by river." Alba squinted at the poorly rendered map.

"Hold on there, sister." Niko rolled up the map. "We'll talk about when and if you're leaving soon enough."

If—of course. I shrank against the wall, fiddling with a torn edge of the smock. Niko was too calculating to save us just to be nice.

"How did you know we would be there? And that we would need help?" Better to start here, on neutral ground.

"Kristos promised you'd come. Said he'd be pulling into port in Hazelwhite on a Serafan vessel with you and others— but you didn't show. So we kept an eye here, figure we'll have to redirect you around the blockades, and instead we find a pair of nuns with an armed escort," he said. "Good thing we were on the lookout or you'd not have made it long before the gallows."

"For conspiracy against the king." I nodded. I sat up a

bit straighter. "Who's in charge in the city? You alone, some committee?"

Niko smirked. "You don't think I could be in charge?"

"I know full well you could be. I want to confirm who I'm talking to. Commander, dictator?"

His mouth twisted into a scowl. "You always were a snob," he said. "I'm head of operations here. Of the Reformist army, if it has a head."

Alba snorted. I shook my head slightly. It wasn't wise to challenge him now.

"So why are we here?" I asked quietly.

Niko waved a hand. The others, in their linen frocks and work shirts and the unifying theme of the red cap, filed out.

"I figure, if you were on your way north, you had a reason to be heading that way. And with the Kvys?" He raked a hand through his thick black hair, disrupting beads of sweat on his forehead. "What were you planning?"

I pressed my lips together. "I was going to Kvyset with Alba. People keep trying to kill me," I explained drily.

"Ah." Niko snorted. "If it was just you, Sophie, I'd believe you could be that selfish. You certainly were last winter." I forced back protests. "But Sastra-set Alba? She's a devotee."

"Then you know one another," I confirmed.

"You know that I knew her cousin? Yes, you do," he said with a glance at my strained expression. "He made the introductions via letter, and Divine Natures, but she was helpful."

"Yes," Alba said quickly. "We've discussed this already. I made my apologies to Sophie for the...unexpected turn of events last winter and my part in that."

"Unexpected, yes," Niko mused. There was a knowing glint in his eyes—perhaps not so unexpected. He had moved quickly last winter, and he moved quickly now, with the nimble ingenuity of the Galatine streets, the adaptability of the children of Pellian immigrants. "I cannot imagine that Sastra-set Alba agreed to anything that wasn't of some long-term benefit to our great cause."

"Sastra-set Alba," I said deliberately, "is a true believer in the reforms and the rights of all. And so she wishes to offer me some protection as she is able."

"Sastra-set Alba," Niko replied, "can answer for herself."

"It's of no use keeping it from him, Sophie." Alba sighed. My eyes widened. I didn't want Niko to know, to use us for his aims. I didn't want any of my power under his control. "I am returning to Kvyset to attempt to broach alliances with the Fenians."

"Fenians?" Niko coughed. "They barely have a military."

"Yes, but they have industry. Forgive my blunt observation, but you have a distinct lack of uniforms. I imagine it reflects a lack of arms and ammunition and all sorts of other necessities." Niko's mouth formed a hard line. "Kristos and I discussed this at length," she added, maneuvering that piece on the board, just a nudge, just to remind him he wasn't solitary in his leadership.

"And you need to go to Kvyset for that?"

"It would allow me to work with fewer...encumbrances than in a besieged city."

"We're not besieged."

Alba folded her hands patiently. "Your port is cut off by an enemy navy. How long, do you think, until you are under siege? The Royalist army is gathering in the south. Your position is not strong." The tilt of her head and faint tone of apology almost suggested a mother watching a fumbling child play at marbles.

Niko didn't acknowledge the weaknesses of his position, like a dockworker refusing to admit that a handcart was too heavy for him, but he pounced on the opportunity Alba presented. "And you think you could secure us a navy? Cannon?"

"I don't think I can. I know I can."

Niko nodded. "Then we'll get you to Kvyset."

I waited. "I'll go with Alba," I said when no one spoke.

"Why does she possibly need you? You're not worth much to the Fenians—I'm guessing her pull is mostly in the large coffers of the convent."

"Sophie is a bit of a folk hero to the Kvys and the Fenians. I need her to smile and wave and play the part." A weak reason, and not entirely true, but a reason.

"I can't imagine I can do you much good here," I added.

Niko watched me as though reevaluating a series of moves, assessing his judgment anew. "You proved that you have some use at Midwinter. It may have taken some convincing then, but you see now that we were right, don't you?"

I inhaled, the scent of charred wood and dust on the breeze coating my nostrils. "Your prediction that this would end in violence was correct." Niko replied with a silent, insouciant shrug.

"I didn't say you were right," I retorted. "I said your predictions came true, not that I agreed with your tactics or your ethics."

"Ethics." Niko flicked the rolled map. "You're right, ethics aren't my first concern when my comrades are dying in the streets fighting a nobility that won't concede to the law. What does a novelty seamstress know about ethics, anyway?"

He still hated me. I was still the silk-wearing, ale-snubbing sister who refused to help those long months ago. I couldn't blame him—here I was, unscathed in the wake of revolt and now in the face of civil war, even as his friends had lost their lives. I softened toward him, just a little. "I can manipulate the light and dark that underpin the universe. So yes, I have rules that I follow." Did I still have those ethics? Had my view shifted to the pragmatism of my brother and Niko, putting my abilities in service to a political cause?

"And that, that's why we need you," he said, suddenly less distant. "Your friend—she's right, we can only hold so long against a blockade of the harbor. If—when—the Royalists turn the focus of their army here, we'll be caught in a pincer. And that's after weeks, or months, of continued fighting here. We hold the city, but they attempt incursions nearly every day. Probably to keep us weakened for when they finally do make a big push."

I swallowed. I didn't want to reveal the full extent of our plan, not to Niko. I still didn't trust him, didn't know what he would do with the knowledge. "I promise that my work with Alba will give you what you need to fight properly," I said instead.

"No, it won't. Not like having you here to curse the enemy would."

"Curse?" I shook my head. "Niko, back to that again, I—"

"Your rules be damned!" He slammed the table with his hand. "No more arguing about that now, it's ridiculous! In the face of death, of annihilation of our cause, you would still debate ethics?"

"I can't!" I cried. "I can't just wind up and throw a curse at them. What, you want me to curse a bunch of clothes and hand them out, hope they'll wear them?"

"No, that's stupid, but—"

"Because that is what I do. The plan to even get a curse into the palace—do you have any idea the lengths Pyord went to to orchestrate that? The curse itself was the smallest part. The best chance I can give you is to go with Sastra-set Alba."

"You go when I say you can go," Niko shouted.

"I don't come and go by your leave," I countered.

"Here, you'd best. You may be legend among some of the Red Caps, but among others you're traitor. Abandoned us when we needed you the most, run off to the safety of Serafe with your lover."

"That's not at all how it happened!"

"I know!" Niko shouted. "I direct an army, but I don't control the rumors. Stories have lives of their own, and hearsay could give a rat for my marching orders." He took a breath. "If I had any doubts, you've proven me wrong. You didn't have to come back here. But you don't leave without my say-so, for your own safety as well as our needs."

"I cannot wait long, so you had best give your say-so swiftly," I said. I had learned something as a consort to the prince—that speaking with confidence in one's authority cost nothing and often had some effect.

"As soon as I can." Sourness replaced the brief flash of empathy in his face. "Until then—you can make yourself useful and prove to this army you didn't run at the first sign of trouble." He pounded on the door, and a red-capped boy entered. "Take her to the warehouse, show her the workrooms." He turned back to me. "Sister, we'll arrange your passage."

"I will not leave without Sophie," Alba reiterated as the boy waited for me to follow him.

"Then you can stay with her," Niko spat. "Of all the blights and bothers, I get stubborn women."

61

—⁓—

THE CITY STREETS WERE NEARLY EMPTY AS THE BOY, CALLED FIG, ushered us to the center of the Red Cap army's warehouses, more abandoned storefronts lining Fountain Square. These shops had served, mainly, the upper-class households, including nobles. The storefront Viola had secured for me was nearby. I was sure Alice and Emmi had abandoned it, like all of these shop owners. The Lord of Coin's offices, where I had spent long hours waiting in line, was now a makeshift field hospital. That, I thought with the closest feeling to a small victory I'd experienced in this battle-scarred city, was a far better use for the place.

"The worst of the fighting happened here," Fig said as we grew closer to Fountain Square. "The Stone Castle was well garrisoned and put up a fight. Of course we couldn't just storm the place, it's too fortified for that. But someone got inside and opened a passageway onto River Street."

I started—the door onto River Street was a secret known to only a handful of nobles, and Theodor and I had used it in our attempt to forestall the revolt at Midwinter. "Any idea who?" I asked.

"I always figured one of Commander Otni's best," Fig said proudly. I glanced at Alba and shook my head—the Red Caps had a silent ally in the nobility. I wondered who, my thoughts skimming Ambrose, though we had not heard a whisper from him. "Anyway, after we surprised them inside the Stone Castle, the fighting moved into the streets, and we drove them out." I took one last look at the old fortress, its narrow windows and high walls imposing and hung with red banners, their frayed edges dancing in the breeze.

The fountain at the center of the square was nearly destroyed, the carved stone stags and swans broken and charred. The store-fronts nearest the fountain were lined with stocks, the crude devices usually used to punish drunks and pickpockets and other petty transgressors put to a new use. I choked as I saw them, and even Alba turned her face away, pale and trembling.

The stocks held dead men and women. Nobles, their silks and fine cottons moldering in the sun and the rain. Coarse versions of their family devices were painted on the walls behind them, with crude epithets painted alongside them. The people themselves...I gagged and forced bile back down my throat. The bodies had been left out for well over a week, and the flesh was decaying, peeling away, bloated in some places and shrunken in others like badly made puppets. I recognized one—Hardinghold. The device, a pair of dancing bears, had been redrawn with bears hung from gibbets. Two corpses were stationed below it, and I couldn't discern if the woman in torn and stained blue silk was Pauline.

"You set them up like dolls after they were dead? Like wax figures?" I demanded.

Fig ducked his head. "No, they were..." His mouth knotted around the answer, and he started over. "That was the method of execution for anyone found aiding the Royalists."

"Mercy of the Creator," murmured Alba. I didn't have words. I saw another family sigil I recognized—Crestmont. The pair of figures below slumped like thin rag dolls. Crestmont had hung his own noose, I thought bitterly. If he had come with us to the summit instead of staying behind to foment insurrection, he wouldn't have been killed. But I couldn't look away from the fine silk embroidery on his stained silk stockings. When he had gotten dressed, that last morning, had he known he was facing execution?

I wanted to cry. This was not my Galitha City, my friends and neighbors. They were not capable of such cruelty. These people had fought against the reforms, broken the law, turned traitor to their own country, and they deserved, I allowed, execution. But not like this. Not torture for the sake of pain, disgrace for the sake of spectacle.

"Why?" I begged.

"Commander Otni says that everyone must join or fall, that there is no room for indecision now. This was..."

"This was a good way to convince anyone still undecided of the virtue of the cause," Alba supplied. "Mercy on you all."

Fig ignored her, but I searched for her arm. She gripped my hand. "Commander Otni says this is how war is," Fig insisted.

"It's how he'll fight a war," I replied, but the bitterness I would have felt toward Niko half a year ago was tempered, knowing what he was facing. An uncertain war and his own, likely ugly, death if the gambit failed. He had few advantages and leveraged them all now. "The nobles you've...executed," I said. "Were all of them actively aiding the Royalists? None of them were killed simply for being of noble houses?"

Fig stuck out his chin. "Of course. Captured and tried fairly."

The lack of clear methods and the rapidity of the trials didn't inspire confidence. I didn't want to ask the next question, but I did. "Prince Theodor's brother Ambrose was still in the city when we left."

"So?" Fig kicked a stone.

"I won't find him in one of those stocks, will I?"

Fig paled. "Not if he was one of us—look, Miss Sophie, Commander Otni can't help that some people may have gotten a little out of hand. But we didn't execute anyone in the royal family, all right?" I shuddered at his use of *we*; a twelve-year-old boy should have had no part in wartime executions. "Commander Otni can't keep track of every casualty."

"The lists of the dead are, I am sure, poorly kept in a city at war. Yet even so, those who would grieve wish to keep their vigils," Alba said.

Fig returned her quiet reprimand with a baffled shrug. "The warehouse," he said, gesturing toward the cathedral.

"I'm sorry, I'm not from Galitha, but that looks like a place of worship," Alba said.

"Commander Otni says we need a defensible storehouse more than we need incense and hymns. Says the Galatine Divine can be better served working than praying."

"So he's a philosopher now, too," I muttered. We stepped inside, and I found the well-lit cavern of space inside bustling with activity. A cadre of men picked at old muskets, taking apart the rusted locks, scouring them clean and daubing them with oil. Across from them, a group of elderly men and a few women made lead shot, the heated metal poured into molds and carefully counted by one old woman who seemed to be blind. And toward the front of the cathedral, near altars stripped of embroidered cloths and incense but piled with bolts of linen, women sewed.

Leaning against the altar, a pile of coarse unbleached linen in her lap, was Alice. She stitched a long serviceable seam, tying a messy knot before she noticed me. It was passable work on utilitarian cloth, but nothing like the fine stitching and practiced hand I knew she was capable of. A pile of cut pieces sat beside her—work shirts. A makeshift uniform for a ragtag army.

Before I could speak, Emmi trotted toward the altar from a side aisle, her hands full of spools of thread and a lopsided pincushion. "Sophie!" she cried, dropping the pincushion. It didn't roll far, settling on its flat side near Alice. Alice looked up, startled, grabbed the pincushion, and then realized that Emmi was looking at me.

"Why are you here?" Emmi called, darting toward me.

"Are you finished with your work?" a dour Pellian woman scolded Emmi, who paused, conflicted, in the aisle.

"Let her be, Mags," Alice said, carefully setting her work aside as she rose. "That's Sophie Balstrade."

Mags, whatever position she may have held in the hierarchies of Niko's army, did not supersede the authority of myth. Whatever most of these people had thought of me, traitor or hero, a hush swept the cathedral to silence and their work stilled as their attention turned, inescapably, toward me. I felt strangely small and oversize at once, aware of my own awkward movement and yet not nearly great enough to fill the expectations these people held of me. Somewhere, far back in a side aisle, a baby cried.

"Alice," I said. "Are you all right? And you, Emmi?" With only moments to decide my strategy, I chose to pretend the mythical Sophie didn't exist and behave as normally as I could. Alba followed at a polite distance, settling herself in the alcove of the cathedral where candles used to wait for penitents to light them in prayer. Now the wall was empty, even the candleholders torn down, used, I presumed, by Niko's army.

Alice took my hand. "Things fell apart so quickly, I—we— we shut up the shop and just holed up while the worst of the fighting was going on."

"I couldn't get home," Emmi added, "so I stayed with Alice. It's all right now," she added in a rush.

"What of everyone else?"

Alice's lips were pressed into a thin line. "Our old neighborhood is half burned down, and I'm sick thinking of how many likely died in the fire alone, without even considering those shot and bludgeoned and who knows what else."

"The Pellian quarter has been left alone, mostly—Commander Otni and the nobles didn't fight there much." Commander Otni. If Emmi was using a title for Niko, his self-made leadership had stuck. "All our friends there are safe."

Another thought struck me—if Niko was demanding my help, had he sought out the charm casters in the Pellian quarter? He knew full well that they were there. "Venia and Heda and Lieta and the rest—are they working here, too?" I asked. "Has Niko asked you all to cast for him?"

Emmi stabbed her pincushion with an errant pin. "We've made a few tablets for a few of our own friends, but most of the Galatines don't believe the superstitions. Commander Otni says it's all right to give anyone a tablet who wants one, but he doesn't want to force Pellian customs on a Galatine army. I think Venia and Heda are working in the laundry, and Lieta cooks for the hospital."

That sounded like Niko—he was happy to leverage charms in other ways, I was sure, but savvy enough to recognize that his Galatine soldiers weren't going to wear clunky clay tablets.

"I'm not sure, but Theodor's brother may still have been in the city. Ambrose?" I asked.

Emmi shook her head, and Alice shrugged. "I've heard nothing of him. I would have assumed Otni would publicize either his loyalty or his execution."

"Which means he doesn't know, either. And you? Truth be

told, I never thought you a great devotee of the cause. What changed?" I asked Alice.

"You saw what's out there. There's common folk and nobles alike. More hung from the walls for aiding the enemy, more killed by mobs." Alice met my eyes. "You're with the Red Caps or you might well be a spy, a collaborator—and a target. Otni hasn't ordered that, but he hasn't stopped it, either."

"And you worked for me." I sighed.

"That wouldn't have mattered," Alice lied carefully.

"And more than that, the Red Caps collected all the food in the city that they could. If you want your share, you have to work." Emmi bit her lip. "It's the only way to ration it, if the port stays blockaded. We can't get much in overland, with the Royalist army south of us."

I exhaled carefully. A city nearly cut off, food in short supply, professional soldiers continuing to harry volunteer fighters— that Niko had managed to hold the city at all was close to a miracle.

"At any rate," Alice said, picking the shirt back up to sew, "you can avoid trouble all you want but if it's going to come banging down the door, you may as well put your oar in some-where you can do some good. Or at least earn your supper."

"Let me help you," I said, picking up a threaded needle.

Before I could finish a seam, the air around us seemed to tremble and the foundation creaked under the strain of a distant thunder. "What was—"

"They're firing mortars over the far wall again," Emmi said. There was a furrow between her brows that hadn't been there before.

"We're out of range here," Alice added.

I stared at both of them, their focus still on their sewing, as though this were another day in the atelier, the work in their hands yet another silk gown, the disturbance nothing more than the tinker getting in a row with the rag man on the street corner. "It's been like this the better part of the week," Emmi explained. "The city's been cleared of the Royalists, but they still hammer at us with some light artillery fire."

"*Light* artillery fire?" I managed to say.

Emmi cracked a smile. "From what I understand. I'm just repeating what the men who go out on patrols say."

Fig dashed up with urgency flooding his young face. "Commander Otni says you're to come with him right away," he said. Alba rose to join us. "The nun can stay here."

"I cannot come with you, then?"

"Commander Otni—"

"Did not request me. Very well." She sat next to Emmi. "I will remain in the company of these ladies, then." She met my eyes—she would learn what she could here. There were few moments that passed that could not, for Sastra-set Alba, be turned to some use.

"Where are we going?" I asked Fig as he tugged my sleeve in haste.

"The wall," he replied. "Otni says you could be of some use there."

62

FIG WAS JOINED BY A PAIR OF MEN CARRYING MUSKETS, THEIR red caps the only indicator of a uniform and their bearing more like those of dockworkers carting a shipment than soldiers under arms. No matter—those muskets, if loaded and primed, were just as deadly carried by a dockworker as a professional soldier, and I took Niko's meaning in their presence. My company was not requested but summoned.

The vacant city we moved through was much like what I'd already seen, broken windows and half-burned buildings. A small square near the public gardens held gallows, and I turned my face away. As we moved closer to the fortified wall surrounding the city, however, the damage grew more substantial, artillery fire knocking craters into the cobblestone streets and whole blocks splintered and burned.

"These were houses," I said. "The people—"

"Mostly moved toward the city center, where it's safer," Fig said.

"Mostly." I glanced at the soldiers walking beside us, matching Fig's quick pace with long strides. "And you? Are your families safe?"

The man nearest me started, not expecting the Sophie

Balstrade he'd imagined to care enough to inquire. Did he imagine a traitor, or a witch, or a spoiled princess in training, I wondered? "They're all near Fountain Square," he said. "We've turned those shops into warehouses for supplies and dormitories. Keeps everyone safer, I wager."

"I would say so," I said, glancing at a chair, overturned and smashed to kindling in the middle of what had been someone's front room.

Niko met us as the street corroded into broken gravel in front of us. "Well done, Fig, go on back and have a rest."

"I can stay and keep running messages, sir, if you like."

Niko smiled with something close to indulgence and patted Fig's shoulder. "Not needed. Have a nap." Fig scurried off, and Niko beckoned me to follow him. It didn't escape me that the two soldiers had not been dismissed. They stood behind me, and I could almost sense the weapons in their hands. "Take a look," he said, almost nonchalant. Almost, except for a strain of something like hope in his voice.

The street dipped uphill a few steps from us, and along that upturn, there was another set of barricades, this time built in successive layers like the terraces the Serafans used for their elaborate gardens. I couldn't stop the sharp intake of my breath as I realized that one section had, very recently, been hit. Bits of wood splintered into long shards over scarred ground, and stretcher bearers were running the last of the wounded toward the hospital on Fountain Square.

They passed close, and I made out the outline of a ragged piece of wood embedded deep in the man's side, his linen shirt punctured by the splinter and stained with blood. He cried out with each jolt and turn of the stretcher, and I forced myself to keep my eyes on his pale, drawn face instead of turning away.

Niko stopped the stretcher bearers and swiftly, silently clasped the wounded man's hand. He spoke to him, in a low voice I couldn't hear, but it had some effect. The man's mouth set itself in a stoic line and he looked, for the moment, determined. Niko stepped away and turned on his heel toward me. "Now that you see what we're facing, what can you do?"

"What can I do?" I gaped. I could try to work a protection charm into the rickety barricades, I supposed. But I had little faith that it would stand up to repeated artillery fire—it was luck I could add, nothing more. A few hours, maybe, a few more missed aims. "You dragged me out here to see—" I swallowed. "If I could do anything for that poor man, to prevent more pain for anyone, I would."

"Then do it!" Niko roared, and I saw him, suddenly, differently. He was tired, nearly broken by the suffering around him. All of his pragmatism could only shore him up so far to make brutally necessary decisions time and again.

There was another shot from the artillery, not so very far away, its deep, thunderous voice pounding alongside my heartbeat, and a round struck the pockmarked, vacant land nearest the wall. "Believe me. If I could end this right now, I would break every rule I have to do so. But I can't."

"You can. You will. It's the last hope I have," he added, desperation finally overtaking the control in his voice. He gestured to the men, who primed their weapons. "I'll force you. I will."

"Force me to do what? Niko—"

"Level on her."

"Not like this!" I stared at the rusted barrels of the old muskets, wishing desperately that I was wearing charmed clothing that might, maybe, induce a misfire in these battered firelocks. "I can use my magic to help, but not here. Not like this. Just listen—"

"If not now, when? The time for deliberation is over. You're either with our cause or you're a traitor to your own people." He took a breath and stepped away from me. "Make ready." I watched the locks clack into place, ready to fire under the unwavering hands of the soldiers.

"You're right that I'm the last hope you have," I said, forcing my voice to stay steady. "I'm going with Alba not to just secure supplies, but to embed enough charm magic in them to give you an advantage. Uniforms with protection spells. Shot charmed for accuracy. Anything I can."

He stared at me for a long time. "Secure your firelocks," he finally ordered. "How can I know you're telling the truth, that you'll come back here with what we need?"

I met his eyes. "Niko, trust me."

He evaded my gaze. "I have a hard time trusting you."

"I know!" I laughed, bitter and hard. "I know. That's been the damn crux of it from the start, hasn't it?" Niko thumbed the bayonet at his belt, the hilt slapping his waist. Repetitive, futile. "We can't keep repeating this, Niko. Your best gamble is letting me go with Alba."

He assessed me, the long, searching look of someone who very badly wanted to be the confident architect Pyord had been and knowing he lacked the innate skills. Niko was something else, a clever, swift-moving Galitha City dockworker. A rapidly adapting child of Pellian immigrants like me.

"Don't try to be him," I said on impulse. "Pyord. You can lead this army better than he could have. He dealt in complicated plans and subterfuge. You're past that now."

Niko's brows constricted. He didn't reply to this; I hadn't expected him to. "And you say you and Alba can get us the supplies we need?"

"We can," I said. "We can outfit an army that will win, not an army that will make a valiant last stand."

Niko nodded, slowly. Adjusting. "Very well. My people will help you get out of the city via the river. There's very little movement north of us, you'll have little enough trouble reaching Kvyset."

63

~m~

THERE WAS NO NEED FOR DECEPTION OR COMPLICATED SCHEMES
to leave the city. I simply changed into a simple, loose short
gown and petticoat Alice leant me, with a subdued farewell.
Leaving the Kvys disguise behind, I set out into the city with
Alba and Niko. War made for clear lines drawn between com-
batant and comrade, between territories carved out on each
side. It made for a strange sense of relief amid the chaos; I knew
where I stood, the borders between friend and foe neatly demar-
cated for the first time in recent memory.

"It is not so far from the river to the Kvys border," Alba said
as we made our plan with Niko, "that we cannot walk as the
pilgrims do."

"And be robbed and beaten as pilgrims surely are." Niko
snorted. "No, the river runs north toward the coastline. A small
vessel could carry you to a Kvys port. Provided you can pay."

"That I can promise," Alba said. "And we will have help
waiting for us in Afenstrid. But the Galatine navy?"

"They've massed here. They've not blockaded the mouth of
the river; they can't without sacrificing too much of their current strength."

"Patrols?" I asked.

Niko shook his head. "Stretched too thin to patrol the coastline effectively."

"Perhaps ineffectively—but they must patrol. Then there is some risk in a sea voyage, too." Alba smiled. "The pilgrim way puts us in no one else's debt or constraint. What if we cannot trust the man we hire?"

"You'll be able to," Niko said. "Between who I know here and your funds, we'll have a trustworthy boat captain."

"And then there's the time it takes," I said. "A sea voyage, you agree, would be shorter. The sooner we can get ourselves out of Galitha, the sooner we can begin establishing suppliers for the army."

Niko grinned. "That's true. And you've already noticed, sister, how badly we need the help." Alba agreed, reticently, and I wondered if she was right to be more cautious of a sea voyage or if her wariness was borne out of yielding control to Niko and the boat captain. Necessity didn't always make for comfort in these freshly brokered alliances.

Niko himself accompanied us to the riverfront docks. These had been little used when the city was not at war; river vessels dropped their cargo here and carried people toward the eastern river cities and, occasionally, to Kvyset. The boats were smaller, dealing in the currency of muscle as they were rowed up and down the river. An old cob plodded along, drawing ferry boats across the river in a system of pulleys that had remained for decades.

A farmer unloaded sacks of early potatoes and greens from the ferry, part of a tenuous network of suppliers bringing food from the thin northern farmlands. He watched us blandly as Niko spoke in rushed, quiet tones with the owner of a nearby skiff.

"He will want more payment than your friend is willing to part with," Alba said, watching the exchange.

"I don't think he's my friend," I replied. "But I suppose you're right. Care to assist?"

Alba folded her hands over her gray habit and inclined her head. She had, despite Niko's arguments, replaced the veil. She glided toward them and an arrangement was swiftly reached. I envied her the deep pockets of her house and the graceful confidence that ended arguments so quickly.

As promised, the journey from the river to the coastline was short, and the mouth of the river comfortably fed us into a broad harbor. No Galatine ships blocked this route yet; that could come before the war was over. If the main harbor and the river mouth were both blocked, no supplies could reach Galitha City by the sea, and if the Royalists had their plans laid well, they could siege the city from the other side. If Theodor and Kristos didn't have our troops in the south in fighting order by then, it was likely to be a swift defeat.

Alba spent the short time at sea drafting letters and calculating funds and running all sorts of tabulations that I only half understood. I thought I knew numbers from keeping my shop's finances, but this was at a greater scale and more intricate tangle of investment and risk and payoff. If the Fenians committed to production, what did we owe to whom, in how many foundries and textile mills and shipyards? Each investment in one area meant trimming a bit from another venture—even the coffers of the Order of the Golden Sphere were not without limit.

While Alba ran scenario after scenario on paper in our shared cabin, I holed up in a corner of the skiff not used overmuch by the pair of sailors keeping the vessel moving. And time and again, I pulled light from the ether around me without the aid of a needle or music. As I practiced over the course of a long summer day, it became clear how crude the conjuring I'd done on the ship from Serafe had been. Unlike my stitched charms, which I could imbue with precise charms for protection, love, money, or health, what I messily pulled and pressed into the sails of the brig had been merely vague good fortune.

Moreover, I needed more control over the light itself, and practiced threading it into ever-more refined spirals and whorls before letting it dissipate. If I didn't tack it to a physical object, it quickly faded and released itself back to wherever it had come from. Focusing on the actual work of charm casting, and on this uncharted method, took my mind off of the stinging question of whether I ought to be doing it at all.

I couldn't tell when we crossed the border into Kvys waters, but by sunrise of our second day at sea, we were in sight of Afenstrid.

"It has Fen in the name," I said as Alba pointed out the still-distant smudge of towers and walls.

"Indeed. As I said, Fenians were originally Kvys colonists. The languages have diverged a bit over time, but a Kvys can still understand a Fenian most of the time, and vice versa." She turned her impassive gaze on the shoreline. "Fen simply means rock. A particular connotation of hard, unyielding, yet valuable rock."

"That sounds promising."

"If rock is against you, there is no turning it. But it's a worth-while ally, I would say." She returned to the cabin and packed her papers until we had reached the docks.

I had expected a quiet fishing village or middling port city, like those we had seen in southern Galitha, but Afenstrid was nothing like those towns with their ramshackle wooden dockside buildings and warehouses. Instead, towers of white limestone and painted turrets bloomed behind the orderly docks, hemmed in by high walls of iron-bordered stone.

A pair of women in gray robes matching Alba's waited at

the end of the docks. Their white veils set them apart from the tradesmen and merchants who also wore gray, black, and deep blue, even in the summer. Kvys were not keen on showy clothing, but they showed their wealth nonetheless. Black was not a cheap dye by any means, and I noticed the fine quality of the merchants' summer-weight wool suits and the silk satin trim and intricate blackwork embroidery on the exposed shift and shirt collars and cuffs.

Alba greeted them with a kiss and a torrent of Kvys, then quickly introduced me. If their knowing looks were any indication, the introduction was unnecessary. They had a carriage waiting, and the ride to the convent took most of what remained of the long summer day. Exhausted by my extended charm casting on board ship and unable to converse with the sisters, I stared out the window as the city unfolded into a bright meadow and then a brilliantly green forest of narrow birches. I could understand Alba's reticence to leave this country for Serafe, and as we stopped for lunch in a moss-covered glen bordered by a crystalline brook, I wondered if I might have actually been transported into a fairy tale.

Then I remembered the fire I'd helped to set in Galitha, not so very far away from this idyllic forest, and knew that this was no folk story. If there was any happy ending to be had here, I would have to help write it.

We arrived at the House of the Golden Sphere just as dusk began to deepen the colors of the forest and soften its edges to velvet. I suppose I had expected the convent to look as dour as the sisters' dress, but its dormitories and libraries and chapels were beautifully built of pale wood, with high arching roofs and tall windows so that light could wash each room. It looked as though it had grown out of the forest itself, and the trees pressed close against its outer walls of pale stone.

"I know you must be tired, but there is something I must show you before you retire," Alba said.

Our traveling companions bowed slightly and took their leave, disappearing into a nearby dormitory.

"The convent was built hundreds of years ago," Alba said, "though I know it hardly looks it—we are scrupulous about the upkeep, of course. The oldest building is the basilica, at the center. It was built almost half a millennium ago, to the glory of the Creator. I wish for you to see it."

Though I was bone tired, the clean calm of the convent leant me some energy. I followed Alba to the center of the convent, where the concentric rings of buildings gave way to an open courtyard surrounding a limestone cathedral. It was smaller than the great cathedral in Galitha City, but no less beautifully built. I stepped toward it, taking in the way the light of the setting sun illuminated the swiftly sloping roofline and the arched tips of the windows.

And then I gasped.

The light wasn't from the setting sun at all. It bloomed from the structure itself. Golden light shrouded the poplar frame of the doorway. It shone like a pale halo, exuding a calm beneficence. I stepped through the doorway, exquisitely attuned to the shimmering light, caught nearly breathless as it licked my sleeve and plucked at my hair in its gentle undulation. Inside, the beams supporting the ceiling of the chapel were overlaid with the familiar otherworldly brilliance. Even the leaded glass windows thrummed with charm magic, a delicate fuzz of light covering them like a film.

I traced the nearest window, hand faltering as the magic pooled around my fingertip and receded.

"It was the special practice of the sisters here," Alba said quietly.

I remembered that she was there. In a rush, I remembered that the Kvys hated casting, scorned it, that it was against every understanding I had of Kvys culture to embrace any part of it. I remembered that Alba had known I was a caster—had known this about me longer than I had known Alba—and yet had failed to say anything about this living light. I remembered that I couldn't truly trust my allies as I would friends. That trust turned shaky the moment we stepped away from our uneasy but equal footing.

"You didn't see fit to tell me."

"It has to be seen. To be understood."

"You could have told me something. Anything. You—you can see this, can't you?" I asked.

She nodded slowly. "It has taken years for me to even perceive it. My aptitude for the art of the spheres is very low. So much so that, were I not a sister, not devoted to hours of silence and meditation, I would not see it clearly at all."

I waved my hand, silencing her without words. The hazy golden quiet of the chapel would not be interrupted by my angry voice. "But you can see my work."

"I saw your work on the ship." This was confirmation, not apology. The room seemed to constrict on me. The charm magic was too much, the light too brilliant, the realization too abrupt and biting that I knew nothing. The one thing that I thought I understood, no, that I thought I had mastery over—I knew nothing. Discovering charmed music in Serafe had been surprising, no doubt, but this shook me. "It was how I knew, for certain, that I had made the right choice in bringing you here. In moving ahead with our plans with Fen. You can do all that I had hoped."

Not now, I breathed. For now, only facts, no great plans for me and my skills. "And it's still practiced here?"

"You know that charm casting is not tolerated in Kvyset now. Once, it was permitted, behind the closed doors of the religious orders. It was never allowed outside the orders, and eventually the Church fathers grew...afraid of its potential. At the time of the schism, those who could practice were arrested. The Order of the Golden Sphere was, of course, hit particularly hard. Those who would give up the art were allowed to return, under an oath of silence." She traced a gilded window frame. "Enforced by the removal of their tongues."

I shivered. "I'm not welcome here," I whispered. "I should not have come."

"The schism was centuries ago. Yet even now, any daughter born with an aptitude for seeing the Creator's light is sent here. Sons are sent to our brother house. The fathers of our order test them, traveling to the churches. There is a ceremony of serving at the altar at Midwinter—the Child's Mass—and it is used to determine if the children see the Creator's light. The Order of the Golden Sphere houses them and keeps them safe and stupid in service to a Creator who endowed them with gifts greater than the Church fathers would allow."

I touched the walls again, feeling as well as seeing the light infused in stone and mortar alike. The charm was not vague good fortune like I had manipulated on the ship; it was refined, for security, for safety, for endurance. "The charm has held fast since it was built?"

"It has not aged in five hundred years," Alba confirmed. "It has not crumbled or required repair since it was built. It has withstood hail and snow and direct strikes from lightning. When the door is barred, no one outside can open it."

"You didn't bring me here only because you needed the resources of your house to contact the Fenians, did you?" I breathed in the beauty of the charm surrounding me one more time, acknowledging a masterful work of art that had long out-lasted the hands that had made it.

"If you can revive the art of casting among my sisters, you will have an army of light at your disposal."

And so will you, I agreed silently. Alba stood to gain much by allying herself with me—once the Order of the Golden Sphere unleashed charm casters for Galitha, the Kvys could not hold them back in their own country. And what of the darkness? Those questions would have to wait, I resolved. I had an ally who could help me deliver an army to my nation.

"Sastra-set." A young sister, eyes downcast and hair wrapped in layers of sheer white linen, held out a battered letter.

Alba took it, then corrected the girl with a firm, "*Va'rit-ma. Rit-na* Sophie." She handed the letter to me. "It is yours. Your correspondence will not be subject to inspection here."

The paper was stained and the seal smudged, but I knew Theodor's handwriting as surely as I knew his face or his hands. I prized up the seal, unfolding the letter like the precious arti-fact, borne over time and distance, that it was.

"They're safe," I breathed. Theodor and Kristos had reached the main Reformist army at Hazelwhite, and had been wel-comed by the flagging forces. *One of us would have been, I think, sufficient to raise their spirits, but together we represent much more—a leadership, along with Niko Otni in Galitha City, who will direct them to victory*, he wrote. I could almost hear his voice—cautious opti-mism, steady vision. *My father refuses to parlay, and even if he did, I fear the Royalists would bury him in their name and roll on without him. And so we must fight. Sianh has already begun working with the recruits, training them in field maneuvering and tactics, and will be well worth his pay. Already light troops harry and pick at the Royalist forces in the south; a pack of "foxes" as Sianh calls them even captured a sup-ply wagon with, of all things, gunpowder and turnips.*

I inhaled, slowly, breathing in hope. *It will not be long, and we will be ready to meet the Royalists in open battle. And then, my love, we will need your light and your influence more than ever. We will need supplies, powder, shot, cannon. A navy. My trust is in you to acquire what we cannot win a war without.* My hands stopped shaking; the gold circlet on my wrist ceased trembling. Theodor's words were charge and assurance at once, promising me purpose.

My brother and the man I loved were holding on to their lives by a tenuous thread, waiting for me. Waiting for a war only I could wage.

I love you, he wrote at last. No flourishes, no grand words. No more needed to be said. I folded the letter and put it in my pocket, wanting to keep it close to me. A good-luck charm, even if it lacked magic, then turned to Alba.

"Let us begin now. We have very little time," I said, voice steady and hands firm on the charmed stone my fellow casters had laid before me. This was the foundation on which I would build.

Acknowledgments

I have so much to be grateful for, and so many people to whom I'm so indebted for their knowledge, work, and support. I know I didn't get here alone, and I know I'm not going anywhere without your help!

Thanks to my agent, Jessica Sinsheimer, for your continued encouragement and professional insight and genius soup recipes. Thanks as well to the rest of the team at Sarah Jane Freymann Literary Agency.

I'm exceptionally lucky and grateful for the vision and talent that's behind this book at Orbit. Sarah Guan, editor extraordinaire, thank you for your perception and for the best hard questions. Two-hour phone calls feel like minutes! I have the most beautiful covers in the world thanks to Lauren Panepinto and Lisa Marie Pompilio. Thanks as well to Tim Paul for a map pretty enough to frame. Thanks on the publicity side to Alex Lencicki, Ellen Wright, Laura Fitzgerald, and Paola Crespo (who, seriously, never stops selling books!). To the whole Orbit team, thanks for this incredible opportunity and for letting me be part of a family of book-obsessed humans with you.

Randy, thanks for your love and support. I didn't mean to write a story "inspired by real life," but I guess when it comes to love and dedication overcoming separation, I did...ooops? No regrets. Eleanor and Marjorie, thanks for letting me disappear into a writing cave and have long phone calls about words and generally be a very weird mother.

Thanks to my parents for being my first and biggest fans and for not having Twitter so you can't post my childhood scribblings for anyone else to see. To my family and friends, your support means so much—every time I awkwardly garble my thanks for reading my book, I hope you know how much it means to me.

To my sewing and history nerd friends, I hope you see your work in these pages. To my writing friends, I hope you know how much your kind words, check-ins, and Twitter banter mean to me.

And to all the readers who have come this far with me, thank you! I'm continually inspired by your support.

The story continues in...

RULE

**Book THREE of the
Unraveled Kingdom**

Keep reading for a sneak peek!

extras

orbit

meet the author

Photo Credit: Heidi Hauck

Rowenna Miller grew up in a log cabin in Indiana and still lives in the Midwest with her husband and daughters, where she teaches English composition, trespasses while hiking, and spends too much time researching and re-creating historical textiles.

if you enjoyed
FRAY
look out for

RULE

The Unraveled Kingdom: Book Three

by

Rowenna Miller

The civil war that the charm caster Sophie and the Crown Prince Theodor tried so desperately to avert has come to Galitha. While Theodor joins Sophie's brother and his Reformist comrades in battle, hoping to turn the tide against the better-supplied and better-trained Royalist army, Sophie leverages the only weapon she has: charm and curse casting. She weaves her signature magic into uniforms and supplies procured with the aid of unlikely foreign allies, but soon discovers that the challenges of a full-scale war are far greater than the entrepreneurial concerns of her small Galatine dress shop. The fractured leadership of the Reformist army must coalesce, the people of Galitha unite against enormous odds, and Sophie create more than a little magical luck in order to have a chance of victory.

The autumn sun had ripened the berries in the hedgerows of the Order of the Golden Sphere, dyeing them a rich ruddy purple. The juices, a red more brilliant than even the best scarlet silk, stained my fingers as I plucked them from the deep brambles. Within several yards in any direction, novices of the order filled baskets of their own. A wheat-haired girl with pale-honey eyes had a smear of berry red across the front of her pale gray gown. She sighed and adjusted her starched white veil, leaving another red streak.

I stifled a laugh, then sobered nearly immediately.

A war waged some hundreds of miles south of us, the sisters of the Golden Sphere were deep in study at the art of casting charms under my tutelage, Sastra-set Alba was making final arrangements for an alliance-cementing voyage to Fen, and I was picking berries. The futility of filling my basket galled me. I snagged my thumb on a large curved thorn; nature made needles as effective as any I had used in my atelier, and the point produced a bead of blood almost instantly. I drew my hand carefully away and wrapped the tiny wound in my apron, letting the red stain sink into the linen.

Picking berries. As though that were an acceptable way to spend my afternoon, now of all times. I flicked the corner of the apron away with a frustrated sigh. My basket was already nearly full, but the bushes were still thick with purple. I knew what Alba would say—winter cared little for our war, and all the members of the community fortified the larder against that enemy. I wanted to rebel against that pragmatic logic. The ordered calm of the convent mocked me, the pristine birch-wood and the gardens, teeming with autumn harvest, all carry-ing on an unconcerned life and inviting me to join in.

The quiet, the unassuming, pacific quiet—it infuriated me. Probably, I acknowledged as I resumed plucking fruit for the basket, because it was so inviting. Here I could almost forget—had forgotten, in horrifying, brief instants—that Theodor and Kristos were overseeing skirmishes and readying for greater battles, that Galitha City, under Niko Otni's command, held out against the Royalists pressing in on them from both the sea and the land. That my friends in the city could be killed under bombardment, that my friends in the south could be overrun on the battlefield.

I wanted, desperately, to do something, and I was, but teach-ing the "light-touched" sisters of the convent how to manip-ulate charm magic was plodding, redundant work, removed from the immediacy of the war for Galitha.

The novice with the berry-stained veil motioned me over. Many of the novices took temporary vows of silence, and though it was not required, there were some sisters who main-tained the vow for life, on the premise that silence made com-munion with the Creator's ever-present spirit easier. Despite long hours of silence, on account of having no one to speak with here, I was no closer to any such communion.

I dropped the last few berries from the hedge into my basket and joined her. I raised an eyebrow and pointed to her veil; she flushed pink as she noticed the stain, and pointed toward the narrow road that carved a furrow through the forest.

Still too far away to see through the trees, travelers announced themselves with the rattle of wheels. She looked to me with baleful curiosity, as though I might know anything. As though I might be able to tell her in the stilted, limited Kvys I had picked up in the past months if I did. The other sisters along the hedgerow noted the sound and gave it little heed, turning back to their berries as though the outside world didn't exist.

To them, perhaps, it didn't.

Before I could decide if I had fulfilled my obligation to the order's larder, Alba crested the little rise behind the convent and strode toward me. Her pale linen gown, a more traditional Kvys design than she had worn in West Serafe, more traditional even than most of the sisters, floated behind her on a light breeze. The yoke was decorated with symbols of the Order of the Golden Sphere, circles and crosshatches and thin dotted lines I now understood to be references to the charm magic I could see and cast.

The berry-stained novice bowed her head, as did the other sisters, to a sastra-set, but Alba wasn't looking for them. "The *hyvtha* is gathering," she said, using the Kvys word that usually referred to a band of threshers at harvest or a troupe of musicians. "Let's see if anyone has made any progress since yesterday, shall we?"

"Don't tell me we're disappointing you," I said, deadpan. Trying to teach adults who had been suppressing any inclination toward casting since they were children was nearly impossible. Of our hyvtha of eighteen women and two men from the order's brother monastery, only ten reliably saw the light, three could maintain enough focus to hold on to it, and one had managed a shaky, crude clay tablet. Tantia was proud of her accomplishment, but had yet to repeat it.

Alba expected a battalion of casters capable of the exquisitely fine work in the order's basilica, and I had one caster who struggled with work a trained Pellian girl could churn out at eight.

The travelers appeared on the road, a comfortable carriage drawn by a pair of gray Kvys draft horses. "And those are the Fenians."

"Which Fenians?" I asked, craning my neck as though I could see past the leaded glass windows in the carriage.

"The foundry owner. Well, his son who handles his negotiations, at any rate." Her smile sparkled. "Your cannons are forthcoming."

"So we'll go to Fen—when?"

"I'm still finalizing the deal with the shipyard, and I've two mill owners on the string each trying to underbid the other." She grinned—she enjoyed this game of gold and ink. It made me feel slightly nauseated, betting with money that wasn't mine. My business had been built carefully, brick by precisely planned brick, and these negotiations with Fen felt like a house of cards, ready to topple under the breath of a single wrong word.

"So. I will not be joining the hyvtha this afternoon. See if Tantia can explain her methods to the others."

"I don't think the problem is my Kvys," I protested.

Alba ignored my suggestion—that her plan for a small regiment of charm-casting sisters and brothers of the order was farfetched.

I rinsed the berry juice from my hands at the hand pump in the courtyard of the monastery. Stains remained on my fingertips and palms.

"*Pra-set,*" I said in poor Kvys, the words sticking like taffy, hoping that my meaning, "very good," was clear to the struggling initiate. Immell's hand shook as she drew her stylus across a damp clay tablet, dragging ragged charm magic into the inscription.

Tantia, who had managed to craft another charmed tablet, laid her hand on Immell's arm, reassuring her in a stream of quiet, almost poetic Kvys. I couldn't follow more than a few words, so I nodded dumbly, what I hoped was a comforting smile plastered on my face. Immell's hand steadied, and the pale glow around her stylus grew stronger, brighter. "Pra-set!" I repeated.

Immell finished the inscription, one word in Kvys meaning *Creator's mercy*, which stood in for *luck*. The charm magic receded from her hand as she lifted her stylus from the clay, but the charm remained embedded in the clay. "Pra-set," I said again, examining her work. It was uneven and one letter was barely legible even to my unschooled eye, but it was done.

We were still a long way from what Alba hoped for: a phalanx of charm casters who had mastered what I could do. A complement to the Galatine army, she suggested. A safeguard for her house's authority, I read between the lines. And a challenge, to the laws prohibiting magic in Kvyset.

A few simple actions, a few stones tossed into a pond infinitely larger than myself, and the ripples were still reaching outward, trembling and new, but intent on fomenting change wherever they went.

Tantia and Immell were speaking in rapid Kvys, gesturing at the tablet. Another novice, Adola, joined them, and the three linked hands. "*Da nin?*" I wondered aloud. What now?

Tantia slapped some fresh clay from the bowl on the table, forming a sloppy disk with her free hand. I was about to chide her—orderliness was supposed to cultivate the mind for casting, especially in new learners—but she picked up her stylus and pressed her lips together, squinting into the blank space in front of her.

Light blazed around the stylus and all but drove itself into the clay, sparkling clean and pure in the gray slab. "*Da bravdin-set! Pra bravdin olosc-ni varsi!*" she exclaimed.

"How did you make such a strong charm?" I asked, correcting myself swiftly to Kvys. "*Da olosc bravdin-set?*"

"Is hands holding," Tantia replied, bypassing attempting to explain in Kvys. "Hands. I put hand on Immell. She cast."

"And the three of you—you joined hands and your charm was much stronger."

She nodded, smiling. "Easy cast, too. Than before." She thought a moment, then added, "Easy than alone."

"How have I never come across this before?" I sighed through my nose. Pellian charm casters worked by themselves, except when an older woman was teaching a novice. "You would think," I began, but stopped myself. My time in the Galatine and Serafan archives had taught me that precious little had been recorded on the subject of casting at all. One *would* think something important had been written down, but that didn't mean it had. "I'll look in the archives later," I promised.

The other sisters and the one brother who had joined us drew closer and Tantia explained what had happened. "We practice," she announced.

I nodded, overwhelmed by their near-accidental discovery. Surely a mother held her daughter's hand while teaching her to cast. But perhaps the process of learning was so different in adults that we noticed the effects more, realized that they were amplifying and not only teaching or steadying one another. More research. In Kvys. I sighed.

I fled to my room, the only place I was ever alone in the compound. It was clean and bright and spare, with pale wood furniture carved in woodland animals and starbursts on the posts and rails. White linen and cherry-red wool covered the bed. A Kvys prayer book and hymnal lay on a shelf over the window. I didn't understand more than a few words of the written language.

467

A light scratch on the door, and a dark gray paw shot under the slim crack. Its black claws searched for purchase.

"Kyshi." I sighed, and opened the door. The dark gray squirrel scurried into the room. A thin circlet of hammered brass around his neck glinted as he clambered up my bedspread and began to nose around my pillow as though I might have hidden a trove of nuts under the coverlet.

I opened my trunk and produced my secret larder—a handful of cracked chestnuts. "These are mine, little thief," I chided him. He burrowed under my hand and swiped a nut. "Don't take all my good chestnuts. They're almost fresh."

His sharp teeth made quick work of what was left of the shell, his nimble paws turning the nut over and around as he chewed. He had been abandoned in his drey and hand-raised by Sastra Dyrka, who worked in the kitchens, where he had developed an astute palate for nuts of all kinds, as well as pastries, sugared fruits, and ham. Now he was a communal pet and quite nearly a mascot for the order.

He settled onto my lap after his snack. I stroked his fur, rich and warm as the finest wool. I wanted to bury my fingers in his thick tail, but he chattered disapprovingly every time I tried.

I felt useless. I thought of a time that felt further ago than a single year, when my brother was staying out late in the taverns and drumming up support for change, before Pyord solidified their plans with money and centralized violence. Before I had realized I couldn't escape the questions that nagged my brother, before I understood that, for all I had built with long hours and tiring work, it was on a cracked and crumbling foundation. I had resisted participating then, had rebuked my brother for even asking. Now I craved action. Picking berries, petting the squirrel, teaching novice charm casters—it all felt unimportant, artificial and distant.

My place was with Galitha. My place was fighting for a better country, a better world for my neighbors and my friends and thousands of people I didn't know.

Kyshi started as the door opened, darted up my shoulder, and settled against my neck. "Alba." I acknowledged her as she entered.

"The Fenians are quite amenable to our terms," she said. "Ah, I do like having a freshly inked contract in hand."

"It's done!" I sat upright, dislodging Kyshi, who protested with a profane squirrel screech and his claws in my hair.

"Cannon barrels. Three-, six-, and twelve-pound guns. In the proportions Sianh recommended."

"Mostly sixes," I recalled.

"He felt they would be more maneuverable than the heavy pieces." Alba smiled. "And of course we will oversee the process for at least a portion of the run, on site at the Fenian foundry."

"Of course," I said. I chewed my lip. I still had to figure out if I could charm molten metal, and whether or not it was even a wise idea. I wished I had Sianh nearby, to explain the use and limitations of the iron guns, to discover how best magic might exploit them—or curb their shortcomings.

"We'll finish talks with the mill owners and the ship builders and then—Fen!" She grinned. "You look less than pleased."

"I'm just tired," I lied. "And I admit, I'm a bit nervous about Fen." That, at least, was the truth.

"Fen is dull and they'll ignore you like they ignore anyone who isn't in the process of paying them or bilking them." She shrugged. "Fenians."

"But the law."

"'But the law!'" Alba mimicked my hesitation with a good-natured laugh. "What, you're going to hang out a shingle, 'Charms Cast for Cheap'?" Kyshi trailed down my arm and settled in my lap again, serving Alba a stern look for the volume of her voice.

"No. I wasn't. But if anyone found out..." I let my fingers tremble on Kyshi's soft coat. The Fenian penalties for even illusions, for simple trickster's street magic, included transportation to their cliff colonies, desolate places scoured half-dead by the northern winds. And actual crimes of attempted magical practices—execution, all of them. Galatine gossip pages sometimes carried stories of Fenian women—always women—tried for buying or selling clay tablets, sentenced to drowning in the deep blue waters off Fen's rocky shores.

"No one will find out. Remember, they don't have any idea you can even cast a charm without your needle and thread. And we'll keep it that way."

"Of course. But—" I swallowed. I felt the memory of the cloying heat of West Serafe, the loggias and colonnades full of beautifully dressed people with their ruthless and competing agendas, their secret alliances and barbed gossip. "Isn't it possible they could invent something?"

"Why?"

Why had I been the focus of so much ire from my own country, from nobles to common people? Why had the Serafans piled rumor and ill will on me? "Because I'm a threat," I answered with surprise at my own confidence. "I have power most of them don't. Even if some of them do, they don't like that I can recognize it."

"I assure you that the Fenians are not the Serafans. They aren't hiding centuries-old secret casting methods. And though I cannot guarantee that none of them will realize that my Galatine companion is the rumored witch consort of the Rebel Prince, well. We won't make it well-known."

"You're sure?" I countered. I buried my fingers in Kyshi's

soft fur, searching for comfort. "If they know that I'm a charm caster, that I can do something they cannot, that scares people."

"You're also bringing them significant investments. And in Fen, nothing speaks louder than gold." She caught my free hand in hers. "Trust me. The Fenians are a strange people, to be sure, but not indecipherable."

if you enjoyed
FRAY

look out for

EMPIRE OF SAND
The Books of Ambha

by

Tasha Suri

A nobleman's daughter with magic in her blood.
An empire built on the dreams of enslaved gods.

*The Amrithi are outcasts; nomads descended from desert spirits,
they are coveted and persecuted throughout the Empire for the
power in their blood. Mehr is the illegitimate daughter of an
imperial governor and an exiled Amrithi mother she can barely
remember but whose face and magic she has inherited. Unbe-
knownst to her, she can manipulate the dreams of the gods to alter
the face of the world.*

extras

When Mehr's power comes to the attention of the Emperor's most feared mystics, she is coerced into their service, as they are determined to harness her magic for the glory of the Empire. She must use every ounce of will, subtlety, and power she possesses to resist the mystics' cruel agenda.

Should she fail, the gods themselves may awaken seeking vengeance...

CHAPTER ONE

Mehr woke up to a soft voice calling her name. Without thought, she reached a hand beneath her pillow and closed her fingers carefully around the hilt of her dagger. She could feel the smoothness of the large opal embedded in the hilt, and its familiar weight beneath her fingertips calmed her. She sat up and pushed back the layer of gauze surrounding her divan.

"Who is it?" she called out.

The room was dark apart from one wavering light. As the light approached, Mehr realized it was an oil lantern, held aloft by a maidservant whom Mehr knew by sight but not by name. Through the glare of the lit flame, the maidservant's features looked distorted, her eyes wide with nervousness.

"I'm sorry to disturb you, my lady," the maid said. "But your sister is asking for you."

Mehr paused for a moment. Then she slid off the divan and wound the sash of her sleep robe tight around her waist.

"You work in the nursery?" she asked.

"Yes, my lady."

"Then you should know Lady Maryam won't be pleased

that you've come to me," she said, tucking the dagger into her sash. "If she finds out, you may be punished."

The maidservant swallowed.

"Lady Arwa is asking for you," she repeated. "She won't sleep. She's very distressed, my lady."

"Arwa is a child," Mehr replied. "And children are often distressed. Why risk your position and come to me?"

The light wavered again as the maidservant adjusted her grip on the lantern.

"She says there is a daiva watching her," the maidservant said, her voice trembling. "Who else could I come to?"

Mehr strode over to the maidservant, who flinched back.

"What's your name?"

"Sara, my lady," said the maidservant.

"Give me the lantern, Sara," said Mehr. "I don't need you to light the way."

Mehr found Arwa curled up in her nurse Nahira's lap outside the nursery, surrounded by a gaggle of frightened maidservants. There was a Haran guardswoman standing by, looking on helplessly with her hand tight on the hilt of her blade. Mehr had some sympathy for her. Steel was no good against daiva, and equally useless in the comforting of distressed women.

"Mehr!" Arwa cried out, coming to life in the woman's arms. "You came!"

The nurse holding on to her had to tighten her grip to keep Arwa in place, now that she was squirming like a landed fish. Mehr kneeled down to meet Arwa at eye level.

"Of course I've come," said Mehr. "Sara says you saw a daiva?"

"It won't leave my room," Arwa said, sniffling. Her face was red with tears.

"How old are you now, Arwa?"

"Nine years," said Arwa, frowning. "You know that."

"Much too old to be crying then, little sister." Mehr brushed a tear from Arwa's cheek with her thumb. "Calm yourself."

Arwa sucked in a deep breath and nodded. Mehr looked up at Arwa's nurse. She knew her well. Nahira had been her nurse once too.

"Did you see it?"

Nahira snorted.

"My eyes aren't what they once were, but I'm still Irin. I could smell it." She tapped her nose.

"It has sharp claws," Arwa said suddenly. "And big eyes like fire, and it wouldn't stop looking at me."

Arwa was growing agitated again, so Mehr cupped her sister's face in her hands and made a low soothing sound, like the desert winds at moonrise.

"There's no need to be afraid," she said finally, when Arwa had gone still again.

"There's not?"

"No," Mehr said firmly. "I'm going to make it go away."

"Forever?"

"For a long while, yes."

"How?"

"It isn't important."

"I need to know," Arwa insisted. "What if another one comes and you're not here? How will I make it go away then?"

I'll always be here, thought Mehr. But of course that was a lie. She could promise no such thing. She looked into her sister's teary eyes and came, abruptly, to a decision. "Come with me now, Arwa. I'll show you."

One of the maidservants made a sound of protest, quickly hushed. Nahira gave her a narrow look, her grip on Arwa still deathly tight.

"She won't approve," warned Nahira.

"If my stepmother asks, say I forced you," Mehr told her. She touched light fingers to Arwa's shoulders. "Please, Nahira."

"I imagine Lady Maryam will draw her own conclusions," Nahira said dryly. She let Arwa go. "She doesn't think highly of you, my lady."

"Oh, I know," said Mehr. "Come on now, Arwa. You can carry the lamp."

The nursery was undisturbed. The living room was lit, candle-light flickering on the bright cushions and throws strewn across the marble floor. Arwa's bedroom, in the next room along, was dark.

The guardswoman trailed in reluctantly behind them. Her hand was fixed firmly on her scabbard.

"There's no need for this, my lady," the guardswoman said. "Lady Arwa simply had a nightmare. I'm sure of it."

"Are you?" Mehr replied mildly.

The guardswoman hesitated, then said, "I told Lady Arwa's nursemaid and the maidservants that daiva don't exist, that they should tell her so, but..." She paused, glancing uneasily at Mehr's face. "The Irin are superstitious."

Mehr returned her look.

This one, she thought, *has not been in Irinah long.*

"I ran into the room as soon as she screamed," said the guard, pressing on despite Mehr's pointed silence. "I saw nothing."

Ignoring her, Mehr nudged Arwa gently with her foot.

"Go on, love. Show me where it is."

Arwa took in another deep breath and stood straight, mustering up her courage. Then she went into her bedroom. Mehr followed close behind her, the guardswoman still hovering at her back.

"There," Arwa said, pointing. "It's moved. On the window ledge."

Mehr looked up and found the daiva already watching her.

Pale dawn was coming in through the window lattice at its back. Silhouetted against it, the daiva was a wisp of taloned shadows, its wings bristling darkly against a backdrop of gray-gold light. It was small for a daiva, no larger than Arwa, with nothing human in the shape of its face or in the lidless glare of its golden eyes.

"Stay where you are, Arwa," Mehr said. "Just lift the lamp higher."

Mehr walked toward it—slowly, so as not to startle it from its perch. The daiva's eyes followed her with the constancy of prayer flames.

Three floors above the ground, behind heavily guarded walls, nothing should have been able to reach Arwa's chambers. But daiva didn't obey the rules of human courtesy, and there were no walls in Jah Irinah that could keep them out of a place they wanted to be. Still, Mehr's gut told her this daiva was not dangerous. Curious, perhaps. But not dangerous.

Just to be sure, she held her hands in front of her, arms crossed, her fingers curled in a sigil to ward against evil. The daiva didn't so much as flinch. Good.

"What are you doing?" whispered Arwa.

"Speaking," said Mehr. "Hush now."

She drew her hands close together, thumbs interlocked, fanning out her fingers in the old sigil for *bird*. The daiva rustled its wings in recognition. It knew its name when it saw it.

"Ah," breathed Mehr. Her heart was beating fast in her chest. "You can move now, love. There's nothing to be afraid of."

"It still looks like it wants to bite me," Arwa said warily.

"It's a bird-spirit," Mehr said. "That's what birds do. But there's nothing evil inside it. It's a simple creature. It won't hurt you."

She took another step closer. The daiva cocked its head.

She could smell the air around it, all humid sweetness like incense mingled with water. She sucked in a deep breath and resisted the urge to set her fingers against the soft shadows of its skin.

She held one palm out. *Go.*

But there was no compulsion behind the movement, and the daiva did not look at all inclined to move. It watched her expectantly. Its nostrils, tucked in the shadows of its face, flared wide. It knew what she was. It was waiting.

Mehr drew the dagger from her sash. Arwa gave a squeak, and behind them the guardswoman startled into life, drawing the first inch of her sword out with a hiss of steel.

"Calm, calm," said Mehr soothingly. "I'm just giving it what it wants."

She pressed the sharp edge of her dagger to her left thumb. The skin gave way easily, a bead of blood rising to the surface. She held her thumb up for the daiva.

The daiva lowered its head, smelling her blood.

For a long moment it held still, its eyes never leaving hers. Then the shadows of its flesh broke apart, thin wisps escaping through the lattice. She saw it coalesce back into life beyond the window, dark wings sweeping through the cloudless, brightening air.

Mehr let out a breath she hadn't known she'd been holding. There was no fear in her. Just the racing, aching joy of a small adventure. She pressed her thumb carefully against the window lattice, leaving her mark behind.

"All gone," she said.

"Is it really?" Arwa asked.

"Yes." Mehr wiped the remaining blood from the dagger with her sash. She tucked the blade away again. "If I'm not here and a daiva comes, Arwa, you must offer it a little of your own blood. Then it will leave you alone."

"Why would it want my blood?" Arwa asked, frightened. Her eyes were wide. "Mehr?"

Mehr felt a pang. There was so much Arwa didn't know about her heritage, so much that Mehr was forbidden from teaching her.

To Arwa, daiva were simply monsters, and Irinah's desert was just endless sand stretching off into the horizon, as distant and commonplace as sky or soil. She had never stared out at it, yearning, as Mehr had. She had never known that there was anything to yearn for. She knew nothing of sigils or rites, or the rich inheritance that lived within their shared blood. She only knew what it meant to be an Ambhan nobleman's daughter. She knew what her stepmother wanted her to know, and no more.

Mehr knew it would be foolish to answer her. She bit her lip, lightly, and tasted the faint shadow of iron on her tongue. The pain grounded her, and reminded her of the risks of speaking too freely. There were consequences to disobedience. Mehr knew that. She did not want to face her stepmother's displeasure. She did not want isolation, or pain, or the reminder of her own powerlessness.

But Arwa was looking up at her with soft, fearful eyes, and Mehr did not have the strength to turn away from her yet. *One more transgression*, she decided; she would defy her stepmother one more time, and then she would go.

"Because you have a little bit of them in your blood," Mehr told her. When Arwa wrinkled her nose, Mehr said, "No, Arwa, it's not an insult."

"I'm not a daiva," Arwa protested.

"A little part of you is," Mehr told her. "You see, when the Gods first went to their long sleep, they left their children the daiva behind upon the earth. The daiva were much stronger then. They weren't simply small animal-spirits. Instead they walked the world like men. They had children with humans, and those children were the first Amrithi, our mother's people." She recited the tale from memory, words that weren't her own tripping off her tongue more smoothly than they had any right to. It had been many years since she'd last had Amrithi tales told to her. "Before the daiva weakened, when they were still truly the strong and terrifying sons and daughters of Gods, they made a vow to protect their descendants, and to never willingly harm them." She showed Arwa the thin mark on her thumb, no longer bleeding. "When we give them a piece of our flesh, we're reminding them of their vow. And, little sister, a daiva's vow is unbreakable."

Arwa took hold of her hand, holding it near the glow of the lantern so she could give it a thorough, grave inspection.

"That sounds like a children's story," she said finally, her tone faintly accusing, as if she were sure Mehr was telling her one of the soft lies people told their young.

"It *is* a children's story," said Mehr. "Our mother told it to me when I was a child myself, and I've never forgotten it. But that doesn't make it any less true."

"I don't know if my blood will work like yours," Arwa said doubtfully. She pressed her thumb gently against Mehr's. Where Mehr's skin was dark like earth after rain, Arwa's skin was a bare shade warmer than desert sand. "I don't look like you, do I?"

"Our blood is just the same," Mehr said quietly. "I promise." She squeezed Arwa's hand in hers, once, tightly. Then she stepped back.

"Tell Nahira it's safe to return," she said to the guardswoman. "I'm going back to my chambers."

The guardswoman edged back in fear. She trembled slightly.

If Mehr had been in a more generous mood, she would, perhaps, have told the guardswoman that Irinah was not like the other provinces of the Empire. Perhaps she would have told the guardswoman that what she so derisively called Irin superstition was in truth Irin practicality. In Irinah, the daiva had not faded into myth and history, as they had elsewhere. Weakened though they were, the daiva were holy beings, and it was wise to treat them with both wariness and reverence when one came upon them on Irin soil.

But Mehr was not in a generous mood. She was tired, and the look on the guardswoman's face had left a bitter taste in her mouth.

"Never mind," said Mehr. "I'll go."

"Daiva aren't real," the guardswoman said blankly, as Mehr swept past her. "They're a barbarian superstition."

Mehr didn't even deign to answer her. She walked out into the hallway, Arwa scampering after her, the lamp swinging wildly in her grip. As they left the nursery, Nahira swept Arwa up into her arms and one of the maids plucked the lamp deftly away. Mehr kept on walking until Arwa called out her name, holding out her arms again in a way that made Mehr's traitorous heart twist inside her chest and her legs go leaden beneath her.

It would be best, she told herself, to keep walking. It would be best not to look back. She did not want to be punished. She did not want *Arwa* to be punished.

"Don't go," Arwa said in a small voice. "Can't you stay just one time?"

Mehr stopped. If she turned back—if she stayed—Maryam would ensure that she would not be allowed to visit Arwa again for a long, long time.

Mehr took a deep breath, turned, and walked back to her sister regardless. She closed her eyes and pressed one firm kiss to Arwa's forehead. Her skin was soft; her hair smelled like rosewater.

"Get some sleep," she said to her. "Everything will be better when you wake up."

"Go," Nahira said. "I'll take care of her, my lady." A pause, as Arwa struggled and Mehr hesitated, her feet frozen in place by a compulsion she couldn't name. "Lady Maryam will be awake soon," Nahira said, and that, at last, broke the spell. Mehr turned and walked swiftly back toward her room. She could hear Arwa crying behind her, but as she had told the maidservant Sara, children were often distressed. The hurt would pass. Soon Arwa would forget she had ever been sad at all.

orbit

Follow us:

:fb: **/orbitbooksUS**

:twitter: **/orbitbooks**

:youtube: **/orbitbooks**

Join our mailing list
to receive alerts on our
latest releases and deals.

orbitbooks.net

Enter our monthly
giveaway for the chance
to win some epic prizes.

orbitloot.com